Lord John
and the
Private Matter

Diana Gabaldon

Century · London

Published by Century in 2003

1 3 5 7 9 10 8 6 4 2

First published in the United Kingdom in 2003 by Century

Random House Group Limited
20 Vauxhall Bridge Road, London SW1V 2SA

Random House Australia (Pty) Limited
20 Alfred Street, Milsons Point, Sydney,
New South Wales 2061, Australia

Random House New Zealand Limited
18 Poland Road, Glenfield,
Auckland 10, New Zealand

Random House (Pty) Limited
Endulini, 5A Jubilee Road, Parktown 2193, South Africa

Random House Group Limited Reg. No 954009

www.randomhouse.co.uk

A CIP catalogue record for this book is available from the British Library

Papers used by Random House are natural, recyclable products
made from wood grown in sustainable forests. The manufacturing processes
conform to the regulations of the country of origin

ISBN 1 8441 3388 5

Printed and bound in Great Britain by
Mackays of Chatham Plc, Chatham, Kent

Lord John
and the
Private Matter

DIANA GABALDON is the international bestselling author of five previous historical novels – *Cross Stitch*, *Dragonfly in Amber*, *Voyager*, *Drums of Autumn* and *The Fiery Cross*, and one work of non-fiction, *Through the Stones*. She lives with her family and a lot of other assorted wildlife in Scottsdale, Arizona.

Praise for Diana Gabaldon

'Gabaldon is a born storyteller' *Los Angeles Daily News*

'The writing is superb – lush, evocative, sensual, with a wealth of historical detail' *Library Journal*

'History comes deliciously alive on the page'
New York Daily News

'Triumphant . . . Her use of historical detail and a truly adult love story confirm Diana Gabaldon as a superior writer'
Publishers Weekly

'A blockbuster hit' *Wall Street Journal*

'A story that is both moving and magical' *Northern Echo*

To Margaret Scott Gabaldon and Kay Fears Watkins,
my children's wonderful grandmothers

THE RANDOM HOUSE GROUP

Diana Gabaldon

Dear Readers—

I think it's only fair to warn you that I wrote this book by accident. I *thought* I was writing a short story about Lord John Grey—one of my favorite characters from the OUTLANDER novels. As it was, though . . . Lord John had other ideas.

Even though I was working—and still am—on the next "big" novel starring Jamie and Claire, Lord John's adventures in London in 1757 kept evolving, growing more complex and fascinating with each page. Set during the time just after Lord John has left Jamie Fraser at Helwater as a Jacobite prisoner of war, *Lord John and the Private Matter* is an interpolation: part of the OUTLANDER series, and taking place within its timeline—but focused on an adventure separate from the lives of the main characters.

So I hope you will enjoy this trip through the darker side of London life in the company of Scottish whores, plumed Huns, reprobate Sergeants, Irish apothecaries, transvestite spies . . . and Lord John.

Slainte mhath!

—Diana

P.S. If you've been reading the OUTLANDER novels, you probably already know that *"Slainte mhath!"* means "To your very good health!" in Gaelic, but I thought I'd mention it, just in case. (You normally say this while drinking whisky, but if you want to drink whisky while reading this book, I think that's fine, and I'm sure Lord John wouldn't mind, either.)

Acknowledgments

Interviewers are always asking me how many research assistants I employ. The answer is "None." I do all my own research—because I simply wouldn't have any idea what to tell an assistant to go look for!

However, the answer also is "Hundreds!"—because so many nice people not only answer my random inquiries about this, that, and the other—but then helpfully provide lots more entertaining information that I would never have dreamed of asking for in the first place.

In conjunction with this particular book, I'd especially like to acknowledge the efforts of . . .

. . . Karen Watson, of Her Majesty's Customs and Excise, who kindly spent a lot of time sleuthing round London (and assorted historical records) to verify the feasibility of various of Lord John's movements, and also was of invaluable assistance in locating appropriate venues for skulduggery, as well as suggesting picturesque bits of arcana like the heroically amended statue of Charles I. I have taken small liberties with some of her information regarding London police jurisdictions, but that's my fault, not hers.

. . . John L. Myers, who inadvertently started this a long time ago, by sending me books about queer Dutchmen and Englishmen who were a little odd, too.

. . . Laura Bailey (and her fellow re-enactors), for the lavish details of costume in the eighteenth century.

. . . Elaine Wilkinson, who not only responded to my plea for a "German red", but discovered the existence of Castle Georgen and the family zu Egkh und Hungerbach (Josef, his castle, and his Schilcher wine are real; his disreputable nephew is my own invention. "Schilcher," by the way, means "brilliant" or "sparkling").

. . . Barbara Schnell, my wonderful German translator, for helpful details regarding the conversation and conduct of Stephan von Namtzen, and for the name "Mayrhofer," as well as the German expression for "well-groomed."

. . . My two literary agents, Russell Galen and Danny Baror, who, when I told them I had finished the second Lord John short story, inquired how long it was. Upon being told, they looked at each other, then at me, and said as one, "You *do* realize that that's the length most *normal* books are?" Which is why this is a book, though I make no claims for how normal it is. Not very, I expect.

Lord John
and the
Private Matter

Chapter 1

When First We Practice
to Deceive

London, June 1757
The Society for the Appreciation of
the English Beefsteak, a Gentlemen's Club

It was the sort of thing one hopes momentarily that one has not really seen—because life would be so much more convenient if one hadn't.

The thing was scarcely shocking in itself; Lord John Grey had seen worse, could see worse now, merely by stepping out of the Beefsteak into the street. The flower girl who'd sold him a bunch of violets on his way into the club had had a half-healed gash on the back of her hand, crusted and oozing. The doorman, a veteran of the Americas, had a livid tomahawk scar that ran from hairline to jaw, bisecting the socket of a blinded eye. By contrast, the sore on the Honorable Joseph Trevelyan's privy member was quite small. Almost discreet.

"Not so deep as a well, nor so wide as a door," Grey muttered to himself. "But it will suffice. Damn it."

He emerged from behind the Chinese screen, lifting the violets to his nose. Their sweetness was no match for the pungent scent that followed him from the piss-pots. It was early June, and the Beefsteak, like every other establishment in London, reeked of beer and asparagus-pee.

Trevelyan had left the privacy of the Chinese screen before Lord John, unaware of the latter's discovery. The Honorable Joseph stood across the dining room now, deep in conversation with Lord Hanley and Mr. Pitt, the very picture of taste and sober elegance. Shallow in the chest, Grey thought uncharitably—though the suit of puce superfine was beautifully tailored to flatter the man's slenderness. Spindle-shanked, too; Trevelyan shifted weight, and a shadow winked on his left leg, where the pad of the downy-calf he wore had shifted under a clocked silk stocking.

Lord John turned the posy critically in his hand, as though inspecting it for wilt, watching the man from beneath lowered lashes. He knew well enough how to look without appearing to do so. He wished he were not in the habit of such surreptitious inspection— if not, he wouldn't now be facing this dilemma.

The discovery that an acquaintance suffered from the French disease would normally be grounds for nothing more than distaste at worst, disinterested sympathy at best—along with a heartfelt gratitude that one was not oneself so afflicted. Unfortunately, the Honorable Joseph Trevelyan was not merely a club acquaintance; he was betrothed to Grey's cousin.

The steward murmured something at his elbow; by reflex, he handed the posy to the man and flicked a hand in dismissal.

"No, I shan't dine yet. Colonel Quarry will be joining me."

"Very good, my lord."

Trevelyan had rejoined his companions at a table across the room, his narrow face flushed with laughter at some jest by Pitt.

Grey couldn't stand there glowering at the man; he hesitated, unsure whether to go across to the smoking room to wait for Quarry, or perhaps down the hall to the library. In the event, though, he was prevented by the sudden entry of Malcolm Stubbs, lieutenant of his own regiment, who hailed him with pleased surprise.

"Major Grey! What brings you here, eh? Thought you was quite the fixture at White's. Got tired of the politicals, have you?"

Stubbs was aptly named, no taller than Grey himself, but roughly twice as wide, with a broad cherubic face, wide blue eyes, and a breezy manner that endeared him to his troops, if not always to his senior officers.

"Hallo, Stubbs." Grey smiled, despite his inner disquiet. Stubbs was a casual friend, though their paths seldom crossed outside of regimental business. "No, you confuse me with my brother Hal. I leave the whiggery-pokery up to him."

Stubbs went pink in the face, and made small snorting noises.

"Whiggery-pokery! Oh, that's ripe, Grey, very ripe. Must remember to tell it to the Old One." The Old One was Stubbs's father, a minor baronet with distinct whiggish leanings, and likely a familiar of both White's Club and Lord John's brother.

"So, you a member here, Grey? Or a guest, like me?" Stubbs, recovering from his attack of mirth, waved a hand round the spacious confines of the white-naped dining room, casting an admiring glance at the impressive array of decanters being arranged by the steward at a sideboard.

"Member."

Trevelyan was nodding cordially to the Duke of Gloucester, who returned the salutation. Christ, Trevelyan really did know everyone. With a small effort, Grey returned his attention to Stubbs.

"My godfather enrolled me for the Beefsteak at my birth. Starting at the age of seven, which is when he assumed reason began, he brought me here every Wednesday for luncheon. Got out of the habit while abroad, of course, but I find myself coming back, whenever I'm in Town."

The wine steward was leaning down to offer Trevelyan a decanter of port; Grey recognized the embossed gold tag at its neck—San Isidro, a hundred guineas the cask. Rich, well-connected . . . and infected. Damn, what was he going to do about this?

"Your host not here yet?" He touched Stubbs's elbow, turning him toward the door. "Come, then—let's have a quick one in the library."

They strolled down the pleasantly shabby carpet that lined the hall, chatting inconsequently.

"Why the fancy-dress?" Grey asked casually, flicking at the braid on Stubbs's shoulder. The Beefsteak wasn't a soldier's haunt; though a few officers of the regiment were members, they seldom wore full dress uniform here, save when on their way to some official business. Grey himself was only uniformed because he was meeting Quarry, who never wore anything else in public.

"Got to do a widow's walk later," Stubbs replied, looking resigned. "No time to go back for a change."

"Oh? Who's dead?" A widow's walk was an official visit, paid to the family of a recently deceased member of the regiment, to offer condolences and make inquiry as to the widow's welfare. In the case of an enlisted man, such a visit might include the handing over of a small amount of cash contributed by the man's intimates and immediate superiors—with luck, enough to bury him decently.

"Timothy O'Connell."

"Really? What happened?" O'Connell was a middle-aged

Irishman, surly but competent; a lifelong soldier who had risen to sergeant by dint of his ability to terrify subordinates—an ability Grey had envied as a seventeen-year-old subaltern, and still respected ten years later.

"Killed in a street brawl, night before last."

Grey's brows went up at that. "Must have been set on by a mob," he said, "or taken by surprise; I'd have given long odds on O'Connell in a fight that was even halfway fair."

"Didn't hear any details; I'm meant to ask the widow."

Taking a seat in one of the Beefsteak's ancient but comfortable library wing chairs, Grey beckoned to one of the servants.

"Brandy—you, too, Stubbs? Yes, two brandies, if you please. And tell someone to fetch me when Colonel Quarry comes in, will you?"

"Thanks, old fellow; come round to my club and have one on me next time." Stubbs unbuckled his dress sword and handed it to the hovering servant before making himself comfortable in turn.

"Met your cousin the other day, by the bye," he remarked, wriggling his substantial buttocks deeply into the chair. "Out ridin' in the Row—handsome girl. Nice seat," he added judiciously.

"Indeed. Which cousin would that be?" Grey asked, with a small sinking feeling. He had several female cousins, but only two whom Stubbs might conceivably admire, and the way this day was going . . .

"The Pearsall girl," Stubbs said cheerfully, confirming Grey's presentiment. "Olivia? That the name? I say, isn't she engaged to that chap Trevelyan? Thought I saw him just now in the dining room."

"You did," Grey said shortly, not anxious to speak about the Honorable Joseph at the moment. Once started on a conversational gambit, though, Stubbs was as difficult to deflect from his course as a twenty-pounder on a downhill slope, and Grey was obliged to hear a great deal regarding Trevelyan's activities and social prominence—things of which he was only too well aware.

"Any news from India?" he asked finally, in desperation.

This gambit worked; most of London was aware that Robert Clive was snapping at the Nawab of Bengal's heels, but Stubbs had a brother in the 46th Foot, presently besieging Calcutta with Clive, and was thus in a position to share any number of grisly details that had not yet made the pages of the newspaper.

"... so many British prisoners packed into the space, my brother said, that when they dropped from the heat, there was no place to put the bodies; those left alive were obliged to trample on the fallen underfoot. He said"—Stubbs looked round, lowering his voice slightly—"some poor chaps had gone mad from the thirst. Drank the blood. When one of the fellows died, I mean. They'd slit the throat, the wrists, drain the body, then let it fall. Bryce said they could scarce put a name to half the dead when they pulled them out of that place, and—"

"Think we're bound there, too?" Grey interrupted, draining his glass and beckoning for another pair of drinks, in the faint hope of preserving some vestige of his appetite for luncheon.

"Dunno. Maybe—though I heard a bit of gossip last week, sounded rather as though it might be the Americas." Stubbs shook his head, frowning. "Can't say as there's much to choose between a Hindoo and a Mohawk—howling brutes, the lot—but there's the hell of a lot better chance of distinguishing oneself in India, you ask me."

"If you survive the heat, the insects, the poisonous serpents, and the dysentery, yes," Grey said. He closed his eyes in momentary bliss, savoring the balmy touch of English June that drifted through the open window.

Speculation was rampant and rumors rife as to the regiment's next posting. France, India, the American Colonies . . . perhaps one of the German states, Prague on the Russian front, or even the West Indies. Great Britain was battling France for supremacy on three continents, and life was good for a soldier.

They passed an amiable quarter hour in such idle conjectures, during which Grey's mind was free to return to the difficulties posed by his inconvenient discovery. In the normal course of things, Trevelyan would be Hal's problem to deal with. But his elder brother was abroad at the moment, in France and unreachable, which left Grey as the man on the spot. The marriage between Trevelyan and Olivia Pearsall was set to take place in six weeks' time; something would have to be done, and done quickly.

Perhaps he had better consult Paul or Edgar—but neither of his half-brothers moved in society; Paul rusticated on his estate in Sussex, barely moving a foot as far as the nearest market town. As for Edgar . . . no, Edgar would not be helpful. His notion of dealing discreetly with the matter would be to horsewhip Trevelyan on the steps of Westminster.

The appearance of a steward at the door, announcing the arrival of Colonel Quarry, put a temporary end to his distractions.

Rising, he touched Stubbs's shoulder.

"Fetch me after dinner, will you?" he said. "I'll come along on your widow's walk, if you like. O'Connell was a good soldier."

"Oh, will you? That's sporting, Grey; thanks." Stubbs looked grateful; offering condolences to the bereaved was not his strong suit.

⚬⚬⚬

Trevelyan had fortunately concluded his meal and departed; the stewards were sweeping crumbs off the vacant table as Grey entered the dining room. Just as well; it would have curdled his stomach if he were obliged to look at the man while eating.

He greeted Harry Quarry cordially, and forced himself to make conversation over the soup course, though his mind was still preoccupied. Ought he to seek Harry's counsel in the matter? He hesitated, dipping his spoon. Quarry was bluff and frequently uncouth in manner, but he was a shrewd judge of character and more than knowledgeable in the messier sort of human affairs. He was of good family and knew how the world of society worked. Above all, he could be trusted to keep a confidence.

Well, then. Talking over the matter might at least clarify the situation in his own mind. He swallowed the last mouthful of broth and set down his spoon.

"Do you know Joseph Trevelyan?"

"The Honorable Mr. Trevelyan? Father a baronet, brother in Parliament, a fortune in Cornish tin, up to his eyeballs in the East India Company?" Harry raised his brows in irony. "Only to look at. Why?"

"He is engaged to marry my young cousin, Olivia Pearsall. I . . . merely wondered whether you had heard anything regarding his character."

"Bit late to be makin' that sort of inquiry, ain't it, if they're already betrothed?" Quarry spooned up a bit of unidentifiable vegetation from his soup bowl, eyed it critically, then shrugged and swallowed it. "Not your business anyway, is it? Surely her father's satisfied."

"She has no father. Nor mother. She is an orphan, and has been my brother Hal's ward these past ten years. She lives in my mother's household."

"Mm? Oh. Didn't know that." Quarry chewed bread slowly, thick brows lowered thoughtfully as he looked at his friend. "What's he done? Trevelyan, I mean, not your brother."

Lord John raised his own brows, toying with his soup spoon.

"Nothing, to my knowledge. Why ought he to have done anything?"

"If he hadn't, you wouldn't be inquiring as to his character," Quarry pointed out logically. "Out with it, Johnny; what's he done?"

"Not so much what he's done, as the result of it." Lord John sat back, waiting until the steward had cleared away the course and retreated out of earshot. He leaned forward a little, lowering his voice well past the point of discretion, yet feeling the blood rise in his cheeks nonetheless.

It was absurd, he told himself. Any man might casually glance— but his own predilections rendered him more than delicate in such a situation; he could not bear the notion that anyone might suspect him of deliberate inspection. Not even Quarry—who, finding himself in a similarly accidental situation, would likely have seized Trevelyan by the offending member and loudly demanded to know the meaning of this.

"I . . . happened to retire for a moment, earlier"—he nodded toward the Chinese screen—"and came upon Trevelyan, unexpectedly. I . . . ah . . . caught sight—" Christ, he was blushing like a girl; Quarry was grinning at his discomfiture.

". . . think it is pox," he finished, his voice barely a murmur.

The grin vanished abruptly from Quarry's face, and he glanced at the Chinese screen, from behind which Lord Dewhurst and a friend were presently emerging, deep in conversation. Catching Quarry's gaze upon him, Dewhurst glanced down automatically, to be sure his flies were buttoned. Finding them secure, he glowered at Quarry and turned away toward his table.

"Pox." Quarry pitched his own voice low, but still a good deal louder than Grey would have liked. "You mean the syphilis?"

"I do."

"Sure you weren't seeing things? I mean, glimpse from the corner of the eye, bit of shadow . . . easy to make a mistake, eh?"

"I shouldn't think so," Grey said tersely. At the same time, his mind grasped hopefully at the possibility. It *had* been only a glimpse. Perhaps he could be mistaken. . . . It was a very tempting thought.

Quarry glanced at the Chinese screen again. The windows were all open to the air, and the glorious June sunshine was streaming through them in floods. The air was like crystal; Grey could see individual grains of salt against the linen cloth, where he had upset the saltcellar in his agitation.

"Ah," Quarry said. He fell silent for a moment, tracing a pattern with one forefinger in the spilled salt.

He didn't ask whether Grey would recognize a chancrous sore. Any young serving officer must now and then have been obliged to accompany the surgeon inspecting troops, to take note of any man so diseased as to require discharge. The variety of shapes and sizes—to say nothing of conditions—displayed on such occasions was common fodder for hilarity in the officers' mess on the evening following inspections.

"Well, where does he go whoring?" Quarry asked, looking up and rubbing salt from his finger.

"What?" Grey looked at him blankly.

Quarry raised one thick brow.

"Trevelyan. If he's poxed, he caught it somewhere, didn't he?"

"I daresay."

"Well, then." Quarry sat back in his chair, pleased.

"He needn't have caught it in a brothel," Grey pointed out. "Though I admit it's the most likely place. What difference does it make?"

Quarry raised both brows.

"The first thing is make certain of it, eh, before you stink up the whole of London with a public accusation. I take it you don't want to make overtures to the man yourself, in order to get a better look."

Quarry grinned widely, and Grey felt the blood rise in his chest, washing hot up his neck. "No," he said shortly. Then he collected himself and lounged back a little in his chair. "Not my sort," he drawled, flicking imaginary snuff from his ruffle.

Quarry guffawed, his own face flushed with a mixture of claret and amusement. He hiccuped, chortled again, and slapped both hands down on the table.

"Well, whores ain't so picky. And if a moggy will sell her body, she'll sell anything else she has—including information about her customers."

Grey stared blankly at the Colonel. Then the suggestion dropped into focus.

"You are suggesting that I employ a prostitute to verify my impressions?"

"You're quick, Grey, damn quick." Quarry nodded approval, snapping his fingers for more wine. "I was thinking more of finding a girl who'd seen his prick already, but your way's a long sight easier. All you've got to do is invite Trevelyan along to your favorite convent, slip the lady abbess a word—and a few quid—and there you are!"

"But I—" Grey stopped himself short of admitting that far from patronizing a favored bawdery, he hadn't been in such an establishment in several years. He had successfully suppressed the memory of the last such experience; he couldn't say now even which street the building had been in.

"It'll work a treat," Quarry assured him, ignoring his discomposure. "Not likely to be too dear, either; two pound would probably do it, three at most."

"But once I know whether my suspicion is confirmed—"

"Well, if he ain't poxed, there's no difficulty, and if he is . . ."
Quarry squinted in thought. "Hmm. Well, how's this? If you was
to arrange for the whore to screech and carry on a bit, once she'd
got a good look at him, then you rush out of your own girl's chamber, so as to see what's the matter, eh? House might be afire, after
all." He chortled briefly, envisioning the scene, then returned to
the plan.

"Then, if you've caught him with his breeches down, so to
speak, and the situation revealed beyond doubt, I shouldn't think
he'd have much choice save to find grounds for breaking the engagement himself. What d'ye say to that?"

"I suppose it might work," Grey said slowly, trying to picture
the scene Quarry painted. Given a whore of sufficient histrionic
talent . . . and there would be no need for Grey actually to utilize
the brothel's services personally, after all.

The wine arrived, and both men fell momentarily silent as it
was poured. As the steward departed, though, Quarry leaned
across the table, eyes alight.

"Let me know when you mean to go; I'll come along for the
sport!"

Chapter 2

Widow's Walk

France," Stubbs was saying in disgust, pushing
his way through the crowd in Clare Market.
"Bloody France again, can you believe it? I dined
with DeVries, and he told me he'd had it direct from
old Willie Howard. Guarding the shipyards in frigging Calais, likely!"

"Likely," Grey repeated, sidling past a fishmonger's barrow. "When, do you know?" He aped
Stubbs's annoyance at the thought of a possibly
humdrum French posting, but in fact, this was welcome news.

He was no more immune to the lure of adventure
than any other soldier, and would enjoy to see the
exotic sights of India. However, he was also well
aware that such a foreign posting would likely keep
him away from England for two years or more—
away from Helwater.

A posting in Calais or Rouen, though . . . he could return every few months without much difficulty, fulfilling the promise he had made to his Jacobite prisoner—a man who doubtless would be pleased never to see him again.

He shoved that thought resolutely aside. They had not parted on good terms—well, on any. But he had hopes in the power of time to heal the breach. At least Jamie Fraser was safe; decently fed and sheltered, and in a position where he had what freedom his parole allowed. Grey took comfort in the imagined vision—a long-legged man striding over the high fells of the Lake District, face turned up toward sun and scudding cloud, wind blowing through the richness of his auburn hair, plastering shirt and breeches tight against a lean, hard body.

"Hoy! This way!" A shout from Stubbs pulled him rudely from his thoughts, to find the Lieutenant behind him, gesturing impatiently down a side street. "Wherever is your mind today, Major?"

"Just thinking of the new posting." Grey stepped over a drowsy, moth-eaten bitch, stretched out across his way and equally oblivious both to his passage and to the scrabble of puppies tugging at her dugs. "If it *is* France, at least the wine will be decent."

O'Connell's widow dwelt in rooms above an apothecary's shop in Brewster's Alley, where the buildings faced each other across a space so narrow that the summer sunshine failed to penetrate to ground level. Stubbs and Grey walked in clammy shadow, kicking away bits of rubbish deemed too decrepit to be of use to the denizens of the place.

Grey followed Stubbs through the shop's narrow door, beneath a sign reading F. SCANLON, APOTHECARY, in faded script. He paused to stamp his foot in order to dislodge a strand of rotting vegetation that had slimed itself across his boot, but looked up at the sound of a voice from the shadows near the back of the shop.

"Good day to ye, gentlemen." The voice was soft, with a strong Irish accent.

"Mr. Scanlon?"

Grey blinked in the gloom, and made out the proprietor, a dark, burly man hovering spiderlike over his counter, arms outspread as though ready to snatch up any bit of merchandise required upon the moment.

"Finbar Scanlon, the same." The man inclined his head courteously. "What might I have the pleasure to be doin' for ye, sirs, may I ask?"

"Mrs. O'Connell," Stubbs said briefly, jerking a thumb upward as he headed for the back of the shop, not waiting on an invitation.

"Ah, herself is away just now," the apothecary said, sidling quickly out from behind the counter in order to block the way. Behind him, a faded curtain of striped linen swayed in the breeze from the door, presumably concealing a staircase to the upper premises.

"Gone where?" Grey asked sharply. "Will she return?"

"Oh, aye. She's gone round for to speak to the priest about the funeral. Ye'll know of her loss, I suppose?" Scanlon's eyes flicked from one officer to the other, gauging their purpose.

"Of course," Stubbs said shortly, annoyed at Mrs. O'Connell's absence. He had no wish to prolong their errand. "That's why we've come. Will she be back soon?"

"Oh, I couldn't be saying as to that, sir. Might take some time." The man stepped out into the light from the door. Middle-aged, Grey saw, with silver threads in his neatly tied hair, but well-built, and with an attractive, clean-shaven face and dark eyes.

"Might I be of some help, sir? If ye've condolences for the

widow, I should be happy to deliver them." The man gave Stubbs a look of straightforward openness—but Grey saw the tinge of speculation in it.

"No," he said, forestalling Stubbs's reply. "We'll wait in her rooms for her." He turned toward the striped curtain, but the apothecary's hand gripped his arm, halting him.

"Will ye not take a drink, gentlemen, to cheer your wait? 'Tis the least I can offer, in respect of the departed." The Irishman gestured invitingly toward the cluttered shelves behind his counter, where several bottles of spirit stood among the pots and jars of the apothecary's stock.

"Hmm." Stubbs rubbed his knuckles across his mouth, eyes on the bottle. "It *was* rather a long walk."

It had been, and Grey, too, accepted the offered drink, though with some reluctance, seeing Scanlon's long fingers nimbly selecting an assortment of empty jars and tins to serve as drinking vessels.

"Tim O'Connell," Scanlon said, lifting his own tin, whose label showed a drawing of a woman swooning on a chaise longue. "The finest soldier who ever raised a musket and shot a Frenchman dead. May he rest in peace!"

"Tim O'Connell," Grey and Stubbs muttered in unison, lifting their jars in brief acknowledgment.

Grey turned slightly as he brought the jar to his lips, so that the light from the door illuminated the liquid within. There was a strong smell from whatever had previously filled the jar—anise? camphor?—overlaying the smell of alcohol, but there were no suspicious crumbs floating in it, at least.

"Where was Sergeant O'Connell killed, do you know?" Grey asked, lowering his makeshift cup after a small sip, and clearing his throat. The liquid seemed to be straight grain alcohol, clear and tasteless, but potent. His palate and nasal passages felt as though they had been seared.

Scanlon swallowed, coughed, and blinked, eyes watering—presumably from the liquor, rather than emotion—then shook his head.

"Somewhere near the river, is all I heard. The constable who came to bring the news said he was bashed about somethin' shocking, though. Knocked on the head in some class of a tavern fight and then trampled in the scrum, perhaps. The constable did mention that there was a heelprint on his forehead, God have mercy on the poor man."

"No one arrested?" Stubbs wheezed, face going red with the strain of not coughing.

"No, sir. As I understand the matter, the body was found lyin' half in the water, on the steps by Puddle Dock. Like enough, the tavern owner it was who dragged him out and dumped him, not wantin' the nuisance of a corpse on his premises."

"Likely," Grey echoed. "So no one knows precisely where or how the death occurred?"

The apothecary shook his head solemnly, picking up the bottle.

"No, sir. But then, none of us knows where or when we shall die, do we? The only surety of it is that we shall all one day depart this world, and heaven grant we may be welcome in the next. A drop more, gentlemen?"

Stubbs accepted, settling himself comfortably onto a proffered stool, one booted foot propped against the counter. Grey declined, and strolled casually round the shop, cup in hand, idly inspecting the stock while the other two lapsed into cordial conversation.

The shop appeared to do a roaring business in aids to virility, prophylactics against pregnancy, and remedies for the drip, the clap, and other hazards of sexual congress. Grey deduced the presence of a brothel in the near neighborhood, and was oppressed anew at the thought of the Honorable Joseph Trevelyan, whose existence he had momentarily succeeded in forgetting.

"Those can be supplied with ribbons in regimental colors, sir," Scanlon called, seeing him pause before a jaunty assortment of *Condoms Design'd for Gentlemen,* each sample displayed on a glass mold, the ribbons that secured the neck of each device coiled delicately around the foot of its mold. "Sheep's gut or goat, per your preference, sir—scented, three farthings extra. That would be gratis to you gentlemen, of course," he added urbanely, bowing as he tilted the neck of the bottle over Stubbs's cup again.

"Thank you," Grey said politely. "Perhaps later." He scarcely noticed what he was saying, his attention caught by a row of stoppered bottles.

Mercuric Sulphide, read the labels on several, and *Guiacum* on others. The contents appeared to differ in appearance, but the descriptive wording was the same for both:

> *For swift and efficacious treatment of the gonorrhoea,*
> *soft shanker, syphilis, and all other forms of venereal pox.*

For a moment, he had the wild thought of inviting Trevelyan to dinner, and introducing one of these promising substances into his food. Unfortunately, he had too much experience to put any trust in such remedies; a dear friend, Peter Tewkes, had died the year before, after undergoing a mercuric "salivation" for the treatment of syphilis at St. Bartholomew's Hospital, after several attempts at patent remedy had failed.

Grey had not witnessed the process personally, having been exiled in Scotland at the time, but had heard from mutual friends who had visited Tewkes, and who had talked feelingly of the vile effects of mercury, whether applied within or without.

He couldn't allow Olivia to marry Trevelyan if he was indeed afflicted; still, he had no desire to be arrested himself for attempted poisoning of the man.

Stubbs, always gregarious, was allowing himself to be drawn into a discussion of the Indian campaign; the papers had carried news of Clive's advance toward Calcutta, and the whole of London was buzzing with excitement.

"Aye, and isn't one of me cousins with Himself?" the apothecary was saying, drawing himself up with evident pride. "The Eighty-first, and no finer class of soldiers to be found on God's green earth"—he grinned, flashing good teeth—"savin' your presences, sirs, to be sure."

"Eighty-first?" Stubbs said, looking puzzled. "Thought you said your cousin was with the Sixty-third."

"Both, sir, bless you. I've several cousins, and the family runs to soldiers."

His attention thus returned to the apothecary, Grey slowly became aware that something was slightly wrong about the man. He strolled closer, eyeing Scanlon covertly over the rim of his cup. The man was nervous—why? His hands were steady as he poured the liquor, but there were lines of strain around his eyes, and his jaw was set in a way quite at odds with his stream of casual talk. The day was warm, but it was not so warm in the shop as to justify the slick of sweat at the apothecary's temples.

Grey glanced round the shop, but saw nothing amiss. Was Scanlon concealing some illicit dealings? They were not far from the Thames here; Puddle Dock, where O'Connell's body had been found, was just by the confluence of the Thames and the Fleet, and petty smuggling was likely a way of life for everyone in the neighborhood with a boat. An apothecary would be particularly well-placed to dispose of contraband.

If that was the case, though, why be alarmed by the presence of two army officers? Smuggling would be the concern of the London magistrates, or the Excise, perhaps the naval authorities, but—

A small, distinct thump came from overhead.

"What's that?" he asked sharply, looking up.

"Oh—naught but the cat," the apothecary replied at once, with a dismissive wave of his hand. "Wretched creatures, cats, but mice bein' more wretched creatures still . . ."

"Not a cat." Grey's eyes were fixed on the ceiling, where bunches of dried herbs hung from the beams. As he watched, one bundle trembled briefly, then the one beside it; a fine gold dust sifted down, the motes visible in the beam of light from the door.

"Someone's walking about upstairs." Ignoring the apothecary's protest, he strode to the linen curtain, pushed it aside, and was halfway up the narrow stair, hand on his sword hilt, before Stubbs had gathered his wits sufficiently to follow.

The room above was cramped and dingy, but sunlight shone through a pair of windows onto a battered table and stool—and an even more battered woman, open-mouthed with surprise as she froze in the act of setting down a dish of bread and cheese.

"Mrs. O'Connell?" She turned her head toward him, and Grey froze. Her open mouth was swollen, lips split, a dark-red gap showing in the gum where a lower tooth had been knocked out. Both eyes were puffed to slits, and she peered through a mask of yellowing bruises. By some miracle, her nose had not been broken; the slender bridge and fine nostrils protruded from the wreck, pale-skinned and freakish by contrast.

She lifted a hand to her face, turning away from the light as though ashamed of her appearance.

"I . . . yes. I'm Francine O'Connell," she murmured, through the fan of her fingers.

"Mrs. O'Connell!" Stubbs took a stride toward her, then

stopped, uncertain whether to touch her. "Who—who has done this to you?"

"Her husband. And may his soul rot in hell." The remark came from behind them, in a conversational tone of voice. Grey turned to see the apothecary advance into the room, his manner still superficially casual, but all his attention focused on the woman.

"Her husband, eh?" Stubbs, no fool, for all his geniality, reached out and seized the apothecary's hands, turning the knuckles to the light. The man suffered the inspection calmly enough, then pulled his unmarred hands back from Stubbs's grip. As though the action granted him license, he crossed to the woman and stood beside her, radiating subdued defiance.

"True it is," he said, still outwardly calm. "Tim O'Connell was a fine man when sober, but when the drink was on him . . . a fiend in human form, no less." He shook his head, tight-lipped.

Grey exchanged a glance with Stubbs. This was true; they shared a memory of extricating O'Connell from a gaol in Richmond, following a riotous night's leave. The constable and the gaoler had both borne the marks of the arrest, though neither had been as badly off as O'Connell's wife.

"And what is your relation to Mrs. O'Connell, if I might ask?" Grey inquired politely. It was hardly necessary to ask; he could see the woman's body sway toward the apothecary, like a twining vine deprived of its trellis.

"I am her landlord, to be sure," the man replied blandly, putting a hand on Mrs. O'Connell's elbow. "And a friend of the family."

"A friend of the family," Stubbs echoed. "Quite." His wide blue gaze descended, resting deliberately on the woman's midsection, where her apron bulged with a pregnancy of five or six months' progress. The regiment—and Sergeant O'Connell—had returned to London a scant six weeks before.

Stubbs glanced at Grey, a question in his eyes. Grey lifted one shoulder slightly, then gave the faintest of nods. Whoever had done for Sergeant O'Connell, it was plainly not his wife—and the money was not theirs to withhold, in any case.

Stubbs gave a small growl, but reached into his coat and drew out a purse, which he tossed onto the table.

"A small token of remembrance and esteem," he said, hostility plain in his voice. "From your husband's comrades."

"Shroud money, is it? I don't want it." The woman no longer leaned on Scanlon, but drew herself upright. She was pale beneath the bruises, but her voice was strong. "Take it back. I'll bury me husband meself."

"One might wonder," Grey said politely, "why a soldier's wife should wish to reject assistance from his fellows. Conscience, do you think?"

The apothecary's face darkened at that, and his fists closed at his sides.

"What d'ye say?" he demanded. "That she did him to death, and 'tis the guilt of the knowledge causes her to spurn your coin? Show 'em your hands, Francie!"

He reached down and seized the woman's hands, jerking them up to display. The little finger of one hand was bandaged to a splint of wood; otherwise, her hands bore no marks save the scars of healed burns and the roughened knuckles of daily work—the hands of any housewife too poor to afford a drudge.

"I do not suppose that Mrs. O'Connell beat her husband to death personally, no," Grey replied, still polite. "But the question of conscience need not apply only to her own deeds, need it? It might also apply to deeds performed on her behalf—or at her behest."

"Not conscience." The woman pulled her hands away from Scanlon with sudden violence, the wreck of her face quivering.

Emotions shifted like sea currents beneath the blotched skin as she glanced from one man to the other.

"I will tell ye why I spurn your gift, sirs. And that is not conscience, but pride." The slit eyes rested on Grey, hard and bright as diamonds. "Or do you think a poor woman such as meself is not entitled to her pride?"

"Pride in what?" Stubbs demanded. He looked pointedly again at her belly. "Adultery?"

To Stubbs's displeased surprise, she laughed.

"Adultery, is it? Well, and if it is, I'm not the first to be after doing it. Tim O'Connell left me last year in the spring; took up with a doxy from the stews, he did, and took what money we had to buy her gauds. When he came here two days ago, 'twas the first time I'd seen him in near on a year. If it were not for Mr. Scanlon offerin' me shelter and work, I should no doubt have become the whore ye think me."

"Better a whore to one man than to many, I suppose," Grey said under his breath, putting a hand on Stubbs's arm to prevent further intemperate remarks.

"Still, madam," he went on, raising his voice, "I do not quite see why you object to accepting a gift from your husband's fellows to help bury him—if indeed you have no sense of guilt over his demise."

The woman drew herself up, crossing her arms beneath her bosom.

"Will I take yon purse and use it to have fine words said over the stinkin' corpse of the man? Or worse, light candles and buy Masses for a soul that's flamin' now in the pits of hell, if there is justice in the Lord? That I will not, sir!"

Grey eyed her with interest—and a certain amount of admiration—then glanced at the apothecary, to see how he took this speech. Scanlon had dropped back a step; his eyes were fixed on the woman's bruised face, a slight frown between the heavy brows.

Grey settled the silver gorget that hung at his neck, then leaned forward and picked up the purse from the table, jingling it gently in his palm.

"As you will, madam. Do you wish also to reject the pension to which you are entitled, as a sergeant's widow?" Such a pension was little enough; but given the woman's situation . . .

She stood for a moment, undecided, then her head lifted again.

"That, I'll take," she said, giving him a glittering look through one slitted eye. "I've earned it."

Chapter 3

O What a Tangled Web
We Weave

There was nothing for it but to report the matter. Finding someone to report to was more difficult; with the regiment refitting and furbishing for a new posting, there were constant comings and goings. The usual parade had been temporarily discontinued, and no one was where he ought to be. It was just past sunset of the following day when Grey eventually ran Quarry to earth, in the smoking room at the Beefsteak.

"Were they telling the truth, d'ye think?" Quarry pursed his lips, and blew a thoughtful smoke ring. "Scanlon and the woman?"

Grey shook his head, concentrating on getting his fresh cheroot to draw. Once it seemed well alight, he took it from his lips long enough to answer.

"She was—mostly. He wasn't."

Quarry's brows lifted, then dropped in a frown.

"Sure of it? You said he was nervous; might that be only because he didn't want you to discover Mrs. O'Connell, and thus his relations with her?"

"Yes," Grey said. "But even after we'd spoken with her . . . I can't say precisely what it was that Scanlon was lying *about*—or even that he lied, specifically. But he knew something about O'Connell's death that he wasn't telling straight, or I'm a Dutchman."

Quarry grunted in response to this, and lay back in his chair, smoking fiercely and scowling at the ceiling in concentration. Indolent by nature, Harry Quarry disliked thinking, but he could do it when obliged to.

Respecting the labor involved, Grey said nothing, taking an occasional pull from the Spanish cigar that had been pressed upon him by Quarry, who fancied the exotic weed. He himself normally drank tobacco smoke only medicinally, when suffering from a heavy rheum, but the smoking room at the Beefsteak offered the best chance of private conversation at this time of day, most members being at their suppers.

Grey's stomach growled at the thought of supper, but he ignored it. Time enough for food later.

Quarry removed the cigar from his lips long enough to say, "Damn your brother," then replaced it and resumed his contemplation of the pastoral frolic taking place on the gessoed ceiling above.

Grey nodded, in substantial agreement with this sentiment. Hal was Colonel of the Regiment, as well as the head of Grey's family. Hal was presently in France—had been for a month—and his temporary absence was creating an uncomfortable burden on those required to shoulder those responsibilities that were rightfully his. Nothing to be done about it, though; duty was duty.

In Hal's absence, command of the regiment devolved upon its two regular Colonels, Harry Quarry and Bernard Sydell. Grey had had not the slightest hesitation in choosing to whom to make his report. Sydell was an elderly man, crotchety and strict, with little knowledge of his troops and less interest in them.

Observing the inferno in progress, one of the ever-watchful servants came silently forward to place a small porcelain dish on Quarry's chest, lest the fuming ashes of his cigar set his waistcoat on fire. Quarry ignored this, puffing rhythmically and making occasional small growling noises between his teeth.

Grey's cheroot had burnt itself out by the time Quarry removed the porcelain dish from his chest and the soggy remains of his own cigar from his mouth. He sat up and sighed deeply.

"No help for it," he said. "You'll have to know."

"Know what?"

"We think O'Connell was a spy."

Astonishment and dismay vied for place in Grey's bosom with a certain feeling of satisfaction. He'd known there was something fishy about the situation in Brewster's Alley—and it wasn't codfish.

"A spy for whom?" They were alone; the ubiquitous servant had disappeared momentarily, but Grey nonetheless glanced round and lowered his voice.

"We don't know." Quarry squashed the stump of his cigar into the dish and set it aside. "That was why your brother decided to leave him be for a bit after we began to suspect him—in hopes of discovering his paymaster, once the regiment was back in London."

That made sense; while O'Connell might have gathered useful military information in the field, he would have found it infinitely easier to pass it on in the seething anthill of London—where men of every nation on earth mingled daily in the streams of commerce that flowed up the Thames—than in the shoulder-rubbing confines of a military camp.

"Oh, I see," Grey said, shooting a sharp glance at Quarry as the light dawned. "Hal took advantage of the gossip regarding the regimental posting, didn't he? Stubbs told me after luncheon that he'd heard from DeVries that we were definitely set for France again—likely Calais. I take it that was misdirection, for O'Connell's benefit?"

Quarry regarded him blandly. "Wasn't announced officially, was it?"

"No. And we take it that the coincidence of such an unofficial decision and the sudden demise of Sergeant O'Connell is sufficient to be . . . interesting?"

"Depends on your tastes, I s'pose," Quarry said, heaving a deep sigh. "Damn nuisance, I call it."

The servant came quietly back into the room, bearing a humidor in one hand, a rack of pipes in the other. The supper hour was drawing to a close, and those members who liked a smoke to settle their digestions would be coming down the hallway shortly, each to claim his own pipe and his preferred chair.

Grey sat frowning for a moment.

"Why was . . . the gentleman in question . . . suspected?"

"Can't tell you that." Quarry lifted one shoulder, leaving it unclear as to whether his reticence was a matter of ignorance or of official discretion.

"I see. So perhaps my brother is in France—and perhaps he isn't?"

A slight smile twitched the white scar on Quarry's cheek.

"You'd know better than I would, Grey."

The servant had gone out again, to fetch the other humidors; several members kept their personal blends of tobacco and snuff at the club. He could already hear the stir from the dining room, of scraping chairs and postprandial conversation. Grey leaned forward, ready to rise.

"But you had him followed, of course—O'Connell. Someone must have kept a close eye on him in London."

"Oh, yes." Quarry shook himself into rough order, brushing ash from the knees of his breeches and pulling down his rumpled waistcoat. "Hal found a man. Very discreet, well-placed. A footman employed by a friend of the family—your family, that is."

"And that friend would be . . ."

"The Honorable Joseph Trevelyan." Heaving himself to his feet, Quarry led the way out of the smoking room, leaving Grey to follow as he might, senses reeling from more than tobacco smoke.

It all made a horrid sense, though, he thought, following Quarry toward the door. Trevelyan's family and Grey's had been associated for the last couple of centuries, and it was in some part Joseph Trevelyan's friendship with Hal that had led to his betrothal to Olivia in the first place.

It wasn't a close friendship; one founded on a commonality of association, clubs, and political interests, rather than on personal affection. Still, if Hal had been looking for a discreet man to put on O'Connell's trail, it would have been necessary to look outside the army—for who knew what alliances O'Connell had formed, both within the regiment and outside it? And so, evidently, Hal had spoken to his friend Trevelyan, who had recommended his own footman . . . and it was simply a matter of dreadful irony that he, Grey, should now be obliged to interfere in Trevelyan's personal life.

Outside the Beefsteak, the doorman had procured a commercial carriage; Quarry was already into it, beckoning Grey impatiently.

"Come along, come along! I'm starving. We'll go up to Kettrick's, shall we? They do an excellent eel pie there. I could relish an eel pie, and perhaps a bucket or two of stout to go along. Wash the smoke down, what?"

Grey nodded, setting his hat on the seat beside him where it wouldn't be crushed. Quarry stuck his head out the window and shouted up to the driver, then pulled it in and relapsed back onto the grimy squabs with a sigh.

"So," Quarry went on, raising his voice slightly to be heard over the rattle and squeak of the carriage, "this man, Trevelyan's footman—Byrd, his name is, Jack Byrd—he took up rooms across from the slammerkin O'Connell lived with. Been following the Sergeant to and fro, up and down London, for the past six weeks."

Grey glanced out of the window; the weather had kept fine for several days, but was about to break. Thunder growled in the distance, and he could feel the coming rain in the air that chilled his face and freshened his lungs.

"What does this Byrd say occurred, then, the night that O'Connell was killed?"

"Nothing." Quarry settled his wig more firmly on his head as a gust of moisture-laden wind swept through the carriage.

"He lost O'Connell?"

Quarry's blunt features twisted wryly.

"No, we've lost Jack Byrd. Man hasn't been seen or heard of since the night O'Connell was killed."

The carriage was slowing, the driver chirruping to his team as they made the turn into the Strand. Grey settled his cloak about his shoulders and picked up his hat, in anticipation of their arrival.

"No sign of his body?"

"None. Which rather suggests that whatever happened to O'Connell, it wasn't a simple brawl."

Grey rubbed at his face, rasping the bristles on his jaw. He was hungry, and his linen was grimy after the day's exertions. The clammy feel of it made him feel seedy and irritable.

"Which rather suggests that whatever happened wasn't the fault of Scanlon, then—for why should he be concerned with Byrd?" He wasn't sure whether to be pleased at this deduction or not. He *knew* the apothecary had been lying to him in some way—but at the same time, he felt some sympathy for Mrs. O'Connell. She would be in a bad way if Scanlon was taken up for murder and hanged or transported—and a worse one, were she to be accused of conspiracy in the affair.

The opposite bench was harlequined with light and shadow as they clopped slowly past a group of flambeaux-men, lighting a party home. He saw Quarry shrug, obviously as irritable as he was himself from lack of food.

"If Scanlon had spotted Byrd following O'Connell, he might have put Byrd out of the way, as well—but why bother to hide it? A brawl might produce multiple bodies, easy as one. They often do, God knows."

"But if it was someone else," Grey said slowly, "someone who wanted O'Connell out of the way, either because he asked too much or because they feared he might give them away? . . ."

"The spymaster? Or his representative, at least. Could be. Again, though—why hide the body, if he did for Byrd, too?"

The alternative was obvious.

"He didn't kill Byrd. He bought him off."

"Damn likely. Directly I heard of O'Connell's death, I sent a man to search the place he was living, but he didn't find a thing. And Stubbs had a good look round the widow's place, as well, while you were there—but not a bean, he says. Not a paper in the place."

He'd seen Stubbs poking round as he made arrangements for the payment of O'Connell's pension to his widow, but had paid no particular attention at the time. It was true, though; Mrs. O'Connell's room was spartan in its furnishing, completely lacking in books or papers of any kind.

"What were they searching for?"

The bearlike growl that emerged from the shadows in reply might have been Quarry, or merely his stomach giving voice to its hunger.

"Don't know for sure what it might look like," Quarry admitted reluctantly. "It will be writing of some kind, though."

"You don't know? What sort of thing is it—or am I not allowed to know that?"

Quarry eyed him, fingers drumming slowly on the seat beside him. Then he shrugged; official discretion be damned, evidently.

"Just before we came back from France, O'Connell took the ordnance requisitions into Calais. He was late—all the other regiments had turned in their papers days before. The damn fool clerk had left the lot just sitting on his desk, if you can believe it! Granted, the office was locked, but still . . ."

Returning from a leisurely luncheon, the clerk had discovered the door forced, the desk ransacked—and every scrap of paper in the office gone.

"I shouldn't have thought one man could carry the amount of paper to be found in an office of that sort," Grey said, half-joking.

Quarry flipped one hand, impatient.

"It was a clerk's hole, not the office proper. Nothing else there was important—but the quarterly ordnance requisitions for every British regiment between Calais and Prague! . . ."

Grey pursed his lips, nodding in acknowledgment. It was a serious matter. Information on troop movements and disposition was highly sensitive, but such plans could be changed, if it became known that the intelligence had fallen into the wrong hands. The munitions requirements for a regiment could not be altered—and the sum total of that information would tell an enemy almost to the gun what strength and what weaponry each regiment possessed.

"Even so," he objected. "It must have been a massive amount of paper. Not the sort of thing a man could easily conceal about his person."

"No, it would have taken a large rucksack, or a sail bag—something of that sort—to cart it all away. But cart it away someone did."

The alarm had been raised promptly, of course, and a search instigated, but Calais was a medieval warren of a place, and nothing had been found.

"Meanwhile, O'Connell disappeared—quite properly; he was given three days' leave when he took the requisitions in. We hunted for him; found him on the second day, smelling of drink and looking as though he hadn't slept for the whole of the time."

"Which would be quite as usual."

"Yes, it would. But that's also what you'd expect a man to look like who'd sat up for two days and nights in a hired room, making a précis of that mass of paper and turning it into something a good bit smaller and more portable—feeding the requisitions into the fire as he went."

"So they weren't ever found? The originals?"

"No. We watched O'Connell carefully; he had no chance to pass on the information to anyone after that—and we think it unlikely that he handed it on before we found him."

"Because now he's dead—and because Jack Byrd has disappeared."

"*Rem acu tetigisti,*" Quarry replied, then snorted, half-pleased with himself.

Grey smiled in spite of himself. "You have touched the matter with a needle"; it meant, "you've put your finger on it." Probably the only bit of Latin Quarry recalled from his schooldays, other than *cave canem*.

"And was O'Connell the only suspect?"

"No, damn it. Hence the difficulty. We couldn't simply arrest him and sweat the truth out of him with no more evidence than the fact of his being there. At least six other men—all from different regiments, damn it!—were there during the relevant time, as well."

"I see. So the other regiments are now quietly investigating *their* potential black sheep?"

"They are. On the other hand," Quarry added judiciously, "the other five are still alive. Which might be an indication, eh?"

The coach stopped, and the sounds and smells of Kettrick's Eel-Pye House floated through the window: laughter and talk, the sizzle of food and clank of wooden plates and pie tins. The brine-smell of jellied eels and ale and the solace of floury pies lapped round them, warm and comforting, spiced with the sauce of alcoholic conviviality.

"Do we know for certain how O'Connell was killed? Did anyone from the regiment see the body?" Grey asked suddenly, as Quarry descended heavily to the pavement.

"No," Quarry said, not looking round, but heading for the door with single-minded determination. "You're going to go and do that tomorrow, before they bury the bugger."

❦

Grey waited until the pies had been set down in front of them before he undertook to argue with Quarry's statement that he, Grey, was forthwith relieved of other duties in order to pursue an investigation into the activities and death of Sergeant Timothy O'Connell.

"Why me?" Grey was astonished. "Surely it's sufficiently serious a matter to justify the senior ranking officer's attention—that would be you, Harry," he pointed out, "or possibly Bernard."

Quarry had his eyes closed in momentary bliss, mouth full of eel pie. He chewed slowly, swallowed, then opened his eyes reluctantly.

"Bernard—ha-ha. Very funny." He brushed crumbs from his chest. "As for me . . . well, it might be, ordinarily. Fact is, though— I was in Calais, too, when the requisitions were taken. Could have done it meself. Didn't, of course, but I could have."

"No one in his right mind would suspect you, Harry, surely?"

"Think the War Office is in its right mind, do you?" Quarry raised one cynical eyebrow, along with his spoon.

"I take your point. But still . . ."

"Crenshaw was on home leave," Quarry said, naming one of the captains of the regiment. "Meant to be in England, but who's to say he didn't sneak back to Calais?"

"And Captain Wilmot? You can't all have been on leave!"

"Oh, Wilmot was in camp where he ought to have been, all proper and above suspicion. But he had a fit of some sort at his club this Monday past. Apoplexy, the quack says. Can't walk, can't talk, can't view bodies." Quarry pointed his spoon briefly at Grey's chest. "You're it."

Grey opened his mouth to expostulate further, but finding no good argument to hand, inserted a bite of pie instead, chewing moodily.

With fate's usual turn for irony, the scandal that had sent him to Ardsmuir in disgrace had now placed him beyond suspicion, as the only functioning senior officer of the regiment who could not possibly have had anything to do with the disappearance of the Calais requisitions. He had returned from his Scottish exile by the time of the disappearance, true—but had probably been in London, having not formally rejoined his regiment until a month ago.

Harry had a genius for avoiding unpleasant jobs, but in the present situation, Grey was forced to admit it wasn't entirely Harry's doing.

Kettrick's was crowded, as usual, but they had found a bench in a secluded corner, and their uniforms kept the other diners at a safe distance. The clatter of spoons and pie tins, the crash and scrape of shifting benches, and the raucous conversation bouncing from the low wooden rafters provided more than sufficient cover for a private conversation. Nonetheless, Grey leaned closer and lowered his voice.

"Does the Cornish gentleman of whom we were speaking earlier know that his servant is *incommunicabilis*?" Grey asked circumspectly.

Quarry nodded, champing eel pie industriously. He coughed to clear a bit of pastry from his throat, and took a deep pull at his tankard of stout.

"Oh, yes. We thought the servant in question might have been scared off by whatever it was that happened to the sergeant—in which case, the natural thing would be for him to scuttle off back to . . . his place of employment." Quarry beetled his brows at Grey, indicating that naturally he understood the necessity for discretion—did Grey think him dense? "Sent Stubbs round to ask—no sign of him. Our Cornish friend is disturbed."

Grey nodded, and conversation was temporarily suspended while both men concentrated on their meal. Grey was scraping a bit of bread round his empty pannikin, unwilling to let a drop of the savory broth escape, when Quarry, having polished off two pies and three pints, belched amiably and chose to resume in a more social vein.

"Speakin' of Cornishmen, what have you done about your putative cousin-in-law? Arranged to take him to a brothel yet?"

"He says he doesn't go to brothels," Grey replied tersely, recalled unwillingly to the matter of his cousin's marriage. Christ, weren't spies and suspected murder enough?

"And you're letting him marry your cousin?" Quarry's thick brows drew down. "How d'ye know he's not impotent, or a sodomite, let alone diseased?"

"I am reasonably sure," Lord John said, repressing the sudden insane urge to remark that, after all, the Honorable Mr. Trevelyan had not been watching *him* at the chamber pot.

He had called on Trevelyan earlier in the day, with an invitation to supper and various libidinous "amusements" to bid a proper farewell to Trevelyan's bachelorhood. Trevelyan had agreed with thanks to a cordial supper, but claimed to have promised his mother upon her deathbed to have nothing to do with prostitutes.

Quarry's shaggy brows shot up.

"What sort of mother talks about whores on her deathbed? Your mother wouldn't do that, would she?"

"I have no idea," Grey said. "The situation has fortunately not arisen. But I suppose," he said, attempting to divert the conversation, "that surely there *are* men who do not seek such recreation. . . ."

Quarry gave him a look of jaundiced doubt. "Damn few," he said. "And Trevelyan ain't one of 'em."

"You seem sure of it," Grey said, slightly piqued.

"I am." Quarry settled back, looking pleased with himself. "Asked around a bit—no, no, I was quite discreet, no need to fret. Trevelyan goes to a house in Meacham Street. Good taste; been there meself."

"Oh?" Grey set aside his empty pie pan, and raised a brow in interest. "Why would he not wish to go with me, I wonder?"

"Maybe afraid you'll blab to Olivia, disillusion the girl." Quarry lifted a massive shoulder in dismissal of Trevelyan's possible motives. "Be that as it may—why not go round and speak to the whores there? Chap I talked to says he's seen Trevelyan there at least twice a month—good chance whichever girl he took last can tell you if he's poxed or not."

"Yes, perhaps," Grey said slowly. Quarry took this for immediate agreement, and tossed back the remains of his final pint, belching slightly as he set it down.

"Splendid. We'll go round day after tomorrow, then."

"Day after tomorrow?"

"Got to go to dinner at my brother's house tomorrow—my sister-in-law is having Lord Worplesdon."

"Steamed, boiled, or baked *en croûte*?"

Quarry guffawed, his already ruddy face achieving a deeper hue under the stress of amusement.

"Oh, a good one, Johnny! I'll tell Amanda—come to think, shall I have her invite you? She's fond of you, you know."

"No, no," Grey said hastily. He was in turn fond of Quarry's sister-in-law, Lady Joffrey, but was only too well aware that she regarded him not merely as a friend, but also as prey—a potential husband for one of her myriad sisters and cousins. "I am engaged tomorrow. But this brothel you've discovered—"

"Well, no time like the present, I agree," Harry said, pushing back his bench. "But you'll need your rest tonight, if you're going to look at bodies in the morning. Besides," he added, swirling his cloak over his shoulders, "I'm never at me best in bed after eel pie. Makes me fart."

Chapter 4

A Valet Calls

Next morning, Grey sat in his bedchamber, un-shaven and attired in his nightshirt, banyan, and slippers, drinking tea and debating with himself whether the authoritative benefits conferred by wearing his uniform outweighed the possible conse-quences—both sartorial and social—of wearing it into the slums of London to inspect a three-day-old corpse. He was disturbed in this meditation by his new orderly, Private Adams, who opened the bed-room door and entered without ceremony.

"A person, my lord," Adams reported, and stood smartly to attention.

Never at his best early in the day, Grey took a moody swallow of tea and nodded in acknowledg-ment of this announcement. Adams, new both to Grey and to the job of personal orderly, took this for permission and stood aside, gesturing the person in question into the room.

"Who are you?" Grey gazed in blank astonishment at the young man who stood thus revealed.

"Tom Byrd, me lord," the young man said, and bowed respectfully, hat in hand. Short and stocky, with a head round as a cannonball, he was young enough still to sport freckles across fair, rounded cheeks and over the bridge of his snubbed nose. Despite his obvious youth, though, he radiated a remarkable air of determination.

"Byrd. Byrd. Oh, Byrd!" Lord John's sluggish mental processes began to engage themselves. Tom Byrd. Presumably this young man was some relation to the vanished Jack Byrd. "Why are you— oh. Perhaps Mr. Trevelyan has sent you?"

"Yes, me lord. Colonel Quarry sent him a note last night, saying as how you was going to be looking into the matter of . . . er-hem." He cleared his throat ostentatiously, with a glance at Adams, who had taken up the shaving brush and was industriously swishing it to and fro in the soap mug, working up a great lather of suds. "Mr. Trevelyan said as how I was to come and assist, whatsoever thing it might be your lordship had need of."

"Oh? I see; how kind of him." Grey was amused at Byrd's air of dignity, but favorably impressed at his discretion. "What duties are you accustomed to perform in Mr. Trevelyan's household, Tom?"

"I'm a footman, sir." Byrd stood as straight as he could, chin lifted in an attempt at an extra inch of height; footmen were normally employed for appearance as much as for skill, and tended to be tall and well-formed; Byrd was about Grey's own height.

Grey rubbed his upper lip, then set aside his teacup and glanced at Adams, who had put down the soap mug and was now holding the razor in one hand, strop in the other, apparently unsure how to employ the two effectively in concert. "Tell me, Byrd, have you any experience at valeting?"

"No, me lord—but I can shave a man." Tom Byrd sedulously

avoided looking at Adams, who had discarded the strop and was testing the edge of the razor against the edge of his shoe sole, frowning.

"You can, can you?"

"Yes, me lord. Father's a barber, and us boys'd shave the bristles from the scalded hogs he bought for to make brushes of. For practice, like."

"Hmm." Grey glanced at himself in the looking glass above the chest of drawers. His beard came in only a shade or two darker than his blond hair, but it grew heavily, and the stubble glimmered thick as wheat straw on his jaw in the morning light. No, he really couldn't forgo shaving.

"All right," he said with resignation. "Adams—give the razor to Tom here, if you please. Then go and brush my oldest uniform, and tell the coachman I shall require him. Mr. Byrd and I are going to view a body."

❧

A night lying in the water at Puddle Dock and two days lying in a shed behind Bow Street compter had not improved Timothy O'Connell's appearance, never his strongest point to begin with. At that, he was at least still recognizable—more than could be said for the gentleman lying on a bit of canvas by the wall, who had apparently hanged himself.

"Turn him over, if you please," Grey said tersely, speaking through a handkerchief soaked with oil of wintergreen, which he held against the lower half of his face.

The two prisoners deputed to accompany him to this makeshift morgue looked rebellious—they had already been obliged to take O'Connell from his cheap coffin and remove his shroud for Grey's inspection—but a gruff word from the constable in charge propelled them into reluctant action.

The corpse had been roughly cleansed, at least. The marks of his last battle were clear, even though the body was bloated and the skin extensively discolored.

Grey bent closer, handkerchief firmly clasped to his face, to inspect the bruises across the back. He beckoned to Tom Byrd, who was standing pressed against the wall of the shed, his freckles dark against the paleness of his face.

"See that?" He pointed to the black mottling over the corpse's back and buttocks. "He was kicked and trampled upon, I think."

"Yes, sir?" Byrd said faintly.

"Yes. But you see how the skin is completely discolored upon the dorsal aspect?"

Byrd gave him a look indicating that he saw nothing whatever, including a reason for his own existence.

"His back," Grey amended. "*Dorsum* is the Latin word for back."

"Oh, aye," Byrd said, intelligence returning. "I see it plain, me lord."

"That means that he lay upon his back for some time after death. I have seen men taken up from a battlefield for burial; the portions that have lain bottom-most are always discolored in that way."

Byrd nodded, looking faintly ill.

"But you found him upon his face in the water, is that correct?" Grey turned to the constable.

"Yes, my lord. The coroner's seen him," the man added helpfully. "Death by violence."

"Quite," Grey said. "There was no grievous wound upon the front of his body that might have caused his death, and I see no such wound here, do you, Byrd? Not stabbed, not shot, not choked with a garrote . . ."

Byrd swayed slightly, but caught himself, and was heard to mutter something about ". . . head, mebbe?"

"Perhaps. Here, take this." Grey shoved the handkerchief into Byrd's clammy hand, then turned and, holding his breath, gingerly began to feel about in O'Connell's hair. He was interested to see that an inexpert attempt had been made to do up the corpse's hair in a proper military queue, wrapped round a pad of lamb's wool and bound with a leather lacing, though whoever had done it had lacked the rice powder for a finishing touch. Someone who cared had laid the body out—not Mrs. O'Connell, he thought, but someone.

The scalp had begun to loosen, and shifted unpleasantly under his probing fingers. There were assorted lumps, presumably left by kicks or blows . . . yes, there. And there. In two places, the bone of the skull gave inward in a sickening manner, and a slight ooze moistened Grey's fingertips.

Byrd made a small choking sound as Grey withdrew his hand, and blundered out, handkerchief still clasped to his face.

"Was he wearing his uniform when he was found?" Grey asked the constable. Deprived of his handkerchief, he wiped his fingers fastidiously on the shroud as he nodded to the two prisoners to restore the corpse to its original state.

"Nah, sir." The constable shook his head. "Stripped to his shirt. We knew as he was one of yours, though, from his hair, and askin' about a bit, we found someone as knew his name and regiment."

Grey's ears pricked up at that.

"Do you mean to say that he was known in the neighborhood where he was found?"

The constable frowned.

"I s'pose so," he said, rubbing at his chin to assist thought. "Let me think . . . yes, sir, I'm sure as that's right. When we pulled him out o' the water, and I saw as how he was a soldier, I went round to the Oak and Oyster to inquire, that bein' the nearest place where the soldiers mostly go. Brought a few of the folk in there along to have a look at him; as I recall, 'twas the barmaid from the Oyster what knew him."

The body had been turned over, and one of the prisoners, lips pressed tight against the smell, was drawing up the shroud again, when Grey stopped him with a motion. He bent over the coffin, frowning, and traced the mark on O'Connell's forehead. It was indeed a heelprint, distinctly indented on the livid flesh. He could count the nailheads.

He nodded to himself and straightened up. The body had been moved, so much was plain. But from where? If the Sergeant had been killed in a brawl, as appeared to be the case, perhaps there would have been a report of such an occurrence.

"Might I have a word with your superior, sir?"

"That'd be Constable Magruder, sir—round the front, room on the left. Will you be done with the corpse, sir?" He was already motioning for the two sullen prisoners to restore O'Connell's wrappings and nail down the coffin lid.

"Oh . . . yes. I think so." Grey paused, considering. Ought he perhaps to make some ceremonial gesture of farewell to a comrade in arms? There was nothing in that blank and swollen countenance, though, that seemed to invite such a gesture, and surely the constable did not care. In the end, he gave a slight nod to the corpse, a shilling to the constable for his trouble, and left.

Constable Magruder was a small, foxy-looking man, with narrow eyes that darted constantly from doorway to desk and back again, lest anything escape his notice. Grey took some encouragement from this, hoping that few things *did* escape the constable of the day and the Bow Street Runners under his purview.

The constable knew Grey's errand; he saw the wariness lurking at the back of the narrow eyes—and the quick flick of a glance toward the magistrate's offices next door. It was apparent that he feared Grey might go to the magistrate, Sir John Fielding, with all the consequent trouble this might involve.

Grey did not know Sir John himself, but was reasonably sure that his mother did. Still, at this point, there was no need to invoke him. Realizing what was in Magruder's mind, Grey did his best to show an attitude of relaxed affability and humble gratitude for the constable's continued assistance.

"I thank you, sir, for your gracious accommodation. I hesitate to intrude further on your generosity—but if I might ask just one or two questions?"

"Oh, aye, sir." Magruder went on looking wary, but relaxed a little, relieved that he was not about to be asked to conduct a time-consuming and probably futile investigation.

"I understand that Sergeant O'Connell was likely killed on Saturday night. Are you aware of any disturbances taking place in the neighborhood on that night?"

Magruder's face twitched.

"Disturbances, Major? The whole place is a disturbance come nightfall, sir. Robbery from the person, purse-cutting, fights and street riots, disagreements betwixt whores and their customers, burglary of premises, theft, tavern brawls, malicious mischief, fire-setting, horse-stealing, housebreaking, random assaults . . ."

"Yes, I see. Still, we are reasonably sure that no one set Sergeant O'Connell on fire, nor yet mistook him for a lady of the evening." Grey smiled to abjure any suspicions of sarcasm. "I am only seeking to narrow the possibilities, you see, sir." He spread his hands, deprecatingly. "My duty, you understand."

"Oh, aye." Magruder was not without humor; a small gleam of it lit the narrow eyes and softened the harsh outlines of his face.

He glanced from the papers on his desk to the hallway, down which echoed shouts and bangings from the prisoners in the rear, then back to Grey.

"I'll have to speak to the constable of the night, go through the reports. If I see anything that might be helpful to your inquiry, Major, I'll send round a note, shall I?"

"I should appreciate it very much, sir." Grey rose promptly, and the two men parted with mutual expressions of esteem.

Tom Byrd was sitting on the pavement outside, still pale, but improved. He sprang to his feet at Grey's gesture, and fell into step behind him.

Would Magruder produce anything helpful? Grey wondered. There were so many possibilities. Robbery from the person, Magruder had suggested. Perhaps . . . but knowing what he did of O'Connell's ferocious temperament, Grey was not inclined to think that a gang of robbers would have chosen him at random—there were easier sheep to fleece, by far.

But what if O'Connell had succeeded in meeting the spy-master—if there was one, Grey reminded himself—and had turned over his documents and received a sum of money?

He considered the possibility that the spymaster had then mur-dered O'Connell to retrieve his money or silence a risk—but in that case, why not simply kill O'Connell and take the documents in the first place? Well . . . if O'Connell had been wise enough not to carry the documents on his person, and the spymaster knew it, he would presumably have taken care to obtain the goods before taking any subsequent steps in disposing of the messenger.

By the same token, though, if someone else had discovered that O'Connell was in possession of a sum of money, they might have killed him in the process of a robbery that had nothing to do with the stolen requisitions. But the amount of damage done to the body . . . that suggested whoever had done the deed had meant to make sure that O'Connell was dead. Casual robbers would not have cared; they would have knocked O'Connell on the head and absconded, completely careless of whether he lived or died.

A spymaster might make certain of the matter. And yet—would a spymaster depend upon the services of associates? For clearly, O'Connell had faced more than one assailant—and from the condition of his hands, had left his mark on them.

"What do you think, Tom?" he said, more by way of clarifying his thoughts than because he desired Byrd's opinion. "If secrecy were a concern, would it not be more sensible to use a weapon? Beating a man to death is likely to be a noisy business. Attract a lot of unwelcome attention, wouldn't you say?"

"Yes, me lord. I expect that's so. Though so far as that goes . . ."

"Yes?" He glanced round at Byrd, who hastened his step a bit to come level with Grey.

"Well, it's only—mind, I ain't—haven't, I mean—seen a man beat to death. But when you go to kill a pig, you only get a terrible lot of screeching if you've done it wrong."

"Done it wrong?"

"Yes, me lord. If you do it right, it doesn't take but one good blow. The pig doesn't know what hit 'im, and there's no noise to speak of. You get a man what doesn't know what he's doing, or isn't strong enough—" Byrd made a face at the thought of such incompetence. "Racket like to wake the dead. There's a butcher's across the street from me dad's shop," he offered in explanation. "I've seen pigs killed often."

"A very good point, Tom," Grey said slowly. If either robbery or simple murder was the intent, it could have been accomplished with much less fuss. Ergo, whatever had befallen Tim O'Connell had likely been an accident, in a brawl or street riot, or . . . and yet the body had been moved, sometime after death. Why?

His cogitations were interrupted by the sound of an agitated altercation in the alleyway that led to the back of the gaol.

"What're you doing here, you Irish whore?"

"I've a right to be here—unlike you, ye draggletail thief!"

"Cunt!"

"Bitch!"

Following the sound of strife into the alley, Grey found Timothy O'Connell's sealed coffin lying in the roadway, surrounded by people. In the center of the mob was the pregnant figure of Mrs. O'Connell, swathed in a black shawl and squared off against another woman, similarly attired.

The ladies were not alone, he saw; Scanlon the apothecary was vainly trying to persuade Mrs. O'Connell away from her opponent, with the aid of a tall, rawboned Irishman. The second lady had also brought reinforcement, in the person of a small, fat clergyman, dressed in dog collar and rusty coat, who appeared more entertained than distressed by the exchange of cordialities. A number of other people crowded the alley behind both women—mourners, presumably, come to assist in the burial of Sergeant O'Connell.

"Take your wicked friends and be off with ye! He was my husband, not yours!"

"Oh, and a fine wife *you* were, I'm sure! Didn't care enough to come and wash the mud from his face when they dragged him out of the ditch! It was me laid him out proper, and me that'll bury him, thank you very much! Wife! Ha!"

Tom Byrd stood open-mouthed under the eaves of the shed, watching. He glanced up wide-eyed at Grey.

"And it's me paid for his coffin—think I'll let you take it? Likely you'll give the body to a knacker's shop and sell the box, greedyguts! Take a man from his wife so you can suck the marrow from his bones—"

"Shut your trap!"

"Shut yours!" bellowed the widow O'Connell, and she took a wild swing at the other woman, who dodged adroitly. Seeing a sudden surge among the mourners on both sides, Grey pushed his way between the women.

"Madam," he began, grasping Mrs. O'Connell's arm with determination. "You must—" His admonition was interrupted by a swift elbow in the pit of the stomach, which took him quite by surprise. He staggered back a pace, and stamped inadvertently on the toe of the tall Irishman, who hopped to and fro on one foot, uttering brief blasphemies in what Grey assumed to be the Irish tongue, as it was no form of French.

These were rapidly subsumed by the blasphemies being flung by the two ladies—if that was the word, Grey thought grimly—in an incoherent barrage of insults.

The pistol-shot sound of a slapped cheek rang out, and then the alley erupted in high-pitched shrieks as the women closed with each other, fingers clawed and feet kicking. Grey grabbed for the other woman's sleeve, but it was torn from his grip and he was knocked heavily into a wall. Someone tripped him, and he went down, rolling and rebounding from the wall of the shed before he could get his feet under him.

Regaining his balance, Grey staggered, then landed on the balls of his feet, and snatched out his sword in a slashing arc that made the metal sing. The thin chime of it cut through the racket in the alleyway like a knife through butter, separating the combatants and sending the women stumbling back from each other. In the moment's silence that resulted, Grey stepped firmly between the two women and glared back and forth between them.

Assured that he had put at least a momentary stop to the battle, he turned to the unknown woman. A solid person with curly black hair, she wore a wide-brimmed hat that obscured her face, but not her attitude, which was belligerent in the extreme.

"May I inquire your name, madam? And your purpose here?"

"She's a class of a slut, what else?" Mrs. O'Connell's voice came from behind him, cracked with contempt, but controlled. Silencing the other woman's heated response to this with a peremptory movement of his sword, he cast an irritated glance over his shoulder.

"I asked the lady herself—if you please, Mrs. O'Connell."

"That would be Mrs. Scanlon—if *you* please, my lord." The apothecary's voice was more than polite, but held a note almost of smugness.

"I beg your pardon?" Taken by surprise, he turned completely round to face Scanlon and the widow. Evidently, the other woman was equally shocked, for beyond a loud "*What?*" behind him, she said nothing.

Scanlon was holding Francine O'Connell by the arm; he tightened his grasp a little and bowed to Grey.

"I have the honor to introduce you to my wife, sir," he said gravely. "Wed yestereen we were, by special license, with Father Doyle himself doing of the honors." He nodded at the tall Irishman, who nodded in turn, though keeping a wary eye on the tip of Grey's rapier.

"What, couldn't wait 'til poor old Tim was cold, could you? And who's the slut here, I'd like to know, you with your belly swole up like a farkin' toad!"

"I'm a married woman—*twice* married! And you with no name and no shame—"

"Ah, now, Francie, Francie . . ." Scanlon put his arms around his incensed wife, lugging her back by main force. "Let it be, sweetheart, let it be. Ye don't want to be doing the babe an injury now, do ye?"

At this reminder of her delicate condition, Francine desisted, though she went on huffing beneath her hat brim, much in the manner of a bull who has chased intruders out of a field and means to see that they stay chased.

Grey turned back to the other woman, just as she opened her mouth again. He put the tip of his rapier firmly against the middle of her chest, cutting her expostulations short and eliciting a brief and startled "Eek!"

"Who the hell are you?" he demanded, patience exhausted.

"Iphigenia Stokes," she replied indignantly. "How dare you be takin' liberties with me person, you?" She backed up a step, swatting at his sword with a hand whose essential broadness and redness was not disguised by the black shammy mitt covering it.

"And who are *you*?" Grey swung toward the small clergyman, who had been tranquilly enjoying the show from a place of security behind a barrel.

"Me?" The clerical gentleman looked surprised, but bowed obligingly. "The Reverend Mr. Cobb, sir, curate of St. Giles. I was asked to come and deliver the obsequies for the late Mr. O'Connell, on behalf of Miss Stokes, whom I understand to have had a personal friendship with the deceased."

"You *what*? A frigging *Protestant*?" Francine O'Connell Scanlon stood straight upright, trembling with renewed outrage. Mr. Cobb eyed her warily, but seemed to feel himself safe enough in his retreat, for he bowed politely to her.

"Interment is to be in the churchyard at St. Giles, ma'am—if you and your husband would care to attend?"

At this, the entire Irish contingent pressed forward, obviously intending to seize the casket and carry it off by main force. Nothing daunted, Miss Stokes's escort likewise pushed eagerly to the fore, several of the gentlemen uprooting boards from a sagging fence to serve as makeshift clubs.

Miss Stokes was encouraging her troops with bellows of "Catholic whore!" while Mr. Scanlon appeared to be of two minds in the matter, simultaneously dragging his wife out of the fray while shaking his free fist in the direction of the Protestants and shouting assorted Irish imprecations.

With visions of bloody riot breaking out, Grey leapt atop the casket and swung his sword viciously from side to side, driving back all comers.

"Tom!" he shouted. "Go for the constables!"

Tom Byrd had not waited for instructions, but had apparently gone for reinforcements during the earlier part of the affray; the word "constables" was barely out of Grey's mouth, when the sound of running feet came down the street. Constable Magruder and a pair of his men charged into the alley, clubs and pistols at the ready, with Tom Byrd bringing up the rear, panting.

Seeing the arrival of armed authority, the warring funeral parties drew instantly apart, knives disappearing like magic and clubs dropping to the ground with insouciant casualness.

"Are you in difficulties, Major?" Constable Magruder called, looking distinctly entertained as he glanced between the two competing widows and then up at Grey on his precarious roost.

"No, sir . . . I thank you," Grey replied politely, gasping for breath. He felt the cheap boards of the coffin creak in a sinister fashion as he shifted his weight, and sweat ran down the groove of his back. "If you would care to go on standing there for just a moment longer, though? . . ."

He drew a deep breath and stepped gingerly down from his perch. He had rolled through a puddle; the seat of his breeches was wet, and he could feel the split where the sleeve seam beneath his right arm had given way. Goddamn it, now what?

He was inclined toward the simplicity of a Solomonic decree that would award half of Tim O'Connell to each woman, and rejected this notion only because of the time it would take and the fact that his rapier was completely unsuited to the task of such division. If the widows gave him any further difficulties, though, he was sending Tom to fetch a butcher's cleaver upon the instant, he swore it.

Grey sighed, sheathed his sword, and rubbed the spot between his brows with an index finger.

"Mrs. . . . Scanlon."

"Aye?" The swelling of her face had gone down somewhat; it was suspicion and fury now that narrowed those diamond eyes of hers.

"When I called upon you two days ago, you rejected the gift presented by your husband's comrades in arms, on the grounds that you believed your husband to be in hell and did not wish to waste money upon Masses and candles. Is that not so?"

"It is," she said, reluctantly. "But—"

"Well, then. If you believe him presently to be occupying the infernal regions," Grey pointed out, "that is clearly a permanent condition. The act of having his body interred in a particular location, or with Catholic ritual, will not alter his unfortunate destiny."

"Now, we can't be knowing for certain as a sinner's soul has gone to hell," the priest objected, suddenly seeing the prospects of a fee for burying O'Connell receding. "God's ways are beyond the ken of us poor men, and for all any of us knows, poor Tim O'Connell repented of his wickedness at the last, made a perfect Act of Contrition, and was taken straight up to paradise in the arms of the angels!"

"Excellent." Grey leapt on this incautious speculation like a leopard on its prey. "If he is in paradise, he is still less in need of earthly intervention. So"—he bowed punctiliously to the Scanlons and their priest—"according to you, the deceased may be either damned or saved, but is surely in one of those two conditions.

Whereas *you*"—he turned to Miss Stokes—"are of the opinion that Tim O'Connell is perhaps in some intermediate state where intercessory actions might be efficacious?"

Miss Stokes regarded him for a moment, her mouth hanging slightly open.

"I just want 'im buried proper," she said, sounding suddenly meek. "Sir."

"Well, then. I consider that you, madam"—he shot a sharp look at the new Mrs. Scanlon—"have to some degree forfeited your legal rights in the matter, being now married to Mr. Scanlon. If Miss Stokes were to reimburse you for the cost of the coffin, would you find that acceptable?"

Grey eyed the Irish contingent, and found them dour-faced but silent. Scanlon glanced at the priest, then at his wife, then finally at Grey, and nodded, very slightly.

"Take him," Grey said to Miss Stokes, stepping back with a brief gesture toward the coffin.

He strode purposefully toward Scanlon, hand on the hilt of his sword, but while there was a certain amount of shuffling, muttering, and spitting in the ranks, none of the Irish seemed disposed to offer more than the occasional murmured insult as Miss Stokes's minions took possession of the disputed remains.

"May I offer my felicitations on your marriage, sir?" he said politely.

"I am obliged to ye, sir," Scanlon said, equally polite. Francine stood by his side, simmering beneath her large black hat.

They stood silent then, all watching as Tim O'Connell was borne away. Iphigenia Stokes was surprisingly gracious in triumph, Grey thought; she cast neither glance nor remark toward the defeated Irish, and her attendants followed her lead, moving in silence to pick up the coffin. Miss Stokes took up her place as chief mourner, and the small procession moved off. At the last, the Reverend Mr. Cobb risked a brief glance back and a tiny wave of the hand toward Grey.

"God rest his soul," Father Doyle said piously, crossing himself as the coffin disappeared down the alley.

"God rot him," said Francine O'Connell Scanlon. She turned her head and spat neatly on the ground. *"And* her."

It was not yet noon, and the taverns were still largely empty. Constable Magruder and his assistants graciously accepted a quantity of drink in the Blue Swan in reward of their help, and then returned to their duties, leaving Grey to shuck his coat and attempt repairs to his wardrobe in a modicum of privacy.

"It seems you're a handy fellow with a needle as well as a razor, Tom." Grey slouched comfortably on a bench in the tavern's deserted snug, restoring himself with a second pint of stout. "To say nothing of quick with both wits and feet. If you'd not gone for Magruder when you did, I'd likely be laid out in the alley now, cold as yesterday's turbot."

Tom Byrd squinted over the red coat he was mending by the imperfect light from a leaded-glass window. He didn't look up from his work, but a small glow of gratification appeared to spread itself across his snub features.

"Well, I could see as how you had the matter well in hand, me lord," he said tactfully, "but there was a dreadful lot of them Irish, to say nothin' of the Frenchies."

"Frenchies?" Grey put a fist to his mouth to stifle a rising eructation. "What, you thought Miss Stokes's friends were French? Why?"

Byrd looked up, surprised.

"Why, they was speakin' French to each other—at least a couple of them. Two black-browed coves, curly-haired, what looked as if they was related to that Miss Stokes."

Grey was surprised in turn, and furrowed his brow in concentration, trying to recall any remarks that might have been made in French during the recent contretemps, but failing. He had marked out the two swarthy persons described by Tom, who had squared up behind their—sister, cousin? for surely Tom was right; there *was* an undeniable resemblance—in menacing fashion, but they had looked more like—

"Oh," he said, struck by a thought. "Did it sound perhaps a bit like this?" He recited a brief verse from Homer, doing his best to infuse it with a crude English accent.

Tom's face lighted and he nodded vigorously, the end of the thread in his mouth.

"I did wonder where she'd got Iphigenia," Grey said, smiling. "Shouldn't think her father was a scholar of the classics, after all. It's Greek, Tom," he clarified, seeing his young valet frown in incomprehension. "Likely Miss Stokes and her brothers—if that's what they are—have a Greek mother or grandmother, for I'm sure Stokes is home-grown enough."

"Oh, Greek," Tom said uncertainly, obviously unclear on the distinctions between this and any other form of French. "To be sure, me lord." He delicately removed a bit of thread stuck to his lip, and shook out the folds of the coat. "Here, me lord; I won't say as it's good as new, but you can at least be wearing it without the lining peepin' out."

Grey nodded in thanks, and pushed a full mug of beer in Tom's direction. He shrugged himself carefully into the mended coat, inspecting the torn seam. It was scarcely tailor's work, but the repair looked stout enough.

He wondered whether Iphigenia Stokes might repay closer inspection; if she *did* have family ties to France, it would suggest both
a motive for O'Connell's treachery—if he had been a traitor—and
an avenue by which he might have disposed of the Calais information. But Greek . . . that argued for Stokes *Père* having been a
sailor, perhaps. Likely merchant seaman rather than naval, if he'd
brought home a foreign wife.

Yes, he rather thought the Stokes family would bear looking
into. Seafaring ran in families, and while his observations had necessarily been cursory under the circumstances, he thought that
one or two of the men in the Stokes party had looked like sailors;
one had had a gold ring in his ear, he was sure. And sailors would
be well-placed for smuggling information out of Britain, though in
that case—

"Me lord?"

"Yes, Tom?" He frowned slightly at the interruption to his
thoughts, but answered courteously.

"It's only I was thinking . . . seeing the dead cove, I mean—"

"Sergeant O'Connell, you mean?" Grey amended, not liking to
hear a late comrade in arms referred to carelessly as "the dead
cove," traitor or not.

"Yes, me lord." Tom took a deep swallow of his beer, then
looked up, meeting Grey's eyes directly. "Do you think me
brother's dead, too?"

That brought him up short. He readjusted the coat on his shoulders, thinking what to say. In fact, he did not think Jack Byrd was
dead; he agreed with Harry Quarry that the fellow had probably
either joined forces with whoever had killed O'Connell—or had
killed the Sergeant himself. Neither speculation was likely to be reassuring to Jack Byrd's brother, though.

"No," he said slowly. "I do not. If he had been killed by the persons who brought about Sergeant O'Connell's death, I think his body would have been discovered nearby. There could be no particular reason to hide it, do you think?"

The boy's rigid shoulders relaxed a little, and he shook his head, taking another gulp of his beer.

"No, me lord." He wiped at his mouth with the back of his hand. "Only—if he's not dead, where do ye think he might be?"

"I don't know," Grey answered honestly. "I am hoping we shall discover that soon." It occurred to him that if Jack Byrd had not yet left London, his brother might be a help in determining his whereabouts, witting or not.

"Can you think of places where your brother might go? If he was—frightened, perhaps? Or felt himself to be in danger?"

Tom Byrd shot him a sharp look, and he realized that the boy was a good deal more intelligent than he had at first assumed.

"No, me lord. If he needed help—well, there's six of us boys and Dad, and me father's two brothers and their boys, too; we takes care of our own. But he's not been home; I know that much."

"Quite a thriving rookery of Byrds, it seems. You've spoken to your family, then?" Grey felt gingerly beneath the skirts of his coat; finding his breeches mostly dried, he sat down again opposite Byrd.

"Yes, me lord. Me sister—there's only the one of her—come to Mr. Trevelyan's on Sunday last, a-looking for Jack with a message. That was when Mr. Trevelyan said he'd not heard from Jack since the night before Mr. O'Connell died."

The boy shook his head.

"If it happened Jack ran into summat too much for him, that Dad and us couldn't handle, he would have gone to Mr. Trevelyan, I think. But he didn't do that. If something happened, I think it must've been sudden, like."

A clatter in the passageway announced the return of the barmaid, and prevented Grey answering—which was as well, since he had no useful suggestion to offer.

"Are you hungry, Tom?" The tray of fresh pasties the woman carried were hot and doubtless savory enough, but Grey's nose was still numbed with oil of wintergreen, and the memory of O'Connell's corpse fresh enough in mind to suppress his appetite.

The same appeared true of Byrd, for he shook his head emphatically.

"Well, then. Give the lady back her needle—and a bit for her kindness—and we'll be off."

Grey had not kept the coach, and so they walked back toward Bow Street, where they might find transport. Byrd slouched along, a little behind Grey, kicking at pebbles; obviously thoughts of his brother were weighing on his mind.

"Was your brother accustomed to report back to Mr. Trevelyan regularly?" Grey asked, glancing over his shoulder. "Whilst watching Sergeant O'Connell, I mean?"

Tom shrugged, looking unhappy.

"Dunno, me lord. Jack didn't say what it was he was up to; only that it was a special thing Mr. Joseph wanted him to do, and that was why he wouldn't be in the house for a bit."

"But you know now? What he was doing, and why?"

An expression of wariness flitted through the boy's eyes.

"No, me lord. Mr. Trevelyan only said as I should help you. He didn't say specially what with."

"I see." Grey wondered how much of the situation to impart. It was the anxious look on Tom Byrd's face, as much as anything else, that decided him on full disclosure. Full, that is, bar the precise nature of O'Connell's suspected peculations and Grey's private conjectures regarding the role of Jack Byrd in the matter.

"So you don't think the dead—Sergeant O'Connell, I mean— you don't think he was just knocked on the head by accident, like, me lord?" Byrd had come out of his mope; the clammy look had left his cheeks, and he was walking briskly now, engrossed in the details of Grey's account.

"Well, you see, Tom, I still cannot say so with any certainty. I was hoping that perhaps we should discover some particular mark upon the body that would make it clear that someone had deliberately set out to murder Sergeant O'Connell, and I found nothing of that nature. On the other hand . . ."

"On the other hand, whoever stamped on his face didn't like him much," Tom completed the thought shrewdly. "*That* was no accident, me lord."

"No, it wasn't," Grey agreed dryly. "That was done after death, not in the frenzy of the moment."

Tom's eyes went quite round.

"However do you know that? Me lord," he added hastily.

"You looked closely at the heelprint? Several of the nailheads had broken through the skin, and yet there was no blood extravasated."

Tom gave him a look of mingled bewilderment and suspicion, obviously suspecting that Grey had made up the word upon the moment for the express purpose of tormenting him, but merely said, "Oh?"

"Oh, indeed." Grey felt some slight chagrin at having inadvertently shown up the deficiencies of Tom's vocabulary, but didn't wish to make further issue of the point by apologizing.

"Dead men don't bleed, you see—save they have suffered some grievous wound, such as the loss of a limb, and are picked up soon after. Then you will see some dripping, of course, but the blood soon thickens as it chills, and—" Seeing the pallid look reappear on Tom's face, he coughed, and resumed upon another tack.

"No doubt you are thinking that the nail marks might have bled, but the blood had been cleansed away?"

"Oh. Um . . . yes," Tom said faintly.

"Possible," Grey conceded, "but not likely. Wounds to the head bleed inordinately—like a stuck pig, as the saying is."

"Whoever says it hasn't likely seen a stuck pig," Tom said, rallying stoutly. "I have. Floods of it, there is. Enough to fill a barrel— or two!"

Grey nodded, noting that it was clearly not the notion of blood per se that was disturbing the lad.

"Yes, that's the way of it. I looked very carefully and found no dried blood in the corpse's hair or on the skin of the face—though the cleansing appeared otherwise to be rather crude. So no, I am fairly sure the mark was made some little time after the Sergeant had ceased to breathe."

"Well, it wasn't Jack what made it!"

Grey glanced at him, startled. Well, now he knew what was disturbing the boy; beyond simple worry at his brother's absence, Tom clearly feared that Jack Byrd might be guilty of murder—or at least suspected of it.

"I did not suggest that he did," he replied carefully.

"But I know he didn't! I can prove it, me lord!" Byrd grasped him by the sleeve, carried away by the passion of his speech.

"Jack's shoes have square heels, me lord! Whoever stamped the dead cove had round ones! Wooden ones, too, and Jack's shoes have leather heels!"

He paused, almost panting in his excitement, searching Grey's face with wide eyes, anxious for any sign of agreement.

"I see," Grey said slowly. The boy was still gripping his arm. He put his own hand over the boy's and squeezed lightly. "I am glad to hear it, Tom. Very glad."

Byrd searched his face a moment longer, then evidently found what he had been seeking, for he drew a deep breath and let go of Grey's sleeve with a shaky nod.

They reached Bow Street a few moments later, and Grey waved an arm to summon a carriage, glad of the excuse to discontinue the conversation. For while he was sure that Tom was telling the truth regarding his brother's shoes, one fact remained: The disappearance of Jack Byrd was still the main reason for presuming that O'Connell's death had been no accident.

Harry Quarry was eating supper at his desk while doing paperwork, but put aside both plate and papers to listen to Grey's account of Sergeant O'Connell's dramatic departure.

" 'How dare you be takin' liberties with me person, you?' She really said that?" He wheezed, wiping tears of amusement from the corners of his eyes. "Christ, Johnny, you've had a more entertaining day than I have, by a long shot!"

"You are quite welcome to resume the personal aspects of this investigation at any moment," Grey assured him, leaning over to pluck a radish from the ravaged remains of Quarry's meal. He had had no food since breakfast, and was ravenous. "I won't mind at all."

"No, no," Quarry reassured him. "Wouldn't dream of deprivin' you of the opportunity. What d'ye make of Scanlon and the widow, coming to bury O'Connell like that?"

Grey shrugged, chewing the radish as he brushed flecks of dried mud from the skirts of his coat.

"He'd just married O'Connell's widow, mere days after the sergeant was killed. I suppose he meant to deflect suspicion, assuming that people would scarce suspect him of having killed the man if he had the face to show up looking pious and paying for the funeral, complete with priest and trimmings."

"Mm." Quarry nodded, picking up a stalk of buttered asparagus and inserting it whole into his mouth. "Geddaluk t'shus?"

"Scanlon's shoes? No, I hadn't the opportunity, what with those two harpies trying to murder each other. Stubbs did look at his hands, though, when we were round at his shop. If Scanlon did for O'Connell, someone else did the heavy work."

"D'you think he did it?"

"God knows. Are you going to eat that muffin?"

"Yes," Quarry said, biting into it. Consuming the muffin in two large bites, he tilted back in his chair, squinting at the plate in hopes of discovering something else edible.

"So, this new valet of yours says his brother can't have done it? Well, he would, wouldn't he?"

"Perhaps so—but the same argument obtains as for Scanlon; it took more than one person to kill O'Connell. So far as we know, Jack Byrd was quite alone—and I can't envision a mere footman by himself doing what was done to Tim O'Connell."

Failing to find anything more substantial, Quarry broke a gnawed chicken bone in two and sucked out the marrow.

"So," he summed up, licking his fingers, "what it comes down to is that O'Connell was killed by two or more men, after which someone stamped on his face, then left him to lie for a bit. Some-time later, someone—whether the same someone who killed him, or someone else—picked him up and dropped him into the Fleet Ditch off Puddle Dock."

"That's it. I asked the constable in charge to look through his re-ports, to see whether there was any fighting reported anywhere on the night O'Connell died. Beyond that—" Grey rubbed his fore-head, fighting weariness. "We should look closely at Iphigenia Stokes and her family, I think."

"You don't suppose she did it, do you? Woman scorned and all that—and she has got the sailor brothers. Sailors all wear wooden heels; leather's slippery on deck."

Grey looked at him, surprised.

"However do you come to know that, Harry?"

"Sailed from Edinburgh to France in a new pair of leather-heeled shoes once," Quarry said, picking up a lettuce leaf and peering hopefully beneath it. "Squalls all the way, and nearly broke me leg six times."

Grey plucked the lettuce leaf out of Quarry's hand and ate it.

"An excellent point," he said, swallowing. "And it would account for the apparent personal animosity evident in the crime. But no, I cannot think Miss Stokes had the Sergeant murdered. Scanlon might easily maintain a pose of pious concern for the purpose of disarming suspicion—but not she. She was entirely sincere in her desire to see O'Connell decently buried; I am sure of it."

"Mm." Quarry rubbed thoughtfully at the scar on his cheek. "Perhaps. Might her male relations have discovered that O'Connell had a wife, though, and done him in for honor's sake? They might not have told her what they'd done, if so."

"Hadn't thought of that," Grey admitted. He examined the notion, finding it appealing on several grounds. It would explain the physical circumstances of the Sergeant's death very nicely; not only the battering, done by multiple persons, but the viciousness of the heelprint—and if the killing had been done in or near Miss Stokes's residence, then there was plainly a need to dispose of the body at a safe distance, which would explain its having been moved after death.

"It's not a bad idea at all, Harry. May I have Stubbs, Calvert, and Jowett, then, to help with the inquiries?"

"Take anyone you like. And you'll keep looking for Jack Byrd, of course."

"Yes." Grey dipped a forefinger into the small puddle of sauce that was the only thing remaining on the plate, and sucked it clean. "I doubt there's much to be gained by troubling the Scanlons further, but I wouldn't mind knowing a bit about his close associates, and where they might have been on Saturday night. Last but not least—what about this hypothetical spy-master?"

Quarry blew out his cheeks and heaved a deep sigh.

"I've something in train there—tell you later, if anything comes of it. Meanwhile"—he pushed back his chair and rose, brushing crumbs from his waistcoat—"I've got a dinner party to go to."

"Sure you haven't spoiled your appetite?" Grey asked, bitingly.

"Ha-ha," Quarry said, clapping his wig on his head and bending to peer into the looking glass he kept on the wall near his desk. "Surely you don't think one gets anything to *eat* at a dinner party?"

"That was my impression, yes. I am mistaken?"

"Well, you do," Quarry admitted, "but not for hours. Nothing but sips of wine and bits of toast with capers on before dinner—wouldn't keep a bird alive."

"What sort of bird?" Grey said, eyeing Quarry's muscular but substantial hindquarters. "A great bustard?"

"Care to come along?" Quarry straightened and shrugged on his coat. "Not too late, you know."

"I thank you, no." Grey rose and stretched, feeling every bone in his back creak with the effort. "I'm going home, before I starve to death."

Chapter 5

Eine Kleine Nachtmusik
(A Little Night Music)

It was well past dark when Grey returned to his mother's house in Jermyn Street. In spite of his hunger, he was deliberately late, having no desire to face either his mother or Olivia before he had decided upon a course of action with regard to Joseph Trevelyan.

Not late enough, though. To his dismay, he saw light blazing through all the windows and a liveried footman standing by the portico, obviously there to admit invited guests and repel those unwanted. A voice within was upraised in some sort of song, accompanied by the sounds of flute and harpsichord.

"Oh, God. It isn't Wednesday, is it, Hardy?" he pleaded, ascending the steps toward the footman, who smiled at sight of him, bowing as he opened the door.

"Yes, my lord. Has been all day, I'm afraid."

Normally, he rather enjoyed his mother's weekly musicales. However, he was in no condition to be sociable at the moment. He ought to go and spend the night at the Beefsteak—but that meant an arduous journey back across London, and he was perished with hunger.

"I'll just slip through to the kitchen," he said to Hardy. "*Don't* tell the Countess I'm here."

"No indeed, my lord."

He stole soft-footed into the foyer, pausing for a moment to judge the terrain. Because of the warm weather, the double doors into the main drawing room stood open, to prevent the occupants being suffocated. The music, a lugubrious German duet with a refrain of *"Den Tod"*—"O Death"—would drown the noise of his footsteps, but he would be in plain view for the second or two required to sprint across the foyer and into the hall that led to the kitchens.

He swallowed, mouth watering heavily at the scents of roast meat and steamed pudding that wafted toward him from the recesses of the house.

Another of the footmen, Thomas, was visible through the half-open door of the library, across the foyer from the drawing room. The footman's back was turned to the door, and he carried a Hanoverian military helmet, ornately gilded and festooned with an enormous spray of dyed plumes, obviously wondering where to put the ridiculous object.

Grey pressed himself against the wall and eased farther into the foyer. There was a plan. If he could attract Thomas's attention, he could use the footman as a shield to cross the foyer, thus gain the safety of the staircase, and make it to the sanctuary of his own chamber, whilst Thomas went to fetch him a discreet tray from the kitchen.

This plan of escape was foiled, though, by the sudden appearance of his cousin Olivia on the stair above, elegant in amber silk, blond hair gleaming in a lace cap.

"John!" she cried, beaming at sight of him. "There you are! I was so hoping you'd come home in time."

"In time for what?" he asked, with a sense of foreboding.

"To sing, of course." She skipped down the stairs and seized him affectionately by the arm. "We're having a German evening— and you do the lieder so well, Johnny!"

"Flattery will avail you nothing," he said, smiling despite himself. "I can't sing; I'm starving. Besides, it's nearly over, surely?" He nodded at the case clock by the stair, which read a few minutes past eleven. Supper was almost always served at half-past.

"If you'll sing, I'm sure they'll wait to hear you. Then you can eat afterward. Aunt Bennie has the most marvelous collation laid on—the biggest steamed pudding I've ever seen, with juniper berries, and lamb cutlets with spinach, and a coq au vin, and some absolutely disgusting sausages—for the Germans, you know. . . ."

Grey's stomach rumbled loudly at this enticing catalog of gustation. He still would have demurred, though, had he not at this moment caught sight of an elderly woman with a swatch of ostrich plume in her tidy wig, through the open double doors of the drawing room.

The crowd erupted in applause, but as though the lady sensed his start of recognition, she turned her head toward the door, and her face lighted with pleasure as she saw him.

"She's been hoping you'd come," Olivia murmured behind him.

No help for it. With distinctly mixed feelings, he took Olivia's arm and led her down as Hector's mother hastened out of the drawing room to greet him.

"Lady Mumford! Your servant, ma'am." He smiled and bent over her hand, but she would have none of this formality.

"Nonsense, sweetheart," she said, in that warm throaty voice that held echoes of her dead son's. "Come and kiss me properly, there's a good boy."

He straightened and obligingly bussed her cheek. She put her hands on his own cheeks and kissed him soundly on the mouth. The embrace did not recall Hector's kiss to him, thank God, but was sufficiently unnerving for all that.

"You look well, John," Lady Mumford said, stepping back and giving him a searching look with Hector's blue eyes. "Tired, though. A great deal to be done, I expect, with the regiment set to move?"

"A good deal," he agreed, wondering whether all of London knew that the 47th was due to be reposted. Of course, Lady Mumford had spent most of her life close to the regiment; even with husband and son both dead, she maintained a motherly interest.

"India, I heard," Lady Mumford went on, frowning slightly as she fingered the cloth of his uniform sleeve. "Now, you'll have your new uniform ready ordered, I hope? A nice tropical weight of superfine for your coat and weskit, and linen breeches. You don't want to be spending a summer under the Indian sun, swaddled to the neck in English wool! Take it from me, my dear; I went with Mumford when he was posted there, in '35. Both of us nearly died, between the heat, the flies, and the food. Spent a whole summer in me shift, having the servants pour water over me; poor old Wally wasn't so fortunate, sweating about in full uniform, never could get the stains out. Drank nothing but whisky and coconut milk— bear that in mind, dear, when the time comes. Nourishing and stimulating, you know, and so much more wholesome to the stomach than brandywine."

Realizing that he was merely proxy to the true objects of her bereaved affections—the shades of Hector and his father—he withstood this barrage with patience. It was necessary for Lady Mumford to talk, he knew; however, as he had learned from experience, it was not really necessary for him to listen.

He clasped her hand warmly between his own, nodding and making periodical small noises of interest and assent, while taking in the rest of the assembly with brief glances past Lady Mumford's lace-covered shoulders.

Much the usual mix of society and army, with a few oddities from the London literary world. His mother was fond of books, and tended to collect scribblers, who flocked in ragtag hordes to her gatherings, repaying the bounty of her table with ink-splotched manuscripts—and a very occasional printed book—dedicated to her gracious patronage.

Grey looked warily for the tall, cadaverous figure of Doctor Johnson, who was all too apt to take the floor at supper and begin a declamation of some new epic in progress, covering any lacunae of composition with wide, crumb-showering gestures, but the dictionarist was fortunately absent tonight. That was well, Grey thought, spirits momentarily buoyed. He was fond both of Lady Mumford and of music, but a discourse on the etymology of the vulgar tongue was well above the odds, after the day he had been having.

He caught sight of his mother on the far side of the room, keeping an eye on the serving tables while simultaneously conversing with a tall military gentleman—from his uniform, the Hanoverian owner of the plumed excrescence Grey had observed in the library.

Benedicta, Dowager Countess Melton, was several inches shorter than her youngest son, which placed her inconveniently at about the height of the Hanoverian's middle waistcoat button. Stepping back a bit in order to relieve the strain on her neck, she spotted John, and her face lighted with pleasure.

She jerked her head at him, widening her eyes and compressing her lips in an expression of maternal command that said, as plainly as words, *Come and talk to this horrible person so I can see to the other guests!*

Grey responded with a similar grimace, and the faintest of shrugs, indicating that the demands of civility bound him to his present location for the moment.

His mother rolled her eyes upward in exasperation, then glanced hastily round for another scapegoat. Following the direction of her minatory gaze, he saw that it had lighted on Olivia, who, correctly interpreting her aunt's Jove-like command, left her companion with a word, coming obediently to the Countess's rescue.

"Wait and have your smallclothes made in India, though," Lady Mumford was instructing him. "You can get cotton in Bombay at a fraction of the London price, and the sheer luxury of cotton next the skin, my dear, particularly when one is sweating freely . . . You wouldn't want to get a nasty rash, you know."

"No, indeed not," he murmured, though he scarcely attended to what he was saying. For at this inauspicious moment, his eye lit upon the companion that his cousin had just abandoned—a gentleman in green brocade and powdered wig who stood looking after her, lips thoughtfully pursed.

"Oh, is that Mr. Trevelyan?" Seeing his gaze rigidly fixed over her shoulder, Lady Mumford had turned to discover the reason for this lapse in his attention. "Whatever is he doing, standing there by himself?"

Before Grey could respond, Lady Mumford had seized him by the arm and was towing him determinedly toward the gentleman.

Trevelyan was got up with his customary dash; his buttons were gilt, each with a small emerald at its center, and his cuffs edged with gold lace, his linen scented with a delicate aroma of lavender. Grey was still wearing his oldest uniform, much creased and begrimed by his excursions, and while he usually did not affect a wig, he had on the present occasion not even had opportunity to tidy his hair, let alone bind or powder it properly. He could feel a loose strand hanging down behind his ear.

Feeling distinctly at a disadvantage, Grey bowed and murmured inconsequent pleasantries, as Lady Mumford embarked on a detailed inquisition of Trevelyan, with regard to his upcoming nuptials.

Observing the latter's urbane demeanor, Grey found it increasingly difficult to believe that he had in fact seen what he thought he had seen over the chamber pots. Trevelyan was cordial and mannerly, betraying not the slightest sense of inner disquiet. Perhaps Quarry had been right after all: trick of the light, imagination, some inconsequent blemish, perhaps a birthmark—

"Ho, Major Grey! We have not met, I think? I am von Namtzen."

As though Trevelyan's presence had not been sufficient oppression, a shadow fell across Grey at this point, and he looked up to discover that the very tall German had come to join them, hawk-like blond features set in a grimace of congeniality. Behind von Namtzen, Olivia rolled her eyes at Grey in a gesture of helplessness.

Not caring to be loomed over, Grey took a polite step back, but to no avail. The Hanoverian advanced enthusiastically and seized him in a fraternal embrace.

"We are allies!" von Namtzen announced dramatically to the room at large. "Between the lion of England and the stallion of Hanover, who can stand?" He released Grey, who, with some irritation, perceived that his mother appeared to be finding something amusing in the situation.

"So! Major Grey, I have had the honor this afternoon to be observing the practice of gunnery at Woolwich Arsenal, in company with your Colonel Quarry!"

"Indeed," Grey murmured, noting that one of his waistcoat buttons appeared to be missing. Had he lost it during the contretemps at the gaol, he wondered, or at the hands of this plumed maniac?

"Such booms! I was deafened, quite deafened," von Namtzen assured the assemblage, beaming. "I have heard also the guns of Russia, at St. Petersburg—pah! They are nothing; mere farts, by comparison."

One of the ladies tittered behind her fan. This appeared to encourage von Namtzen, who embarked upon an exegesis of the military personality, giving his unbridled opinions on the virtues of the soldiery of various nations. While the Captain's remarks were ostensibly addressed to Grey, and peppered by occasional interjections of "Do you not agree, Major?", his voice was sufficiently resonant as to overpower all other conversation in his immediate vicinity, with the result that he was shortly surrounded by a company of attentive listeners. Grey, to his relief, was able to retreat inconspicuously.

This relief was short-lived, though; as he accepted a glass of wine from a proffered tray, he discovered that he was standing cheek by jowl again with Joseph Trevelyan, and now alone with the man, both Lady Mumford and Olivia having inconveniently decamped to the supper tables.

"The English?" von Namtzen was saying rhetorically, in answer to some question from Mrs. Haseltine. "Ask a Frenchman what he thinks of the English army, and he will tell you that the English soldier is clumsy, crude, and boorish."

Grey met Trevelyan's eye with an unexpected sympathy of feeling, the two men at once united in their unspoken opinion of the Hanoverian.

"One might ask an English soldier what he thinks of the French, too," Trevelyan murmured in Grey's ear. "But I doubt the answer would be suited to a drawing room."

Taken by surprise, Grey laughed. This was a tactical error, as it drew von Namtzen's attention to him once more.

"However," von Namtzen added, with a gracious nod toward Grey over the heads of the intervening crowd, "whatever else may be said of them, the English are . . . invariably ferocious."

Grey lifted his glass in polite acknowledgment, ignoring his mother, who had gone quite pink in the face with the difficulty of containing her emotions.

He turned half away from the Hanoverian and the Countess, which left him face-to-face with Trevelyan; an awkward position, under the circumstances. Requiring some pretext of conversation, he thanked Trevelyan for his graciousness in sending Byrd.

"Byrd?" Trevelyan said, surprised. "Jack Byrd? You've seen him?"

"No." Grey was surprised in turn. "I referred to Tom Byrd. Another of your footmen—though he says he is brother to Jack."

"Tom Byrd?" Trevelyan's dark brows drew together in puzzlement. "Certainly he is Jack Byrd's brother—but he is no footman. Beyond that . . . I did not send him anywhere. Do you mean to tell me that he has imposed his presence upon you, on the pretext that *I* sent him?"

"He said that Colonel Quarry had sent a note to you, advising you of . . . recent events," he temporized, returning the nod of a passing acquaintance. "And that you had in consequence dispatched him to assist me in my enquiries."

Trevelyan said something that Grey supposed to be a Cornish oath, his lean cheeks growing red beneath his face powder. Glancing about, he drew Grey aside, lowering his voice.

"Harry Quarry did communicate with me—but I said nothing

to Byrd. Tom Byrd is the boy who cleans the boots, for God's sake! I should scarcely take him into my confidence!"

"I see." Grey rubbed a knuckle across his upper lip, suppressing his involuntary smile at the recollection of Tom Byrd, drawing himself up to his full height, claiming to be a footman. "I gather that he somehow informed himself, then, that I was charged with . . . certain enquiries. No doubt he is concerned for his brother's welfare," he added, remembering the young man's white face and subdued manner as they left the Bow Street compter.

"No doubt he is," Trevelyan said, plainly not perceiving this as mitigation. "But that is scarcely an excuse. I cannot believe such behavior! Inform himself—why, he has invaded my private office and read my correspondence—the infernal cheek! I should have him arrested. And then to have left my house without permission, and come here to practice upon you . . . This is unconscionable! Where is he? Bring him to me at once! I shall have him whipped, and dismissed without character!"

Trevelyan was growing more livid by the moment. His anger was surely justified, and yet Grey found himself oddly reluctant to hand Tom Byrd over to justice. The boy must plainly have been aware that he was sacrificing his position—and quite possibly his skin—by his actions, and yet he had not hesitated to act.

"A moment, if you will, sir." He bowed to Trevelyan, and made his way toward Thomas, who was passing through the crowd with a tray of drinks—and not a moment too soon.

"Wine, my lord?" Thomas dipped his tray invitingly.

"Yes, if you haven't anything stronger." Grey took a glass at random and drained it in a manner grossly disrespectful to the vintage, but highly necessary to his state of mind, and took another. "Is Tom Byrd in the house?"

"Yes, my lord. I saw him in the kitchens just now."

"Ah. Well, go and make sure that he stays there, would you?"

"Yes, my lord."

Seeing Thomas off with his tray, Grey returned slowly to Trevelyan, a wineglass in either hand.

"I am sorry," he said, offering one of the glasses to Trevelyan. "The boy seems to have disappeared. Fearful of being discovered in his imposture, I daresay."

Trevelyan was still flushed with indignation, though his breeding had by now overtaken his temper.

"I must apologize," he said stiffly. "I regret most extremely this deplorable situation. That a servant of mine should have practiced upon you in such fashion—I cannot excuse such unwarrantable intrusion, on any grounds."

"Well, he has caused me no inconvenience," Grey said mildly, "and was in fact helpful in some small way." He brushed a thumb unobtrusively over the edge of his jaw, finding it still smooth.

"That is of no importance. He is dismissed at once from my service," Trevelyan said, mouth hardening. "And I beg you will accept my apologies for this base imposition."

Grey was not surprised at Trevelyan's reaction. He *was* surprised at the revelation of Tom Byrd's behavior; the boy must have the strongest of feelings for his brother—and under the circumstances, Grey was inclined to a certain sympathy. He was also impressed at the lad's imagination in conceiving such a scheme—to say nothing of his boldness in carrying it out.

Dismissing Trevelyan's apologies with a gesture, he sought to turn the conversation to other matters.

"You enjoyed the music this evening?" he asked.

"Music?" Trevelyan looked blank for a moment, then recovered his manners. "Yes, certainly. Your mother has exquisite taste—do tell her I said so, will you?"

"Certainly. In truth, I am somewhat surprised that my mother has found time for such social pursuits," Grey said pleasantly, waving a hand at the harpist, who had resumed playing as background to the supper conversation. "My female relations are so obsessed with wedding preparations of late that I should have thought any other preoccupation would be summarily dismissed."

"Oh?" Trevelyan frowned, his mind plainly still on the matter of the Byrds. Then his expression cleared, and he smiled, quite transforming his face. "Oh, yes, I suppose so. Women do love weddings."

"The house is filled from attic to cellar with bridesmaids, bolts of lace, and sempstresses," Grey went on carelessly, keeping a sharp eye on Trevelyan's face for any indications of guilt or hesitancy. "I cannot sit down anywhere without fear of impalement upon stray pins and needles. But I daresay the same conditions obtain at your establishment?"

Trevelyan laughed, and Grey could see that despite the ordinariness of his features, he was possessed of a certain charm.

"They do," he admitted. "With the exception of the bridesmaids. I am spared that, at least. But it will all be over soon." He glanced across the room toward Olivia as he spoke, with a faint wistfulness in his expression that both surprised Grey and reassured him somewhat.

The conversation concluded in a scatter of cordialities, and Trevelyan took his leave with grace, heading across the room to speak to Olivia before departing. Grey looked after him, reluctantly admiring the smoothness of his manners, and wondering whether a man who knew himself to be afflicted with the French disease could possibly discuss his forthcoming wedding with such insouciance. But there was Quarry's finding of the house in Meacham Street—conflicting, rather, with Trevelyan's pious promise to his dying mother.

"Thank God he's gone at last." His own mother had approached without his notice, and stood beside him, fanning herself with satisfaction as she watched Captain von Namtzen's plumes bobbing out of the library toward the front door.

"Beastly Hun," she remarked, smiling and bowing to Mr. and Mrs. Hartsell, who were also departing. "Did you *smell* that dreadful pomade he was using? What was it, some disgusting scent like patchouli? Civet, perhaps?" She turned her head, sniffing suspiciously at a blue damask shoulder. "The man reeks as though he had just emerged from a whorehouse, I swear. And he *would* keep touching me, the hound."

"What would you know of whorehouses?" Grey demanded. Then he saw the gimlet gleam in the Countess's eye and the slight curve of her lips. His mother delighted in answering rhetorical questions.

"No, don't tell me," he said hastily. "I don't want to know." The Countess pouted prettily, then folded her fan with a snap and pressed it against her lips in a token of silence.

"Have you eaten, Johnny?" she asked, flipping the fan open again.

"No," he said, suddenly recalling that he was starving. "I hadn't the chance."

"Well, then." The Countess waved one of the footmen over, selected a small pie from his tray, and handed it to her son. "Yes, I saw you talking to Lady Mumford. Kind of you; the dear old thing dotes upon you."

Dear old thing. Lady Mumford was possibly the Countess's senior by a year. Grey mumbled a response, impeded by pie. It was steak with mushrooms, delectable in flaky pastry.

"Whatever were you talking to Joseph Trevelyan so intently about, though?" the Countess asked, raising her fan in farewell to the Misses Humber. She turned to look at her son, and lifted one brow, then laughed. "Why, you've gone quite red in the face, John—one might think Mr. Trevelyan had made you some indecent proposal!"

"Ha ha," Grey said, thickly, and put the rest of the pie into his mouth.

Chapter 6

A Visit to the Convent

In the event, they did not visit the brothel in Meacham Street until Saturday night.

The doorman gave Quarry an amiable nod of recognition—a welcome expanded upon by the madam, a long-lipped, big-arsed woman in a most unusual green velvet gown, topped by a surprisingly respectable-looking lace-trimmed cap and kerchief that matched the lavish trim of gown and stomacher.

"Well, if it's not Handsome Harry!" she exclaimed in a voice nearly as deep as Quarry's own. "You been neglectin' us, me old son." She gave Quarry a companionable buffet in the ribs, and wrinkled back her upper lip like an ancient horse, exposing two large yellow teeth, these appearing to be the last remaining in her upper jaw.

"Still, I s'pose we must forgive you, mustn't we, for bringing such a sweet poppet as this along!"

She turned her oddly engaging smile on Grey, a shrewd eye taking in the silver buttons on his coat and the fine lawn of his ruffles at a glance.

"And what's your name, then, me sweet child?" she asked, seizing him firmly by the arm and drawing him after her into a small parlor. "You've never come here before, I know; I should recall a pretty face like yours!"

"This is Lord John Grey, Mags," Quarry said, throwing off his cloak and tossing it familiarly over a chair. "A particular friend of mine, eh?"

"Oh, to be sure, to be sure. Well, now, I wonder who might suit? . . ." Mags was sizing Grey up with the skill of a horse trader on fair day; he felt tight in the chest and avoided her glance by affecting an interest in the room's decoration, which was eccentric, to say the least.

He had been in brothels before, though not often. This was a cut above the usual bagnio, with paintings on the walls and a good Turkey carpet before a handsome mantelpiece, on which sat a collection of thumbscrews, irons, tongue-borers, and other implements whose use he didn't wish to imagine. A calico cat was sprawled among these ornaments, eyes closed, one paw dangling indolently over the fire.

"Like me collection, do you?" Mags hovered at his shoulder, nodding at the mantelpiece. "That little 'un's from Newgate; got the irons from the whipping post at Bridewell when the new one was put up last year."

"They ain't for use," Quarry murmured in his other ear. "Just show. Though if your taste runs that way, there's a gel called Josephine—"

"What a handsome cat," Grey said, rather loudly. He extended a forefinger and scratched the beast under the chin. It suffered this attention for a moment, then opened bright yellow eyes and sharply bit him.

"You want to watch out for Batty," Mags said, as Grey jerked back his hand with an exclamation. "Sneaky, that's what she is." She shook her head indulgently at the cat, which had resumed its doze, and poured out two large glasses of porter, which she handed to her guests.

"Now, we've lost Nan, I'm afraid, since you was last here," she said to Quarry. "But I've a sweet lass called Peg, from Devonshire, as I think you'll like."

"Blonde?" Quarry said with interest.

"Oh, to be sure! Tits like melons, too."

Quarry promptly drained his glass and set it down, belching slightly.

"Splendid."

Grey managed to catch Quarry's eye, as he was turning to follow Mags to the parlor door.

"What about Trevelyan?" he mouthed.

"Later," Quarry mouthed back, patting his pocket. He winked, and disappeared into the corridor.

Grey sucked his wounded finger, brooding. Doubtless Quarry was right; the chances of extracting information were better once social relations had been loosened by the expenditure of cash—and it was of course sensible to question the whores; the girls might spill things in privacy that the madam's professional discretion would guard. He just hoped that Harry would remember to ask his blonde about Trevelyan.

He stuck his injured finger in the glass of porter and frowned at the cat, now wallowing on its back among the thumbscrews, inviting the unwary to rub its furry belly.

"The things I do for family," he muttered balefully, and resigned himself to an evening of dubious pleasure.

He did wonder about Quarry's motives in suggesting this expe-
dition. He had no idea how much Harry knew or suspected about
his own predilections; things had been said, during the affair of the
Hellfire Club . . . but he had no notion how much Harry might
have overheard on that occasion, nor yet what he had made of it, if
he had.

On the other hand, given what he himself knew of Quarry's
own character and predilections, it was unlikely that any ulterior
motive was involved. Harry simply liked whores—well, any
woman, actually; he wasn't particular.

The madam returned a moment later to find Grey in fascinated
contemplation of the paintings. Mythological in subject and
mediocre in execution, the paintings nonetheless boasted a remarkable sense of invention on the part of the artist. Grey pulled
himself away from a large study showing a centaur engaged in
amorous coupling with a very game young woman, and forestalled
Mags' suggestions.

"Young," he said firmly. "Quite young. But not a child," he
added hastily. He withdrew his finger from the glass and licked it,
making a face. "And some decent wine, if you please. A lot of it."

Much to his surprise, the wine *was* decent; a rich, fruity red, whose
origin he didn't recognize. The whore was young, as per his request, but also a surprise.

"You won't mind that she's Scotch, me dear?" Mags flung back
the chamber door, exposing a scrawny dark-haired girl crouched on
the bed, wrapped up in a wooly shawl, despite a good fire burning
in the hearth. "Some chaps finds the barbarous accent puts 'em
off, but she's a good girl, Nessie—she'll keep stumm, and you tell
her to."

The madam set the decanter and glasses on a small table and

smiled at the whore with genial threat, receiving a hostile glare in return.

"Not at all," Grey murmured, gesturing the madam out with a courteous bow. "I am sure we shall suit splendidly."

He closed the door and turned to the girl. Despite his outward self-possession, he felt an odd sensation in the pit of his stomach.

"Stumm?" he asked.

" 'Tis the German word for dumb," the girl said, eyeing him narrowly. She jerked her head toward the door, where the madam had vanished. "She's German, though ye wouldna think it, to hear her. Magda, she's called. But she calls the doorkeep Stummle— and he's a mute, to be sure. So, d'ye want me to clapper it, then?" She put a hand across her mouth, slitted eyes above it reminding him of the cat just before it bit him.

"No," he said. "Not at all."

In fact, the sound of her speech had unleashed an extraordinary—and quite unexpected—tumult of sensation in his bosom. A mad mix of memory, arousal, and alarm, it was not an entirely pleasant feeling—but he wanted her to go on talking, at all costs.

"Nessie," he said, pouring out a glass of wine for her. "I've heard that name before—though it was not applied to a person."

Her eyes stayed narrow, but she took the drink.

"I'm a person, no? It's short for Agnes."

"Agnes?" He laughed, from the sheer exhilaration of her presence. Not just her speech—that slit-eyed look of dour suspicion was so ineffably *Scots* that he felt transported. "I thought it was the name the local inhabitants gave to a legendary monster, believed to live in Loch Ness."

The slitted eyes popped open in surprise.

"Ye've heard of it? Ye've been in Scotland?"

"Yes." He took a large swallow of his own wine, warm and rough on his palate. "In the north. A place called Ardsmuir. You know it?"

Evidently she did; she scrambled off the bed and backed away from him, wineglass clenched so hard in one hand, he thought she might break it.

"Get out," she said.

"What?" He stared at her blankly.

"Out!" A skinny arm shot out of the folds of her shawl, finger jabbing toward the door.

"But—"

"Soldiers are the one thing, and bad enough, forbye—but I'm no takin' on one of Butcher Billy's men, and that's flat!"

Her hand dipped back under the shawl, and reemerged with something small and shiny. Lord John froze.

"My dear young woman," he began, slowly reaching out to set down his wineglass, all the time keeping an eye on the knife. "I am afraid you mistake me. I—"

"Oh, no, I dinna mistake ye a bit." She shook her head, making frizzy dark curls fluff round her head like a halo. Her eyes had gone back to slits, and her face was white, with two hectic spots burning over her cheekbones.

"My da and two brothers died at Culloden, *duine na galladh*! Take that English prick out your breeks, and I'll slice it off at the root, I swear I will!"

"I have not the slightest intention of doing so," he assured her, lifting both hands to indicate his lack of offensive intent. "How old are you?" Short and skinny, she looked about eleven, but must be somewhat older, if her father had perished at Culloden.

The question seemed to give her pause. Her lips pursed uncertainly, though her knife hand held steady.

"Fourteen. But ye needna think I dinna ken what to do with this!"

"I should never suspect you of inability in any sphere, I assure you, madam."

There was a moment of silence that lengthened into awkward-ness as they faced each other warily, both unsure how to proceed from this point. He wanted to laugh; she was at once so doubtful and yet so in earnest. At the same time, her passion forbade any sort of disrespect.

Nessie licked her lips and made an uncertain jabbing motion to-ward him with the knife.

"I said ye should get out!"

Keeping a wary eye on the blade, he slowly lowered his hands and reached for his wineglass.

"Believe me, madam, if you are disinclined, I should be the last to force you. It would be a shame to waste such excellent wine, though. Will you not finish your glass, at least?"

She had forgotten the glass she was holding in her other hand. She glanced down at it, surprised, then up at him.

"Ye dinna want to swive me?"

"No, indeed," he assured her, with complete sincerity. "I should be obliged, though, if you would honor me with a few moments' conversation. That is—I suppose that you do not wish me to sum-mon Mrs. Magda at once?"

He gestured toward the door, raising one eyebrow, and she bit her lower lip. Inexperienced as he might be in brothels, he was rea-sonably sure that a madam would look askance at a whore who not only refused custom, but who took a knife to the patrons without evident provocation.

"Mmphm," she said, reluctantly lowering the blade.

Without warning, he felt an unexpected rush of arousal, and turned from her to hide it. Christ, he hadn't heard that uncouth Scottish noise in months—not since his last visit to Helwater—and had certainly not expected it to have such a powerful effect, rendered as it was in a sniffy girlish register, rather than with the tone of gruff menace to which he was accustomed.

He gulped his wine, and busied himself in pouring out another glass, asking casually over his shoulder, "Tell me—given the undoubted strength and justice of your feelings regarding English soldiers, how is it that you find yourself in London?"

Her lips pressed into a seam, and her dark brows lowered, but after a moment she relaxed enough to raise her glass and take a sip.

"Ye dinna want to ken how I came to be a whore—only why I'm here?"

"I should say that the former question, while of undoubted interest, is your own affair," he said politely. "But since the latter question affects my own interests—yes, that is what I am asking."

"Ye're an odd cove, and no mistake." She tilted back her head and drank off the wine quickly, keeping a suspicious eye trained on him all the while. She lowered it with a deep exhalation of satisfaction, licking red-stained lips.

"That's no bad stuff," she said, sounding a little surprised. "It's the madam's private stock—German, aye? Gie us another, then, and I'll tell ye, if ye want to know so bad."

He obliged, refilling his own glass at the same time. It *was* good wine; good enough to warm stomach and limbs, while not unduly clouding the mind. Under its beneficent influence, he felt the tension he had carried in neck and shoulders since entering the brothel gradually fade away.

For her part, the Scottish whore seemed similarly affected. She sipped with a delicate greed that drained her cup twice while she told her tale—a tale he gathered she had told before, recounted as it was with circumstantial embellishments and dramatic anecdotes. In sum, it was simple enough, though; finding life insupportable in the Highlands after Culloden and Cumberland's devastations, her surviving brother had gone away to sea, and she and her mother had come south, begging for their bread, her mother occasionally reduced to the expedient of selling her body when begging was not fruitful.

"Then we fell in with *him*," she said, making a sour grimace of the word, "in Berwick." *He* had been an English soldier named Harte, newly released from service, who took them "under his protection"—a concept that Harte implemented by setting up Nessie's mother in a small cottage where she could entertain his army acquaintances in comfort and privacy.

"He saw what a profit could be made, and so he'd go out now and again, huntin', and come back wi' some poor lass he'd found starvin' on the roads. He'd speak soft to them, buy them shoes and feed them up, and next thing they kent, they were spreading their legs three times a night for the soldiers who'd put a bullet through their husbands' heids—and within two years, Bob Harte was drivin' a coach-and-four."

It might be an approximation of the truth—or it might not.

Having no grounds for personal delusion, it was clear to Grey that a whore's profession was one founded on mendacity. And if one could not believe in a whore's central premise, unspoken though it was, one could scarcely place great credence in anything she said.

Still, it was an absorbing story—as it was meant to be, he thought cynically. He did not stop her, though; beyond the necessity of putting her at ease if he was to get any information from her, the simple fact was that he enjoyed hearing her talk.

"We met Bob Harte when I was nay more than five," she said, putting a fist to her mouth to stifle a belch. "He waited until I was eleven—when I began to bleed—and then . . ." She paused, blinking, as though searching for inspiration.

"And then your mother, bent upon protecting your virtue, slew him in order to preserve you," Grey suggested. "She was taken up and hanged, of course, whereupon you found yourself obliged by necessity to embrace the fate which she had sacrificed herself to prevent?" He lifted his glass to her in ironic toast, leaning back in his seat.

Rather to his surprise, she burst out laughing.

"No," she said, wiping a hand beneath her nose, which had gone quite pink, "but that's no bad. Better than the truth, aye? I'll remember that one." She lifted her glass in acknowledgment, then tilted back her head and drained it.

He reached for the bottle, only to find it empty. Rather to his surprise, the other was empty, too.

"I'll get more," Nessie said promptly. She bounced off the bed and was out of the room before he could protest. She had left the knife, he saw; it lay on the table, next to a covered basket. Leaning over and lifting the napkin from this, he discovered that it contained a pot of some slippery unguent, and various interesting appliances, a few of obvious intent, others quite mysterious in function.

He was holding one of the more obvious of these engines, admiring the artistry of it—which was remarkably detailed, even to the turgid veins visible upon the surface of the bronze—when she came back, a large jug clasped to her bosom.

"Oh, is that what ye like?" she asked, nodding at the object in his hand.

His mouth opened, but fortunately no words emerged. He dropped the heavy object, which struck him painfully in the thigh before hitting the carpeted floor with a thump.

Nessie finished pouring two fresh glasses of wine and took a gulp from hers before bending to pick the thing up.

"Oh, good, ye've warmed it a bit," she said with approval. "That bronze is mortal cold." Holding her full glass carefully in one hand and the phallic engine in the other, she knee-walked over the bed and settled herself among the pillows. Sipping her wine, she took hold of the engine with her other hand and used the tip to inch her shift languidly up the reaches of her skinny thighs.

"Shall I say things?" she inquired, in a businesslike tone. "Or d'ye want just to watch and I'll pretend ye're no there?"

"No!" Emerging suddenly from his tongue-tied state, Grey spoke more loudly than he had intended to. "I mean—no. Please. Don't . . . do that."

She looked surprised, then mildly irritated, but relinquished her hold on the object and sat up.

"Well, what then?" She pushed back the brambles of her hair, eyeing him in speculation. "I suppose I could suckle ye a bit," she said reluctantly. "But only if ye wash it well first. With soap, mind."

Feeling suddenly that he had drunk a great deal, and much more quickly than he had intended, Grey shook his head, fumbling in his coat.

"No, not that. What I want—" He withdrew the miniature of Joseph Trevelyan, which he had abstracted from his cousin's bedroom, and laid it on the bed before her. "I want to know if this man has the pox. Not clap—syphilis."

Nessie's eyes, hitherto narrowed, went round with surprise. She glanced at the picture, then at Grey.

"Ye think I can tell from lookin' at his *face*?" she inquired incredulously.

A more comprehensive explanation given, Nessie sat back on her heels, blinking meditatively at the miniature of Trevelyan.

"So ye dinna want him to marry your cousin, and he's poxed, eh?"

"That is the situation, yes."

She nodded gravely at Grey.

"That's verra sweet of you. And you an Englishman, too!"

"Englishmen are capable of loyalty," he assured her dryly. "At least to their families. Do you know the man?"

"I've no had him, myself, but aye, I think I've maybe seen him once or twice." She closed one eye, considering the portrait again. She was swaying slightly, and Grey began to fear that his wine strategy had miscarried of its own success.

"Hmm!" she said, and nodded to herself. Tucking the miniature into the neck of her shift—given the meagerness of her aspect, he couldn't imagine what held it there—she slid off the bed and took a soft blue wrapper from its peg.

"Some of the lasses will be busy the noo, but I'll go and have a word wi' those still in the sallong, shall I?"

"The . . . oh, the salon. Yes, that would be very helpful. Can you be discreet about your inquiries, though?"

She drew herself up with tipsy dignity.

"O' course I can. Leave me a bit o' the wine, aye?" Waving at the jug, she pulled the wrapper around her and swayed from the room in an exaggerated manner better suited to someone with hips.

Sighing, Grey sat back in his chair and poured another glass of wine. He had no idea what the vintage was costing him, but it was worth it.

He held his glass to the light, examining it. Wonderful color, and the nose of it was excellent—fruity and deep. He took another sip, contemplating progress to date. So far, so good. With luck, he would have an answer regarding Trevelyan almost at once—though it might be necessary to return, if Nessie could not manage to speak to whichever girls had most recently been with him.

The prospect of a return visit to the brothel gave him no qualms, though, since he and Nessie had reached their unspoken understanding.

He did wonder what she would have done, had he been truly interested in a carnal encounter rather than information. She had appeared deeply sincere in her objections to servicing one of Cumberland's men—and in all honesty, he thought those objections not unreasonable.

The Highland campaign following Culloden had been his first, and he had seen such sights during it as would have made him ashamed to be a soldier, had he been in any frame of mind at the time as to encompass them. As it was, he had been shocked to numbness, and by the time he saw real action in battle, he was in France, and fighting against an honorable enemy—not the women and children of a defeated foe.

Culloden had been his first battle, in a way—though he had not seen action there, thanks to the scruples of his elder brother, who had brought him along to have a taste of military life but drew the line at letting him fight.

"If you think I am risking having to take your mutilated body home to Mother, you are demented," Hal had grimly informed him. "You haven't a commission; it's not your duty yet to go and get your arse shot off, so you're not going to. Stir one foot out of camp, and I'll have Sergeant O'Connell thrash you in front of the entire regiment, I promise you."

Fool that he was at sixteen, he had regarded this as monstrous injustice. And when he was at length allowed to set foot on the field, in the aftermath of the battle, he had gone out with pulse pounding, pistol cold in a sweating hand.

He and Hector had discussed it before, lying close together in a nest of spring grass under the stars, a little apart from the others. Hector had killed two men, face-to-face—God knew how many more, in the smoke of battle.

"You can't tell, really," Hector had explained, from the lofty heights of his four years' advantage and his second lieutenant's commission. "Not unless it's face-to-face, with a bayonet, say, or your sword. Otherwise, it's all black smoke and noise and you've no idea what you're doing—you just watch your officer and run when he tells you, fire and reload—and sometimes you see a Scot go down, but you never know if it was your shot that took him. He might just have stepped in a mole hole, for all you know!"

"But you do know—when it's close." He had given Hector a rude nudge with his knee. "So what was it like then? Your first? Don't dare to tell me you don't remember!"

Hector had grabbed him and squeezed the muscle of his thigh until he squealed like a rabbit, then gathered him in close, laughing, forcing John's face into the hollow of his shoulder.

"All right, I do remember, then. Wait, though." He was quiet for a moment, his breath stirring John's hair warm above the ear. It was too early in the year for midges, but the wind moved over them fresh and cool, tickling their skins with ends of waving grass.

"It was—well, it was fast. Lieutenant Bork had sent me and another fellow round a bit of copse to see if anything was doing, and I was in the lead. I heard a sort of thump and a cough behind me, and I thought Meadows—he was following me—I thought he'd stumbled. I turned to tell him to be quiet, and there he was lying on the ground, with blood all over his head, and a Scot just dropping the thumping great rock he'd hit Meadows with, and bending down to snatch his gun.

"They're like animals, you know; all wild whiskers and dirt, generally barefoot and half-naked to boot. This one glanced up and saw me, and tried to seize the musket up and brain me, only Meadows had fallen on it, and I—well, I just screamed and lunged at him. I didn't think a bit about it; it was just like the drills—only it felt a lot different when the bayonet went into him."

John had felt a small shudder run through the body pressed against him, and put his arm round Hector's waist, squeezing in reassurance.

"Did he die right away?" he asked.

"No," Hector said softly, and John felt him swallow. "He fell back and sat down hard on the ground, and—and I lost hold of the gun, so he was sitting there with the bayonet sticking in him, and the gun's butt . . . it was on the ground, bracing him, almost, like a shooting stick."

"What did you do?" He stroked Hector's chest, trying in some clumsy way to comfort him, but that was far beyond his powers at the moment.

"I knew I should do something—try to finish him, somehow— but I couldn't think how. All I could do was to stand there, like a ninny, and him staring up at me out of that dirty face, and I . . ."

Hector swallowed again, hard.

"I was crying," he said, all in a rush. "I kept saying, 'I'm sorry, I'm sorry,' and crying. And he sort of shook his head, and he said something to me, but it was in that barbarous Erse, and I couldn't understand if he knew what I'd said, or was cursing me, or if he wanted something, water maybe . . . I had water . . ."

Hector's voice trailed off, but John could tell from the thick-ened sound of his breath that he was near to crying now. His hand was fastened hard around John's upper arm, clinging hard enough to leave a bruise, but John stayed still, perfectly still, until Hector's breathing eased and the iron-hard grip relaxed at last.

"It seemed to take a long time," he said, and cleared his throat. "Though I suppose it wasn't, really. After a bit, his head just fell forward, very slowly, and stayed that way."

He took a deep, wet breath, as though cleansing himself of the memory, and gave John a reassuring hug.

"Yes, you do remember the first one. But I'm sure it will be easier for you—you'll do it better."

Grey lay on Nessie's bed, wineglass in hand, sipping slowly. He stared up at the soot-stained ceiling, but was seeing instead the gray skies over Culloden. It *had* been easier—to do, at least, if not to recall.

"You'll go with Windom's detail," Hal had said, handing him a long pistol. "Your job is to give the *coup de grâce,* if you find any still alive. Through one eye is surest, but behind the ear will answer well enough, if you find you can't bear the eyes."

His brother's face was drawn with strain, white under the smudges of powder smoke; Hal was only twenty-five, but looked twice that, uniform plastered to him with rain and filthy with mud from the field. He gave his orders in a calm, clear voice, but Grey felt his brother's hand tremble as he gave him the gun.

"Hal," he said, as his brother turned away.

"Yes?" Hal turned back, patient but empty-eyed.

"You all right, Hal?" he asked, lowering his voice lest anyone nearby hear him.

Hal seemed to be looking somewhere far beyond him; it took a visible effort for him to bring his gaze back from that distant place, to fix it on his younger brother's face.

"Fine," he said. The edge of his mouth trembled, as though he wanted to smile in reassurance, but it fell back in exhaustion. He clapped a hand on John's shoulder and squeezed hard; John felt oddly as though he were providing support to his brother, rather than the other way round.

"Just remember, Johnny—it's a mercy that you give them. A mercy," he repeated softly, then dropped his hand and left.

It lacked perhaps two hours 'til sunset when Corporal Windom's detail set out onto the field, slogging through mud and moor plants that clung and grasped at their boots as they passed. The rain had stopped, but a freezing wind plastered his damp cloak to his body. He remembered the mixture of dread and excitement in his belly, superseded by the numbness of his fingers and his fear that he would not be able to prime the pistol again, if he had to use it more than once.

As it was, he had no need to use it at all for some time; all the men they came across were clearly dead. Nearly all Scots, though here and there a red coat burned like flame among the dull moor plants. The fallen of the English were taken away with respect, on stretchers. The enemy were thrown in heaps, the soldiers blue-fingered and mumbling curses in puffs of white breath as they dragged the bodies like so many felled logs, naked limbs like pale branches, stiff and awkward in the handling. He was not sure if he should help with this work, but no one seemed to expect him to; he trailed after the soldiers, gun in hand, growing colder by the moment.

He had seen battlefields before, at Preston and Falkirk, though neither had had so many bodies. One dead man was much like another, though, and within a short time, he was no longer bothered by their presence.

He had grown so numb, in fact, that he was barely startled when one of the soldiers shouted, "Hey, Cheeky! Got one for you!" His cold-slowed mind had not had time to interpret this before he found himself face-to-face with the man, the Scot.

He had vaguely supposed that everyone on the field was unconscious, if not dead; execution would be no more than a matter of kneel by the body, place the pistol, pull the trigger, step back and reload.

This man sat bolt upright in the heather, weight braced on the heels of his hands, the smashed leg that had prevented his escape twisted in front of him, streaked with blood. He was staring at

Grey, dark eyes lively and watchful. He was young, perhaps
Hector's age. The eyes went from Grey's face to the gun in his
hand, then back to his face. The man lifted his chin, setting his
mouth hard.

Behind the ear will answer well enough, if you find you can't bear the
eyes.

How? How was he to reach behind the ear, with him sitting like
that? Grey lifted the pistol awkwardly, and stepped to the side,
crouching a bit. The man's head turned, eyes following him.

Grey stopped—but he couldn't stop, the soldiers were watching.

"H-head, or heart?" he asked, trying to keep his voice steady.
His hands were shaking; it was cold, though, so very cold.

The dark eyes closed for an instant, opened again, piercing
through him.

"Christ, do I care?"

He lifted the pistol, the muzzle wavering a little, and pointed it
carefully at the center of the man's body. The Scot's mouth compressed, and he shifted his weight to one hand. Before Grey could
jerk away, he had lifted his free hand to seize Grey's wrist.

Startled, Grey made no move to pull away. Breathing hard with
effort, teeth gritted against the pain, the Scot guided the barrel so
it came to rest against his forehead, just between the eyes. And
stared at him.

And what Grey recalled most clearly was not the eyes, but the
feel of the fingers, colder even than his own chilled flesh, curling
gently round his wrist. There was no strength left now in the
touch, but it stilled his shaking. The fingers squeezed, very gently.
Offering mercy.

An hour later, they had gone back in darkness, and he had
learned of Hector's death.

The candle had been guttering for some time. There was another on the table, but he made no move to reach for it. Instead,

he lay staring as the flame went out, and went on drinking wine in the musky dark.

⤜⊷

He woke with a splitting head, somewhere in the dark hours before dawn. The candle had gone out, and for a disorienting moment, he had no idea where he was—or with whom. A warm, moist weight was curled against him, and his hand rested on bare flesh.

Possibilities erupted in his mind like a flight of startled quail, then disappeared as he took a deep breath and smelt cheap scent, expensive wine, and female musk. Girl. Yes, of course. The Scottish whore.

He lay still for a moment, muddled, trying to gain his bearings in the unfamiliar dark. There—a thin line of gray marked the shuttered window, a shade lighter than the night inside. Door . . . where was the door? He turned his head and saw a faint flicker of light across the floorboards, the exhausted glow of a guttering candle in the hallway. He vaguely remembered some uproar, singing and stamping from below, but that had ceased now. The brothel had subsided into quiet, though it was an odd, uneasy hush, like the troubled sleep of a drunken man. Speaking of which . . . he worked his tongue, trying to muster enough saliva from his parched and sticky membranes to swallow. His heart was beating with an unpleasant insistence that seemed to cause his eyeballs to protrude, bulging painfully with each throb of the organ. He hastily closed his eyes, but it didn't help.

It was warm and close in the room, but a faint stirring of air from the shuttered window touched his body, a cool finger raising the hairs of chest and leg. He was naked, but didn't recall undressing.

She was lying on his arm. Moving slowly, he disengaged himself from the girl, taking care not to rouse her. He sat for a moment on the bed, clutching his head in a soundless moan, then rose to his feet, taking great care lest it fall off.

Christ! What had he been about, to drink so much of that ungodly swill? It would have been better to swive the girl and have done with it, he thought, feeling his way across the room through bursts of brilliant white light that lit up the inside of his skull like fireworks on the Thames. His probing foot struck the table leg, and he felt blindly about beneath it until he found the chamber pot.

Somewhat relieved, but still desperately thirsty, he put it down and groped for the ewer and basin. The water in the pitcher was warm and tasted faintly of metal, but he drank it greedily, spilling it down his chin and chest, gulping until his guts began to protest the tepid onslaught.

He wiped a hand down his face and smeared the wetness across his chest, then loosened the shutters, taking deep, shuddering breaths of the cool gray air. Better.

He turned to look for his clothes, but realized belatedly that he couldn't leave without Quarry. The thought of searching the house for his friend, flinging open doors and surprising sleep-sodden whores and their customers, was more than he could countenance in his present condition. Well, the madam would rout Harry out in short order, come daybreak. Nothing for it but wait.

Since he must wait, he might as well do it lying down; his innards were shifting and gurgling in ominous fashion, and his legs felt weak.

The girl was naked, too. She lay curled on her side, back to him, smooth and pale as a smelt on a fishmonger's slab. He crawled cautiously onto the bed and eased himself down beside her. She shifted and murmured, but didn't wake.

The air was much cooler now, with dawn coming on and the shutters ajar. He would have covered himself, but the girl was lying on the rumpled sheet. She shifted again, and he saw the gooseflesh prickling over her skin. She was thinner even than she had seemed the night before, ribs shadowing her sides and the shoulder blades sharp as wings in her bony little back.

He turned on his side and drew her against him, fumbling with one hand to disentangle the damp sheet and draw it over them both—as much to cover her skinniness as for its dubious warmth.

Her loosened hair was thick and curly, soft against his face. The feel of it disturbed him, though it was a moment before he realized why. She'd had hair like that—the Woman. Fraser's wife. Grey knew her name—Fraser had told him—and yet he stubbornly refused to think of her as anything but "the Woman." As though it were her fault—and the fault of her sex alone, at that.

But that was in another country, he thought, pulling the scrawny whore closer to him, *and besides, the wench is dead.* Fraser had said so.

He'd seen the look in Jamie Fraser's eyes, though. Fraser had not ceased to love his wife merely because she was dead—no more than Grey could or would cease to love Hector. Memory was one thing, though, and flesh another; the body had no conscience.

He wrapped one arm over the girl's fine-boned form, holding her tight against him. Nearly breastless, and narrow-arsed as a boy, he thought, and felt a tiny flame of desire, wine-fueled, lick up the insides of his thighs. Why not? he thought. He was paying for it, after all.

But, *I'm a person, no?* she'd said. And she was neither of the persons he longed for.

He closed his eyes, and kissed the shoulder near his face, very gently. Then he slept again, drifting on the troubled clouds of her hair.

Chapter 7

Green Velvet

He woke to broad daylight and a rumbling stir in the brothel below. The girl was gone—no, not gone. He rolled over and saw her by the window, dressed in her shift, her lips pressed tight in concentration as she plaited her hair, using the reflection in the chamber pot as her looking glass.

"Awake at last, are ye?" she asked, squinting at her reflection. "Thought I might need to poke a darning needle under your toenail to rouse ye." Tying a red ribbon at the end of her plait, she turned and grinned at him.

"Ready for a bit o' breakfast, then, chuck?"

"Don't even mention it." He sat up, slowly, one hand pressed to his forehead.

"Oh, a wee bit peaky this morn, are we?" A brown glass bottle and a pair of wooden tumblers had appeared on the washstand; she poured out something the color of ditch water and thrust the cup into his hand. "Try that; hair o' the dog that bit ye is the best cure, or so they say." She slopped a generous tot into her own glass and drank it off as though it were water.

It wasn't water. He thought it was possibly turpentine, from the smell. Still, he wouldn't be put to shame by a fourteen-year-old whore; he tossed it back in a gulp.

Not turpentine; vitriol. The liquid burned a fiery path straight down his gullet and into his bowels, sending a gust of brimstone fumes through the cavities of his head. Whisky, that's what it was, and very raw whisky, at that.

"Aye, that's the stuff," she said approvingly, watching him. "Have another?"

Incapable of speech, he blinked watering eyes and held out his cup. Another fuming swallow, and he found that he had recovered sufficient presence of mind to inquire after his vanished clothes.

"Oh, aye. Just here." She hopped up, bright as a sparrow, and pulled open a panel in the wall that hid a row of clothes pegs, upon which his uniform and linen had been hung with care.

"Did you undress me?"

"I dinna see anyone else here, do you?" She put a hand above her eyes, peering about the room in exaggerated fashion. He ignored this, pulling the shirt over his head.

"Why?"

He thought the glint of a smile showed in her eyes, though no trace of it touched her lips.

"So much as ye drank, I kent ye'd wake soon to have a piss, and like enough to stagger off then, if ye could. If ye stayed the night through, though, Magda wouldna bring anyone else up for me." She shrugged, shift sliding off one scrawny shoulder. "Best sleep I've had in months."

"I am deeply gratified to have been of benefit to you, madam,"

Grey said dryly, assuming his breeches. "And what is likely to be the cost of an entire night spent in your charming company?"

"Two pound," she said promptly. "Ye can pay me now, if ye like."

He gave her a jaundiced look, one hand on his pocketbook.

"Two pound? Ten shillings, more like. Try again."

"Ten shillings?" She tried to look insulted, but failed, thus informing him that he had been close in his estimate. "Well . . . one and six, then. Or perhaps one and ten"—she eyed him, her small pink tongue darting out to touch her upper lip in speculation—"if I can find out for ye where he goes?"

"Where who goes?"

"The Cornish lad ye were asking after—Trevelyan."

Grey's headache seemed suddenly diminished. He stared at her for a moment, then reached slowly into his pocketbook. He drew out three pound notes and tossed them into her lap.

"Tell me what you know."

Agnes clasped her thighs together, hands between them, tight on the money, eyes sparkling with pleasure.

"What I ken is that he comes here, aye, maybe twa, three times in a month, but he doesna go wi' any of the lasses—so as I couldna find out about the state of his prick, ye ken." She looked apologetic.

Grey left off fastening his garter buckles, surprised.

"What does he do, then?"

"Weel, he goes into Mrs. Magda's room, same as the rich ones always do—and a wee while later, out comes a woman in one of Maggie's gowns and a big lace cap . . . but it's no our Maggie. She's near the same height, aye, but nay bosom to her and nay bum at all—and narrow in the shoulder, where Mags has the meat of a well-fed bullock."

She raised one perfect eyebrow, obviously entertained by the look on his face.

"And then this . . . lady . . . goes out the back way, intae the alley, where there's a chair waitin'. I've seen her do it," she added, with a sardonic emphasis on the pronoun. "Though I didna ken who it was at the time."

"And does . . . she . . . come back?" Grey asked, with the same emphasis.

"Aye, she does. She leaves past dark, and comes back just before dawn. I heard the chairmen in the alley, a week past, and bein' as I happened for once to be alone"—she made a brief moue—"I got up and had a keek down from my window to see who it was. I couldna see any more than the top of her cap and a flash of green skirt—but whoever it was, her step was quick and long, like a man's."

She stopped then, looking expectant. Grey rubbed a hand through his tousled hair. The ribbon had come off as he slept, and was nowhere in sight.

"But you think that you can discover where this . . . person . . . goes to?"

She nodded, certain of herself.

"Oh, aye. I may not have seen the lady's face, but I saw one of the chairmen, plain. Happen he's a big auld lad called Rab, from up near Fife. He hasna often got the price of a whore, but when he does, he asks for me. Homesick, see?"

"Yes, I do see." Grey wiped the hair out of his face, then reached into his pocketbook once more. She spread her legs just in time, catching the handful of silver neatly in the basket of her skirt.

"See that Rab has the price of you soon," Grey suggested. "Aye?"

A rap came on the door, which sprang open to reveal Harry Quarry, bewhiskered and bleary-eyed, coat hung over one shoulder. His shirt was unbuttoned at the neck and only half-tucked into his breeches, the neckcloth discarded. While Quarry did have his wig on, it sat crookedly astride one ear.

"Not interrupting, am I?" he said, stifling a belch.

Grey hastily took up his own coat and stuffed his feet into his shoes.

"No, not at all. Just coming."

Quarry scratched his ribs, rucking up his shirt in unconscious fashion to show a segment of hairy paunch. He blinked vaguely in Nessie's direction.

"Had a good night, then, Grey? Not much to that one, is there?"

Lord John pressed two fingers between his throbbing brows and essayed what he hoped was an expression of satiated lewdness.

"Ah, well, you know the saying—'the nearer the bone, the sweeter the meat.' "

"Really?" Despite his dishevelment, Quarry perked up a little, peering over Lord John's shoulder into the chamber. "Perhaps I'll give her a try next time, then. What's your name, chuck?"

Half-turning, Lord John saw Nessie's eyes widen at the sight of Quarry, bloodshot and leering. Her mouth twisted in revulsion; she really had no tact, for a whore. He laid a hand on Quarry's arm to distract him.

"Don't think you'd like her, old fellow," he said. "She's Scotch."

Quarry's momentary interest disappeared like a snuffed-out candle.

"Oh, Scotch," he said, belching slightly. "Christ, no. The sound of that barbarous tongue would wilt me on the spot. No, no. Give me a nice, fat English girl, good round bum, plenty of flesh on her, something to get hold of." He aimed a jovial slap at the bum of a passing maid who clearly met these requirements, but she dodged adroitly and he staggered, narrowly avoiding ignominious collapse by catching hold of Grey, who in turn seized the doorjamb with both hands to keep from being overborne. He heard a giggle from Nessie, and straightened up, pulling his clothes into what order he could.

Following this rather undignified departure, they found themselves in a coach, rattling up Meacham Street in a manner highly unsuited to the state of Grey's head.

"Find out anything useful?" Quarry asked, closing one eye to assist in concentration as he redid the buttons of his fly, which had been somehow fastened askew.

"Yes," Grey said, averting his eyes. "But God knows what it means."

He explained his inconclusive findings briefly, causing Quarry to blink owlishly at him.

"I don't know what it means, either," Quarry said, scratching his balding head. "But you might drop a word to that constable friend of yours—ask if any of his men have heard of a woman in green velvet. If she—or he—is up to something . . ."

The coach turned, sending a piercing ray of light through Grey's eyes and straight into the center of his brain. He emitted a low moan. What had Constable Magruder suggested? Housebreaking, horse-stealing, robbery from the person . . .

"Right," he said, closing his eyes and breathing deeply, envisioning the Honorable Joseph Trevelyan under arrest for fire-setting or public riot. "I'll do that."

Chapter 8

Enter the Chairman

Grey came down late to breakfast on Monday. The Countess had long since finished her meal and departed; his cousin Olivia was at table, though, informally clad in a muslin wrapper with her hair in a plait down her back, opening letters and nibbling toast.

"Late night?" he said, nodding to her as he slid into his chair.

"Yes." She yawned, covering her mouth daintily with a small fist. "A party at Lady Quinton's. What about you?"

"Nothing so entertaining, I'm afraid." After a long and blissfully restorative sleep, he had spent the Sunday evening at Bernard Sydell's house, listening to interminable complaints about the lack of discipline in the modern army, the moral shortcomings of the younger officers, the miserliness of politicians who expected wars to be fought without adequate materials, the shortsightedness of the current government, lamentations for the departure of Pitt as Prime Minister—who had been just as roundly excoriated when in office—and further remarks in a similar vein.

At one point during these declamations, Malcolm Stubbs had leaned aside and murmured to Grey, "Why don't someone just fetch a pistol and put him out of his misery?"

"Toss you a shilling for the honor," Grey had murmured back, causing Stubbs to choke on the vile sherry Sydell thought appropriate to such gatherings.

Harry Quarry hadn't been there. Grey hoped that Harry was busy with his "something in train," rather than merely avoiding the sherry—for if something definite was not discovered soon regarding O'Connell's death, it was likely to come to the attention not only of Sydell, but of people with the capacity to cause a great deal more trouble.

"What do you think of these two, John?" Olivia's voice interrupted his thoughts, and he withdrew his attention from the coddled egg before him to look across the table. She was frowning thoughtfully at two narrow lengths of lace, one draped across the silver coffeepot, another suspended from one hand.

"Mm." Grey swallowed egg and tried to focus his attention. "For what?"

"Edging for handkerchiefs."

"That one." He pointed with his spoon at the sample on the coffeepot. "The other is too masculine." In fact, the first one reminded him vividly—though not unpleasantly—of the lace trim on the gown worn by Magda, madam of the Meacham Street brothel.

Olivia's face broke into a beaming smile.

"Exactly what I thought! Excellent; I want to have a dozen handkerchiefs made for Joseph—I'll have an extra half-dozen made up for you as well, shall I?"

"Spending Joseph's money already, are you?" he teased. "The poor man will be bankrupt before you've been married a month."

"Not a bit of it," she said loftily. "This is my own money, from Papa. A gift from the bride to the bridegroom. D'you think he'll like it?"

"I'm sure he'll be charmed at the thought." And lace-trimmed handkerchiefs would go so well with emerald velvet, he thought, stricken by a sudden qualm. All around him, preparations for the wedding were proceeding like the drawing up of battle lines, with regiments of cooks, battalions of sempstresses, and dozens of people with no discernible function but a great deal of self-important busy-ness swarming through the house each day. Five weeks until the wedding.

"You have a bit of egg on your ruffle, Johnny."

"Have I?" He peered downward, flicking at the offending particle. "There, is it gone?"

"Yes. Aunt Bennie says you have a new valet," she said, still looking him over with an air of appraisal. "That odd little person. Is he not a trifle young and—unpolished—for such a position?"

"Mr. Byrd may lack something in terms of years and experience," Grey admitted, "but he does know how to administer a proper shave."

His cousin peered closely at him—like his mother, she was a trifle short of sight—then leaned across the table to stroke his cheek, a liberty he suffered with good grace.

"Oh, that *is* nice," she said with approval. "Like satin. Is he good with your wardrobe?"

"Splendid," he assured her, with a mental picture of Tom Byrd frowning over his mending of the torn coat seam. "Most assiduous."

"Oh, good. You must tell him, then, to make sure your gray velvet is in good repair. I should like you to wear it for the wedding supper, and last time you had it on, I noticed that the hem had come unstitched in back."

"I shall call it to his attention," he assured her gravely. "Is this concern lest my appearance disgrace your nuptials, or are you practicing care of domestic detail in preparation for assuming command of your own household?"

She laughed, but flushed, very prettily.

"I *am* sorry, Johnny. How overbearing of me! I confess, I do worry. Joseph tells me I need not trouble over anything, his butler is a marvel—but I do not wish to be the sort of wife who is nothing more than an ornament."

She looked quite anxious as she said this, and he felt a deep qualm of misgiving. Caught up in his own responsibilities, he had scarcely taken time to think how his investigation of Joseph Trevelyan might affect his cousin personally, should the man indeed prove to be poxed.

"You are never less than ornamental," he said, a little gruffly, "but I am sure that any man of worth must discern the true nature of your character, and value it much more highly than your outward appearance."

"Oh." She flushed more deeply, and lowered her lashes. "Why— thank you. What a kind thing to say!"

"Not at all. Will I fetch you a kipper?"

They ate in a pleasant silence for a few moments, and Grey's thoughts had begun to drift toward a contemplation of the day's activities, when Olivia's voice pulled him back to the present moment.

"Have you never thought of marriage for yourself, John?"

He plucked a bun from the basket on the table, taking care not to roll his eyes. The newly betrothed and married of either sex invariably believed it their sacred duty to urge others to share their happy state.

"No," he said equably, breaking the bread. "I see no pressing need to acquire a wife. I have no estate or household that requires a mistress, and Hal is making an adequate job of continuing the family name." Hal's wife, Minnie, had just presented her husband with a third son—the family ran to boys.

Olivia laughed.

"Well, that is true," she agreed. "And I suppose you enjoy playing the gay bachelor, with all the ladies swooning after you. They do, you know."

"Oh, la." He made a dismissive gesture with the butter knife, and resumed his attention to the bun. Olivia seemed to take the hint, and retired into the mysteries of a fruit compote, leaving him to organize his thoughts.

The chief business of the day must be the O'Connell affair, of course. His inquiries into Trevelyan's private life had yielded more mystery than answer so far, but his investigation of the Sergeant's murder had produced still less in the way of results.

Inquiries into the Stokes family had revealed them to be a polyglot crew descended from a Greek sailor who had jumped ship in London some forty years earlier, whereupon he had promptly met and married a girl from Cheapside, taken her name—very sensibly, as his own was Aristopolous Xenokratides—and settled down to produce a numerous family, most of whom had promptly returned to the sea like spawning efts. Iphigenia, stranded on shore by the accident of her gender, ostensibly earned her living by the needle, with occasional financial augmentations offered by assorted gentlemen with whom she had lived, Sergeant O'Connell being the most recent of these.

Grey had set Malcolm Stubbs to explore the family's further connexions, but he had little hope of this producing anything helpful.

As for Finbar Scanlon and his wife—

"Have you ever been in love, John?"

He looked up, startled, to see Olivia looking earnestly at him over the teapot. Evidently she had not abandoned her inquiries, after all, but had merely been occupied with the consumption of breakfast.

"Well . . . yes," he said slowly, unsure whether this was mere familial curiosity or something more.

"But you did not marry. Why was that?"

Why was that, indeed. He took a deep breath.

"It wasn't possible," he said simply. "My lover died."

Her face clouded, full lip trembling with sympathy.

"Oh," she murmured, looking down at her empty plate. "That's *awfully* sad, Johnny. I'm so sorry."

He shrugged with a slight smile, acknowledging her sympathy but not encouraging further questions.

"Any interesting letters?" he asked, raising his chin toward the small sheaf of papers by her plate.

"Oh! Yes, I almost forgot—here are yours." Burrowing through the stack, she unearthed two missives addressed to him and handed them across.

The first note, from Magruder, was brief but riveting. Sergeant O'Connell's uniform—or at least the coat to it—had been found. The pawnbroker in whose shop it was discovered said that it had been brought in by an Irish soldier, himself wearing a uniform.

I went myself to inquire, Magruder wrote, *but the man was unable to be sure of the rank or regiment of this Irishman—and I were loath to press him, for fear of his recollection transforming the man into a Welsh lance-corporal or a Cornish grenadier, under the pressure of forced recollection. For what the observation be worth, he believed the man to be selling an old coat of his own.*

Impatient as he was for more detail, Grey was forced to admit the soundness and delicacy of Magruder's instinct. Press questions too far, and a man would tell you what he thought you wanted to hear. It was much better to ask questions briefly, in a number of short sessions, rather than to bombard a witness with interrogation—but time was short.

Still, Magruder had got what he could be sure of. While all insignia and buttons had naturally been stripped from the coat, it was identifiable as having belonged to a sergeant of the 47th. While the government dictated certain specifics of army dress, those gentlemen who raised and financed their own regiments held the privilege of designing the uniforms for said regiments. In the case of the 47th, it was Hal's wife who had patterned the officers' coats, with a narrow buff stripe up the outside of the sleeve, which helped to draw the eye when an arm was waved in command. A sergeant's coat, poorer in material and less stylish in cut, still bore that stripe.

Grey made a mental note to have someone check the other regimental sergeants, to be sure that none had sold an old coat—but this was merely for the sake of thoroughness. Magruder had not only described the coat and included a brief sketch of the garment, but noted also that the lining of the coat had been unstitched at one side, the stitches appearing to have been cut, rather than torn.

Well, that explained where O'Connell had been keeping his booty, if not where it was now. Grey took a bite of cold toast and reached for the second note, sporting Harry Quarry's bold black scrawl. This one was still more brief.

Meet me at St. Martin-in-the-Fields, tomorrow at six o'clock, it read, the signature rendered merely as a large, slapdash "Q . . ." *P.S. wear old uniform.*

He was still frowning at this terse communication when Tom Byrd's round head poked into the room, looking apologetic.

"Me lord? Sorry, sir, but you did say as how if a big Scotchman was to come—"

Grey was already on his feet, leaving Olivia open-mouthed behind him.

Rab the chairman was tall and solid, with a stupid, sullen face that barely brightened into dourness at Grey's greeting.

"Agnes said ye'd pay for a word," he muttered, not quite able to keep from staring at the bronze orrery that stood upon the table by the library window, its graceful arms and swooping orbs catching the morning sun.

"I will," Grey said promptly, wanting to dispose of the man before his mother should come downstairs and start asking questions. "What is the word?"

Rab's bloodshot eyes met his, displaying a bit more intelligence than did the rest of his countenance.

"Ye dinna want to know the price first?"

"Very well. How much do you want?" He could hear the Countess's voice upstairs, raised in song.

The man's thick tongue poked out, touching his upper lip in contemplation.

"Two pound?" he said, trying to sound indifferently truculent, but unable to conceal the tentative note in his voice. Obviously, two pounds was a nearly unthinkable fortune; he had no faith that it might actually be forthcoming, but was willing to hazard the chance.

"How much of that does Agnes get?" Grey asked pointedly. "I shall see her again, mind, and I'll ask to make certain that she's had her share."

"Oh. Ah . . ." Rab struggled with the problem of division for a moment, then he shrugged. "Half, then."

Grey was surprised at this generosity—and surprised further that Rab was able to discern his response.

"I mean to marry her," the chairman said gruffly, fixing him with a stare and narrowing one eye as though daring him to make something of this statement. "When she's bought free of her contract, aye?"

Grey bit his tongue to forestall an incautious response to this startling revelation, merely nodding as he dug into his pocketbook. He laid the silver on the desk, but kept his hand over it.

"What are you to tell me, then?"

"A house called 'Lavender,' in Barbican Street. Near to Lincoln's Inn. Big place—not so much to look at from outside, but verra rich within."

Grey felt a sudden cold weight in the pit of his stomach, as though he had swallowed lead shot.

"You have been inside?"

Rab moved one burly shoulder, shaking his head.

"Nah, then. Only to the door. But I could see as there were carpets like that"—he nodded at the silk Kermanshah on the floor by the desk—"and pictures on the wall." He lifted a chin like a battering ram, indicating the painting over the mantelpiece, of Grey's paternal grandfather seated on horseback. The chairman frowned with the effort of recall.

"I could see a bit into one of the rooms. There was a . . . thing. No quite like that thing"—he nodded at the orrery—"but along the same lines, ken? Bits o' clockwork, like."

The sensation of cold heaviness was worse. Not that there could have been any doubt about it from the beginning of Rab's account.

"The . . . woman you fetched from this place," Grey forced himself to ask. "Do you know her name? Did you deliver her there, as well?"

Rab shook his head, indifferent. There was no sign on his oxlike face that he knew that the person he had transported was not indeed a woman, nor that Lavender House was not merely another wealthy London house.

Grey essayed a few more questions, for form's sake, but received no further information of value, and at last he removed his hand and stood back, nodding to indicate that Rab might take his pay.

The chairman was likely a few years younger than Grey himself, but his hands were gnarled, frozen in a curve, as though in permanent execution of his occupation. Grey watched him fumble, thick fingers slowly pinching up the coins one by one, and curled his own hands into fists among the folds of his banyan, to restrain the impulse to do it for him.

The skin of Rab's hands was thick as horn, the palms yellow with callus. The hands themselves were broad and bluntly powerful, with black hairs sprouting over knobbled joints. Grey saw the chairman to the door himself, all the while imagining those hands upon Nessie's silken skin, with a sense of morbid wonder.

He shut the door and stood with his back against it, as though he had just escaped from close pursuit. His heart was beating fast. Then he realized that he was imagining Rab's brutal grasp upon his own wrists, and closed his eyes.

A dew of sweat prickled on his upper lip and temples, though the sense of inner cold had not diminished. He knew the house near Lincoln's Inn, called "Lavender." And had thought never to see or hear of it again.

Chapter 9

Molly-Walk

The horses clip-clopped through the darkened square at a good rate, but not so fast that he couldn't make out the row of bog-houses—or the vague figures that surrounded them, dim as the moths that flitted through his mother's garden at nightfall, drawn by the perfume of the flowers. He drew a deep, deliberate breath through the open window. Quite a different perfume reached him from the bog-houses, acrid and sour, and under it the remembered smell of the sweat of panic and desire—no less compelling in its way than the scent of nicotiana to the moths.

The bog-houses of Lincoln's Inn were notorious; even more so than Blackfriars Bridge, or the shadowed recesses of the arcades at the Royal Exchange.

A little distance farther on, he rapped on the ceiling with his stick, and the carriage drew to a halt. He paid the driver and stood waiting until the carriage had quite disappeared before turning into Barbican Street.

Barbican Street was a curving lane, less than a quarter mile long, and interrupted by the passage through it of the Fleet Ditch. Covered over for part of its length, the remnants of the river were still open here, spanned by a narrow bridge. The street was various, one end of it a mix of tradesmen's shops and noisy taverns, these yielding place gradually to the houses of minor City merchants, and terminating abruptly beyond the bridge in a small crescent of large houses that turned their backs upon the street, facing superciliously inward to a small private park. One of these was Lavender House.

Grey could as easily have arrived at the crescent by carriage, but he had wanted to begin at the far end of Barbican Street, approaching his goal more slowly afoot. The journey would give him time to prepare—or so he hoped.

It had been nearly five years since he had last set foot in Barbican Street, and he had changed a great deal in the interim. Had the character of the neighborhood altered as well?

It had not, judging by his first impressions. The street was a dark one, lit only by random spills of window-light and the wash of a cloudy half-moon, but it bustled with life, at least at the near end of the street, where numerous taverns insured traffic. People—mostly men—strolled up and down, brushing shoulders and shouting greetings to friends, or lounged in small gangs around the entrances to the public houses. The smell of ale rose sweet and pungent on the air, mixed with the scents of smoke, roast meat—and bodies, hot with drink and the sweat of a day's labor.

He had borrowed a suit of rough clothes from one of his mother's servants, and wore his hair tied back in a heavy tail, bound with a scrap of leather, with a slouch hat to hide its fairness.

There was nothing to distinguish him outwardly from the dyers and fullers, smiths and weavers, bakers and butchers whose haunt this was, and he walked anonymous through the churning throng. Anonymous unless he spoke—but there should be no need for speech, until he reached Lavender House. Until then, the swirl of Barbican Street rose round him, dark and intoxicating as the beer-drenched air.

A trio of laughing men brushed by him, leaving a smell of yeast, sweat, and fresh bread in their wake—bakers.

"D'ye hear what that *bitch* said to me?" one was demanding in mock outrage. "How he dares!"

"Ah, come on, then, Betty. Ye don't want 'em smackin' your sweet round arse, don't wave it about!"

"Wave it—I'll wave *you*, you cheeky cull!"

They disappeared into the dark, laughing and shoving each other. Grey walked on, feeling suddenly more comfortable, despite the seriousness of his errand.

Mollies. There were four or five molly-walks in London, well-known to those so inclined, but it had been a long time since he had entered one past dark. Of the six taverns on Barbican Street, three at least were molly-houses, patronized by men who sought food and drink and the enjoyment of one another's companion-ship—and one another's flesh—unashamed in like company.

Laughter lapped round him as he passed unnoticed, and here and there he caught the "maiden names" many mollies used among themselves, exchanged in joke or casual insinuation. Nancy, Fanny, Betty, Mrs. Anne, Miss Thing . . . he found himself smiling at the boisterous badinage he overheard, though he had never been inclined to that particular fancy himself.

Was Joseph Trevelyan so inclined? He would have sworn not; even now, he found the notion inconceivable. Still, he knew that almost all his own acquaintance in London society and army circles would swear with one voice on a Bible that Lord John Grey would never, could not possibly . . .

"Would you *look* at our Miss Irons tonight?" A carrying voice, raised in grudging admiration, made him turn his head. Holding riotous court in the torchlit yard of the Three Goats was "Miss Irons"—a stout young man with broad shoulders and a bulbous nose, who had evidently paused with his companions for refreshment en route to a masquerade at Vauxhall.

Powdered and painted with joyous abandon, and rigged out in a gown of crimson satin with a ruffled headdress in cloth of gold, Miss Irons was presently seated on a barrel, from which perch she was rejecting the devotions of several masked gentlemen, with an air of flirtatious scorn that would have suited a duchess.

Grey came up short at the sight, then, recollecting himself, faded hastily across the road, seeking to disappear into the shadows.

Despite the finery, he recognized "Miss Irons"—who was by day one Egbert Jones, the cheerful young Welsh blacksmith who had come to repair the wrought-iron fence around his mother's herb garden. He rather thought that Miss Irons might recognize him in turn despite his disguise—and in her current well-lubricated mood, this was the last thing he desired to happen.

He reached the refuge of the bridge, helpfully shadowed by tall stone pillars at either end, and ducked behind one. His heart was thumping and his cheeks flushed, from alarm rather than exertion. No shout came from behind, though, and he leaned over to brace his hands upon the wall, letting the cool air off the river rise over his heated face.

A pungent smell of sewage and decay rose, too. Ten feet below the arch of the bridge, the dark and fetid waters of the Fleet crawled past, reminding him of Tim O'Connell's sordid end, and he straightened, slowly.

What had that end been? A spy's wages, paid in blood to prevent the threat of disclosure? Or something more personal?

Very personal. The thought came to him with sudden certainty, as he saw once more in memory that heelprint on O'Connell's forehead. Anyone might have killed the Sergeant, for any of several motives—but that final indignity was a deliberate insult, left as signature to the crime.

Scanlon's hands were unmarked; so were Francine O'Connell's. But O'Connell's death had come at the hands of more than one, and the Irish gathered like fleas in the city; where you found one, there were a dozen more nearby. Scanlon doubtless had friends or relations. He should very much like to examine the heels of Scanlon's shoes.

There were several men standing, as he was, near the wall; one turned aside, tugging at his breeches as though to make water, another sidling toward him. Grey felt the nearness of someone at his own shoulder, and turned his back sharply; he felt the hesitation of the man behind him, and then the small huff of breath, an audible shrug, as the stranger turned away.

Best to keep walking. He had barely resumed his journey, though, when he heard a startled exclamation from the shadows a few feet behind him, followed by a brief scuffling noise.

"Oh, you bold pullet!"

"What are—hey! Mmph!"

"Oh? Well, if you'd rather, my dear . . ."

"Oy! Leggo!"

The agitated voice raised the hairs on the nape of Grey's neck in recognition. He whirled on his heel and was moving toward the altercation by reflex, before his conscious mind had realized what he was about.

Two shadowy figures swayed together, grappling and shuffling. He seized the taller of these just above the elbow, gripping hard.

"Leave him," he said, in his soldier's voice. The steel of it made the man start and step back, shaking off Grey's grip. Pale moonlight showed a long face, caught between puzzlement and anger.

"Why, I wasn't but—"

"Leave him," Grey repeated, more softly, but with no less menace. The man's face changed, assuming an air of injured dignity, as he did up his breeches.

"Sorry, I'm sure. Didn't know he was your cull." He turned away, rubbing ostentatiously at his arm, but Grey paid no attention, being otherwise concerned.

"What in Christ's name are you doing here?" he said, keeping his voice low.

Tom Byrd appeared not to have heard; his round face was open-mouthed with amazement.

"That bloke come straight up to me and put his pego into me hand!" He stared into his open palm, as though expecting to find the object in question still within his grasp.

"Oh?"

"Yes! I swear as a Christian, he did! And then he kissed me, and went for to put his hand into me breeches and grabbed me by the bollocks! Whatever would he want to do that for?"

Grey was tempted to reply that he had not the slightest idea, but instead took Byrd by the arm and towed him out of earshot of the interested parties on the bridge.

"I repeat—what are you doing here?" he asked, as they reached the refuge of a residence whose gate was sheltered by a pair of flowering laburnums, white in the moonlight.

"Oh, ah." Byrd was recovering rapidly from his shock. He rubbed the palm of his hand on his thigh and stood up straight.

"Well, sir—me lord, I mean—I saw you go out, and thought as how you might have need of someone at your back, as it was. I mean"—he darted a quick glance at Grey's unorthodox costume—

"I thought you must be headin' to somewhere as might be dangerous." He looked back over his shoulder at the bridge, obviously
feeling that recent events there had confirmed this suspicion.

"I assure you, Tom, I am in no danger." Byrd was; while most
mollies were simply looking for a good time, there was rough trade
to be found in such places and persons who would not take no for
an answer—to say nothing of simple footpads.

Grey glanced down the street; he could not send the boy back
past the taverns, not alone.

"Come with me, then," he said, making up his mind upon the
moment. "You may accompany me to the house; from there, you
will go home."

Byrd followed him without demur; Grey was obliged to take the
young man's arm and draw him up beside—otherwise the boy fell
by habit into step behind him, which would not do.

A middle-aged man in a cocked hat strolled past them, giving
Byrd a penetrating glance. Grey felt the boy meet the glance, then
jerk his eyes away.

"Me lord," he whispered.

"Yes?"

"These coves hereabouts. Are they . . . sodomites?"

"Many of them, yes."

Byrd asked no further questions. Grey let go the boy's arm after
a bit, and they walked in silence through the quieter end of the
street. Grey felt all his earlier tension return, made the more uncomfortable for the brief interlude before Byrd's appearance had
recalled him to himself.

He had not remembered. Hardly surprising; he had done his
best to forget those years after Hector's death. He had sleepwalked
through the year after Culloden, spent with Cumberland's troops
as they cleansed the Highlands of rebels, doing his soldier's duty,
but doing it as in a dream. Returning at last to London, though, he

could no longer keep from waking to the reality of a world in which Hector was not.

He had come here in that bad time, looking for surcease at best, oblivion at worst. He had found the latter, both in liquor and in flesh, and realized his luck in surviving both experiences unscathed—though at the time, survival had been the least of his concerns.

What he had forgotten in the years since then, though, was the simple, unutterable comfort of existing—for however brief a time—without pretense. With Byrd's appearance, he felt that he had hastily clapped on a mask, but wore it now somewhat awry.

"Me lord?"

"Yes?"

Byrd drew a deep and trembling breath, which made Grey turn to look at the boy. Dark as their surroundings were, his strong emotion was evident in the clenched fists.

"Me brother. Jack. D'ye think he—have ye come to find him here?" Byrd blurted.

"No." Grey hesitated, then touched Byrd's shoulder gently. "Have you any reason to suppose that he would be here—or in another such place?"

Byrd shook his head, not in negation, but in sheer helplessness.

"I dunno. I never—but I never thought . . . I dunno, sir, that's the truth."

"Has he a woman? A girl, perhaps, with whom he walks out?"

"No," Byrd said miserably. "But he's a cove to save his money, Jack. Always said as how he'd take a wife when he could afford one, and before then why tempt trouble?"

"Your brother sounds a wise man," Grey said, letting the hint of a smile show in his voice. "And an honorable one."

Byrd drew another deep breath, and swiped his knuckles furtively beneath his nose.

"Aye, sir, Jack's that."

"Well, then." Grey turned away, but waited for a moment, until Byrd moved to follow.

Lavender House was large, but in no way ostentatious. Only the marble tubs of fragrant lavender that stood on either side of its door distinguished it in any way from the houses to either side. The curtains were drawn, but shadows passed now and then beyond them, and the murmur of male conversation and occasional bursts of laughter seeped through the hanging velvet.

"It sounds like what goes on at those gentlemen's clubs in Curzon Street," Byrd said, sounding faintly puzzled. "I've heard 'em."

"It is a gentlemen's club," Grey replied, with a certain grimness. "For gentlemen of a particular sort." He removed his hat, and, untying his hair, shook it free over his shoulders; the time for disguise was past.

"Now you must go home, Tom." He pointed the way, across the park. "Do you see that light, at the end? Just beyond is an alley; it will take you to a main street. Here—take some money for a cab."

Byrd accepted the coin, but shook his head.

"No, me lord. I'll go to the door with you."

He glanced at Byrd, surprised. There was sufficient light from the curtained windows to see both the dried tears on Byrd's round face and the determined expression under them.

"I mean to be sure as these sodomitical sons of bitches shall be aware that somebody knows where you are. Just in case, me lord."

The door opened promptly to his knock, revealing a liveried butler, who gave Grey's clothes a disparaging glance. Then the man's eyes rose to his face, and Grey saw the subtle change of expression. Grey was not one to trade on his looks, but he was aware of their effect in some quarters.

"Good evening," he said, stepping across the threshold as though he owned the place. "I wish to speak to the current proprietor of this establishment."

The butler gave way in astonishment, and Grey saw the man's calculations undergo a rapid shift in the face of his accent and manner, so much at variance with his dress. Still, the man had been well-trained, and wasn't to be so easily bamboozled.

"Indeed, sir," the butler said, not quite bowing. "And your name?"

"George Everett," Grey said.

The butler's face went blank.

"Indeed, sir," he said woodenly. He hesitated, plainly uncertain what to do. Grey didn't recognize the man, but the man clearly had known George—or known of him.

"Give that name to your master, if you please," Grey said pleasantly. "I will await him in the library."

On a table by the door stood the clockwork figure Rab the chairman had noted—not an orrery, but a clockwork man, elaborately enameled and gilded, made to drop his breeches and bend over when the key was wound. Grey made as though to go to the left of this figure, toward where he knew the library to be. The butler put out a hand as though to stop him, but then halted, distracted by something outside.

"Who is that?" he said, thoroughly startled.

Grey turned to see Tom Byrd standing at the edge of the light-spill from the door, glowering fiercely, fists clenched and his jaw set in a way that brought his lower teeth up to fix in the flesh of his upper lip. Mud-spattered from his adventures, he looked like a gargoyle knocked from his perch.

"That, sir, is my valet," Grey said politely, and, turning, strode down the hall.

There were a few men in the library, sprawled in chairs near the hearth, chatting over their newspapers and brandy. It might have been the library at the Beefsteak, save that conversation stopped abruptly with Grey's entrance, and half a dozen pairs of eyes fixed upon him in open appraisal.

Fortunately, he recognized none of them, nor they him.

"Gentlemen," he said, bowing. "Your servant." He turned at once to the sideboard, where the decanters stood, and in defiance of convention and good manners, poured out a glass of some liquid, not taking the time to ascertain what it was. He turned back to find them all still staring at him, trying to reconcile the contradictions of his appearance, his manner, and his voice. He stared back.

One of the men recovered himself quickly, and rose from his seat.

"Welcome . . . sir."

"And what's your name, sweet boy?" another chimed in, smiling as he tossed down his paper.

"That is my own affair . . . sir." Grey returned the smile, with a razor edge to it, and took a sip of his drink. It was porter, curse the luck.

The rest of them had risen now and came to circle round him, nosing in the manner of dogs smelling something freshly dead. Half curious, half wary, thoroughly intrigued. He felt a trickle of sweat roll down the nape of his neck, and a nervous clenching of the belly. All of them were dressed quite ordinarily, though that meant nothing. Lavender House had many rooms, and catered to an assortment of fancies.

All were well-dressed, but none of them wore wigs or paint, and a couple showed some disorder in their dress; stocks discarded, and shirts and waistcoats opened to allow liberties that wouldn't be countenanced in the Beefsteak.

The golden-haired youth to his left was studying him with

narrowed eyes and obvious appetite; the stocky brown-haired lad saw, and didn't like it. Grey saw him move closer, deliberately jostling Goldie-Locks, to distract his attention. Goldie-Locks put a soothing hand on his playfellow's leg, but didn't take his eyes off Grey.

"Well, if you will not give your name, let me make you a present of mine." A curly-haired young man with a sweet mouth and soft brown eyes stepped forward, smiling, and took his hand. "Percy Wainwright—at your service, ma'am." He bent over Grey's hand in the most graceful of gestures, and kissed the knuckles.

The feel of the boy's warm breath on his skin made the hairs stand up on Grey's forearm. He would have liked to grasp Percy's hand and draw him in, but that wouldn't do, not just now.

He let his own hand lie inert in Wainwright's for a moment, to offer neither insult nor invitation, then drew it back.

"Your servant . . . madam."

That made them laugh, though still with an edge of wariness. They were not sure yet if he was fish or fowl, and he meant to keep it that way as long as possible.

He was a good deal more cautious now than he had been when George Everett had first brought him here. Then he had not cared for anything in particular—save George, perhaps. Now, having come so close to losing his for good, he had some appreciation for the value of a reputation; not merely his, but those of his family and his regiment, as well.

"What brings you here, my dear?" Goldie-Locks stepped closer, blue eyes burning like twin candle flames.

"Looking for a lady," Grey drawled, leaning back against the sideboard in assumed casualness. "In a green velvet gown."

There was a sputter of laughter at this, and glances among them, but nothing that looked like dawning recognition.

"Green doesn't suit me," Goldie-Locks said, and licked a

pointed tongue briefly across his upper lip. "But I've a *charming* blue satin with laced pinners that I'm *sure* you'd like."

"Oh, I'm sure," the brown-haired boy said, eyeing both Grey and Goldie-Locks with clear dislike. "You cunt, Neil."

"Language, ladies, language." Percy Wainwright edged Goldie-Locks back with a deft elbow, smiling at Grey. "This lady in green—have you a name for her?"

"Josephine, I believe," Grey said, glancing from one face to another. "Josephine, from Cornwall."

That provoked a chorus of mildly derisive "Oooh"s, and one man began to sing "My Little Black Ewe," in an off-key voice. Then the door opened, and everyone turned to see who had come in.

It was Richard Caswell, the proprietor of Lavender House. Grey knew him at once—and he recalled Grey, it was plain. Still, Caswell didn't greet him by name, but merely nodded pleasantly.

"Seppings said that you wished to speak with me. If you would care to join me? . . ." Caswell stood aside, indicating the door.

A low whistle of insinuating admiration followed Grey as he left, succeeded by whoops of laughter.

You cunt, Neil, he thought, and then dismissed all thought of anything save the matter at hand.

Chapter 10

The Affairs of Men

I was not sure that you still owned this place, else I should have inquired for you by name." Grey settled himself into the chair indicated by his host, and took the opportunity to discard the unwanted glass of porter onto a nearby table crowded with knickknacks.

"Surprised I'm still alive, I expect," Caswell said dryly, taking his own seat across the hearth.

This was the truth, and Grey didn't bother to deny it. The fire burned low and lent a deceptively ruddy hue to Caswell's wasted features, but Grey had seen him by clear candlelight in the library. He looked worse than he had when last seen, years before—but not much worse.

"You don't look a day over a thousand, Mother Caswell," Grey said lightly. That was the truth, too; beneath his modish bag-wig and an extravagant suit of striped blue silk, the man might as well have been an Egyptian mummy. Bony brown wrists and hands like bundles of dry sticks protruded from the sleeves; while the suit had undoubtedly been made by an excellent tailor, it hung upon his shrunken form like a scarecrow's burlap.

"You shameless flatterer." Caswell looked him over, amusement flickering in his eyes. "Can't say the same for you, my dear. You look as fresh and innocent as the day I first saw you. How old were you then, eighteen?" Caswell's eyes were just the same; small, black, and clever, perpetually bloodshot from smoke and late hours, sunk in pouches of deep violet.

"I lead a wholesome life. Keeps the skin clear."

Caswell laughed, then began to cough. With a practiced economy of motion, he drew a crumpled handkerchief from his waistcoat and clapped it to his mouth. He lifted a sketchy brow at Grey, half-shrugging as though to apologize for the delay of their conversation, meanwhile suffering the racking spasms with the indifference of long custom.

The coughing done at last, he inspected the resultant blood spots on the handkerchief and, evidently finding them no worse than expected, tossed the cloth into the fire.

"I need a drink," he said hoarsely, rising from his chair and heading toward the big mahogany desk, where a silver tray held a decanter and several glasses.

Unlike Magda's sanctum, Caswell's room held nothing at all that indicated the nature of Lavender House or of its members; it might have belonged to a director of the Bank of London, for all its soberness and elegance of furnishing.

"You're not enjoying that swill, are you?" Caswell nodded toward the discarded glass of porter. He filled a pair of crystal wine-glasses with a deep crimson liquid, and held one out. "Here, have some of this."

Grey took the proffered glass with a sense of unreality; he had taken wine here, in this room, when George had first brought him to Lavender House—a prelude to their retiring to one of the chambers upstairs. The sense of mild disorientation was succeeded by a sharp shock when he took the first sip.

"That's very good," he said, holding the glass up to the fire as though to appraise the color. "What is it?"

"Don't know the name," Caswell said, sniffing at the wine with appreciation. "German stuff, not bad. Had it before?"

Grey closed his eyes and drank deeply, frowning and affecting to wash it about his tongue in an effort at placement. Not that he entertained the slightest doubt. He had a good nose for wine, and a better palate—and he had drunk enough of this particular vintage with Nessie to be more than sure of recognizing it again.

"Might have," he said, opening his eyes and meeting Caswell's penetrating gaze with an innocent blink. "Can't recall. Decent stuff, though. Where'd you find it?"

"One of our members prefers it. He brings it by the cask, and we keep it in the cellar for him. Fond of it myself." Caswell took another sip, then set down his glass. "Well . . . my lord. How might I have the pleasure of serving you?" The fleshless lips rose in a smile. "Do you mean to seek membership in the Lavender Club? I'm sure the committee would look upon your application with the most cordial favor."

"Was that the committee I met in the library?" Grey asked dryly.

"Some of them." Caswell uttered a short laugh, but choked it off, unwilling to start another coughing fit. "Mind you, they might require you to submit to a series of personal interviews, but I'm sure you would have no objection to that?"

The glass felt slippery in his hand. He'd once seen a young man bent over a leather ottoman in that library and subjected to a number of personal interviews, to the vast entertainment of all present. They still had the ottoman; he'd noticed.

"I am exceedingly flattered at the suggestion," he said politely. "As it happens, though, what I require at the moment is information, rather than companionship, delightful as that prospect might be."

Caswell coughed, sitting up a little straighter. The smile was still there, but the black eyes had grown brighter.

"Yes?" he said. Grey could almost hear the whisper of steel drawn from a scabbard. The *pourparlers* were done; let the duel begin.

"The Honorable Mr. Trevelyan," he said, laying his own blade against Caswell's. "He comes here regularly; I know that already. I wish to know whom he meets."

Caswell actually blinked, not having expected such an immediate thrust, but recovered smoothly with a sidestep.

"Trevelyan? I know no one of that name."

"Oh, you know him. Whether he uses that name here is of no account; you know everything of interest about everyone who comes here. Certainly you know their real surnames."

"Flatterer," Caswell said again, though he looked less amused.

"The gentlemen in the library were not reserved," Grey said, trying for advantage. "If I were to seek them out, outside the confines of your house, I imagine some of them might tell me what I wish to know."

Caswell laughed, deeply enough to start a small fit of coughing.

"No, they won't," Caswell wheezed, groping for a fresh handkerchief. He mopped at his eyes and his shriveled mouth, drawn up in a smile once more. "No doubt one or two would tell you anything they thought you'd like to hear, if it would loosen your breeches, but they won't tell you that."

"Won't they?" Grey affected indifference, sipping at his wine.

"Trevelyan's affairs must be of more importance than I thought, if it's worth your threatening your members to keep his secrets."

"Oh, perish the thought, perish the thought!" Caswell flapped a bony hand. "Threats? Me? You know better than that, dear boy. If I were given to threats, I should have ended in the Fleet Ditch with my head caved in, long since."

A tingle of alertness shot through Grey at this remark, though he fought to keep his face blandly expressionless. Was this mere hyperbole, or warning? Caswell's withered face gave nothing away, though the sparkling eyes watched his own for any clue to his intent.

He breathed deeply to slow the rapid beating of his heart, and took another sip of wine. It might be nothing more than a coincidence, a mere accident of speech; the Fleet was at hand, after all—and for what it was worth, Caswell was correct: He serviced men of wealth and influence, and if he were given to threats or blackmail, he would have been quietly put out of business long since, in one way or another.

Information, though, was something else. George had once told him that Caswell's main stock in trade was information—and the profits from Lavender House likely were not great enough to provide the lavish furnishings evident in Caswell's private quarters. *Everyone knows Dickie Caswell*, George had said, lolling indolently on the bed in one of the upstairs rooms. *And Dickie knows everyone—and everything. Anything you want to know—for a price.*

"Your tact and discretion are most commendable," Grey said, seeking new footing for a fresh attack. "Why do you say they will not tell me, though?"

"Why, because it isn't true," Caswell replied promptly. "They've never seen a man called Trevelyan here—how could they tell you anything about him?"

"Not a man, no. I rather imagine they have seen him as a woman."

He felt a small rush of exhilaration, seeing the violet swags under Caswell's eyes deepen in hue as the color paled from his cheeks. First blood; he'd pinked his man.

"In a green velvet gown," he added, pressing the advantage. "I told you—I know he comes here; the fact is not in question."

"You are quite mistaken," Caswell said, but a cough bubbling to the surface gave the words a quavering aspect.

"Let it go, Dickie," Grey said, flicking his rapier with a touch of insolence. He lounged a little, looking tolerantly over his glass. "I say I know; you will scarcely convince me I do not. I require only a few small additional details."

"But—"

"You need not trouble yourself that you will be blamed. If I have learned the main facts about Trevelyan from another source—as indeed I have—then why should I not have learned everything from this same source?"

Caswell had opened his mouth to say something, but instead narrowed his eyes and pursed his mouth in thought.

"Nor do you need to fear that I mean any harm to Mr. Trevelyan. He is about to become a part of my family, after all—perhaps you are aware that he is engaged to my cousin?"

Caswell nodded, almost imperceptibly. His mouth was pursed so tightly that it resembled nothing so much as a dog's anus, which Grey thought very disagreeable. Still, it scarcely mattered what the evil old creature looked like, so long as he coughed up the necessary details.

"I am sure you will understand that my efforts in this regard are intended solely to protect my family." Grey glanced away, toward a massive silver epergne filled with hothouse fruit, then back at Caswell. Time for the *coup*.

"So, then," he said, spreading his hands with a graceful gesture. "It remains only to decide the price, does it not?"

Caswell made a deep, catarrhal noise, and spat thickly into a new handkerchief, which he then balled up and cast into the fire after its fellows. Grey thought cynically that he must require a good deal of money merely to keep himself in linen.

"The price." Caswell took a deep swallow of wine and put down the glass, licking his lips. "What do you have to offer? Always assuming that I have something to sell, mind."

No more pretence of ignorance. The duel was over. Grey could not help a brief sigh, and was surprised to discover that not only were his palms damp but that he was sweating freely beneath his shirt, though the room was not warm.

"I have money—" he began, but Caswell interrupted him.

"Trevelyan gives me money. A lot of money. What else can you offer me?"

The small black eyes were fixed on him, unblinking, and he saw the tip of Caswell's tongue steal out, barely visible, to lick away a drop of wine from the corner of his mouth.

Sweet Jesus. He sat dumbstruck for an instant, caught in those eyes, then glanced down, as though suddenly remembering his own wine. He lifted his glass, lowering his lashes to hide his eyes.

In defense of King, country, and family, he would unhesitatingly have sacrificed his virtue to Nessie, had that been required. If it was a question of Olivia marrying a man with syphilis and half the British army being exterminated in battle, versus himself experiencing a "personal interview" with Richard Caswell, though, he rather thought Olivia and the King had best look to their own devices.

He put down his glass, hoping that this conclusion was not reflected upon his features.

"I have something other than money," he said, meeting Caswell's gaze squarely. "Do you want to know how George Everett really died?"

If there was a flicker of disappointment in those black marble orbs, it was swamped at once beneath a wave of interest. Caswell tried to hide it, but there was no disguising the glint of curiosity, mixed with avarice.

"I heard that it was a hunting accident; broke his neck out in the country. Where was it? Wyvern?"

"Francis Dashwood's place—Medmenham Abbey. It wasn't his neck, and it was no accident. He was killed on purpose—a sword-thrust through the heart. I was there."

These last three words were dropped like pebbles into a lake; he could feel their impact send ripples through the air of the room. Caswell sat immobile, scarcely breathing, contemplating the possibilities.

"Dashwood," he whispered at last. "The Hellfire Club?"

Grey nodded. "I can tell you who was there—and everything that happened that night at Medmenham. *Everything.*"

Caswell fairly quivered with excitement, black eyes moist.

George had been right. Caswell was one of those who loved secrets, who hoarded information, who kept confidential information for the sheer joy of knowing things that no one else knew. And when the time might come that such things could be sold for a profit . . .

"Have we a bargain, Dickie?"

That recalled Caswell somewhat to himself. He took a deep breath, coughed twice, and nodded, pushing back his chair.

"That we have, my little love. Come along, then."

❦

The upper floors consisted mostly of private rooms; Grey couldn't tell whether much had been changed—he had been in no condition to notice very much on the occasions of his previous visits to Lavender House.

Tonight was different; he noticed everything.

It was peculiar, he thought, following Caswell through an upper hall. The feel of this house was quite different from that of the brothel, even though the purpose of the establishments was the same. He could hear music below, and intimate sounds in some of the rooms they passed—and yet it was not the same at all.

Magda's brothel had been much more explicit, with everything in the place intended to provoke libidinous intent. No molly-house he had ever been in did such things—there was seldom any ornamentation, nor even much furnishing beyond the simplest of beds. Sometimes, not even that; many were no more than taverns, with a room opening off the main taproom, where men could re-pair for sport, often to the applause and shouted comments of on-lookers in the tavern.

He believed that even very poor brothels had doors. Was it that women insisted upon privacy, he wondered? Yet he doubted that many whores found stimulation in the sorts of objects Magda pro-vided for the delectation of her customers. Perhaps there truly was a difference between men who were lured by women, and those who preferred the touch of their own sex? Or was it the women—did they perhaps require some decoration of the exchange?

As far as sexual feeling went . . . this house fairly vibrated with it. There were male voices and the scents of men everywhere; two lovers embraced at the end of the corridor, entwined against a wall, and his own skin prickled and jumped; he could not stop sweating.

Caswell led him to a staircase, past the lovers. One was Goldie-Locks, Neil the Cunt, who looked up, disheveled, mouth swollen, and gave him a languorous smile before returning to his compan-ion—who was not the brown-haired lad. Grey carefully did not look back as they started up the stair.

Things were quieter on the topmost floor of the house. The furnishing seemed more luxurious, as well; a wide oriental carpet ran the length of the corridor, and tasteful pictures decorated the walls, above small tables that held vases of flowers.

"Up here, we have several suites of rooms; sometimes a gentleman will come in from the provinces to stay for a few days, a week . . ."

"Quite the little home away from home. I see. And Trevelyan engages one of these suites now and again?"

"Oh, no." Caswell stopped at a varnished door, and shook loose a large key from the bunch he carried. "He keeps this particular suite on a permanent basis."

The door swung open on darkness, showing the pale rectangle of a window on the far wall. It had clouded over, and Grey could see the moon, now high and small in the sky, nearly lost amid layers of hazy cloud.

Caswell had brought a taper; he touched it to a candlestick near the door, and the light caught and grew, shedding a wavering light over a large room with a canopied bed. The room was clean and empty; Grey breathed in, but smelled nothing other than wax and floor polish, with a faint whiff of long-dead fires. The hearth was freshly swept, and a fire laid, but the room was cold; clearly no one had been here recently.

Grey prowled the room, but there was no evidence of its occupants.

"Does he entertain the same companion each time?" he asked. The keeping of a suite argued some long-term affair.

"Yes, I believe he does." There was an odd tone in Caswell's voice that made him glance sharply at the man.

"You believe? You have not seen his companion?"

"No—he is very particular, our Mr. Trevelyan." Caswell's voice was ironic. "He always arrives first, changes his clothes, and then goes down to wait near the door. He brings his companion in and up the stairs at once; all the servants have instructions to be elsewhere."

That was a disappointment. He had hoped for a name. Still, a tendency to thoroughness made him turn back to Caswell, probing for further information.

"I am sure your servants are meticulous in observing your instructions," he said. "But you, Dickie? Surely you don't expect me to believe that anyone comes into your house without your finding out everything there is to know about them. You've only heard my Christian name before, to my knowledge—and yet, if you know about Trevelyan's engagement to my cousin, plainly you know who I am."

"Oh, yes—my lord." Caswell smiled, lips drawn into a puckish point. The bargain struck, he was enjoying his revelations as much as he had his earlier reticence.

"You are right, to a degree. In fact, I do not know the name of Mr. Trevelyan's *inamorata*; he is very careful. I do, however, know one rather important thing about her."

"Which is?"

"That she *is* an *inamorata*—rather than an *inamorato*."

Grey stared at him for an instant, deciphering this.

"What? Trevelyan is meeting a *woman*? A real woman? *Here?*"

Caswell inclined his head, hands folded gravely at his waist like a butler.

"How do you know?" Grey demanded. "Are you sure?"

The candlelight danced like laughter in Caswell's small black eyes.

"Ever smelt a woman? Close to, I mean." Caswell shook his head, the loose folds of skin on his neck quivering with the movement. "Let alone a room where someone's been swiving one of the creatures for hours on end. Of course I'm sure."

"Of course you are," Grey murmured, repelled by the mental image of Caswell nosing ratlike through sheets and pillows in the vacated rooms of his house, pilfering crumbs of information from the rubble left by careless love.

"She has dark hair," Caswell offered helpfully. "Nearly black. Your cousin is fair, I believe?"

Grey didn't bother answering that.

"And?" he asked tersely.

Caswell pursed his lips, considering.

"She wears considerable paint—but I cannot say, of course, whether that is her normal habit, or part of the guise she adopts when coming here."

Grey nodded, taking the point. Those mollies who liked to dress as women normally were painted like French noblewomen; a woman hoping to be mistaken for one would likely do the same.

"And?"

"She wears a very expensive scent. Civet, vetiver, and orange, if I am not mistaken." Caswell cast his eyes up toward the ceiling, considering. "Oh, yes—she has a taste for that German wine I gave you."

"You said you kept it for a member. Trevelyan, I presume? How do you know it isn't he alone who drinks it?"

Caswell's hairy nostrils quivered with amusement.

"A man who drank as much as is brought up to this suite would be incapable for days. And judging from the evidence"—he nodded delicately at the bed—"our Mr. Trevelyan is far from incapable."

"She arrives by sedan chair?" Grey asked, ignoring the allusion.

"Yes. Different bearers each time, though; if she keeps men of her own, she does not use them when coming here—which argues a high degree of discretion, does it not?"

A lady with a good deal to lose, were the *affaire* discovered. But the intricacy of Trevelyan's arrangements was sufficient to tell him that already.

"And that is all I know," Caswell said, in tones of finality. "Now, as to your part of the bargain, my lord? . . ."

His mind still reeling from the shock of revelation, Grey recalled his promise to Tom Byrd and gathered sufficient wits to ask one more question, pulled almost at random from the swirl of fact and speculation that presently inhabited his cranium.

"All you know about the woman. About Mr. Trevelyan, though—have you ever seen a man with him, a servant? Somewhat taller than myself, lean-faced and dark, with a missing eyetooth on the left side?"

Caswell looked surprised.

"A servant?" He frowned, ransacking his memory. "No. I . . . no, wait. Yes . . . yes, I believe I have seen the man, though I think he has come only once." He looked up, nodding with decision.

"Yes, that was it; he came to fetch his master, with a note of some kind—some emergency to do with business, I think. I sent him down to the kitchens to wait for Trevelyan—he was comely enough, tooth or no, but I rather thought he was not disposed to such sport as he might encounter abovestairs."

Tom Byrd would be relieved to hear that expert opinion, Grey thought.

"When was this? Do you recall?"

Caswell's lips puckered in thought, causing Grey briefly to avert his glance.

"In late April, I think it was, though I cannot—oh. Yes, I *can* be sure." He grinned, triumphantly displaying a set of decaying teeth. "That was it. He brought word of the Austrian defeat at Prague, arrived by special courier. The newspapers had it within days, but naturally Mr. Trevelyan would wish to know of it at once."

Grey nodded. For a man with Trevelyan's business interests, information like that would be worth its weight in gold—or even more, depending on its timeliness.

"One last thing, then. When he left so hastily—did the woman leave then, too? And did she go with him, rather than seeking separate transport?"

Caswell was obliged to ponder that one for a moment, leaning against the wall.

"Ye-es, they did leave together," he said at last. "I seem to recall that the servant ran off to fetch a hired carriage, and they entered it together. She'd a shawl over her head. Quite small, though; I might easily have taken her for a boy—save that her figure was quite rounded."

Caswell drew himself up straight then, and cast a last glance about the vacant room, as though to satisfy himself that it would yield no further secrets.

"Well, that's my end of the bargain kept, my love. And yours?" His hand hovered over the candlestick, scrawny claw poised to pinch out the flame. Grey saw the polished obsidian eyes fix on him in invitation, and was all too conscious of the large bed, close behind him.

"Of course," Grey said, moving purposefully toward the door. "Shall we adjourn to your office?"

Caswell's expression might have been termed a pout, had he had the fullness of lip to achieve such a thing.

"If you insist," he said with a sigh, and extinguished the candle in a burst of fragrant smoke.

Dawn was beginning to lighten over the housetops of London by the time Grey left Dickie Caswell's sanctum, alone. He paused at the end of the corridor, resting his forehead against the cool glass of the casement, watching the City as it emerged by imperceptible degrees from its cloak of night. Muted by clouds that had thickened during the night, the light grew in shades of gray, relieved only by the faintest tinge of pink over the distant Thames. In his present state of mind, it reminded Grey of the last vestiges of life fading from a corpse's cheeks.

Caswell had been delighted with his half of the bargain, as well he should be. Grey had held back nothing of his Medmenham adventures, save the name of the man who had actually killed George Everett. There, he said only that the man had been robed and masked; impossible to say for sure who it had been.

He felt no compunction in thus blackening George's name; to his manner of thinking, George had accomplished that reasonably well for himself—and if a posthumous revelation of his actions could help to save the innocent, that might compensate in some small way for the innocent lives Everett had taken or ruined as the price of his ambition.

As for Dashwood and the others . . . let them look to themselves. *He who sups wi' the De'il, needs bring a lang spoon.* Grey smiled faintly, hearing the Scots proverb in memory. Jamie Fraser had said it on the occasion of their first meal together—casting Grey as the Devil, he supposed, though he had not asked.

Grey was not a religious man, but he harbored a persistent vision: an avenging angel presiding over a balance on which the deeds of a man's life were weighed—the bad to one side, the good to the other—and George Everett stood before the angel naked, bound and wide-eyed, waiting to see where the wavering balance might finally come to rest. He hoped this night's work should be laid to George's credit, and wondered briefly how long the accounting might go on, if it was true that a man's deeds lived after him.

Jamie Fraser had told him once of purgatory, that Catholic conception of a place prior to final judgment, where souls remained for a time after death, and where the fate of a soul might still be affected by the prayers and Masses said for it. Perhaps it was true; a place where the soul waited, while each action taken during life played itself out, the unexpected consequences and complications following one another like a collapsing chain of dominoes down through the years. But that would imply that a man was responsible not only for his conscious actions, but for all the good and evil that might spring from them forever, unintended and unforeseen; a terrible thought.

He straightened, feeling at once drained and keyed up. He was exhausted, but completely awake—in fact, sleep had never seemed so far away. Every nerve was raw, and all his muscles ached with unrelieved tension.

The house lay silent around him, its inhabitants still sleeping the drugged sleep of wine and sated sensuality. Rain began to fall, the soft ping of raindrops striking the glass accompanied by a harsh, fresh scent that came cold through the cracks of the casement, cutting through the stale air of the house and through the fog that filled his brain.

"Nothing like a long walk home in a driving rain to clear the cobwebs," he murmured to himself. He had left his hat somewhere—perhaps in the library—but felt no desire to go in search of it. He made his way to the stair, down to the second floor, and along the gallery toward the main staircase that would take him down to the door.

The door of one of the rooms on the gallery was open, and as he passed by, a shadow fell across the boards at his feet. He glanced up and met the eye of a young man who lounged in the doorway, clad in nothing but his shirt, dark curls loose upon his shoulders. The young man's eyes, black and long-lashed, passed over him, and he felt the heat of them on his skin.

He made as though to go by, but the young man reached out and grasped him by the arm.

"Come in," the young man said softly.

"No, I—"

"Come. For a moment only."

The young man stepped out onto the gallery, his bare feet long and graceful, standing so close that his thigh pressed Grey's. He leaned forward, and the warmth of his breath brushed Grey's ear, the tip of his tongue touched the whorl of it with a crackling sound like the spark that springs from the fingers on a dry day when metal is touched.

"Come," he murmured, and stepped backward, drawing Grey after him into the room.

It was clean and plainly furnished, but he saw nothing save the dark eyes, so close, and the hand that moved from his arm, sliding down to entwine its fingers with his own, the swarthiness of it startling by contrast with his own fairness, the palm broad and hard against his.

Then the young man moved away and, smiling at Grey, took hold of the hem of the shirt and drew it upward over his head.

Grey felt as though the cloth of his stock were choking him. The room was cool, and yet a dew of sweat broke out on his body, hot damp in the small of his back, slick in the creases of his skin.

"What will you, sir?" the young man whispered, still smiling. He put down one hand and stroked himself, inviting.

Grey reached slowly up and fumbled for a moment with the fastening of his stock, until it suddenly came free, leaving his neck exposed, bare and vulnerable. Cool air struck his skin as he shed his coat and loosened his shirt; he felt gooseflesh prickle on his arms and rush pell-mell down the length of his spine.

The young man knelt now on the bed. He turned his back and stretched himself catlike, arching, and the rain-light from the window played upon the broad flat muscle of thigh and shoulder, the groove of back and furrowed buttocks. He looked back over one shoulder, eyelids half-lowered, long and sleepy-looking.

The mattress gave beneath Grey's weight, and the young man's mouth moved under his, soft and wet.

"Shall I talk, sir?"

"No," Grey whispered, closing his eyes, pressing down with hips and hands. "Be silent. Pretend . . . I am not here."

Chapter 11

German Red

There were, Grey calculated, approximately a thousand wineshops in the City of London. However, if one considered only those dealing in wines of quality, the number was likely more manageable. A brief inquiry with his own wine merchant proving unfruitful, though, he decided upon consultation with an expert.

"Mother—when you had the German evening last week, did you by any chance serve German wine?"

The Countess was sitting in her boudoir reading a book, stockinged feet comfortably propped upon the shaggy back of her favorite dog, an elderly spaniel named Eustace, who opened one sleepy eye and panted genially in response to Grey's entrance. She looked up at her son's appearance, and shoved the spectacles she wore for reading up onto her forehead, blinking a little at the shift from the world of the printed page.

"German wine? Well, yes; we had a nice Rhenish one, to go with the lamb. Why?"

"No red wine?"

"Three of them—but not German. Two French, and a rather raw Spanish; crude, but it went well with the sausages." Benedicta ran the tip of her tongue thoughtfully along her upper lip in recollection. "Captain von Namtzen didn't seem to like the sausages; very odd. But then, he's from Hanover. Perhaps I inadvertently had sausages done in the style of Saxony or Prussia, and he thought it an insult. I think Cook considers all Germans to be the same thing."

"Cook thinks that anyone who isn't an Englishman is a frog; she doesn't draw distinctions beyond that." Dismissing the cook's prejudices for the moment, Grey unearthed a stool from under a heap of tattered books and manuscripts, and sat on it.

"I am in search of a German red—full-bodied, fruity nose, about the color of one of those roses." He pointed at the vase of deep-crimson roses spilling petals over his mother's mahogany secretary.

"Really? I don't believe I've ever even seen a German red wine, let alone tasted one—though I suppose they do exist." The Countess closed her book, keeping a finger between the pages to mark her place. "Are you planning your supper party? Olivia said you'd invited Joseph to dine with you and your friends—that was very kind of you, dear."

Grey felt as though he'd received a sudden punch to the midsection. Christ, he'd forgotten all about his invitation to Trevelyan.

"Whyever do you want a German wine, though?" The Countess laid her head on one side, one fair brow lifted in curiosity.

"That is another matter, quite separate," Grey said hastily. "Are you still getting your wine from Cannel's?"

"For the most part. Gentry's, now and then, and sometimes Hemshaw and Crook. Let me see, though . . ." She ran the tip of a forefinger slowly down the bridge of her nose, then pressed the tip, having arrived at the sought-for conclusion.

"There is a newish wine merchant, rather small, down in Fish Street. The neighborhood isn't very nice, but they do have some quite extraordinary wines; things you can't find elsewhere. I should ask there, if I were you. Fraser et Cie is the name."

"Fraser?" It was a fairly common Scots name, after all. Still, the mere sound of it gave him a faint thrill. "I'll ask there. Thank you, Mother." He leaned forward to kiss her cheek, taking in her characteristic perfume: lily of the valley, mixed with ink—the latter fragrance more intense than usual, owing to the newness of the book in her lap.

"What's that you're reading?" he asked, glancing at it.

"Oh, young Edmund's latest bit of light entertainment," she said, closing the cover to display the title: *A Philosophical Enquiry into the Origin of Our Ideas of the Sublime and Beautiful*, by Edmund Burke. "I don't expect you'd like it—too frivolous by half." Taking up her silver penknife, she neatly cut the next page. "I have a new printing of John Cleland's *Fanny Hill*, though, if you find yourself in want of reading matter. You know, *Memoirs of a Woman of Pleasure*?"

"Very amusing, Mother," he said tolerantly, scratching Eustace behind the ears. "Do you mean to read the Cleland thing, or do you intend merely to leave it artfully displayed in the salon, in order to drive off Lady Roswell in a state of shock?"

"Oh, *what* a good idea!" she said, giving him a look of approval. "I hadn't thought of that. Unfortunately, it hasn't got the title on the cover, and she's much too stupidly incurious simply to pick up a book and open it."

She reached over and rummaged through the stacked books on her secretary, pulling out a handsome calf-bound quarto volume, which she handed to him.

"It's a special presentation edition," she explained. "Blank spine, plain cover. So one can read it in dull company, I suppose, without arousing suspicion—as long as one doesn't let the illustrations show, at least. Why don't you take it, though? I read it when it first came out, and you'll be needing some sort of present for Joseph's bachelor party. That seems rather appropriate, if half what I hear of such parties is true."

He had been about to rise, but stopped, holding the book.

"Mother," he said carefully. "About Mr. Trevelyan. Do you think Livy is terribly in love with him?"

She looked at him with raised brows; then, very slowly, closed her book, took her feet off Eustace, and sat up straight.

"Why?" she asked, in a tone that managed to communicate all of the wariness and cynical suspicion regarding the male sex that was the natural endowment of a woman who had raised four sons and buried two husbands.

"I . . . have some reason to think that Mr. Trevelyan has . . . an irregular attachment," he said carefully. "The matter is not yet quite certain."

The Countess inhaled deeply, closed her eyes for a moment, then opened them and regarded him with a pale, clear blue gaze of pragmatism, tinged only slightly with regret.

"He is a dozen years her senior; it would be not merely unusual, but most remarkable, if he had not had several mistresses. Men of your age do have *affaires*, after all." Her lashes lowered briefly in delicate reference to the hushed-up scandal that had sent him to Ardsmuir.

"I could hope that his marriage would cause him to abandon any such irregular liaisons, but if it does not . . ." She shrugged, her shoulders sloping in sudden tiredness. "I trust he will be discreet."

For the first time, it occurred to Grey to wonder whether either his father or her first husband, Captain DeVane . . . but this was not the time for such speculations.

"I think Mr. Trevelyan is highly discreet," he said, clearing his throat a little. "I only wondered if . . . if Livy would be heartbroken, should . . . anything happen." He liked his cousin, but knew very little about her; she had come to live with his mother after he himself had left to take up his first commission.

"She's sixteen," his mother said dryly. "*Signor* Dante and his Beatrice notwithstanding, most girls of sixteen are not capable of grand passion. They merely think they are."

"So—"

"So," she said, cutting him neatly off, "Olivia actually knows nothing whatever of her intended husband, beyond the fact that he is rich, well-dressed, not bad-looking, and highly attentive to herself. She knows nothing of his character, nor of the real nature of marriage, and if she is truly in love with anything at the moment, it is with her wedding dress."

Grey felt somewhat reassured at this. At the same time, he was well aware that the cancellation of his cousin's nuptials might easily cause a scandal that would dwarf the controversy over the dismissal of Pitt as Prime Minister two months before—and the brush of scandal was not discriminating; Olivia could be tarred with it, blameless or not, to the real ruin of her chances for a decent marriage.

"I see," he said. "If I were to discover anything further, then—"

"You should keep quiet about it," his mother said firmly. "Once they are married, if she should discover anything amiss regarding her new husband, she will ignore it."

"Some things are rather difficult to ignore, Mother," he said, with more of an edge than he intended. She glanced at him sharply, and the air seemed for an instant to solidify around him, as though there were suddenly nothing to breathe. Her eyes met his straight on and held them for a moment of silence. Then she looked away, setting aside her volume of Burke.

"If she finds she cannot ignore it," she said steadily, "she will be convinced that her life is ruined. Eventually, with luck, she will have a child, and discover that it is not. Shoo, Eustace." Pushing the somnolent spaniel aside with her foot, she rose, glancing at the small chiming clock on the table as she did so.

"Go and look for your German wine, John. The wretched sempstress is coming round at three, for what I sincerely hope is the antepenultimate fitting for Livy's dress."

"Yes. Well . . . yes." He stood awkwardly for a moment, then turned to take his leave, but halted suddenly at the door of the boudoir, turning as a question struck him.

"Mother?"

"Mm?" The Countess was picking up things at random, peering nearsightedly beneath a heap of embroidery. "Do you see my spectacles, John? I know I had them!"

"They're on your cap," he said, smiling despite himself. "Mother—how old were you when you married Captain DeVane?"

She clapped one hand to her head, as though to trap the errant spectacles before they could take flight. Her face was unguarded, taken by surprise by his question. He could see the waves of memory pass across it, tinged with pleasure and ruefulness. Her lips pursed a little, and then widened in a smile.

"Fifteen," she said. The faint dimple that showed only when she was most deeply amused glimmered in her cheek. "I had a *wonderful* dress!"

Chapter 12

Along Came a Spider

There was unfortunately not time to visit Fraser et Cie before his appointment with Quarry, whom he found waiting in front of the church of St. Martin-in-the-Fields, as advertised.

"Are we attending a wedding or a funeral?" he asked, stepping down from the coach that had brought him.

"Must be a wedding—I see you've brought a present. Or is that for me?" Quarry nodded at the book beneath his arm.

"You may have it, if you like." Grey surrendered the presentation copy of *Fanny Hill* with some relief; he had been obliged to leave the house with it, as Olivia had come upon him as he passed through the hall and then had accompanied him to the door, flourishing further samples of lace beneath his nose while asking his opinion.

Quarry opened the book, blinked, then looked up at Grey, leering.

"Why, Johnny. Didn't know you cared!"

"What?" Seeing Quarry's grin, he snatched the book back, discovering only then that there was an inscription on the title page. Evidently the Countess had been in ignorance of it, too—or at least he hoped so.

It was a fairly explicit verse from Catullus, inscribed to the Countess, and signed with the initial "J."

"Too bad my name's not Benedicta," Quarry remarked. "Looks quite an interesting volume!"

Gritting his teeth and hastily reviewing a mental list of his mother's acquaintance for persons beginning with "J," Grey carefully tore the title page from the book, stuffed it in his pocket, and handed the volume firmly back to Quarry.

"Who are we going to see?" he inquired. He had, as instructed, come in his oldest uniform, and picked critically at an unraveling thread at his cuff. Tom Byrd was an excellent barber, but his skill at valeting left something to be desired.

"Someone," Quarry said vaguely, looking at one of the illustrations. "Don't know his name. Richard put me onto him; said he knew all about the Calais business; might be helpful." Richard was Lord Joffrey, Quarry's elder half-brother, and a force in politics. While not directly involved with army or navy, he knew everyone of consequence who was, and generally was informed of any brewing scandals weeks before they erupted in public.

"Something in government, then, this person?" Grey asked, because they were turning into Whitehall Street, which contained little else.

Quarry closed the book and gave him a wary look.

"Don't know, exactly."

Grey gave up asking questions, but hoped that the business wouldn't take too long. He had had a frustrating day; the morning spent in futile inquiries, the afternoon in being fitted for a suit that he was increasingly sure would never be worn at the wedding for which it was intended. He was, all in all, in the mood for a hearty tea and a stiff drink—not interviews with nameless persons holding nonexistent positions.

He was a soldier, though, and knew duty when it called.

Whitehall Street was architecturally undistinguished, bar the remnants of the Palace and the great Banqueting Hall, left over from a previous century. Their destination was neither of these, nor yet any of the faintly moldy buildings in the neighborhood that housed the minor functions of government. To Grey's surprise, Quarry turned in instead at the door of the Golden Cross, a dilapidated tavern that stood across from St. Martin-in-the-Fields.

Quarry led the way to the snug, calling to the barman for a pair of pint-pots, and took a bench, behaving for all the world as though this were his local place of refreshment—and there were in fact a number of military persons among the clientele, though most of these were minor naval officers. Quarry kept up the pretense so far as to hold a loudly jocose conversation with Grey regarding horse-racing, though his gaze roamed ceaselessly round the room, taking note of everyone who entered or left.

After a few minutes of this pantomime, Quarry said very quietly, "Wait two minutes, then follow me." He gulped the rest of his drink, shoved the empty glass carelessly away, and went out, going down the back passage as though in search of the privy.

Grey, rather bemused, drank the rest of his ale in a leisurely manner, then rose himself.

The sun was setting, but there was enough light to see that the cramped yard behind the Golden Cross was empty, bar the usual detritus of rubbish, wet ash, and broken barrels. The door to the privy hung ajar, showing that to be empty too—bar a cloud of flies, encouraged by the mild weather. Grey was waving off several of these inquisitive insects, when he saw a small movement in the shadows at the end of the yard.

Advancing cautiously, he discovered a personable young man, neatly but unobtrusively dressed, who smiled at him, but turned without greeting. He followed this escort, and found himself climbing a rickety stair that ran between the wall of the tavern and the neighboring building, ending at a door that presumably guarded the tavern owner's private quarters. The young man opened this and, going through, beckoned him to follow.

He was not sure what this preliminary mystification had led him to expect, but the reality was sadly lacking in excitement. The room was dark, low-raftered, and squalid, furnished with the well-used objects of a shabby life—a battered sideboard, a deal table with bench and stools, a chipped chamber pot, a smoky lamp, and a tray holding smudged glasses and a decanter full of murky wine. By way of incongruous decoration, a small silver vase sat on the table, holding a bunch of brilliant yellow tulips.

Harry Quarry sat just by the flowers, close in conversation with a small, fusty-looking man whose pudgy back was turned to Grey. Quarry glanced up and flicked an eyebrow, acknowledging Grey, but made a small motion with one hand, indicating that Grey was to stay back for a moment.

The discreet young man who had brought him in had disappeared through a door into the next room; another young man was busy at the far end of the room, sorting an array of papers and portfolios at the sideboard.

Something about this gentleman piqued his memory, and he

took a step in that direction. The young man suddenly turned around, hands full of papers, looked up, and stood stock-still, gaping like a goldfish. A neat wig covered the golden curls, but Grey had no difficulty in recognizing the white face beneath it.

"Mr. Stapleton?" The pudgy little man at the table did not turn round, but lifted a hand. "Have you found it?"

"Yes, Mr. Bowles," the young man said, hot blue eyes still fixed on Grey's face. He swallowed, Adam's apple bobbing in his throat. "Just coming."

Grey, having no idea whom this Mr. Bowles might be, nor what was going on, gave Stapleton a small, enigmatic smile. The young man tore his eyes away, and went to give the pudgy man the papers in his hand, but could not resist a quick, disbelieving glance over his shoulder.

"Thank you, Mr. Stapleton," the little man said, a clear tone of dismissal in his voice. Mr. Stapleton, alias Neil the Cunt, gave a short, jerky bow and moved away, eyes flickering to and from Grey with the air of one who has just seen an apparition but hopes it will have the good manners to disappear before the next glance.

Quarry and the shabby Mr. Bowles still murmured, heads together. Grey sauntered unobtrusively to an open window, where he stood, hands folded behind him, ostensibly seeking air as an antidote to the fug inside the room.

The sun was nearly down, the last of it gleaming off the rump of the bronze horse bearing the statue of Charles I that stood in the street below. He had always felt a sneaking fondness for that statue, having been informed by some forgotten tutor that the monarch, who had been two inches short of Grey's own current height, had had himself rendered on horseback in order to look more imposing—in the process, having his height unobtrusively amended to an even six feet.

A slight clearing of the throat behind him informed him that Neil the Cunt had joined him, as intended.

"Will you take some wine, sir?"

He half-turned, in such a way that it seemed natural for the young man, bearing his tray, to step forward and set it down on the broad sill. Grey made a small gesture of assent, looking coolly on as the wine was poured.

Stapleton's eyes flicked sideways to insure that no one was watching, then darted back to fix on Grey's with an expression of unspoken desperation.

Please. His lips moved soundlessly, as he held out the tumbler. The wine trembled, washing to and fro against the cloudy glass.

Grey didn't move to take it at once, but flicked his own glance sideways toward Mr. Bowles's bowed head, and back at Stapleton, raising his brows in question.

A look of horror at the thought filled Stapleton's eyes, and he shook his head, very slightly.

Grey reached out and wrapped his hand around the glass, covering the tips of Neil's fingers as he did so. He squeezed them briefly, then took the glass, lowering his gaze.

"I thank you, sir," he said politely.

"Your servant, sir," Stapleton said, with equal politeness, and bowed before turning to lift the tray. Grey caught the faint scent of Stapleton's sweat, rank with fear, but the decanter and remaining glasses stayed steady as he carried them away.

From this angle of view, he could see the pillory that stood near Charles's statue. Grey barely tasted the foul wine, half-choked as he was by the beating of the pulse in his own throat. What in God's name was going on? He didn't think this meeting was to do with him; surely Harry would have warned him. But perhaps Stapleton had—no, or he would scarcely have been so terrorized at Grey's appearance. But then, what—

A scraping of chairs fortunately interrupted his speculations before they became any more incoherent.

"Lord John?" Quarry had stood up, addressing him formally. "May I present Mr. Hubert Bowles? Major Grey."

Mr. Bowles had stood up, too, though he scarcely appeared to have done so, he being so short that there was little change in height from his seated aspect. Grey bowed courteously, murmuring, "Your servant, sir."

He took the indicated stool, and found himself facing a pair of soft blue eyes, the vague slaty color of a newborn child's, set in a face bearing as much distinction of feature as a suet pudding. There was an odd scent in the air—something like very old sweat, but with a hint of putrid decay. He couldn't tell whether it came from the furnishings or from the man in front of him.

"My lord," Bowles said, in a lisping voice little more than a whisper. "It is kind of you to attend us."

As though I were here of choice, Grey thought cynically, but merely bowed and murmured a courtesy in reply, trying meanwhile to breathe exclusively through his mouth.

"Colonel Quarry has been recounting your efforts and discoveries," Bowles said, turning over a sheet of paper with short-fingered delicacy. "You have been most assiduous."

"You flatter me too much, sir," Grey said. "I have found out nothing certain—I take it we are discussing the death of Timothy O'Connell?"

"Among other things." Bowles smiled pleasantly, but the vague expression in his eyes did not alter.

Grey cleared his throat, belatedly tasting the nastiness of the wine he had swallowed. "I imagine that Colonel Quarry has informed you that I have discovered no proof of O'Connell's involvement in—the matter at hand?"

"He has." Bowles's gaze had drifted away from Grey, and rested idly on the yellow tulips. They had orange throats, Grey saw, and glowed like molten gold in the last of the light. If they had a scent, it wasn't strong enough to perceive, unfortunately. "Colonel Quarry thinks that your efforts might be aided were we to inform you of the results of our other . . . inquiries."

"I see," Grey said, though he saw nothing at all, so far. "Our other inquiries." And who were "we," exactly? Harry sat hunched on his own stool, an untasted glass of wine in his hand, face carefully expressionless.

"As the Colonel told you, I believe, there were several suspects in the original theft." Bowles's small, soft paw spread itself on the papers. "Inquiries were instituted at once, through a variety of channels, regarding all of these men."

"I supposed that to be the case."

It was very warm in the chamber, despite the open window, and Grey could feel his shirt sticking to his back, sweat tickling his temples. He wanted to wipe his face on his sleeve, but somehow the presence of this odd little man constrained him to do no more than nod, sitting rigidly at attention.

"Without divulging details"—a tiny smile flitted across Bowles's face at that, as though the thought of withholding details was something secretly delicious—"I can inform you, Major, that it is now all but certain that Sergeant O'Connell was the guilty party."

"I see," Grey said again, guardedly.

"We lost track of him, of course, when the man who was following him—Jack Byrd, was that the name?—disappeared on Saturday." Grey was quite sure that Bowles knew the name; knew a lot more than that, in all likelihood.

"However," Bowles continued, extending a stubby finger to touch one of the shimmering petals, "we have recently received a report from another source, placing O'Connell at a particular location on the Friday. The day before his death."

A drop of sweat was hanging from Grey's chin; he could feel it trembling there like the grains of pollen trembling on the soft black anthers of the tulips.

"A rather unusual location," Bowles went on, stroking the petal with dreamy gentleness. "A place called Lavender House, near Lincoln's Inn. Have you heard of it?"

Oh. Christ. He heard the words distinctly, and hoped he hadn't spoken them aloud. This was it, then.

He sat up straighter still and wiped the drop of sweat from his chin with the back of his hand, setting himself for the worst.

"I have, yes. I visited Lavender House myself last week—in the course of my inquiries."

Bowles did not—of course!—look astonished by this. Grey was conscious of Quarry by his side, looking curious but not alarmed. He was reasonably sure that Harry had no idea of the nature of Lavender House. He was quite sure that Bowles did.

Bowles nodded amiably.

"Quite. What I am wondering, Major, is what you discovered regarding O'Connell that led you to that destination?"

"It—was not O'Connell about whom I was inquiring." Quarry shifted a little at that, and emitted a small "Hmph!"

No help for it. Commending his soul to God, Grey took a deep breath and recounted the entire story of his explorations into the life and behavior of Joseph Trevelyan.

"A green velvet dress," Bowles said, sounding only mildly curious. "God bless my soul." His hand had dropped from the tulips, and was now curled possessively around the fat little belly of the silver vase.

Grey's shirt was soaked through by now, but he was no longer anxious. He felt an odd sort of calm, in fact, as though matters had been taken quite out of his own control. What happened next lay in the hands of Fate, or God—or Hubert Bowles, whoever in God's name he was.

Stapleton was plainly in the employ of Mr. Bowles's office—whatever nameless office that might be—and Grey's second thought, after the shock of seeing him, had been that Stapleton had gone to Lavender House as an agent of Bowles.

But Stapleton had been terrified by Grey's sudden appearance; that meant that Stapleton thought Bowles to be in ignorance of his own nature. Why else that silent plea?

That being so, Stapleton would never have mentioned Grey's presence at Lavender House; he could not do so without incriminating himself. And that in turn meant that his presence there had been purely personal. Given room to think for a moment, Grey realized—with the stomach-dropping relief of one stepping back from the trap of a scaffold—that Mr. Bowles was not in fact inquiring into his own behavior, save as it pertained to the O'Connell affair. And with an obvious reason for his presence at Lavender House given . . .

"I b-beg your pardon, sir?" he stammered, realizing belatedly that Bowles had said something to him.

"I asked whether you were convinced that these Irish were conspicuously involved, Major? The Scanlons?"

"I think that they are," he replied cautiously. "But that is an impression only, sir. I have said to Colonel Quarry that it might be useful to question them more officially, though—and not only the Scanlons, but Miss Iphigenia Stokes and her family."

"Ah, Miss Stokes." The pendulous cheeks quivered faintly. "No, we are familiar with the Stokes family. Petty smugglers, to a man, but nothing whatever in the political line. Nor have they any connexion to the . . . persons at Lavender House."

Persons. That, Grey realized, almost certainly meant Dickie

Caswell. For Bowles to know about O'Connell's presence at Lavender House, someone there must have told him. The obvious conclusion was that Caswell was the "source" who had provided the information regarding O'Connell—which in turn implied that Caswell was a regular source of information for Mr. Bowles and his shadowy office. That was rather worrying, but there was no time to think of such things just now.

"You said that Mr. O'Connell visited Lavender House upon the Friday," Grey said, taking a fresh grip on the conversation. "Do you know whom he spoke with there?"

"No." Bowles's lips thinned to nothing. "He went to the back door of the establishment, and when asked his errand, replied that he was looking for a gentleman named Meyer, or something of the sort. The servant who saw him told him to wait and went away to inquire; when he returned, O'Connell had gone."

"Meyer?" Quarry leaned forward, interjecting himself into the conversation. "German? A Jew? I've heard of a fellow of that name—traveling coin-dealer. Think he works in France. Very good disguise for a secret agent, that—going about to big houses, carrying a pack, what?"

"There you have me, sir." Bowles seemed mildly annoyed by the admission. "There was no such person at Lavender House, nor was any such known by that name. It does seem most suspicious, though, given the circumstances."

"Oh, rather," Quarry said, with a tinge of sarcasm. "So, then. What d'you suggest we do?"

Bowles gave Quarry a cold look.

"It is of the utmost importance that we discover the man to whom O'Connell intended to sell his secrets, sir. It seems clear that this was a crime of impulse, rather than deliberate espionage—no one could have known that the requisitions would be exposed and unattended."

Quarry gave a grunt of agreement, and sat back, arms folded across his chest.

"Aye, so?"

"Having recognized the value of the information, though, and removed the documents, the thief—call him O'Connell, for convenience—would then be faced with the necessity of finding someone to pay for them."

Bowles pulled several sheets of rough foolscap from the stack before him, and spread them out. They were covered with a round scrawl, done in pencil, and sufficiently illegible that Grey could make out only the occasional word, read upside down.

"These are the reports that Jack Byrd supplied to us through Mr. Trevelyan," Bowles said, dealing the sheets upon the table one by one. "He describes O'Connell's movements, and notes the appearance—and often the name—of each person with whom he observed the Sergeant conversing. Agents of this office"—Grey noticed that he didn't specify *which* office—"have located and identified most of these persons. There were several among them who do indeed have tenuous connexions with foreign interests—but none who would themselves be able to accomplish a contract of such magnitude."

"O'Connell was looking for a purchaser," Grey summarized. "Perhaps one of these small fish gave him the name of this Meyer for whom he was searching?"

Bowles inclined his round little head an inch in Grey's direction.

"That was my assumption as well, Major," he said politely. " 'Small fish.' A very picturesque and appropriate image, if I may say so. And this Meyer may well be the shark in our sea of intrigue."

Grey caught a brief glimpse from the corner of his eye of Harry making faces, and coughed, turning a bit to lead Bowles's gaze in his own direction.

"Your . . . um . . . source, then—could he not discover any such person, if the suspect had an association with Lavender House?"

"I should certainly expect so," Bowles said, complacency returning. "My source disclaims all knowledge of such a person, though—which leads me to believe either that O'Connell was misdirected, or that this Meyer goes by an alias of some sort. Hardly an unlikely possibility, given the . . . ah . . . nature of that place."

"That place" was spoken with such an intonation—something between condemnation and . . . fascination? gloating?—that Grey felt a brief crawling sensation, and rubbed instinctively at the back of his hand, as though brushing away some noxious insect.

Bowles was reaching into yet another folder, but the paper he withdrew this time was of somewhat higher quality; good parchment, and sealed with the Royal Seal.

"This, my lord, is a letter empowering you to make inquiries in the matter of Timothy O'Connell," Bowles said, handing it to Grey. "The language is purposely rather vague, but I trust you may employ it to good use."

"Thank you," Grey said, accepting the document with profound misgivings. He wasn't sure yet why, but his instincts warned him that the red seal indicated danger.

"Well, then, d'ye want Lord John to go back there and rummage the place?" Quarry asked, impatient. "We've a tame constable; shall we ask him to collect the Jews in his district and put their feet to the fire until they cough up this Meyer? What shall we *do*, for God's sake?"

Mr. Bowles disliked being hurried, Grey could see. His lips thinned again, but before he could reply, Grey made his own interjection.

"Sir—if I might? I have something—it may be nothing, of

course—but there seems to be an odd connexion . . ." He explained, as well as he could, the appearance of an unusual German wine at Lavender House and its apparent connexion with Trevelyan's mysterious companion. And Jack Byrd, of course, was connected to Trevelyan.

"So I am wondering, sir, whether it might be possible to trace buyers of this wine, and thus perhaps to fall upon the scent of the mysterious Mr. Meyer?"

The small bulge of flesh that served Mr. Bowles for a brow underwent convulsions like a snail thinking fierce thoughts—but then relaxed.

"Yes, I think that might be a profitable channel of inquiry," he conceded. "In the meantime, Colonel"—he turned to Quarry with an air of command—"I recommend that you apprehend Mr. Scanlon and his wife, and make such representations to them as may be appropriate."

"Up to and including thumbscrews?" Harry inquired, standing up. "Or shall I stop at knouting?"

"I shall leave that to your impeccable professional judgment, Colonel," Bowles said politely. "I shall handle further investigations at Lavender House. And Major Grey—I think it best that you pursue the matter of Mr. Trevelyan's potential involvement in the matter; you seem best placed to handle it discreetly."

Meaning, Grey thought, *that I now have "scapegoat" written on my forehead in illuminated capitals. If it all blows up, the blame can be safely pinned to my coat, and I can be shipped off to Scotland or Canada permanently, with no loss to society.*

"Thank you," Grey said, handling the compliment as though it were a dead rat. Harry snorted, and they took their leave.

Before they had quite reached the door, though, Mr. Bowles spoke again.

"Lord John. If you will accept a bit of well-meant advice, sir?" Grey turned. The vague blue eyes seemed focused at a spot over his left shoulder, and he had to steel himself not to turn and look to see whether there was in fact someone behind him.

"Of course, Mr. Bowles."

"I think I should hesitate to allow Mr. Joseph Trevelyan to become a relation by marriage. Speaking only for myself, you understand."

"I thank you for your kind interest, sir," Grey said, and bowed, most correctly.

He followed Harry down the rickety stair and out of the noisome yard to the street, where they both stood for a moment, breathing deeply.

"Knouting?" Grey said.

"Russian flogging," Quarry explained, tugging at his wilted stock. "With a whip made of hippopotamus hide. Saw it once; flayed the poor bugger to the bone in three strokes."

"I see the appeal," Grey agreed, feeling an unexpected kinship with his half-brother Edgar. "You haven't got a spare knout you might lend me, before I go speak to Trevelyan?"

"No, but Maggie might have such a thing in her collection. Shall I ask?" Freed of Bowles's oppressive den, Quarry's natural exuberance was reasserting itself.

Grey made a dissentient motion of the hand.

"Don't trouble." He fell in beside Harry and they turned down the street, back toward the river.

"If the recent Mr. Bowles were to be dried and stuffed, he would make an excellent addition to that collection. What *is* he, do you know?"

"Not fish nor fowl, so I suppose he must be flesh," Quarry said with a shrug. "Beyond that, I think it's best not to inquire."

Grey nodded understanding. He felt wrung out—and horribly thirsty.

"Stand you a drink at the Beefsteak, Harry?"

"Make it a cask," Quarry said, clapping him on the back, "and I'll stand supper. Let's go."

Chapter 13

Barber, Barber,
Shave a Pig

The wineshop of Fraser et Cie was small and
dark, but cleanly kept—and the air inside was
dizzyingly rich with the perfume of grapes.

"Welcome, sir, welcome. Will you have the kindness to give me your honest opinion of this vintage?"

A small man in a tidy wig and coat had popped
up out of the gloom, appearing at his elbow with the
suddenness of a gnome springing out of the earth,
offering a cup with a small quantity of dark wine.

"What?" Startled, Grey took the cup by reflex.

"A new vintage," the little man explained, bowing. "I think it very fine myself—very fine! But taste
is such an individual matter, do you not find it so?"

"Ah . . . yes. To be sure." Grey raised the cup cautiously to his face, only to have an aroma of amazing
warmth and spice insinuate itself so deeply into his

nostrils that he found the cup pressed to his lips in an involuntary effort to bring the elusive scent closer.

It spread over mouth and palate and rose up in a magic cloud inside his head, the flavor unfolding like a series of blooming flowers, each scented with a different heady perfume: vanilla, plum, apple, pear . . . and the most delicate aftertaste, which he could describe only as the succulent feeling left on the tongue by the swallowing of fresh buttered toast.

"I will have a cask of it," he said, lowering the cup and opening his eyes as the last of the perfume evaporated on his palate. "What is it?"

"Oh, you like it!" The little man was all but clapping his hands with delight. "I am so pleased. Now, if you find that particular vintage to your liking, I am *convinced* that you will enjoy this. . . . Not everyone does, it takes a particularly educated palate to appreciate the subtleties, but *you*, sir . . ." The empty cup was snatched from his hand, and another substituted for it before he could draw breath to speak.

Wondering just how much he had already spent, he obligingly lifted the fresh cup.

Half an hour later, with flattened pocketbook and a pleasantly inflated head, he floated out of the shop, feeling rather like a soap bubble—light, airy, and gleaming with iridescent colors. Under his arm was a corked bottle of Schilcher, the mysterious German red, and in his pocket a list of those customers of Fraser et Cie known to have purchased it.

It was a short list, though there were more than he would have suspected—half a dozen names, including that of Richard Caswell, dealer in information. What else had Caswell carefully not told him? he wondered.

The enthusiastic wine-seller, who had eventually introduced

himself as Mr. Congreve, was regretfully unable to tell him much regarding the other buyers of the German red: "Most of our customers merely send a servant, you know; such a pity that more will not come in person, like yourself, my lord!"

Still, it was apparent from the names that at least four of the six were in fact Germans, though none was called Meyer. If his mother could not identify them, chances were good that Captain von Namtzen could; wealthy foreigners in London tended to club together, or at least to be aware of each other, and if Prussia and Saxony found themselves on different sides of the present conflict, their inhabitants did at least still speak the same language.

A bundle of rags crouched by the pavement stirred as though to move toward him, and his eyes went to it at once, with a fixed stare that made the bundle hunch and mutter to itself. His mother had been accurate in describing the environs of Fraser et Cie as "not very nice," and the ice-blue suit with silver buttons, which had proven so helpful in establishing his immediate bona fides with Mr. Congreve, was attracting rather less-desirable attention from the less-reputable inhabitants of the neighborhood.

He had taken the precaution of wearing his sword as visible warning, and had a dagger in the waist of his breeches in addition to a jerkin of thickened leather beneath his waistcoat—though he knew well enough that a manner demonstrating instant willingness to do violence was better armor than any of these. He'd learned that at the age of eight; fine-boned and lightly built as he was, it had been a matter of self-preservation, and the lesson had served him well ever since.

He gave a hostile glare to two loungers eyeing him, and put a hand on his sword hilt; their eyes slid away. He would have welcomed Tom Byrd's company, but had reckoned that time was more important than safety. He had sent Byrd to the other wine-sellers his mother had recommended; perhaps he would turn up more names to investigate.

It was minor progress in his quest to untangle the affairs of Joseph Trevelyan, but at this point, any information that seemed straightforward and unambiguous was a relief. He had quite made up his mind that Trevelyan would not marry Olivia under any circumstance—but a means of discreetly severing the engagement while not harming Livy's reputation remained to be found.

Merely to announce the dissolution of the betrothal himself would not do; if no reason was given, rumor would spread like wildfire, and rumor was the ruin of a young woman. Lacking explanation, it would be assumed that Joseph Trevelyan had discovered some grievous fault in her, for engagements in this stratum of society were neither undertaken nor discarded lightly. Olivia's wedding contract had taken two months and four lawyers to draw up.

Likewise, he could not let the true cause of the severance be publicly known—and in terms of society, there was no privacy; if anyone outside the families concerned learned the truth, within days, everyone would know of it.

While the Greys were not without influence, they did not approach the wealth and power of the Cornish Trevelyans. Letting the truth be known was to invite enmity from the Trevelyans on a scale that would compromise his own family's affairs for decades—and would still damage Livy, for the Trevelyans would hold her responsible as the agent of Joseph's exposure and disgrace, no matter that she had known nothing of it.

He could force Joseph Trevelyan to break the engagement by privately threatening exposure; but that too would cast Livy's reputation in doubt, if no plausible explanation was given. No, Trevelyan must dissolve the engagement voluntarily, and must do so in a fashion that absolved Livy of any blame in the matter. There would still be talk and speculation, but with luck, it would not be so injurious as to prevent Livy eventually making a reasonable match elsewhere.

What such grounds might be, and how he was to induce Trevelyan to discover them . . . he had no good ideas, but was in hopes that finding Trevelyan's *inamorata* might provide one. Clearly, she was a married woman, and just as clearly, in a position of considerable social delicacy; if he could discover her identity, a visit to her husband might possibly suggest a means of bringing pressure to bear upon the Trevelyans without need of Grey appearing to act directly in the matter.

A growing racket jerked him from his thoughts, and he looked up to see a group of three youths coming toward him, joking and shoving each other in lighthearted disportment. They seemed so innocent as to arouse immediate suspicion, and glancing quickly round, he spotted the accomplice: a filthy girl of twelve or so, lurking nearby, ready to dash in and cut his buttons or snatch his wine, as soon as his attention should be distracted by her playfellows.

He took hold of his sword with one hand, and clutched the neck of the bottle club-like in the other, giving the girl a gimlet stare. She pouted impudently at him, but stepped back, and the gang of young pickpockets clattered past, talking loudly and patently ignoring him.

A sudden silence made him turn to look after them, though, and he saw the girl's petticoat tail just disappearing into an alleyway. The youths were nowhere in sight, but the sound of hasty footsteps thumped softly, running away down the dark alley.

He swore silently to himself, glancing round. Where might that alley come out again? The lane he was in showed several dark openings between his present location and the turn into the next street. Evidently, they meant to dash ahead, then lie in wait until he had passed their hiding place, jumping out to commit ambush from behind.

Forewarned was forearmed, but there were still three of them—four, counting the girl—and he doubted that the pie-sellers and rag-and-bone men on the street would feel compelled to come to his aid. With quick decision, he turned upon his heel and ducked into the alley where the pickpockets had disappeared, lifting the bottom edge of his waistcoat to render the dagger hilt ready to his hand.

The lane had been shabby; the alley was noisome, narrow, dark, and half-choked with refuse. A rat, disturbed by the earlier passage of the pickpockets, hissed at him from a mound of rubble; he swung the bottle and sent the rat flying into the wall, which it struck with a satisfyingly juicy thump before falling limp at his feet. He kicked it aside and went on, bottle at the ready and hand on his dagger, listening for any sound of footfalls ahead.

The alleyway forked, with a jog hard right, back toward the lane; he paused, listening, then risked a quick glance round the corner. Yes, there they were, crouched at the ready, sticks in hand. The girl, curse her, had a knife or a bit of broken glass in her hand; he saw the light glint from it as she moved.

A moment more, and they would realize he was not coming down the lane. He stepped silently past the fork and made his way as fast as he could through the rubble of the left-hand alley. He was obliged to climb over stacks of wet refuse and worm sideways through the hanging goods in a fuller's yard, to the gross disfigurement of his suit, but emerged at last into a wider thoroughfare.

He didn't recognize the street, but was able to see the dome of St. Paul's looming in the distance, and thus to judge his way. Breathing somewhat easier in spite of the mephitis of dog turds and rotten cabbage that surrounded him, he set his steps eastward, and turned his thoughts to the next item on the day's agenda of unpleasant duties, which was to resume the search for a break in the clouds obscuring the truth of Timothy O'Connell's life and death.

A note had come that morning from the enigmatic Mr. Bowles, to the effect that no further connexions had been discovered to exist between the late Sergeant and any known agents of a foreign power. Grey wondered grimly just how many unknown agents there might be in London.

Constable Magruder had come in person the night before, to report a lack of result from inquiries into the Turk's Head, scene of Saturday's brawl. The tavern's owner insisted stubbornly that O'Connell had left the place drunk, but moving under his own power—and while admitting that a brawl had occurred on the premises on the night in question, insisted that the only damage done had been to the window of the establishment, when one patron had thrust another through it, headfirst. No witnesses had been found who had seen O'Connell later in the evening—or who would admit to it.

Grey sighed, his mood of mellow buoyancy deflating. Bowles was convinced that O'Connell was the traitor—and possibly he was. But the longer the investigation continued, the more apparent it seemed to Grey that O'Connell's death had been a strictly personal matter. And if that was the case, the suspects were obvious.

So was the next step—the arrest of Finbar Scanlon and his wife. Well, if it must be done, it must.

It would likely be a simple matter, given the circumstances. Apprehend them, and then question them separately. Quarry would make it clear to Scanlon that Francine would probably hang for O'Connell's murder, unless it could be proved that she had no involvement in the crime—and what proof was there, other than Scanlon's own confession of guilt?

Of course, success depended upon the assumption that if Scanlon loved the woman enough to kill for her, he would also die for her—and that might not be the case. It was, however, the best place to start; and if it did not work, why, then the same suggestion might be employed to better effect upon the wife, with respect to her new husband.

It was a sordid matter, and he took no pleasure in its resolution. It was necessary, though—and the process did hold one small gleam of hope. If O'Connell had indeed abstracted the requisitions, and had not passed the information on at the time of his death, then in all probability either Scanlon, Francine, or Iphigenia Stokes knew where it was, even if none of them had killed him for it.

If he or Quarry could extract anything resembling a confession from his suspects, they might be offered official clemency in the form of a commuted sentence—if the stolen records were restored. He was sure that between them, Harry Quarry and the mysterious Mr. Bowles could arrange for a sentence of transportation rather than hanging, and he hoped it would fall out so.

He was very much afraid, though, that the stolen requisitions were presently in France, having been taken there by Jack Byrd. And in that case . . .

In spite of the convoluted nature of his thoughts, he had not abandoned his alertness, and the sound of running footsteps on the roadway behind him made him turn sharply, both hands on his weapons.

His pursuer was not one of the pickpockets, though, but rather his valet, Tom Byrd.

"Me lord," the boy gasped, coming to a halt beside him. He bent over, hands on his knees, panting like a dog to recover breath. "I was lookin' for—saw you—and ran—what—you been—a-doing to your *suit*?"

"Never mind that," Grey said shortly. "Has something happened?"

Byrd nodded, gulping air. His face was still bright red and streaming sweat, but he could at least form words.

"Constable Magruder. He sent—says come as quick as may be. He's found a woman. A dead woman—in a green velvet dress."

Stray bodies would normally be taken to the nearest coroner—but mindful of the possible importance of his discovery and the need for discretion, Constable Magruder had helpfully had the body brought first to the regiment's quarters near Cadogan Square, where it had been placed in the hay shed—to the horror of Corporal Hicks, who was in charge of the horses. Harry Quarry, summoned from his tea to deal with this new circumstance, told Grey as much upon his arrival in the courtyard.

"What happened to your suit?" Quarry asked, casting an interested eye over the assorted stains. He rubbed a finger beneath his nose. "Phew."

"Never mind that," Grey said tersely. "Do you know the woman?"

"Don't think her own mother would know her," Quarry said, turning to lead the way into the stables. "Pretty sure I've seen the dress, at Maggie's place. Certainly isn't Maggie, though—no tits at all."

A sudden fear turned Grey's bowels to water. Christ, could it be Nessie?

"When you say her mother wouldn't know her—had she . . . been in the water long?"

Quarry cast him a puzzled look.

"She wasn't in the water at all. Had her face beaten in."

He felt bile rise at the back of his throat. Had the little whore gone nosing about, in hopes of helping him further, and been murdered for her interference? If she had died on his account, and in such a way . . . Uncorking the bottle of wine, he took a deep swallow, and another, then handed it to Quarry.

"Good idea. She's niffy as a Frenchman's arse; been dead a day or two." Harry tilted up the bottle and drank, looking somewhat happier afterward. "Nice stuff, that."

Grey saw Tom Byrd cast a look of longing at the bottle, but Quarry kept firm hold of it as he led the way through the brick-paved stables.

Magruder was waiting for them outside the shed, with one of his constables.

"My lord." Magruder inclined his head, looking curiously at Grey. "What happened to—"

"Where did you find her?" Grey interrupted.

"In Saint James's Park," the constable replied. "In the bushes by the path."

"Where?" Grey said incredulously. Saint James's was the preserve of merchants and aristocrats, where the young, the rich, and the fashionable strolled to see and be seen. Magruder shrugged, slightly defensive.

"People out for an early walk found her—or rather, their dog did." He stepped back, ushering the soldiers ahead of him through the door to the tack room. "There was considerable blood."

Grey's first thought upon seeing the body was that the constable was a master of understatement. His second was a sense of profound relief; the body was in fact fairly flat-chested, but was much too tall to be Nessie. The hair was darker than the Scottish whore's, too—nearly black—and while it was thick and wavy, it was nothing like Nessie's wild curly mane.

The face was essentially gone; obliterated in a frenzy of blows from something like the back of a spade or a fireplace poker.

Suppressing his distaste—Quarry had been right about the smell—
Grey circled slowly about the table on which the corpse had been
laid.

"Think it's the same?" Quarry asked, watching him. "The dress,
I mean. You've an eye for such things."

"I am fairly sure that it is. The lace . . ." He nodded at the wide
trim on the gown, which matched the edging of the kerchief. The
kerchief itself straggled loose across the table, torn and soaked
in blood, but still pinned precariously to the gown. "It's
Valenciennes. I noticed it particularly at the brothel, because it's
very like that on my cousin's wedding gown—there are swathes of
it all over my mother's house. Expensive stuff, though."

"Not common, then." Quarry fingered the tattered rag of the
kerchief.

"Not at all."

Quarry nodded, turning to Magruder.

"I think we shall be wanting a word with a madam named
Maggie—house in Meacham Street, you know it? Rather a pity,
that," he added, turning back to Grey with a sigh. "Did like that
blonde with the big tits."

Grey nodded, only half-hearing. The gown itself was so crusted
with blood and dirt that the color was almost indistinguishable;
only the draggled folds of the skirt still showed emerald green. The
smell was very strong in the confined quarters—Quarry had been
right, she did reek like a . . .

He bent closer, hands on the table, sniffing deeply. Civet. He'd
swear he smelt civet—and something else as well. The corpse was
wearing perfume, though the scent was nearly obscured by the
earthier reeks of blood and ordure.

She wears a very expensive scent. Civet, vetiver, and orange, if I am not
mistaken. He could hear Richard Caswell's voice in his head, dry as

grave flowers. *She has dark hair. Nearly black. Your cousin is fair, I believe?"*

Excitement and dread tightened his belly as he leaned over the dead woman. It had to be; this was Trevelyan's mysterious lover. But what had happened to her? Had her husband—if she had one—discovered the affair and taken his revenge? Or had Trevelyan . . .

He sniffed again, eager for confirmation.

Where did women wear perfume? Behind the ears—no, not a chance; the corpse had only one ear and the other was in no condition . . . Between the breasts, perhaps; he'd seen his mother tuck a scented cloth down into the top of her stays before a party.

He ducked his head to inhale more deeply, and saw the small, blackened hole in the center of the bodice, inconspicuous amidst the general carnage.

"I will be damned," he said, looking up at the phalanx of bemused faces hovering over him. "She's been shot."

"Do you want to know summat else, me lord?" The whisper came at his elbow. Tom Byrd, by now somewhat inured to nasty sights, had edged his way close, and was looking at the corpse's smashed face in fascination.

"What's that, Tom?"

The boy's finger floated tentatively across the table, pointing at what Grey had taken for a smudge of dirt behind the jaw.

"She's got whiskers."

∞

The corpse was, in fact, that of a man. Striking as that was, though, it was not the main point of remark, once the rags of the green gown had been removed to verify the fact.

"I've never seen anything like that in me life," Harry Quarry

said, eyeing the dead man with a combination of disgust and fascination. "You, Magruder?"

"Well, on a woman, now and then," the constable said, pursing
his lips fastidiously. "Some of the whores do it regular, I understand. Bit of a curiosity, like."

"Oh, whores, yes, of course." Quarry flapped a hand, indicating
that such usage was not only familiar to him, but positively com-
monplace. "But this is a man, dammit! You've never seen such a
thing, have you, Grey?"

Grey had, in fact, seen such a thing, and more than once,
though it was not an affectation that appealed to him personally. It
would scarcely do to say so, though, and he shook his head, widening his eyes in a semblance of shocked incomprehension at the per-
versity of mankind.

"Mr. Byrd," he said, making space for Tom to approach closer.
"You are our chief expert on the art of shaving; what can you tell us
about this?"

Nostrils pinched against the reek of the corpse, Tom the barber's son motioned for the lantern to be brought closer, and leaned
down, squinting in professional fashion along the planes of the
body.

"Well," he said judiciously, "he does it—did it, I mean—regular.
More like, someone did it for him—a nice, professional bit of
work. See, there's no cuts, nor yet no scraping—and that's an awkward bit, round there." He pointed, frowning. "Hard to manage by
yourself, I should think."

Quarry made a noise that might have been a laugh, but con-
verted it hastily into a wheezing cough.

Byrd, ignoring this, stretched out a hand and ran it very delicately up the corpse's leg.

"Oh, yes," he said, in tones of satisfaction. "Feel that, me lord?
You can feel the stubble, sharp-ended, like, when you goes against

the grain. It gets like that when a man shaves regular. If he shaves no more than once or twice a month, he's like to get bumps—the hair curls up under the skin as it grows, see? But no bumps here."

There were not. The corpse's skin was smooth, devoid of hairs on arms, legs, chest, buttocks and privates. Other than smears of dried blood and caked ordure, and the small black hole of the bullet wound in his chest, only the deep purple-brown of the nipples and the riper tones of the rather well-endowed expanse between the man's legs interrupted the pale olive perfection of his flesh. Grey thought the gentleman would likely have been quite popular, in certain circles.

"He has stubble. So the shaving took place before death?" Grey asked.

"Oh, yes, me lord. Like I said—he does it regular."

Quarry scratched his head.

"I will be damned. D'ye think he's a he-whore, then? A sodomite of some type?"

Grey would have taken a substantial wager to that effect, were it not for one observation. The man was slight, but well-built and muscular, like Grey himself. However, the muscles of chest and arms had begun to sag from lack of use, and there was a definite roll of fat around the middle. Adding to these observations the fact that the man's neck was deeply seamed and, despite an impeccable manicure, the backs of his hands thickly veined and knobbed, Grey was reasonably sure that the body was that of a man in his late thirties or early forties. Male prostitutes seldom lasted far beyond twenty.

"Nah, too old," Magruder objected, fortunately saving Grey from the necessity of finding some way of saying the same thing, without disclosing how he knew it. "This cove would be one as hires such, not one himself."

Quarry shook his head in disapproval.

"Should never have suspected Maggie of dealing in that sort of thing," he said, as much in regret as condemnation. "You sure about the dress, then, Grey?"

"Reasonably. It is not impossible that a dressmaker should make more than one gown, of course—but whoever made this one made the one that Magda was wearing."

"Magda?" Quarry blinked at him.

Grey cleared his throat, a hideous realization coming suddenly over him. Quarry hadn't known.

"The . . . ah . . . Scottish woman I met there informed me that the madam was called Magda, and is in fact a, um, a German of some type."

Quarry's face looked pinched in the lantern light.

"Of some type," he repeated bleakly. It made considerable difference *which* type, and Quarry was well aware of it. Prussia and Hanover—of course—had allied themselves with England, while the duchy of Saxony had chosen up sides with France and Russia, in support of its neighbor Austria. For an English colonel to be patronizing a brothel owned by a German of unknown background and allegiance, and now with an evident involvement in criminal matters, was a dicey proposition, and one that Quarry must devoutly hope would never come to official notice. Or the notice of the unblinking Mr. Bowles.

It wouldn't do Grey's reputation any good, either. He realized now that he ought to have mentioned the situation to Quarry at the time, rather than assuming that he must know of Magda's background already. But he had allowed himself to be distracted by alcoholic excess, and by Nessie's disclosure about Trevelyan—and now he could but hope there wasn't the devil to pay for it.

Harry Quarry drew a deep breath and blew it out again, squaring his shoulders. One of Harry's many good points was that he never wasted time in recrimination, and—unlike Bernard Sydell—never blamed subordinates, even when they deserved it.

"Well, then," he said, and turned to Magruder. "I think we must have Mrs. Magda taken into custody and questioned without delay. We shall need to search her premises, as well, I should think—will you require a warrant?"

"Yes, sir. Given the circumstances"—Magruder nodded delicately at the dead man—"I shouldn't think the magistrate would be reluctant."

Quarry nodded, straightening the coat on his shoulders.

"Aye. I'll come myself and speak to him now." He drummed his fingers restlessly on the table, making the corpse's slack hand tremble with the vibration. "Grey—I think we shall have the Scanlons taken up, too, as you advised. You'll question them; go round to the gaol tomorrow, once Magruder has had a chance to lay them by the heels. As for . . . the Cornish gentleman . . . use your best judgment there, will you?"

Grey managed a nod, cursing himself for his idiocy, and then Quarry and Magruder were gone, leaving the faceless corpse naked and staring in the flickering light.

"You in trouble, me lord?" Tom Byrd was frowning worriedly at him from the shadows, having evidently divined some hint of the undercurrents in the preceding conversation.

"I hope not." He stood looking down at the dead man. Who the devil was he? Grey had been convinced that the body was that of Trevelyan's lover—and it might still be, he reminded himself. True, Caswell had insisted that it was a woman whom Trevelyan entertained at Lavender House, but Caswell might have been mistaken in his own powers of olfactory discernment—or lying, for reasons unknown.

Use his best judgment, Harry said. His best judgment was that

Trevelyan was in this up to his neck—but there was no direct evidence.

There was certainly no evidence to connect the Scanlons with this business, and precious little to connect them with O'Connell's murder—but Harry's motive in ordering an arrest there was apparent; if inquiries were eventually made into the conduct of the investigation, it would be prudent to make it look as though affairs were being pursued aggressively. The muddier the waters, the less likely anyone might be to take up the matter of Magda's inconvenient nationality.

"Major?" He turned, to see Corporal Hicks frowning at him from the doorway. "You aren't going to leave that thing *here*, are you?"

"Oh. No, Corporal. You may remove it to the coroner's. Fetch some men."

"Right, sir." Hicks disappeared with alacrity, but Grey hesitated. Was there any further information that the body itself could offer?

"You think it was the same cove what did for that Sergeant O'Connell what did for this 'un, me lord?" Tom Byrd had come to stand alongside him.

"I have no particular reason to think so," Grey said, a little startled at this supposition. "Why?"

"Well, the, uh, face." Tom gestured, a little awkwardly, at the remains, and swallowed audibly. One eyeball had been dislodged so far from its parent socket as to dangle out onto the crushed cheek, staring accusingly off into the shadows of the hay shed. "Seems like whoever did this didn't care for him much—same as whoever stamped on the Sergeant."

Grey considered that, pursing his lips. Reluctantly, he shook his head.

"I don't think so, Tom. I think that whoever did this"—he gestured at the corpse—"did it in order to disguise the gentleman's identity, not out of personal dislike. It's heavy work, to crush a skull like that, and this was a very thorough job. One would have to be in an absolute frenzy of hatred—and if that was the case, why shoot him first?"

"Did they? Shoot him first, I mean, me lord. 'Coz what you said about dead men don't bleed—this one surely did, so he can't have been dead when they . . . erm." He glanced at the smashed face, and then away. "But he couldn't live long like that—so why shoot him, then?"

Grey stared at Tom. The boy was pale, but bright-eyed, intent on his argument.

"You have a very logical sort of mind, Tom," he said. "Why, indeed?" He stood for a moment looking down at the corpse, trying to reconcile the disparate bits of information at hand. What Tom said made obvious sense—and yet he was convinced that whoever had killed this man had not beaten in his face from anger. Just as he was convinced that whoever had stamped on Tim O'Connell's face had acted from precisely that emotion.

Tom Byrd stood patiently by, keeping quiet as Grey circled the table, viewing the corpse from all angles. Nothing seemed to make sense of the puzzle, though, and when Hicks's men came in, he allowed them to bundle up the body into a canvas.

"D'you want us to take this, as well, sir?" One of the men picked up the sodden hem of the green dress, gingerly, between two fingers.

"Not even the mort-man'd want *that*," the other objected, wrinkling his nose at the reek.

"You couldn't sell it to a ragpicker, even was you to wash it."

"No," Grey said, "leave it, for now."

"You don't mean to leave it in here, do you, sir?" Hicks stood by, arms folded, glowering at the sodden pile of velvet.

"No, I suppose not," Grey said, with a sigh. "Don't want to put the horses off their feed, do we?"

It was full dark as they left the stables, but with a gibbous moon rising. No coach would take them as passengers with their malodorous burden, even with it wrapped in tarred canvas, and so they were obliged to walk to Jermyn Street.

They made the journey for the most part in silence, Grey mulling over the events of the day, trying vainly to fit the dead man somehow into the puzzle. Two things alone seemed clear about the matter: one, that a great effort had been made to disguise the man's identity. Two, that there was some connexion between the dead man and the brothel in Meacham Street—which in turn meant that there must be some connexion with Joseph Trevelyan.

This seemed vaguely wrong; if one's chief motive was to disguise identity, why clothe the corpse in such a distinctive gown? His mind supplied the answer, belatedly reminding him of what he had seen but not consciously noted at the time. The man had not been dressed in the gown after death—he had been wearing it when he was shot.

There was no doubt about it. The bullet hole in the dress was singed round the edges, and there were powder grains in the fabric of the dress for some distance around it; likewise, the wound in the chest had shreds of fabric driven into it.

That began to make matters seem more sensible. If the victim had been wearing the gown when shot, and there was some reason not to remove it—then the smashing of the man's face to obscure identity was a reasonable step.

Look at it from the other direction, he thought. If Magruder had not been on the alert for any mention of a green velvet gown—for no one could have known that there was any official interest in such a thing—what might have been expected to happen?

The corpse would have been discovered, and taken to the nearest morgue—which was . . . where, exactly? Near Vauxhall, perhaps?

That was promising; Vauxhall was a rowdy district, full of theaters and amusement parks, much patronized by ladies of the evening *and* by painted mollies out for an evening's jollification at one of the many masked balls. He must ask Magruder to discover whether there had been a ball on Tuesday night.

So, then. If not for Magruder's interference, the body would have been taken to a morgue, where it would likely have been assumed to be that of a prostitute, such women not uncommonly meeting with violent ends. Everyone who had seen the body had in fact assumed it to be that of a woman, until Tom the barber's son had spotted the tiny patch of telltale stubble.

That was it, he thought, with a small spurt of excitement. That was why the gown was not removed and why the face was smashed; to disguise not the identity per se, but the sex of the victim!

He felt Tom glance at him in curiosity, and realized that he must have made some exclamation. He shook his head at the boy and paced on, too engrossed in his speculations to suffer the distraction of conversation.

Even if the truth of the corpse's sex had been discovered, he thought, it would likely have been assumed that the body belonged to the shady half-world of transvestite commerce—no one of consequence, no one who would be missed.

The body would then have been promptly disposed of, taken off to a dissection room or a potter's field, depending on its state—but in either case, safely gone, with no chance of its ever being identified.

All of which gave him an unpleasant sensation in the pit of the stomach. A number of boys and young men from that shadow world disappeared in London every year, their fates—when they were noticed at all—usually concealed in official wording that sought to soothe society's sensibilities by ignoring any hint that they had been involved in abominable perversion.

Which meant that for such trouble to be taken in disguising this particular death—the dead man *was* someone of consequence. Someone who would be missed. The bundle under his arm seemed suddenly heavier, dragging at him like the weight of a severed head.

"Me lord?" Tom Byrd laid a tentative hand on the bundle, offering to take it from him.

"No, Tom, that's all right." He shifted the bundle, tucking it more firmly under his arm. "I smell like a slaughterhouse already; no need for you to spoil your clothes as well."

The boy took his hand away, with an alacrity that informed Grey of the nobility of the original offer. The bundle *did* stink abominably. He smiled to himself, face hidden in the darkness.

"I'm afraid we will have missed our supper—but I suppose Cook will let us have something."

"Yes, me lord."

Piccadilly lay just ahead; the streets were opening out, lined with the shops of clothiers and merchants, rather than the libkens and taverns of the narrower ways near Queen Street. At this time of night, the streets were busy with foot traffic, horses and carriages; random snatches of conversation, shouts and cheerful bustle drifted past.

A light rain was falling, and mist rose from the pavements round their feet. The lightermen had come already; the streetlamps flickered and glowed under the glass of their canopies and shone upon the wet stones, helping to dispel the lurking horror of that conference in the hay shed.

"Do you get used to it, me lord?" Tom glanced at him, round face troubled in the transient glow.

"To what? Death, do you mean, and bodies?"

"Well . . . that sort of death, I suppose." The boy made a diffi-dent gesture toward the bundle. "I'd think this was maybe differ-ent than what you see in battle—but maybe I'm wrong?"

"Maybe." Grey slowed his pace to let a group of gay blades pass, laughing as they crossed the street, dodging an oncoming detach-ment of mounted Horse Guards, harness glittering in the wet.

"I suppose it is no different in the essentials," he said, stepping out as the sound of hooves clattered off down Piccadilly. "I have seen more dreadful things on a battlefield, often. And yes, you do get used to that—you must."

"But it *is* different?" Tom persisted. "This?"

Grey took a deep breath, and a firmer hold on his burden.

"Yes," he said. "And I should not like to meet the man to whom this is routine."

Chapter 14

A Troth Is Blighted

Grey was rudely roused from his bed just after dawn, to find Corporal Jowett arrived on the doorstep with bad news.

"Ruddy birds had flown, sir," Jowett said, handing over a note from Malcolm Stubbs to the same effect. "Lieutenant Stubbs and I went round with a couple of soldiers, along with that Magruder fellow and two constables, thinking to take the Scanlons unawares whilst it was still dark." Jowett looked like an emaciated bulldog at the best of times; his face now was positively savage. "Found the door locked and broke it in—only to find the place empty as a ruddy tomb on Easter morning."

Not only had the Scanlons themselves decamped; the entire stock of the apothecary's shop was missing, leaving behind only empty bottles and bits of scattered rubbish.

"They had warning, eh?" Jowett said. "Somebody tipped 'em—but who?"

"I don't know," Grey said grimly, tying the sash of his banyan. "You spoke to the neighbors?"

Jowett snorted.

"For what good it did. Irishmen, all of 'em, and liars born. Magruder arrested a couple of them, but it won't do any good—you could see that."

"Did they say at least *when* the Scanlons had decamped?"

"Most of them said they hadn't the faintest—but we found one old granny down the end of the street as said she'd seen folk carrying boxes out of the house on the Tuesday."

"Right. I'll speak to Magruder later." Grey glanced out the window; it was raining, and the street outside was a dismal gray, but he could see the houses on the other side—the sun was up. "Will you have some breakfast, Jowett? A cup of tea, at least."

Jowett's bloodshot eyes brightened slightly.

"I wouldn't say no, Major," he allowed. "It's been a busy night."

Grey sent the Corporal off to the kitchen in the charge of a yawning servant, and stood staring out the window at the downpour outside, wondering what the devil to make of this.

On the positive side, this hasty disappearance clearly incriminated the Scanlons—but in what? They had a motive for O'Connell's death, and yet they had simply denied any involvement, Scanlon looking cool as a plateful of sliced cucumbers. Nothing had happened since that might alarm them in that regard; why should they flee now?

What *had* happened was the discovery of the dead man in the green velvet dress—but what could the Scanlons have had to do with that?

Still, it seemed very likely that the man had been killed sometime on Tuesday—and Tuesday appeared to be when the Scanlons had fled. Grey rubbed a hand through his hair, trying to stimulate his mental processes. All right. That was simply too great a coincidence to *be* a coincidence, he thought. Which meant . . . what?

That the Scanlons—or Finbar Scanlon, at least—were involved in some way with the death of the man in green velvet. And who the hell was he? A gentleman—or someone with similar pretensions, he thought. The corpse was no workingman, that was sure.

"Me lord?" Tom Byrd had come in with a tray. He hadn't yet washed his face, and his hair stuck up on end, but he seemed wide-awake. "I heard you get up. D'ye want some tea?"

"Christ, yes." He seized the steaming cup and inhaled its fragrant steam, the heat of the china wonderful in his chilled hands.

The rain poured in sheets from the eaves. When had they left? he wondered. Were Scanlon and his wife out in this, or were they safe in some place of refuge? Chances were, they had decamped immediately following the death of the man in green velvet—and yet, they had taken the time to pack, to remove the valuable stock from the shop. . . . These were not the panicked actions of murderers, surely?

Of course, he was obliged to admit to himself, he hadn't dealt with many murderers before—unless . . . The recollection flashed through his mind, as it did now and then, of what Harry Quarry had told him about Jamie Fraser and the death of a Sergeant Murchison at Ardsmuir. If it was true—and even Quarry had not been sure—then Fraser also had remained cool and unpanicked, and had gotten away with the crime in consequence. What if Scanlon had a similar temperament, an equal capacity?

He shook his head impatiently, dismissing the thought. Fraser was not a murderer, whatever else he might be. And Scanlon? For the life of him, Grey could not decide.

"Which is why we have courts of law, I suppose," he said aloud, and drained the rest of the cup.

"Me lord?" Tom Byrd, who had just succeeded in lighting the fire, scrambled to his feet and picked up the tray.

"I was merely observing that our legal system rests on evidence, rather than emotion," Grey said, setting the empty cup back on the tray. "Which means, I think, that I must go and find some." Brave words, considering that he had no good ideas as to where to look for it.

"Oh, aye, sir? Will you be wanting your good uniform, then?"

"No, I think not yet." Grey scratched thoughtfully at his jaw. The only hope of a clue that he had at present was the German wine. Thanks to the helpful Mr. Congreve, he knew what it was, and who had bought it. If he could not find the Scanlons, perhaps he could discover something about the mysterious man in green.

"I'll wear it when we call upon Captain von Namtzen. But first—"

But first it was high time to discharge an unpleasant duty.

"I'll wear the ice-blue now, if it's decent," he decided. "But first, I need a shave."

"Very good, me lord," said Byrd, in his best valet's voice, and bowed, upsetting the teacup.

Tom Byrd had mostly succeeded in removing the odor from the ice-blue suit. Mostly.

Grey sniffed discreetly at the shoulder of his coat. No, that was all right; perhaps it was just a miasma from the object in his pocket. He had cut a square from the green velvet dress, crusty with dried blood, and brought it with him, wrapped in a bit of oil-cloth.

He had, after some hesitation, also brought a walking stick, a slender affair of ebony, with a chased silver handle in the shape of a brooding heron. He did not intend to strike Trevelyan with it, no matter how the interview progressed. He was, however, aware that having some object with which to occupy one's hands was useful in times of social difficulty—and this occasion promised to be rather more difficult than the usual.

He'd thought of his sword, merely because that was an accustomed tool, and the weight of it at his side a comfort. This wasn't an occasion for uniform, though.

Not that he wasn't an oddity among the crush of seamen, porters, barrowmen, and oysterwomen near the docks, but there were at least a few gentlemen here as well. A pair of prosperous-looking merchants strolled together toward him, one holding a chart, which he seemed to be explaining to the other. A man whom he recognized as a banker picked his way through the mud and slime underfoot, careful of his coat as he brushed past a barrow full of slick black mussels, dripping weed and water.

He was aware of people looking at him in curiosity as he passed, but that was all right; it wasn't the sort of curiosity that would cause talk.

He had gone first to Trevelyan's house, only to be informed that the master had gone down to his warehouse and was not expected before the evening. Would he leave his card?

He had declined, and taken a carriage to the docks, unable to bear the thought of waiting all day to do what must be done.

And what *was* he going to do? He felt hollow at the thought of the coming interview, but clung firmly to the one thing he did know. The engagement must be broken, officially. Beyond that, he would get what information he could from Trevelyan, but to protect Olivia was the most important thing—and the only thing that he, personally, could insure.

He wasn't looking forward to going home afterward and telling Olivia and his mother what he had done—let alone why. He'd learned in the army not to anticipate more than one unpleasant contingency at a time, though, and resolutely ignored the thought of anything that lay beyond the next half hour. Do what must be done, and then deal with the consequences.

It was one of the larger warehouses in the district, and despite the shabby look of such buildings in general, well-maintained. Inside, it was a vast cavern of riches; despite his errand, Grey took time to be impressed. There were stacked chests and wooden boxes, stenciled with cryptic symbols of ownership and destination; bundles wrapped in canvas and oilcloth; sheets of rolled copper; and stacks of boards, barrels, and hogsheads tiered five and six high against the walls.

Beyond the sheer abundance, he was as much impressed by the sense of orderliness amid confusion. Men came and went, burdened like ants, fetching and taking away in a constant stream. The floor was inches deep in the fragrant straw used for packing, and the air filled with golden motes of it, kicked up by the treading feet.

Grey brushed bits of straw from his coat, taking deep breaths with pleasure; the air was perfumed with the intoxicating scents of tea, wine, and spice, gently larded with the more oleaginous tones of whale oil and candle wax, with a solid bottom note of honest tar. On a different occasion, Grey would have liked to poke about in the fascinating clutter, but not today, alas. With a last regretful lungful, he turned aside in pursuit of his duty.

He made his way through the bustle to a small enclosure of clerks, all seated on high stools and madly scribbling. Boys roamed among them like dairymaids through a herd of cows, milking them of their output and carrying off stacks of papers toward a door in the wall, where the foot of a staircase hinted at the presence of offices above.

His heart gave an unpleasant thump as he spotted Trevelyan himself, deep in conversation with an ink-stained functionary.

Taking a deep breath of the scented air, he threaded his way through the maze of stools, and tapped Trevelyan on the shoulder. Trevelyan swung round at once, clearly accustomed to interruption, but halted, surprised, at sight of Grey.

"Why, John!" he said, and smiled. "Whatever brings you here?"

Slightly taken aback by the use of his Christian name, Grey bowed formally.

"A private matter, sir. Might we—?" He raised his brows at the ranks of laboring clerks, and nodded toward the stair.

"Of course." Looking mildly puzzled, Trevelyan waved away a hovering assistant, and led the way up the stair and into his own office.

It was a surprisingly plain room; large, but simply furnished, the only ornaments an ivory-and-crystal inkwell and a small bronze statue of some many-armed Indian deity. Grey had expected something much more ornate, in keeping with Trevelyan's wealth. On the other hand, he supposed that perhaps that was one reason why Trevelyan *was* wealthy.

Trevelyan waved him toward a chair, going to take his own seat behind the large, battered desk. Grey stood stiffly, though, the blood thumping softly in his ears.

"No, sir, I thank you. The matter will not take long."

Trevelyan glanced at him in surprise. The Cornishman's eyes narrowed, seeming for the first time to take in Grey's stiffness.

"Is something the matter, Lord John?"

"I have come to inform you that your engagement to my cousin is at an end," Grey said bluntly.

Trevelyan blinked, expressionless.

What would he do? Grey wondered. Say "Oh," and leave it at that? Demand an explanation? Become furious and call him out? Summon servants to remove him from the premises?

"Do sit down, John," Trevelyan said at last, sounding quite as cordial as he had before. He took his own chair and leaned back a little, gesturing in invitation.

Seeing no alternative, Grey sat, resting the walking stick across his knees.

Trevelyan was stroking his long, narrow chin, looking at Grey as though he were a particularly interesting shipment of Chinese pottery.

"I am of course somewhat surprised," he said politely. "Have you spoken to Hal about this?"

"In my brother's absence, I am the head of the family," Grey said firmly. "And I have decided that under the circumstances, your betrothal to my cousin ought not to be continued."

"Really?" Trevelyan went on looking polite, though he raised one eyebrow dubiously. "I do wonder what your brother is likely to say, upon his return. Tell me, is he not expected back fairly soon?"

Grey set the tip of his walking stick on the floor and leaned upon it, gripping hard. *The devil with a sword,* he thought, keeping a similar grip upon his temper. *I should have brought a knout.*

"Mr. Trevelyan," he said, steel in his voice, "I have told you my decision. It is final. You will cease at once to pay addresses to Miss Pearsall. The wedding will not take place. Do I make myself clear?"

"No, I can't say that you do, really." Trevelyan steepled his fingers and placed them precisely below the tip of his nose, so that he looked at Grey over them. He was wearing a cabochon seal ring with the incised figure of a Cornish chough, and the green stone glowed as he leaned back. "Has something occurred that causes you to take this—I hope you will excuse my characterizing it as rather rash—step?"

Grey stared at him for a moment, considering. At last, he reached into his pocket and removed the oilcloth parcel. He laid it on the desk in front of Trevelyan, and flipped it open, releasing a crude stink of corruption that overwhelmed any hint of spice or straw.

Trevelyan stared down at the scrap of green velvet, still expressionless. His nostrils twitched slightly, and he took a deep breath, seeming to inhale something.

"Excuse me a moment, will you, John?" he said, rising. "I'll just see that we are not disturbed." He vanished onto the landing, allowing the door to close behind him.

Grey's heart was still beating fast, but he had himself in better hand, now that it was begun. Trevelyan had recognized the scrap of velvet; there was no doubt of that.

This came as a considerable relief, on the one hand; there would be no need to address the matter of Trevelyan's disease. It was grounds for great wariness, though; he needed to extract as much information from the Cornishman as he could. How? No way of knowing what would be effective; he must just trust to the inspiration of the moment—and if the man proved obdurate, perhaps a mention of the Scanlons would be beneficial.

It was no more than a few minutes, but seemed an age before Trevelyan returned, carrying with him a jug and a pair of wooden cups.

"Have a drink, John," he said, setting them on the desk. "Let us speak as friends."

Grey had it in mind to refuse, but on second thought, it might be helpful. If Trevelyan felt relaxed, he might divulge more than otherwise—and wine had certainly worked to induce a spirit of cooperation in Nessie.

He gave a small nod of acquiescence, and accepted the cup, though he did not drink from it until Trevelyan was likewise equipped. The Cornishman sat back, looking quite unruffled, and lifted his cup a little.

"What shall we drink to, John?"

The gall of the man was staggering—and rather admirable, he had to admit. He lifted his own cup, unsmiling.

"To the truth, sir."

"Oh? Oh, by all means—to the truth!" Still smiling, though with a slight expression of wariness, Trevelyan drained his cup.

It was a tawny sherry, and a good one, though it hadn't settled adequately.

"Just off a ship from Jerez," Trevelyan said, waving at the jug with an air of apology. "The best I had to hand, I'm afraid."

"It is very good. Thank you," Grey said repressively. "Now—"

"Have another?" Not pausing for reply, Trevelyan refilled both cups. He lowered the jug, and at last took notice of the square of discolored velvet, sitting on his desk like a toad. He prodded it gingerly with a forefinger.

"I . . . ah . . . confess that I am at something of a loss, John. Does this object have some significance of which I should be aware?"

Grey cursed himself silently for letting the man leave the room; damn it, he'd had time to think, and had obviously decided that a ploy of determined ignorance was best.

"That bit of cloth was taken from the garment on a corpse," he said, keeping his voice level. "A murdered woman."

Sure enough, Trevelyan's left eye twitched, just slightly, and a small, fierce surge of satisfaction burned in Grey's heart. He *did* know!

"God rest her soul, poor creature." Trevelyan folded the cloth over once, quite gently, so the worst of the blood was hidden. "Who was she? What happened to her?"

"The magistrate is choosing to keep that information private for the moment," Grey said pleasantly, and was rewarded by the jumping of a muscle in Trevelyan's jaw at the word "magistrate."

"However, I understand that certain evidence was discovered, suggesting a connexion between this woman and yourself. Given the sordid circumstances, I am afraid that I cannot allow your attachment to my cousin to continue."

"What evidence?" Trevelyan had got control of himself again, and was exhibiting precisely the right degree of outrage. "There cannot possibly be anything linking . . . whoever this creature is, to me!"

"I regret that I am unable to acquaint you with the particulars," Grey said, grimly pleased. Two could play the game of ignorance. "But Sir John Fielding is a close friend of the family; he has a natural concern for my cousin's happiness and reputation." He shrugged delicately, implying that the magistrate had tipped him the wink, while withholding any number of sordidly incriminating details. "I thought it better to sever the betrothal, before anything of a scandalous nature should emerge. I am sure you—"

"That is—" Trevelyan wore no powder in the warehouse; his face was becoming blotched with emotion. "That is unspeakable! I have nothing to do with any murdered woman!"

That was true—but only because it hadn't been a woman. To the truth, indeed!

"As I say, I am unable to deal in particulars," Grey said. "However, I did hear a name, in connexion with the matter. Are you acquainted with a Mr. Scanlon, perhaps? An apothecary?" He took up his cup and sipped, feigning indifference, but watching carefully beneath his lashes.

Trevelyan was master of his face, but not his blood. He kept the expression of outraged bafflement firmly fixed—but his face had gone dead-white.

"I am not, sir," he said firmly.

"Or an establishment called Lavender House?"

"I am not." The bones stood out in Trevelyan's narrow face, and his eyes gleamed dark. Grey thought that if they had been alone in some alley, the man would likely have attacked him.

They sat in silence for a moment. Trevelyan drummed his fingers on the desk, narrow mouth set tight as he thought. The blood began to come back into his face, and he picked up the jug and re-filled Grey's cup, without asking.

"See here, John," he said, leaning forward a little. "I do not know to whom you have been speaking, but I can assure you that there is no truth whatever to any rumor you may have heard."

"You would naturally say as much," Grey remarked.

"So would any innocent man," Trevelyan replied evenly.

"Or a guilty one."

"Are you accusing me, John, of having done someone to death? For I will swear to you—on the Book, on your cousin's life, your mother's head, on whatever you like—that I have done no such thing." A slightly different note had entered Trevelyan's voice; he leaned forward and spoke with passion, eyes blazing. For a moment, Grey felt a slight qualm—either the man was a splendid actor, or he was telling the truth. Or part of it.

"I do not accuse you of murder," he said, cautiously seeking another way past Trevelyan's defenses. "However, for your name to be entangled in the matter is clearly a serious concern."

Trevelyan gave a small grunt, settling back a little.

"Any fool can bandy a man's name—many do, God knows. I should not have thought you so credulous, John."

Grey took a sip of sherry, resisting the urge to respond to the insult. "I should have thought, sir, that you would at once be aroused to make inquiry—should you be quite innocent of the matter."

Trevelyan uttered a short laugh.

"Oh, I am aroused, I assure you of that. Why, I should be calling for my carriage at this moment, to go round and speak to Sir John face-to-face—were I not aware that he is presently in Bath, and has been for the last week."

Grey bit the inside of his cheek and tasted blood. God damn him for a fool! How could he have forgotten—Joseph Trevelyan knew everyone.

He was still holding the cup of sherry. He drank it off at a gulp, feeling the liquor sear the bitten place, and set it down with a thump.

"Very well, then," he said, a little hoarsely. "You leave me no choice. I had sought to spare your sensibilities—"

"Spare me? *Spare* me? Why, you—"

"—but I see I cannot. I forbid you to marry Olivia—"

"You think you can forbid me? You? When your brother—"

"—because you are poxed."

Trevelyan stopped speaking so abruptly that it seemed he had been turned into a pillar of salt. He sat utterly immobile, dark eyes fixed on Grey with a stare so penetrating that Grey felt he meant to see through flesh and bone, plucking out truth from Grey's heart and brain by means of sheer will.

The silver handle of his stick was slick with sweat, and he saw that Trevelyan had gripped the bronze statue so tightly that his knuckles were white. He shifted one hand on his stick for leverage; one move by Trevelyan to brain him, and he'd lay the man out.

As though the small movement had broken some evil spell, Trevelyan blinked, his hand letting go the little bronze goddess. He continued to look at Grey, but now with an expression of concern.

"My dear John," he said quietly. "My dear fellow." He sat back, rubbing a hand across his brow, as though overcome.

He said nothing more, though, leaving Grey to sit there, the sound of his denunciation ringing in his ears.

"Have you nothing to say, Mr. Trevelyan?" he demanded at last.

"Say?" Trevelyan dropped his hand, and looked at him, mouth a little open. He closed it, shook his head slightly, and poured fresh sherry, pushing Grey's cup across to him.

"What have I to say?" he repeated, staring into the depths of his own cup. "Well, I could deny it, of course—and I do. In your present state of mind, though, I am afraid that no statement would be adequate. Would it?" He glanced up, inquiringly.

Grey shook his head.

"Well, then," Trevelyan said, almost kindly. "I do not know where you have acquired these remarkable notions, John. Of course, if you truly believe them, then you have no choice but to act as you are—I see that."

"You do?"

"Yes." Trevelyan hesitated, choosing his words carefully. "Did you . . . seek counsel of anyone, before coming here?"

What the devil did the fellow mean by that?

"If you are inquiring whether anyone is cognizant of my where-abouts," Grey said coldly, "they are." In fact, they were not; no one knew he was at the warehouse. On the other hand, a dozen clerks and countless laborers had seen him downstairs; it would take a madman to try to do away with him here—and he didn't think Trevelyan was mad. Dangerous, but not mad.

Trevelyan's eyes widened.

"What? You thought I meant—good gracious." He glanced away, rubbing a knuckle over his lips. He cleared his throat, twice, then looked up. "I merely meant to ask whether you had shared these incredible . . . delusions of yours with anyone. I think you have not. For if you had, surely anyone would have tried to per-suade you not to pursue such a disastrous course."

Trevelyan shook his head, an expression of worried dismay pursing his lips.

"Have you a carriage? No, of course not. Never mind; I shall summon mine. The coachman will see you safely to your mother's house. Might I recommend Doctor Masonby, of Smedley Street? He has an excellent history with nervous disorders."

Grey was so stricken with amazement that he scarcely felt outraged.

"Are you attempting to suggest that I am insane?"

"No, no! Of course not, certainly not."

Still Trevelyan went on looking at him in that worried, pitying sort of way, and he felt the amazement melting away. He should perhaps be furious, but felt instead an urge to laugh incredulously.

"I am pleased to hear it," Grey said dryly, and rose to his feet. "I shall bear your kind advice in mind. In the meantime, however— your betrothal is at an end."

He had nearly reached the door when Trevelyan called out behind him.

"Lord John! Wait a moment!"

He paused and looked back, though without turning.

"Yes?"

The Cornishman had his lower lip caught in his teeth, and was watching Grey with the air of one judging a wild animal. Would it attack, or run? He beckoned, gesturing to the chair Grey had vacated.

"Come back a moment. Please."

He stood, undecided, hearing the thrum of business below, longing to escape this room and this man and lose himself in comings and goings, once more a peaceful part of the clockwork, and not a grain of sand in the cogs. But duty dictated otherwise, and he walked back, stick held tight.

"Sit. Please." Trevelyan waited for him to do so, then sat down slowly himself.

"Lord John. You say that your concern is for your cousin's reputation. So is mine." He leaned across the desk, eyes intent. "Such a sudden breach cannot but give rise to scandal—you know this, surely?"

Grey did, but forbore to nod, merely watching impassively. Trevelyan ignored his lack of response, and carried on, speaking more hurriedly.

"Well, then. If you are convinced of the wisdom of your intention, then plainly I cannot dissuade you. Will you give me a short time, though, to devise some reasonable grounds for the dissolution of the betrothal? Something that will discredit neither party?"

Grey drew breath, feeling the beginnings of something like relief. This was the resolution he had hoped for from the moment he had discovered the sore on Trevelyan's prick. He realized that the situation now bore far more aspects than he had ever thought, and such a resolution would not touch most of them. Still, Olivia would be safe.

Trevelyan sensed his softening, and pushed the advantage.

"You know that merely to announce a severance will give rise to talk," he said persuasively. "Some public reason, something plausible, must be offered to prevent it."

Doubtless the man had an ulterior motive; perhaps he meant to flee the country? But then Grey felt again the vibrations beneath his feet, the boomings of rolling wine casks and thud of heaved crates, the muffled shouts of men in the warehouse below. Would a man of such substance readily abandon his interests, merely to avoid accusation?

Probably not; more likely he had it in mind to use the grace period to cover his tracks completely, or dispose of dangerous complications such as the Scanlons. If he hadn't already done so, Grey thought suddenly.

But there was no good reason to refuse such a request. And he could alert Magruder and Quarry at once—have the man followed.

"Very well. You have three days."

Trevelyan drew breath, as if to protest, but then nodded, accepting it.

"As you say. I thank you." He took the jug and poured more sherry, slopping it a little. "Here—let us drink on the bargain."

Grey had no wish to linger in the man's company, and took no more than a token sip before pushing his cup away and rising. He took his leave, but turned back briefly at the door, to see Trevelyan looking after him, with eyes that would have burned a hole in the door to hell.

Chapter 15

One Man's Poison

If Captain von Namtzen was surprised to see Grey and his valet, there was no evidence of it in his manner.

"Major Grey! How great a pleasure to see you again! Please, you will have some wine—a biscuit?" The tall Hanoverian clasped him by hand and forearm, beaming, and had Tom dispatched to the kitchen and Grey himself seated in the drawing room with refreshments before he could gracefully decline, let alone explain his objective in calling. Once he managed to do so, though, the Captain was helpfulness itself.

"But certainly, certainly! Let me see this list."

He took the paper from Grey and carried it to the window for scrutiny. It was well past teatime, but so near to Midsummer Day, late-afternoon light still flooded in, haloing von Namtzen like a saint in a medieval painting.

He looked like one of those German saints, too, Grey thought a little abstractedly, admiring the cleanly ascetic lines of the German's face, with its broad brow and wide, calm eyes. The mouth was not particularly sensitive, but it did show humor in the creases beside it.

"I know these names, yes. You wish me to tell you . . . what?"

"Anything that you can." Tiredness dragged at him, but Grey rose and came to stand beside the Captain, looking at the list. "All I know of these people is that they have purchased a particular wine. I cannot say precisely what the connexion may be, but this wine seems to have something to do with . . . a confidential matter. I'm afraid I can say no more." He shrugged apologetically.

Von Namtzen glanced sharply at him, but then nodded, and returned his attention to the paper before him.

"Wine, you say? Well, that is strange."

"What is strange?"

The Captain tapped a long, immaculate finger on the paper.

"This name—Hungerbach. It is the family name of an old noble house; zu Egkh und Hungerbach. Not German at all, you understand; they are Austrian."

"Austrian?" Grey felt his heart lurch, and leaned forward, as though to make certain of the name on the paper. "You are sure?"

Von Namtzen looked amused.

"Of course. The estate near Graz is very famous for its wines; that is why I say it is strange you bring me this name and say it is about wine. The best of the St. Georgen wines—that is the name of the castle there, St. Georgen—is very famous. A very good red wine they make—the color of fresh blood."

Grey felt an odd rushing in his ears, as though his own blood were draining suddenly from his head, and put a hand on the table to steady himself.

"Don't tell me," he said, feeling a slight numbness about his lips. "The wine is called Schilcher?"

"Why, yes. However did you know that?"

Grey made a small motion with one hand, indicating that it was of no importance. There seemed to be a number of gnats in the room, though he had not noticed them before; they swarmed in the light from the window, dancing motes of black.

"These—the Hungerbach family—some are here, then, in London?"

"Yes. Baron Joseph zu Egkh und Hungerbach is the head of the family, but his heir is a distant cousin, named Reinhardt Mayrhofer—he keeps a quite large house in Mecklenberg Square. I have been there sometimes—though of course with the situation as it now is . . ." He lifted one shoulder in acknowledgment of the delicate diplomatic issues involved.

"And this . . . Reinhardt. He—is he a small man? Dark, with long . . . curling . . . h-hair." The gnats had become suddenly more numerous, and illuminated, a nearly solid mass of flickering lights before his eyes.

"However did you—Major! Are you quite well?" Dropping the paper, he grabbed Grey by the arm and guided him hurriedly to the sofa. "Sit, please. Water I will have brought, and brandy. Wilhelm, *mach schnell!*" A servant appeared briefly in the doorway, then disappeared at once at von Namtzen's urgent gesture.

"I am quite—quite all right," Grey protested. "Really, there is . . . not . . . the slightest . . . n-need—" But the Hanoverian put a large, firm hand in the center of Grey's chest and pushed him flat on the sofa. Stooping swiftly, he seized Grey's boots and hoisted his feet up as well, all the while bellowing in German for assorted incomprehensible things.

"I—really, sir, you must—" And yet he felt a gray mist rising before his eyes, and a whirling in his head that made it difficult to order his thoughts. He could taste blood in his mouth, how odd. . . . It mingled with the smell of pig's blood, and he felt his gorge rising.

"Me lord, me lord!" Tom Byrd's voice rang through the mist, shrill with panic. "What you done to him, you bloody Huns?"

A confusion of deeper voices surrounded him, speaking words that slipped away before he could grasp their meaning, and a spasm seized him, twisting his guts with such brutal force that his knees rose toward his chest, trying vainly to contain it.

"Oh, dear," said von Namtzen's voice, quite near, in tones of mild dismay. "Well, it was not such a nice sofa, was it? You, boy—there is a doctor who is living two doors down, you run and fetch him right quick, *ja*?"

⁂

Events thereafter assumed a nightmarish quality, with a great deal of noise. Monstrous faces peered at him through a nacreous fog, with words such as "emesis" and "egg whites" shooting past his ears like darting fish. There was a terrible burning feeling in his mouth and throat, superseded periodically by bouts of griping lower down, so intense that he now and then lost consciousness for a few moments, only to be roused again by a flood of sulfurous bile that rose with so much violence that his throat alone provided insufficient egress, and it burst from his nostrils in a searing spew.

These bouts were succeeded by copious outpourings of saliva, welcome at first for their dilution of the brimstone heavings, but then a source of horror as they threatened drowning. He had a dim sense of himself at one point, lying with his head hanging over the edge of the sofa, drooling like a maddened dog, before someone pulled him upright and tried once more to pour something down his throat. It was cool and glutinous, and at the touch of it on his palate, his inward parts again revolted. At last the dense perfume of poppies spread itself like a bandage across the raw membranes of his nose; he sucked feebly at the spoon in his mouth and fell with relief into a darkness shot with fire.

He woke some unimaginable time later from the disorientation of opium visions, to find one of the monstrous faces of his dreams still present, bending over him—a pallid countenance with bulging yellow eyes and lips the color of raw liver. A clammy hand clutched him by the privates.

"Do you suffer from a chronic venereal complaint, my lord?" the countenance inquired. A thumb prodded him familiarly in the scrotum.

"I do not," Grey said, sitting bolt upright and pressing the tail of his shirt protectively between his legs. The blood rushed from his head and he swayed alarmingly. He seized the edge of a small table by the bed to keep upright, only then noting that in addition to the clammy hands, the dreadful countenance was possessed of an outsize wig and a wizened body clad in rusty black and reeking of medicaments.

"I have been poisoned. What sort of infamous quack are you, that you cannot tell the difference between a derangement of the internal organs and the pox, for God's sake?" he demanded.

"Poisoned?" The doctor looked mildly bemused. "Do you mean that you did not take an excess of the substance deliberately?"

"What substance?"

"Why, sulphide of mercury, to be sure. It is used to treat syphilis. The results of the gastric lavage— What are you about, sir? You must not exert yourself, sir, really, you must not!"

Grey had thrust his legs out of bed and attempted to rise, only to be overcome by another wave of dizziness. The doctor seized him by the arm, as much to keep him from toppling over as to prevent his escape.

"Now, then, sir, just lie back . . . yes, yes, that is the way, to be sure. You have had a very narrow escape, sir; you must not imperil your health by hasty—"

"Von Namtzen!" Grey resisted the hands pushing him back into bed, and shouted for assistance. His throat felt as though a large wood-rasp had been thrust down it. "Von Namtzen, for God's sake, where are you?"

"I am here, Major." A large hand planted itself firmly on his shoulder from the other side, and he turned to see the Hanoverian's handsome face looking down at him, creased in a frown.

"You were poisoned, you say? Who is it that would do this thing?"

"A man called Trevelyan. I must go. Will you find me my clothes?"

"But, my lord—"

"But, Major, you have been—"

Grey gripped von Namtzen's wrist, hard. His hand trembled, but he summoned what strength he could.

"I must go, and go at once," he said hoarsely. "It is a matter of duty."

The Hanoverian's face changed at once, and he nodded, standing up.

"Quite so. I will go with you, then."

His statement of intent had quite exhausted Grey's meager reserve of strength, but fortunately von Namtzen took charge, dismissing the doctor, sending for his own coach, and summoning Tom Byrd, who went off at once to fetch Grey's uniform—which had luckily been cleaned—and help him into it.

"I'm very glad as you're alive, me lord, but I will say as you're a man what is hard on his clothes," Byrd said reproachfully. "And this your best uniform, too! Or was," he added, critically examining a faint stain on the front of the waistcoat before holding it up for Grey to insert his arms therein.

Grey, having no energy to spare, said nothing until they were rattling down the road in von Namtzen's coach. The Hanoverian was also wearing his full dress uniform, and had brought the plumed helmet, set upon the seat beside him in the coach. He had also brought a large china bowl of eggs, which he set neatly upon his knees.

"What—?" Grey nodded at the eggs, feeling too weak for more precise inquiry.

"The doctor says that you must have egg whites, frequently and in great quantity," von Namtzen explained, matter-of-factly. "It is the antidote for the mercuric sulphide. And you must not drink water nor wine for two days, only milk. Here." With admirable dexterity, considering the shaking of the coach, he removed an egg from the bowl, cracked it against the rim, and slopped the white into a small pewter cup. He handed this to Grey, thriftily gulped the leftover yolk, and tossed the fragments of eggshell out the window.

The pewter felt cool in his hand, but Grey viewed the egg white within with a marked lack of enthusiasm. Tom Byrd glared at him from the opposite seat.

"You swallow that," he said, in tones of menace. "Me lord."

Grey glared back, but grudgingly obeyed. It felt mildly unpleasant, but he was relieved to discover that the nausea had evidently left him for good.

"How long—?" he asked, glancing out the window. It had been late afternoon of the Thursday; now it was mid-morning—but of which morning?

"It is Friday," von Namtzen said.

Grey relaxed a little, hearing this. He had lost all sense of time, and was relieved to discover that his experience had not in fact lasted the eon it had seemed. Trevelyan would have had time to flee, but perhaps not to escape altogether.

Von Namtzen coughed, tactfully.

"It is perhaps not proper for me to inquire—you must forgive me, if so—but if we are to meet Herr Trevelyan shortly, I think perhaps it would be good to understand *why* he has been seeking to kill you?"

"I don't know whether he did mean to kill me," Grey said, accepting another cup of egg white with no more than a faint grimace of distaste. "He may only have meant to incapacitate me for a time, in order to give himself time to escape."

Von Namtzen nodded, though a slight frown formed itself between his heavy brows.

"We shall hope so," he said. "Though if so, his judgment is regrettably imprecise. If you think he wishes to escape, will he be still in his house?"

"Perhaps not." Grey closed his eyes, trying to think. It was difficult; the nausea had passed, but the dizziness showed a tendency to return periodically. He felt as though his brain were an egg, fragile and runny after being dropped from a height. *"One can't make an omelette without breaking eggs,"* he murmured.

"Oh?" Von Namtzen said politely. "Just so, Major."

If Trevelyan *had* meant to kill him, then the man might well be still at his house; for if Grey were dead, Trevelyan would have sufficient leisure to follow his original plans—whatever they were. If not, though, or if he were not sure that the mercuric sulphide would have a fatal effect, he might have fled at once. In which case—

Grey opened his eyes and sat up.

"Tell the coachman to go to Mecklenberg Square," he said urgently. "If you please."

Von Namtzen didn't question this change of plan, but thrust his head out of the window and shouted to the coachman in German. The heavy coach swayed as it slowed, making the turn.

Six eggs later, it drew to a stop before the house of Reinhardt Mayrhofer.

Von Namtzen sprang lithely from the coach, put on his helmet, and strode like bold Achilles toward the door of the house, plumes waving. Grey assumed his own hat, paltry and insignificant as this object seemed by comparison, and followed, holding tightly to Tom Byrd's arm lest his knees give way.

By the time Grey reached the doorstep, the door was open, and von Namtzen was haranguing the butler in a flood of German menace. Grey's own German extended to no more than a smattering of parlor conversation, but he was able to follow von Namtzen's demands that the butler summon Reinhardt Mayrhofer, and do it forthwith, if not sooner.

The butler, a square person of middle age with a stubborn cast to his brow, was stoutly withstanding this preliminary barrage by insisting that his master was not at home, but clearly the man had no notion of the true nature of the forces ranged against him.

"I am Stephan, Landgrave von Erdberg," von Namtzen announced haughtily, drawing himself up to his full height—which Grey estimated as roughly seven feet, including feathers. "I will come in."

He promptly did so, bending his neck only sufficiently to prevent the obliteration of his helmet. The butler fell back, sputtering and waving his hands in agitated protest. Grey nodded coolly to the man as he passed, and managed to uphold the dignity of His Majesty's army by navigating the length of the entry hall without support. Reaching the morning room, he made for the first seat in evidence, and managed to sit down upon it before his legs gave way.

Von Namtzen was lobbing mortar shells into the butler's position, which appeared to be rapidly crumbling but was still being defended. No, the butler said, now visibly wringing his hands, no, the master was most certainly not at home, and no, nor was the mistress, alas. . . .

Tom Byrd had followed Grey and was looking round the room in some awe, taking in the set of malachite-topped tables with gold feet, the white damask draperies, and the gigantic paintings in gilded frames that covered every wall.

Grey was sweating heavily from the effort of walking, and the dizziness set his head spinning afresh. He took an iron grip upon his will, though, and stayed upright.

"Tom," he said, low-voiced, so as not to draw the attention of the embattled butler. "Go and search the house. Come and tell me what—or who—you find."

Byrd gave him a suspicious look, obviously thinking this a device to get rid of him so that Grey could die surreptitiously—but Grey stayed rigidly upright, jaw set tight, and after a moment, the boy nodded and slipped quietly out, unnoticed by the fulminating butler.

Grey let out a deep breath, and closed his eyes, holding tight to his knees until the spinning sensation eased. It seemed to last a shorter time now; only a few moments, and he could open his eyes again.

Von Namtzen in the meantime appeared to have vanquished the butler, and was now demanding in stentorian tones the immediate assembly of the entire household. He cast a glance over his shoulder at Grey, and interrupted his tirade for an instant.

"Oh—and you will bring me the whites of three eggs, please, in a cup."

"Bitte?" said the butler, faintly.

"Eggs. You are deaf?" von Namtzen inquired, in biting tones. "Only the whites. *Schnell!"*

Stung at this public solicitude for his weakened condition, Grey forced himself to his feet, coming to stand beside the Hanoverian, who—with the butler in full rout—had now removed his helmet and was looking quite pleased with himself.

"You are better now, Major?" he inquired, dabbing sweat delicately from his hairline with a linen handkerchief.

"Much, I thank you. I take it that both Reinhardt Mayrhofer and his wife are out?" Reinhardt, he reflected, was almost certainly out. But the wife—

"So the butler says. If he is not out, he is a coward," von Namtzen said with satisfaction, putting away his handkerchief. "I will root him out of his hiding place like a turnip, though, and then—what will you do, then?" he inquired.

"Probably nothing," Grey said. "I believe him to be dead. Is that the gentleman in question, by chance?" He nodded at a small framed portrait on a table by the window, its frame set with pearls.

"Yes, that is Mayrhofer and his wife, Maria. They are cousins," he added, unnecessarily, in view of the close resemblance of the two faces in the portrait.

While both had a delicacy of feature, with long necks and rounded chins, Reinhardt was possessed of an imposing nose and an aristocratic scowl. Maria was a lovely woman, though, Grey thought; she was wigged in the portrait, of course, but had the same warm skin tones and brown eyes as her husband, and so was also likely dark-haired.

"Reinhardt is dead?" von Namtzen asked with interest, looking at the portrait. "How did he die?"

"Shot," Grey replied briefly. "Quite possibly by the gentleman who poisoned me."

"What a very industrious sort of fellow." Von Namtzen's attention was distracted at this point by the entrance of a parlor maid, white-faced with nerves and clutching a small dish containing the requested egg whites. She glanced from one man to the other, then held out the dish timidly toward von Namtzen.

"*Danke,*" he said. He handed the dish to Grey, then proceeded at once to catechize the maid, bending toward her in a way that made her press herself against the nearest wall, terrorized into speechlessness and capable only of shaking her head yes and no.

Unable to follow the nuances of this one-sided conversation, Grey turned away, viewing the contents of his dish with distaste. The sound of footsteps in the corridor and agitated voices indicated that the butler was indeed assembling the household, as ordered. Depositing the dish behind an alabaster vase on the desk, he stepped out into the corridor, to find a small crowd of household servants milling about, all chattering in excited German.

At sight of him, they stopped abruptly and stared, with a mixture of curiosity, suspicion, and what looked like simple fright on some faces. Why? he wondered. Was it the uniform?

"*Guten Tag,*" he said, smiling pleasantly. "Are any of you English?"

There were shifty glances to and fro, the focus of which seemed to be a pair of young chambermaids. He smiled reassuringly at them, beckoning them to one side. They looked at him wide-eyed, like a pair of young deer confronted by a hunter, but a glance at von Namtzen, emerging from the morning room behind him, hastily decided them that Lord John was the lesser of the evils on offer, and they followed close on his heels back into the room, leaving von Namtzen to deal with the crowd in the entry hall.

Their names, the girls admitted, with much stammering and blushing, were Annie and Tab. They were both from Cheapside, bosom friends, and had been in the employ of Herr Mayrhofer for the last three months.

"I gather that Herr Mayrhofer is not, in fact, at home today," Grey said, still smiling. "When did he go out?"

The girls glanced at each other in confusion.

"Yesterday?" Grey suggested. "This morning?"

"Oh, no, sir," Annie said. She seemed a trifle the braver of the two, though she could not bring herself to meet his eyes for more than a fraction of a second. "The master's been g-gone since Tuesday."

And Magruder's men had discovered the corpse on Wednesday morning.

"Ah, I see. Do you know where he went?"

Naturally, they did not. They did, however, say—after much shuffling and contradicting of each other—that Herr Mayrhofer was often given to short journeys, leaving home for several days at a time, two or three times a month.

"Indeed," Grey said. "And what is Herr Mayrhofer's business, pray?"

Baffled looks, followed by shrugs. Herr Mayrhofer had money, plainly; where it came from was no concern of theirs. Grey felt a growing metallic taste at the back of his tongue, and swallowed, trying to force it down.

"Well, then. When he left the house this time, did he go out in the morning? Or later in the day?"

The girls frowned and conferred with each other in murmurs, before deciding that, well, in fact, they had neither of them actually seen Herr Reinhardt leave the house, and no, they had not heard the carriage draw up, but—

"He must have done, though, Annie," Tab said, sufficiently engrossed in the argument as to lose some of her timidity. " 'Coz he wasn't in his bedroom in the afternoon, was he? Herr Reinhardt likes to have a bit of a sleep in the afternoon," she explained, turning to Grey. "I turns down the bed right after lunch, and I did it that day—but it wasn't mussed when I went up after teatime. So he must have gone in the morning, then, mustn't he?"

The questioning proceeded in this tedious fashion for some time, but Grey succeeded in eliciting only a few helpful pieces of information, most of these negative in nature.

No, they did not think their mistress owned a green velvet gown, though of course she might have ordered one made; her personal maid would know. No, the mistress really wasn't at home today, or at least they didn't think so. No, they did not know for sure when she had left the house—but yes, she was here yesterday, and last night, yes. Had she been in the house on Tuesday last? They thought so, but could not really remember.

"Has a gentleman by the name of Joseph Trevelyan ever visited the house?" he asked. The girls exchanged shrugs and looked at him, baffled. How would they know? Their work was all above-stairs; they would seldom see any visitors to the house, save those who stayed overnight.

"Your mistress—you say that she was at home last night. When is the last time you saw her?"

The girls frowned, as one. Annie glanced at Tab; Tab made a small moue of puzzlement at Annie. Both shrugged.

"Well . . . I don't rightly know, my lord," Annie said. "She's been poorly, the mistress. She's been a-staying in her room all day, with trays brought up. I go in to change the linens regular, to be sure, but she'd be in her boudoir, or the privy closet. I suppose I haven't seen her proper since—well, maybe since . . . Monday?" She raised her brows at Tab, who shrugged.

"Poorly," Grey repeated. "She was ill?"

"Yes, sir," Tab said, taking heart from having an actual piece of information to impart. "The doctor came, and all."

He inquired further, but to no avail. Neither, it seemed, had actually seen the doctor, nor heard anything regarding their mistress's ailment; they had only heard of it from Cook . . . or was it from Ilse, the mistress's lady's maid?

Abandoning this line of questioning, Grey was inspired by the mention of gossip to inquire further about their master.

"You would not know this from personal experience, of course," he said, altering his smile to one of courteous apology, "but perhaps Herr Mayrhofer's valet might have let something drop. . . . I am wondering whether your master has any particular marks or oddities? Upon his body, I mean."

Both girls' faces went completely blank, and then suffused with blood, so rapidly that they were transformed within seconds into a pair of tomatoes, ripe to bursting point. They exchanged brief glances, and Annie let out a high-pitched squeak that might have been a strangled giggle.

He hardly needed further confirmation at this point, but the girls—with many stifled half-shrieks and muffling of their mouths with their hands—did eventually confess that, well, yes, the valet, Herr Waldemar, *had* explained to Hilde the parlor maid exactly why he required so much shaving soap. . . .

He dismissed the girls, who went out giggling, and sank down for a moment's respite on the brocaded chair by the desk, resting his head on his folded arms as he waited for his heart to cease pounding quite so hard.

So, the identity of the corpse was established, at least. And a connexion of some sort between Reinhardt Mayrhofer, the brothel in Meacham Street—and Joseph Trevelyan. But that connexion rested solely on a whore's word, and on his own identification of the green velvet gown, he reminded himself.

What if Nessie was wrong, and the man who left the brothel dressed in green was not Trevelyan? But it was, he reminded himself. Richard Caswell had admitted it. And now a rich Austrian had turned up dead, dressed in what certainly appeared to be the same green gown worn by Magda, the madam of Meacham Street—which was in turn presumably the same gown worn by Trevelyan. And Mayrhofer was an Austrian who left his home on frequent mysterious journeys.

Grey was reasonably sure that he had discovered Mr. Bowles's unknown shark. And if Reinhardt Mayrhofer was indeed a spymaster . . . then the solution to the death of Tim O'Connell most likely lay in the black realm of statecraft and treachery, rather than the blood-red one of lust and revenge.

But the Scanlons were gone, he reminded himself. And what part, in the name of God, did Joseph Trevelyan play in all this?

His heart was slowing again; he swallowed the metallic taste in his mouth and raised his head, to find himself looking at what he had half-seen but not consciously registered before: a large painting that hung above the desk, erotic in nature, mediocre in craftsmanship—and with the initials "RM" worked cunningly into a bunch of flowers in the corner.

He rose, wiping sweaty palms on the skirt of his coat, and glanced quickly round the room. There were two more of the same nature, indisputably by the same hand as the paintings that decorated Magda's boudoir. All signed "RM."

It was additional evidence of Mayrhofer's connexions, were any needed. But it caused him also to wonder afresh about Trevelyan. He had only Caswell's word for it that Trevelyan's *inamorata* was a woman—otherwise, he would be sure that the Cornishman's rendezvous were kept with Mayrhofer . . . for whatever purpose.

"And the day you trust Dickie Caswell's word about anything, you foolish sod . . ." he muttered, pushing himself up from the chair. On his way out the door, he spotted the dish of congealing egg whites, and took a moment to thrust it hastily into the drawer of the desk.

Von Namtzen had herded the rest of the servants into the library for further inquisition. Hearing Grey come in, he turned to greet him.

"They are both gone, certainly. He, some days ago, she, sometime in the night—no one saw. Or so these servants say." Here he turned to bend a hard eye on the butler, who flinched.

"Ask them about the doctor, if you please," Grey said, glancing from face to face.

"Doctor? You are unwell again?" Von Namtzen snapped his fingers and pointed at a stout woman in an apron, who must be the cook. "You—more eggs!"

"No, no! I am quite well, I thank you. The chambermaids said that Mrs. Mayrhofer was ill this week, and that a doctor had come. I wish to know if any of them saw him."

"Ah?" Von Namtzen looked interested at this, and at once began peppering the ranks before him with questions. Grey leaned inconspicuously on a bookshelf, affecting an air of keen attention, while the next bout of dizziness spent itself.

The butler and the lady's maid had seen the doctor, von Namtzen reported, turning to interpret his results to Grey. He had come several times to attend Frau Mayrhofer.

Grey swallowed. Perhaps he should have drunk the last batch of egg whites; they could not taste half so foul as the copper tang in his mouth.

"Did the doctor give his name?" he asked.

No, he had not. He did not dress quite like a doctor, the butler offered, but had seemed confident in his manner.

"Did not dress like a doctor? What does he mean by that?" Grey asked, straightening up.

More interrogation, answered by helpless shrugs from the butler. He did not wear a black suit, was the essential answer, but rather a rough blue coat and homespun breeches. The butler knit his brow, trying to recall further details.

"He did not smell of blood!" von Namtzen reported. "He smelled instead of . . . plants? Can that be correct?"

Grey closed his eyes briefly, and saw bunches of dried herbs hanging from darkened rafters, the fragrant gold dust drifting down from their leaves in answer to footsteps on the floor above.

"Was the doctor Irish?" he asked, opening his eyes.

Now even von Namtzen looked slightly puzzled.

"How would they tell the difference between an Irishman and an Englishman?" he said. "It is the same language."

Grey drew a deep breath, but rather than attempt to explain the obvious, changed tack and gave a brief description of Finbar Scanlon. This, translated, resulted in immediate nods of recognition from butler and maid.

"This is important?" von Namtzen asked, watching Grey's face.

"Very." Grey folded his hands into fists, trying to think. "It is of the greatest importance that we discover where Frau Mayrhofer is. This 'doctor' is very likely a spy, in the Mayrhofers' employ, and I very much suspect that the lady is in possession of something that His Majesty would strongly prefer to have back."

He glanced over the ranks of the servants, who had started whispering among themselves, casting looks of awe, annoyance, or puzzlement at the two officers.

"Are you convinced that they are ignorant of the lady's whereabouts?"

Von Namtzen narrowed his eyes, considering, but before he could reply, Grey became aware of a slight stir among the servants, several of whom were looking toward the door behind him.

He turned to see Tom Byrd standing there, freckles dark on his round face, and fairly quivering with excitement. In his hands were a pair of worn shoes.

"Me lord!" he said, holding them out. "Look! They're Jack's!"

Grey seized the shoes, which were large and very worn, the leather across the toes scuffed and cracked. Sure enough, the initials "JB" had been burnt into the soles. One of the heels was loose, hanging from its parent shoe by a single nail. Leather, and round at the back, as Tom had said.

"Who is Jack?" von Namtzen inquired, looking from Tom Byrd to the shoes, with obvious puzzlement.

"Mr. Byrd's brother," Grey explained, still turning the shoes over in his hands. "We have been in search of him for some time. Could you please inquire of the servants as to the whereabouts of the man who owns these shoes?"

Von Namtzen was in many ways an admirable associate, Grey thought; he asked no further questions of his own, but merely nodded and returned to the fray, pointing at the shoes and firing questions in a sharp but businesslike manner, as though he fully expected prompt answers.

Such was his air of command, he got them. The household, originally alarmed and then demoralized, had now fallen under von Namtzen's sway, and appeared to have quite accepted him as temporary master of both the house and the situation.

"The shoes belong to a young man, an Englishman," he reported to Grey, following a brief colloquy with butler and cook. "He was brought into the house more than a week ago, by a friend of Frau Mayrhofer; the Frau told Herr Burkhardt"—he inclined his head toward the butler, who bowed in acknowledgment—"that the

young man was to be treated as a servant of the house, fed and ac-
commodated. She did not explain why he was here, saying only
that the situation would be temporary."

The butler at this point interjected something; von Namtzen
nodded, waving a hand to quell further remarks.

"Herr Burkhardt says that the young man was not given specific
duties, but that he was helpful to the maids. He would not leave
the house, nor would he go far away from Frau Mayrhofer's rooms,
insisting upon sleeping in the closet at the end of the hall near her
suite. Herr Burkhardt had the feeling that the young man was
guarding Frau Mayrhofer—but from what, he does not know."

Tom Byrd had been listening to all of this with visible impa-
tience, and could contain himself no longer.

"The devil with what he was doing here—where's Jack gone?"
he demanded.

Grey had his own pressing question, as well.

"This friend of Frau Mayrhofer—do they know his name? Can
they describe him?"

With strict attention to social precedence, von Namtzen ob-
tained the answer to Grey's question first.

"The gentleman gave his name as Mr. Josephs. However, the
butler says that he does not think this is his true name—the gentleman hesitated when asked for his name. He was very . . ." Von
Namtzen hesitated himself, groping for translation. "*Fein heraus-
geputzt*. Very . . . polished."

"Well dressed," Grey amended. The room seemed very warm,
and sweat was trickling down the seam of his back.

Von Namtzen nodded. "A bottle-green silk coat, with gilt buttons. A good wig."

"Trevelyan," Grey said, with a sense of inevitability that was
composed in equal parts of relief and dismay. He took a deep
breath; his heart was racing again. "And Jack Byrd?"

Von Namtzen shrugged.

"Gone. They suppose that he went with Frau Mayrhofer, for no one has seen him since last night."

"Why'd he leave his shoes behind? Ask 'em that!" Tom Byrd was so upset that he neglected to add a "sir," but von Namtzen, seeing the boy's distress, graciously overlooked it.

"He exchanged these shoes for the working pair belonging to this footman." The Hanoverian nodded at a tall young man who was following the conversation intently, brows knitted in the effort of comprehension. "He did not say why he wished it—perhaps because of the damaged heel; the other pair were also very worn, but serviceable."

"Why did this young man agree to the exchange?" Grey asked, nodding at the footman. The nod was a mistake; the dizziness rolled suddenly out of its hiding place and revolved slowly round the inside of his skull like a tilting quintain.

A question, an answer. "Because these are leather, with metal buckles," von Namtzen reported. "The shoes he exchanged were simple clogs, with wooden soles and heels."

At this point, Grey's knees gave up the struggle, and he lowered himself into a chair, covering his eyes with the heels of his hands. He breathed shallowly, his thoughts spinning round in slow circles like the orbs of his father's orrery, light flashing from memory to memory, hearing Harry Quarry say, *Sailors all wear wooden heels; leather's slippery on deck,* and then, *Trevelyan? Father a baronet, brother in Parliament, a fortune in Cornish tin, up to his eyeballs in the East India Company?*

"Oh, Christ," he said, and dropped his hands. "They're sailing."

Chapter 16

Lust Is Perjur'd

It took no little effort to persuade both von Namtzen and Tom Byrd that he was capable of independent movement and would not fall facedown in the street—the more so as he was not entirely sure of it himself. In the end, though, Tom Byrd went reluctantly to Jermyn Street to pack a bag, and von Namtzen—even more reluctantly—was convinced that his own path of duty lay in perusing the contents of Mayrhofer's desk.

"No one else is capable of reading whatever papers may be there," Grey pointed out. "The man is dead, and was very likely a spy. I will send someone from the regiment at once to take charge of the premises—but if there is anything urgent in those papers . . ."

Von Namtzen compressed his lips, but nodded.

"You will take care?" he asked earnestly, putting a large, warm hand on the nape of Grey's neck, and bending down to look searchingly into his face. The Hanoverian's eyes were a troubled gray, with small lines of worry round them.

"I will," Grey said, and did his best to smile in reassurance. He handed Tom a scribbled note, desiring Harry Quarry to send a German speaker at once to Mecklenberg Square, and took his leave.

Three choices, he thought, breathing deeply to control the dizziness as he stepped into a commercial coach. The offices of the East India Company, in Lamb's Conduit Street. Trevelyan's chief man of business, a fellow named Royce, who kept offices in the Temple. Or Neil the Cunt.

The sun was nearly down, an evening fog dulling its glow like the steam off a fresh-fired cannonball. That made the choice simple; he could not hope to reach Westminster or the Temple before everyone had gone home for the night. But he knew where Stapleton lived; he had made it his business to find out, after the unsettling interview with Bowles.

"You want what?" Stapleton had been asleep when Grey pounded on his door; he was in his shirt and barefoot. He knuckled one bleary eye, regarding Grey incredulously with the other.

"The names and sailing dates for any ships licensed to the East India Company leaving England this month. Now."

Stapleton had both eyes open now. He blinked slowly, scratching his ribs.

"How would I know such a thing?"

"I don't suppose you would. Someone in Bowles's employ does, though, and I expect you can find out where the information is, without undue loss of time. The matter is urgent."

"Oh, is it?" Neil's mouth twisted, and the lower lip protruded a little. His weight shifted subtly, so that he stood suddenly nearer. "How . . . urgent?"

"Much too urgent for games, Mr. Stapleton. Put on your clothes, please; I have a coach waiting."

Neil did not reply, but smiled and lifted a hand. He touched Grey's face, cupping his cheek, a thumb drawing languidly beneath the edge of his mouth. He was very warm, and smelt of bed.

"Not all that much of a rush, surely, Mary?"

Grey gripped the hand and pulled it away from his face, squeezing hard, so that the knucklebones cracked in his grasp.

"You will come with me at once," he said, very clearly, "or I will inform Mr. Bowles officially of the circumstances under which we first met. Do you understand me, sir?"

He stared at Stapleton, eye to eye. The man was awake now, blue eyes snapping-bright and furious. He freed himself from Grey's grasp with a wrench and took a half-step backward, trembling with rage.

"You wouldn't."

"Try me."

Stapleton's tongue flicked across his upper lip—not in attempted flirtation, but in desperation. The light was dying, but not yet so far gone that Grey could not see Stapleton's face clearly, and discern the bone-deep fright that underlay the fury.

Stapleton glanced round, to be sure they were not overheard, and gripping Grey's sleeve, drew him into the shelter of the doorway. Standing so near, it was plain that the man wore nothing beneath his shirt; Grey could see the smoothness of his chest in the open neck, golden skin falling away to alluring shadows farther down.

"Do you know what could happen to me if you were to do such a thing?" he hissed.

Grey did. Loss of position and social ruination were the least of it; imprisonment, public whipping, and the pillory were likely. And if it was discovered that Stapleton's irregular attachments had contributed to a breach of confidence in his duties—which was precisely what Grey was inciting him to do—he would be fortunate to escape hanging for treason.

"I know what will happen to you if you don't do as I tell you," Grey said coldly. He pulled his sleeve away and stepped back. "Be quick about it; I have no time to waste."

It took no more than an hour before they reached a dingy lane and a shabby building that housed a printing shop, closed and shuttered for the night. Without a glance at Grey, Stapleton jumped out of the coach and banged at the door. Within moments, a light showed between the cracks of the shutters, and the door opened. Stapleton murmured something to the old woman who stood there, and slipped inside.

Grey sat well back in the shadows, a slouch hat drawn down to hide his face. The coach was a livery affair, ramshackle enough—but still an oddity in the neighborhood. He could only hope that Stapleton was quick enough in his errand to allow them to remove before some inquisitive footpad thought to try his luck.

The rumble and stink of a night-soil wagon floated through the air, and he tugged the window shut against them.

He was relieved that Stapleton had given in without more struggle; the man was certainly clever enough to have realized that the sword Grey held over his head was a two-edged one. True, Grey claimed to have been in Lavender House only as a matter of inquiry—and the only person who could prove otherwise was the young man with dark hair—but Stapleton didn't know that.

Still, if it came to a conflict of allegations between himself and Stapleton, there was no doubt who would be believed, and Stapleton obviously realized that, as well.

What he *didn't* realize, just as obviously, was that Richard

Caswell was one of the flies in Mr. Bowles's web. Grey would wager half a year's income that that fat little spider with the vague blue eyes knew the name of every man who had ever walked through the doors of Lavender House—and what they had done there. The thought gave him a cold feeling at the base of the neck, and he shivered, drawing his coat closer in spite of the mildness of the night.

A sudden slap at the window beside him jerked him upright, pistol drawn and pointed. No one was there, though; only the smeared print of a hand, excrement-smeared fingers leaving long dark streaks on the glass as they dragged away. A clump of noxious waste slid slowly down the window, and the guffaws of the night-soil men mingled with the bellows of the coach's driver.

The coach heaved on its springs as the driver stood up, and then there was the crack of a whip and a sharp yelp of surprise from someone on the ground. Nothing like avoiding notice! Grey thought grimly, crouching back in his seat as a barrage of night soil thumped and splattered against the side of the coach, the night-soil men hooting and gibbering like Barbary apes as the coachman cursed, clinging to his reins to stop the team from bolting.

A rattling at the coach's door brought his hand to his pistol again, but it was only Stapleton, flushed and breathless. The young man hurled himself onto the bench across from Grey, and tossed a scribbled sheet of paper into his lap.

"Only two," he said brusquely. "The *Antioch,* sailing from the Pool of London in three weeks time, or the *Nampara,* from Southampton, day after tomorrow. That what you wanted?"

The coachman, hearing Stapleton's return, drew up the reins and shouted to his horses. All too willing to escape the brouhaha, the team threw themselves forward and the coach leapt away, flinging Grey and Stapleton into a heap on the floor.

Grey hastily disentangled himself, still grasping the slip of paper tightly, and clambered back to his seat. Neil's eyes gleamed up at him from the floor of the coach, where he swayed on hands and knees.

"I said—that's what you wanted?" His voice was barely loud enough to carry over the rumble of the coach's wheels, but Grey heard him well enough.

"It is," he said. "I thank you." He might have put out a hand to help Stapleton up, but didn't. The young man rose by himself, long body swaying in the dark, and flung himself back into his seat.

They did not speak on the way back into London. Stapleton sat back, arms folded across his chest, head turned to stare out of the window. The moon was full, and dim light touched the aquiline nose and the sensual, spoilt mouth beneath it. He was a beautiful young man, to be sure, Grey thought—and knew it.

Ought he try to warn Stapleton, he wondered? He felt in some fashion guilty over his use of the man—and yet, warning him that Bowles was undoubtedly aware of his true nature would accomplish nothing. The spider would keep that knowledge to himself, hoarding it, until and unless he chose to make use of it. And once he did—no matter what that use might be—no power on earth would free Stapleton from the web.

The coach came to a stop outside Stapleton's lodging, and the young man got out without speaking, though he cast a single, angry glance at Grey just before the coach door closed between them.

Grey rapped on the ceiling, and the driver's panel slid back.

"To Jermyn Street," he ordered, and sat silent on the drive back, scarcely noticing the stink of shit surrounding him.

Chapter 17

Nemesis

In frank revolt, Grey declined to consume further egg whites. In intractable opposition, Tom Byrd refused to allow him to drink wine. An uneasy compromise was achieved by the time they reached the first posthouse, and Grey dined nursery-fashion upon bread and milk for supper, to the outspoken amusement of his fellow coach passengers.

He ignored both the jibes and the continuous feeling of unease in head and stomach, scratching ferociously with a borrowed, battered quill and wretched ink, holding a lump of milk-sodden bread with his free hand as he wrote.

A note to Quarry first; then to Magruder, in case the first should go astray. There was no time for code or careful wording—just the blunt facts, and a plea for reinforcements to be sent as quickly as possible.

He signed the notes, folded them, and sealed them with daubs of sooty candle wax, stamped with the smiling half-moon of his ring. It made him think of Trevelyan, and his emerald ring, incised with the Cornish chough. Would they be in time?

For the thousandth time, he racked his brain, trying to think if there was some quicker way—and for the thousandth time, reluctantly concluded that there wasn't. He was a decent horseman, but the chances of his managing a hell-bent ride from London to Southampton in his present condition were virtually nil, even had he had a good mount instantly available.

It must be Southampton, he thought, reassuring himself for the hundredth time. Trevelyan had agreed to three days; not enough time to prevent pursuit—unless he had planned on Grey being dead? But in that case, why bargain for time? Why not simply dismiss him, knowing that he would soon be incapable of giving chase?

No, he must be right in his surmise. Now he could only urge the post coach on by force of will, and hope that he would recover sufficiently by the time they arrived to allow him to do what must be done.

"Ready, me lord?" Tom Byrd popped up by his elbow, holding his greatcoat, ready to wrap round him. "It's time to go."

Grey dropped the bread into his bowl with a splash, and rose.

"See that these are sent back to London, please," he ordered, handing the notes to the postboy with a coin.

"Aren't you a-going to finish that?" Byrd asked, sternly eyeing the half-full bowl of bread and milk. "You'll be needing your strength, me lord, and you mean to—"

"All right!" Grey seized a final piece of bread, dunked it hastily in the bowl, and made his way to the waiting coach, cramming it into his mouth as he went.

❧

The *Nampara* was an East Indiaman, tall in silhouette against a sky of fleeting clouds, her masts dwarfing the other ship traffic. Much too large to approach the quay, she was anchored well out; the doryman rowing Grey and Byrd toward the ship called out to a skiff heading back to shore, receiving an incomprehensible bellow in return across the water.

"Dunno, sir," the doryman reported, shaking his head. "She means to leave on the tide, and it's ebbin' now." He lifted one dripping oar, briefly indicating the gray water racing past, though Grey could not have told which way it was going, under oath.

Still queasy from rocking and bumping for a night and half a day in the post coach to Southampton, Grey was disinclined to look at it; everything in sight seemed to be moving, all in contrary and unsettling directions—water, clouds, wind, the heaving boat beneath them. He thought he might vomit if he opened his mouth, so he settled for a scowl in the doryman's direction and a significant clutching of his purse, which answered well enough.

"She'll be away, mebbe, before we reach her—but we'll try, sir, aye, we'll give it a go!" The man redoubled his efforts, digging hard, and Grey closed his eyes, clinging tight to the scale-crusted slat on which he sat and trying to ignore the stink of dead fish seeping into his breeches.

"Ahoy! Ahoy!" The doryman's shriek roused him from dogged misery, to see the side of the great merchantman rising like a cliff before them. They were still rods away, and yet the massive thing blotted out the sun, casting a cold, dark shadow over them.

Even a lubber such as himself could see that the *Nampara* was on the point of departure. Shoals of smaller boats that he supposed had been supplying the great Indiaman were rowing past them toward shore, scattering like tiny fish fleeing from the vicinity of some huge sea monster on the point of awaking.

A flimsy ladder of rope still hung from the side; as the doryman heaved to, keeping the boat skillfully away from the monster's side with one oar, Grey stood up, tossed the doryman his pay, and seized a rung. The dory was sucked out from under his feet by a falling wave, and he found himself clinging for dear life, rising and falling with the ship itself.

A small flotilla of turds drifted past below his feet, detritus from the ship's head. He set his face upward and climbed, stiff and slow, Tom Byrd pressing close behind lest he fall, and came at last to the top with his body slimed with cold sweat, the taste of blood like metal in his mouth.

"I will see the owner," he said to the merchant officer who came hurrying hugger-mugger from the confusion of masts and the webs of swaying ropes. "Now, by the order of His Majesty."

The man shook his head, not attending to what he said, only concerned that they not interfere. He was already turning away, beckoning with one hand for someone to come remove them.

"The captain is busy, sir. We are on the point of sailing. Henderson! Come and—"

"Not the captain," Grey said, closing his eyes briefly against the dizzying swirl of the cobweb ropes overhead. He reached into his coat, groping for his much-creased letter of appointment. "The owner. I will see Mr. Trevelyan—now."

The officer swung his head round, looking at him narrowly, and seemed in Grey's vision to sway like the dark mast beside him.

"Are you quite well, sir?" The words sounded as though they were spoken from the bottom of a rain barrel. Grey wetted his lips with his tongue, preparing to reply, but was eclipsed.

"Of course he ain't well, you starin' fool," Byrd said fiercely from his side. "But that's no matter. You take the Major where he says, and do it smart!"

"Who are you, boy?" The officer puffed up, glaring at Byrd, who was having none of it.

"That's no matter, either. He says he's got a letter from the King, and he does, so you hop it, mate!"

The officer snatched the paper from Grey's fingers, glanced at the Royal Seal, and dropped it as though it were on fire. Tom Byrd set his foot on it before it could blow away, and picked it up, while the officer backed away, muttering apologies—or possibly curses; Grey couldn't tell, for the ringing in his ears.

"Had you best sit down, me lord?" Byrd asked anxiously, trying to dust the footmark off the parchment. "There's a barrel over there that nobody's using just now."

"No, I thank you, Tom, I'm better now." He was; strength was returning after the effort of the climb, as the cold breeze dried the sweat and cleared his head. The ship was a great deal steadier underfoot than the dory. His ears still buzzed, but he clenched his belly muscles and glanced after the officer. "Did you see where that man went? Let us follow; it's best if Trevelyan is not given too much warning."

The ship seemed in complete confusion, though Grey supposed there was some method in it. Seamen scampered to and fro, dropping out of the rigging with the random suddenness of ripe fruit, and shouts rang through the air in such profusion that he did not see how anyone could make out one from another. One benefit of the bedlam, though, was that no one tried to stop them, or even appeared to notice their presence, as Tom Byrd led the way through a pair of half-height doors and down a ladder into the shadowed depths belowdecks. It was like going down a rathole, he thought dimly—are Tom and I the ferrets?

A short passageway, and another ladder—was Tom indeed tracking the officer by smell through the bowels of the ship?—and a turn, and sure enough: The officer stood by a narrow door from which light flooded into the cavernous belowdecks, talking to someone who stood within.

"There he is, me lord," Tom said, sounding breathless. "That'll be him."

"Tom! Tom, lad, is that you?"

A loud voice spoke incredulously behind them, and Grey swung round to see his valet engulfed in the embrace of a tall young man whose face revealed his kinship.

"Jack! I thought you was dead! Or a murderer." Tom wriggled out of his brother's hug, face glowing but anxious. "Are you a murderer, Jack?"

"I am not. What the devil do you mean by that, you pie-faced little snot?"

"Don't you speak to me like that. I'm valet to his lordship, and you're no but a footman, so there!"

"You're what? No, you're never!"

Grey would have liked to hear the developments of this conversation, but duty lay in the other direction. Heart thundering in his chest, he turned his back on the Byrds, and pushed his way past the ship's officer, ignoring his objections.

The cabin was spacious, with stern windows that flooded the space with light, and he blinked against the sudden brightness. There were other people—he sensed them dimly—but his sole attention was fixed on Trevelyan.

Trevelyan was seated on a sea chest, coatless, with the sleeve of his shirt rolled up, one hand clamping a bloodstained cloth to his forearm.

"Good Christ," Trevelyan said, staring at him. "Nemesis, as I live and breathe."

"If you like." Grey swallowed a rush of saliva and took a deep breath. "I arrest you, Joseph Trevelyan, for the murder of Reinhardt Mayrhofer, by the power of . . ." Grey put a hand into his pocket, but Tom Byrd still had his letter. No matter; it was near enough.

A trembling vibration rose under his feet before he could speak further, and the boards seemed to shift beneath him. He staggered, catching himself on the corner of a desk. Trevelyan smiled, a little ruefully.

"We are aweigh, John. That is the anchor chain you hear. And this is my ship."

Grey drew another deep breath, realization of his error coming over him with a sense of fatality. He should have insisted upon seeing the captain, whatever the objection. He should have presented his letter and made sure that at all costs the ship was prevented from sailing—but in his haste to make sure of Trevelyan, his judgment had failed. He had been able to think of nothing but finding the man, cornering him, and bringing him to book at last. And now it was too late.

He was alone, save for Tom Byrd, and while Harry Quarry and Constable Magruder would know where he was, that knowledge would not save him—for now they were a-sail, heading away from England and help. And he doubted that Joseph Trevelyan meant ever to come back to face the King's justice.

Still, they would not put him overboard in sight of land, he supposed. And perhaps he could yet reach the captain, or Tom Byrd could. It might be a blessing that Byrd still held his letter; Trevelyan could not destroy it immediately. But would any captain clap the owner of his ship in irons, or abort the sailing of such a juggernaut, on the power of a rather dubious letter of empowerment?

He glanced away from Trevelyan's wry gaze, and saw, with no particular sense of surprise, that the man who stood in the corner of the cabin was Finbar Scanlon, quietly putting a case of instruments and bottles to rights.

"And where is Mrs. Scanlon?" he inquired, putting a bold face on it. "Also aboard, I assume?"

Scanlon shook his head, a slight smile on his lips.

"No, my lord. She is in Ireland, safe. I'd not risk her here, to be sure."

Because of her condition, he supposed the man meant. No woman would choose to bear a child on board ship, no matter how large the vessel.

"A long voyage then, I take it?" In his muddled state, he had not even thought to ask Stapleton for the ship's destination. Had he been in time, that would not have mattered. But now? Where in God's name were they headed?

"Long enough." It was Trevelyan who spoke, taking away the cloth from his arm and peering at the result. The tender skin of his inner forearm had been scarified, Grey saw; blood still oozed from a rectangular pattern of small cuts.

Trevelyan turned to pick up a fresh cloth, and Grey caught sight of the bed beyond him. A woman lay behind the drapes of gauze net, unmoving, and he took the few steps that brought him to the bedside, unsteady on his feet as the ship shuddered and quickened, taking sail.

"This would be Mrs. Mayrhofer, I suppose?" he asked quietly, though she seemed in a sleep too deep to rouse from easily.

"Maria," Trevelyan said softly at his elbow, wrapping his arm with a bandage as he looked down at her.

She was drawn and wasted by illness, and looked little like her portrait. Still, Grey thought she was likely beautiful, when in health. The bones of her face were too prominent now, but the shape of them graceful, and the hair that swept back from a high brow dark and lush, though matted by sweat. She had been let blood, too; a clean bandage wrapped the crook of her elbow. Her hands lay open on the coverlet, and he saw that she wore Trevelyan's signet, loose on her finger—the emerald cabochon, marked with the Cornish chough.

"What is the matter with her?" he asked, for Scanlon had come to stand by his other side.

"Malaria," the apothecary replied, matter-of-factly. "Tertian fever. Are you well, sir?"

So close, he could smell it, as well as see it; the woman's skin was yellow, and a fine sweat glazed her temples. The strange musky odor of jaundice reached him through the veil of perfume that she wore—the same perfume he had smelt on her husband, lying dead in a blood-soaked dress of green velvet.

"Will she live?" he asked. Ironic, he thought, if Trevelyan had killed her husband in order to have her, only to lose her to a deadly disease.

"She's in the hands of God now," Scanlon said, shaking his head. "As is he." He nodded at Trevelyan, and Grey glanced sharply at him.

"What do you mean by that?"

Trevelyan sighed, rolling down his sleeve over the bandage.

"Come and have a drink with me, John. There is time enough now; time enough. I'll tell you all you wish to know."

"I should prefer to be knocked straightforwardly on the head, rather than poisoned again—if it is all the same to you, sir," Grey said, giving him an unfriendly eye. To his annoyance, Trevelyan laughed, though he muted it at once, with a glance at the woman in the bed.

"I'd forgotten," he said, a smile still tugging at the corner of his mouth. "I do apologize, John. Though for what the explanation is worth," he added, "I was not intending to kill you—only to delay you."

"Perhaps it was not your intent," Grey said coldly, "but I suspect you did not mind if you did kill me."

"No, I didn't," Trevelyan agreed frankly. "I needed time, you see—and I couldn't take the chance that you wouldn't act, despite our bargain. You would not speak openly—but if you had told your mother, everyone in London would have known it by night-fall. And I could not be delayed."

"And why should you trifle at my death, after all?" Grey asked, anger at his own stupidity making him rash. "What's one more?"

Trevelyan had opened a cupboard and was reaching into it. At this, he stopped, turning a puzzled face to Grey.

"One more? I have killed no one, John. And I am pleased not to have killed you—I would have regretted that."

He turned back to the cupboard, removing from it a bottle and a pair of pewter cups.

"You won't mind brandy? I have wine, but it is not yet settled."

Despite both anger and apprehension, Grey found himself nodding acceptance as Trevelyan poured the amber drink. Trevelyan sat down and took a mouthful from his cup, holding the aromatic liquid in his mouth, eyes half-closed in pleasure. After a moment, he swallowed, and glanced up at Grey, who still stood, glaring down at him.

With a slight shrug, he reached down and pulled open the drawer of the desk. He took out a small roll of grubby paper and pushed it across the desk toward Grey.

"Do sit down, John," he said. "You look a trifle pale, if you will pardon my mentioning it."

Feeling somehow foolish, and resenting both that feeling and the weakness of his knees, Grey lowered himself slowly onto the proffered stool, and picked up the roll of paper.

There were six sheets of rough paper, hard-used. Torn from a journal or notebook, they bore close writing on both sides. The paper had been folded, then unfolded and tightly rolled at some point; he had to flatten it with both hands in order to read it, but a glance was sufficient to tell him what it was.

He glanced up, to see Trevelyan watching him, with a slightly melancholy smile.

"That is what you have been seeking?" the Cornishman asked.

"You know that it is." Grey released the papers, which curled themselves back into a cylinder. "Where did you get them?"

"From Mr. O'Connell, of course."

The little cylinder of papers rolled gently to and fro with the motion of the ship, and the cloud-shattered light from the stern windows seemed suddenly very bright.

Trevelyan sat sipping his own drink, seeming to take no further notice of Grey, absorbed in his own thoughts.

"You said—you would tell me whatever I wished to know," Grey said, picking up his own cup.

Trevelyan closed his eyes briefly, then nodded, and opened them, looking at Grey.

"Of course," he said simply. "There is no reason why not—now."

"You say you have killed no one," Grey began carefully.

"Not yet." Trevelyan glanced at the woman in the bed. "It remains to be seen whether I have killed my wife."

"*Your* wife?" Grey blurted.

Trevelyan nodded, and Grey caught a glimpse of the fierce pride of five centuries of Cornish pirates, normally hidden beneath the suave facade of the merchant prince.

"Mine. We were married Tuesday evening—by an Irish priest Mr. Scanlon brought."

Grey turned on his stool, gawking at Scanlon, who shrugged and smiled, but said nothing.

"I imagine my family—good Protestants that they've all been since King Henry's time—would be outraged," Trevelyan said, with a faint smile. "And it may not be completely legal. But needs must when the devil drives—and she is Catholic. She wished to be married, before . . ." His voice died away as he looked at the woman on the bed. She was restless now; limbs twitching beneath the coverlet, head turning uncomfortably upon her pillow.

"Not long," Scanlon said quietly, seeing the direction of his glance.

"Until what?" Grey asked, suddenly dreading to hear the answer.

"Until the fever comes on again," the apothecary replied. A faint frown creased his brow. "It is a tertian fever—it comes on, passes off, and then returns again upon the third day. And so again—and yet again. She was able to travel yesterday, but as you see . . ." He shook his head. "I have Jesuit bark for her; it may work."

"I am sorry," Grey said formally to Trevelyan, who inclined his head in grave receipt. Grey cleared his throat.

"Perhaps you would be good enough, then, to explain how Reinhardt Mayrhofer met his death, if not by your hand? And just how these papers came into your possession?"

Trevelyan sat for a moment, breathing slowly, then lifted his face briefly to the light from the windows, closing his eyes like a man savoring to the full the last moments of life before his execution.

"I suppose I must begin at the beginning, then," he said at last, eyes still closed. "And that must be the afternoon when I first set eyes upon Maria. That occasion was the ninth of May last year, at one of Lady Bracknell's salons."

A faint smile flitted across his face, as though he saw the occasion pass again before his eyes. He opened them, regarding Grey with an easy frankness.

"I never go to such things," he said. "Never. But a gentleman with whom I had business dealings had come to lunch with me at the Beefsteak, and we found we had more to speak of than would fit comfortably within the length of a luncheon. And so when he invited me to go with him to his further engagement, I did. And . . . she was there."

He opened his eyes and glanced at the bed where the woman lay, still and yellow.

"I did not know such a thing was possible," he remarked, sounding almost surprised. "If anyone had suggested such a thing to me, I would have scoffed at them—and yet . . . ."

He had seen the woman sitting in the corner and been struck by her beauty—but much more by her sadness. It was not like the Honorable Joseph Trevelyan to be touched by emotion—his own or others'—and yet the poignant grief that marked her features drew him as much as it disturbed him.

He had not approached her himself, but had not been able to take his eyes off her for long. His attention was noticed, and his hostess had obligingly told him that the woman was Frau Mayrhofer, wife of a minor Austrian noble.

"Do go and speak to her," the hostess had urged, a worried kindness evident in her manner as she glanced at the lovely, sorrowful guest. "This is her first excursion into society since her sad loss—her first child, poor thing—and I am sure that a bit of attention would do her so much good!"

He had crossed the room with no notion what he might say or do—he had no knowledge of the language of condolence, no skill at social small talk; his metier was business and politics. And yet, when his hostess had introduced them and left, he found himself still holding the hand he had kissed, looking into soft brown eyes that drowned his soul. And without further thought or hesitation had said, "God help me, I am in love with you."

"She laughed," Trevelyan said, his own face lighting at the recollection. "She laughed, and said, 'God help *me*, then!' It transformed her in an instant. And if I had been in love with La Dolorosa, I was . . . ravished . . . by La Allegretta. I would have done anything to keep the sorrow from returning to her eyes." He

looked at the woman on the bed again, and his fists curled uncon-
sciously. "I would have done anything to have her."

She was Catholic, and a married woman; it had taken several
months before she yielded to him—but he was a man accustomed
to getting what he wanted. And her husband—

"Reinhardt Mayrhofer was a degenerate," Trevelyan said, his
narrow face hardening. "A womanizer and worse."

And so their affair had begun.

"This would be before you became betrothed to my cousin?"
Grey asked, a slight edge in his voice.

Trevelyan blinked, seeming slightly surprised.

"Yes. Had I had any hopes of inducing Maria to leave
Mayrhofer, then of course I should never have contracted the betrothal. As it was, though, she was adamant; she loved me, but
could not in conscience leave her husband. That being so . . ." He
shrugged.

That being so, he had seen nothing wrong with marrying Olivia,
thus enhancing his own fortunes and laying the foundation of his
future dynasty with someone of impeccable family—while maintaining his passionate affair with Maria Mayrhofer.

"Don't look so disapproving, John," Trevelyan said, long mouth
curling a little. "I should have made Olivia a good husband. She
would have been quite happy and content."

This was doubtless true; Grey knew a dozen couples, at least,
where the husband kept a mistress, with or without his wife's
knowledge. And his own mother had said . . .

"I gather that Reinhardt Mayrhofer was not so complaisant?"
he said.

Trevelyan uttered a short laugh.

"We were more than discreet. Though he would likely not have
cared—save that it offered him a means of profit."

"So," Grey hazarded a guess, "he discovered the truth, and undertook to blackmail you?"

"Nothing quite so simple as that."

Instead, Trevelyan had learned from his lover something of her husband's interests and activities—and, interested himself by this information, had set out to gain more.

"He was not a bad intriguer, Mayrhofer," Trevelyan said, turning the cup gently in his hands so as to release the bouquet of the brandy. "He moved well in society, and had a nose for bits of information that meant little by themselves but that could be built up into something of importance—and either sold or, if of military importance, passed on to the Austrians."

"It did not, of course, occur to you to mention this to anyone in authority? That *is* treason, after all."

Trevelyan took a deep breath, inhaling the spice of his brandy.

"Oh, I thought I would just watch him for a bit," he said blandly. "See exactly what he was up to, you know."

"See whether he was doing anything that might be of benefit to you, you mean."

Trevelyan pursed his lips, and shook his head slowly over the brandy.

"You have a very suspicious sort of mind, John—has anyone ever told you that?" Not waiting for an answer, he went on. "So when Hal came to me with his suspicions about your Sergeant O'Connell, it occurred to me to wonder whether I might possibly kill two birds with one stone, you see?"

Hal had accepted his offer of Jack Byrd at once, and Trevelyan had set his most trusted servant the task of following the Sergeant. If O'Connell did have the Calais papers, then it might be arranged for Reinhardt Mayrhofer to hear about them.

"It seemed desirable to discover what Mayrhofer might do with such a find; who he would go to, I mean."

"Hmm," Grey said skeptically. He eyed his own brandy suspiciously, but there was no sediment. He took a cautious sip, and found that it burned agreeably on his palate, obliterating the murky smells of sea, sickness, and sewage. He felt immeasurably better at once.

Trevelyan had left off his wig. He wore his hair polled close; it was flat and a nondescript sort of brown, but it quite altered his appearance. Some men—Quarry, for instance—were who they were, no matter how attired, but not Trevelyan. Properly wigged, he was an elegant gentleman; shirtsleeved and bareheaded, with the bloodstained bandage about his arm, he might have been a buccaneer plotting the downfall of a prey, narrow face alight with determination.

"So I set Jack Byrd to watch O'Connell, as Hal had asked—but the bugger didn't do anything! Just went about his business, and when he wasn't doing that, spent his time drinking and whoring, before going home to that little seamstress he'd taken up with."

"Hmm," Grey said again, trying and failing notably to envision Iphigenia Stokes as a little anything.

"I told Byrd to try to get round the Stokes woman—see if she might be induced to wheedle O'Connell into action—but she was surprisingly indifferent to our Jack," Trevelyan said, pursing his lips.

"Perhaps she actually loved Tim O'Connell," Grey remarked, eliciting a pair of raised eyebrows and a puff of disbelief from Trevelyan. Love, evidently, was the exclusive province of the upper classes.

"Anyway"—Trevelyan dismissed such considerations with a wave of the hand—"finally Jack Byrd reported to me that O'Connell had scraped acquaintance with a man whom he met in a tavern. Unimportant in himself, but known to have vague connexions with parties sympathetic to France."

"Known by whom?" Grey interrupted. "Not you, I don't suppose."

Trevelyan gave him a quick glance, wary but interested.

"No, not me. Do you know a man named Bowles, by any chance?"

"I do, yes. How the hell do you know him?"

Trevelyan smiled faintly.

"Government and commerce work hand in hand, John, and what affects one affects the other. Mr. Bowles and I have had an understanding for some years now, regarding the trade of small bits of information."

He would have gone on with his story, but Grey had had a sudden flash of insight.

"An understanding, you say. This understanding—did it have something to do, perhaps, with an establishment known as Lavender House?"

Trevelyan stared at him, one brow raised.

"That's very perceptive of you, John," he said, looking amused. "Dickie Caswell said you were much more intelligent than you looked—not that you appear in any way witless," he hastened to add, seeing the look of offense on Grey's face. "Merely that Dickie is somewhat susceptible to male beauty, and thus inclined to be blinded to a man's other qualities if he is the possessor of such beauty. But I do not employ him to make such distinctions, after all; merely to report to me such matters as might be of interest."

"Good Lord." Grey felt the dizziness threatening to overwhelm him again, and was obliged to close his eyes for a moment. *Such matters as might be of interest.* The mere fact that a man had visited Lavender House—let alone what he might have done there— would be a "matter of interest," to be sure. With such knowledge, Mr. Bowles—or his agents—could bring pressure to bear on such men, the threat of exposure obliging them to undertake any actions suggested. How many men did the spider hold, enmeshed in his blackmailer's web?

"So you employ Caswell?" he asked, opening his eyes and swallowing the metallic taste at the back of his throat. "You are the owner of Lavender House, then?"

"And of the brothel in Meacham Street," Trevelyan said, his look of amusement deepening. "A great help in business. You have no idea, John, of the things that men will let slip when in the grip of lust or drunkenness."

"Don't I?" Grey said. He took a sparing sip of the brandy. "I am surprised, then, that Caswell should have revealed to me what he did, regarding your own activities. It was he who told me that you visited a woman there."

"Did he?" Trevelyan looked displeased at that. "He didn't tell me that." He leaned back a little, frowning. Then he gave a short laugh and shook his head.

"Well, it's as my old Nan used to say to me: 'Lie down with pigs, and you'll rise up mucky.' I daresay it would have suited Dickie very well to have me arrested and imprisoned, or executed—and I suppose he thought the opportunity was ripe at last. He believes that Lavender House will go to him, should anything happen to me; I think it is that belief alone that's kept him alive so long."

"He believes it. It is not so?"

Trevelyan shrugged, suddenly indifferent.

"No matter now." He rose, restless, and went to stand by the bed again. He could not keep from touching her, Grey saw; his fingers lifted a damp wisp of hair away from her cheek and smoothed it back behind her ear. She stirred in her sleep, eyelids fluttering, and Trevelyan took her hand, kneeling down to murmur to her, stroking her knuckles with his thumb.

Scanlon was watching, too, Grey saw. The apothecary had started brewing some potion over a spirit lamp; a bitter-smelling steam began to rise from the pot, fogging the windows. Glancing back toward the bed, he saw that England had fallen far behind by now; only a narrow hump of land was still visible through the windows, above the roiling sea.

"And you, Mr. Scanlon," Grey said, rising, and moving carefully toward the apothecary, cup in hand. "How do you find yourself entangled in this affair?"

The Irishman gave him a wry look.

"Ah, and isn't love a grand bitch, then?"

"I daresay. You would be referring to the present Mrs. Scanlon, I collect?"

"Francie, aye." A warmth glowed in the Irishman's eyes as he spoke his wife's name. "We took up together, her and me, after her wretch of a husband left. It didn't matter that we couldn't marry, though she'd have liked it. But then the bastard comes back!"

The apothecary's big clean hands curled up into fists at the thought.

"Waited until I was out, the shite. I come back from tending to an ague, and what do I find but my Francie on the floor, a-welter in her own blood and her precious face smashed in—" He stopped abruptly, trembling with recalled rage.

"There was a man bent over her; I thought he'd done it, and went for him. I'd have killed him, sure, had Francie not come round enough to wheeze out to me as it weren't him but Tim O'Connell who'd beaten her."

The man was Jack Byrd, who had followed O'Connell to the apothecary's shop, and then, hearing the sounds of violence and a woman screaming, had rushed up the stairs, surprising Tim O'Connell and driving him away.

"Bless him, he was in time to save her life," Scanlon said, crossing himself. "And I said to him, I did, that he was free of me and all I had, for what he'd done, though he'd take no reward for it."

At this, Grey swung around to Trevelyan, who had risen from his own wife's side and come to rejoin them.

"A very useful fellow, Jack Byrd," Grey said. "It seems to run in the family."

Trevelyan nodded.

"I gather so. That was Tom Byrd I heard in the corridor outside?"

Grey nodded in turn, but was impatient to return to the main story.

"Yes. Why on earth did O'Connell come back to his wife, do you know?"

Trevelyan and the apothecary exchanged glances, but it was Trevelyan who answered.

"We can't say for sure—but given what transpired later, it is my supposition that he had not gone there in order to see his wife, but rather to seek a hiding place for the papers he had. I said that he had made contact with a petty spy."

Jack Byrd had reported as much to Harry Quarry—and thus to Mr. Bowles—but, loyal servant that he was, had reported it also to his employer. This was his long-standing habit; in addition to his duties as footman, he was instructed to pick up such gossip in taverns as might prove of interest or value, to be followed up in such manner as Trevelyan might decide.

"So it is not merely Cornish tin or India spices that you deal in," Grey said, giving Trevelyan a hard eye. "Did my brother know that you trade in information as well, when he asked your help?"

"He may have done," Trevelyan replied blandly. "I have been able to draw Hal's attention to a small matter of interest now and then—and he has done the same for me."

It was not precisely a surprise to Grey that men of substance should regard matters of state principally in terms of their personal benefit, but he had seldom been brought so rudely face-to-face with the knowledge. But surely Hal would not have had any part in blackmail—He choked the thought off, returning doggedly to the matter at hand.

"So, O'Connell made some overture to this minor *intrigant,* and you learned of it. What then?"

O'Connell had not made it clear what information he possessed; only that he had something which might be worth money to the proper parties.

"That would fit with what the army suspected," Grey said. "O'Connell wasn't a professional spy; he merely recognized the importance of the requisitions and seized the chance. Perhaps he knew someone in France to whom he thought to sell them—but then the regiment was brought home before he had the chance to contact his buyer."

"Quite." Trevelyan nodded, impatient of the interruption. "I, of course, knew what the material was. But it seemed to me that, rather than simply retrieving the information, it might be more useful to discover who some of the parties interested in it might be."

"It did not, of course, occur to you to share these thoughts with Harry Quarry or anyone else connected with the regiment?" Grey suggested politely.

Trevelyan's nostrils flared.

"Quarry—that lump? No. I suppose I might have told Hal—but he was gone. It seemed best to keep matters in my own hands."

It would, Grey thought cynically. No matter that the welfare of half the British army depended on those matters; naturally, a merchant would have the best judgment!

Trevelyan's next words, though, made it apparent that things ran deeper than either money or military dispositions.

"I had learned from Maria that her husband dealt in secrets," he said, glancing over his shoulder at the bed. "I thought to use

O'Connell and his material as bait, to draw Mayrhofer into some incriminating action. Once revealed as a spy . . ."

"He could be either banished or executed, thus leaving you a good deal more freedom with regard to his wife. Quite."

Trevelyan glanced sharply at him, but chose not to take issue with his tone.

"Quite," he said, matching Grey's irony. "It was, however, a delicate matter to arrange things so that O'Connell and Mayrhofer should be brought together. O'Connell was a wary blackguard; he'd waited a long time to search out a buyer, and was highly suspicious of any overtures."

Trevelyan, restless, got up and moved back to the bed.

"I was obliged to see O'Connell myself, posing as a putative middleman, in order to draw the Sergeant in and assure him that there was money available—but I went disguised, and gave him a false name, of course. Meanwhile, though, I had succeeded from the other end, in interesting Mayrhofer in the matter. *He* decided to cut me out—duplicitous bastard that he was!—and set one of his own servants to find O'Connell."

Hearing Mayrhofer's name from another source, and realizing that the man he spoke to was acting under an assumed identity, O'Connell had rather logically deduced that Trevelyan *was* Mayrhofer, negotiating incognito in hopes of keeping down the price. He therefore followed Trevelyan from the place of their last meeting—and tracked him with patience and skill to Lavender House.

Discerning the nature of the place from questions in the neighborhood, O'Connell had thought himself possessed of a marked advantage over the man he assumed to be Mayrhofer. He could confront the man at the scene of his presumed crimes, and then demand what he liked, without necessarily giving up anything in return.

He had, of course, been thwarted in this scheme when he found no one at Lavender House who had heard the name Mayrhofer. Baffled but persistent, O'Connell had hung about long enough to see Trevelyan depart, and had followed him back to the brothel in Meacham Street.

"I should never have gone directly to Lavender House," Trevelyan admitted with a shrug. "But the business with O'Connell had taken longer than I thought—and I was in a hurry." The Cornishman could not keep his eyes from the woman. Even from where he sat, Grey could see the flush of fever rising in her pallid cheeks.

"Normally, you would have gone to the brothel first, thence to Lavender House, and back again, in your disguise?" Grey asked.

"Yes. That was our usual arrangement. No one questions a gentleman's going to a bordello—or a whore coming out of one, being taken to meet a customer." Trevelyan said. "But Maria naturally could not meet me there. At the same time, no one would suspect a woman of entering Lavender House—no one who knew what sort of place it is."

"An ingenious solution," Grey said, with thinly veiled sarcasm. "One thing—why did you always employ a green velvet dress? Or dresses, as the case may be? Did you and Mrs. Mayrhofer both employ that disguise?"

Trevelyan looked uncomprehending for a moment, but then smiled.

"Yes, we did," he said. "As for why green—" He shrugged. "I like green. It's my favorite color."

At the brothel, O'Connell had inquired doggedly for a gentleman in a green dress, possibly named Mayrhofer—only to have it strongly implied by Magda and her staff that he was insane. The result was naturally to leave O'Connell in some agitation of mind.

"He was not a practiced spy, as you note," Trevelyan said, shaking his head with a sigh. "Already suspicious, he became convinced that some perfidy was afoot—"

"Which it was," Grey put in, earning himself a brief glance of annoyance from Trevelyan, who nonetheless continued.

"And so I surmise that he decided he required some safer place of concealment for the papers he held—and thus returned to his wife's lodgings in Brewster's Alley."

Where he had discovered his abandoned wife in an advanced state of pregnancy by another man, and with the irrationality of jealousy, proceeded to batter her senseless.

Grey massaged his forehead, closing his eyes briefly in order to counteract a tendency for his head to spin.

"All right," he said. "The affair is reasonably clear to me so far. But," he added, opening his eyes, "we have still two dead men to account for. Obviously, Magda told *you* that O'Connell had rumbled you. And yet you say you did not kill him? Nor yet Mayrhofer?"

A sudden rustling from the bed interrupted him, and he turned, startled.

"It was I who killed my husband, good sir."

The voice from the bed was soft and husky, with no more than a hint of foreign accent, but all three men jerked, startled as though it had been a trumpet blast. Maria Mayrhofer lay upon her side, hair tangled over her pillow. Her eyes were huge, glazed with encroaching fever, but still luminous with intelligence.

Trevelyan went at once to kneel beside her, feeling her cheek and forehead.

"Scanlon," he said, a tone of command mingled with one of appeal.

The apothecary went at once to join him, touching her gently beneath the jaw, peering into her eyes—but she turned her head away from him, closing her eyes.

"I am well enough for the moment," she said. "This man—" She waved in Grey's direction. "Who is he?"

Grey stood, keeping his feet awkwardly as the deck rose under him, and bowed to her.

"I am Major John Grey, madam. I am appointed by the Crown to investigate a matter"—he hesitated, uncertain how—or whether—to explain—"a matter that has impinged upon your own affairs. Did I understand you to say that you had killed Herr Mayrhofer?"

"Yes, I did."

Scanlon had withdrawn to check his hell-brew, and she rolled her head to meet Grey's gaze again. She was too weak to lift her head from the pillow, and yet her eyes held something prideful— almost insolent, despite her state—and he had a sudden glimmer of what it was that had so attracted the Cornishman.

"Maria . . ." Trevelyan set a hand on her arm in warning, but she disregarded it, keeping her gaze imperiously on Grey.

"What does it matter?" she asked, her voice still soft, but clear as crystal. "We are on the water now. I feel the waves that bear us on; we have escaped. This is your realm, is it not, Joseph? The sea is your kingdom, and we are safe." A tiny smile played over her lips as she watched Grey, making him feel very odd indeed.

"I have left word," Grey felt obliged to point out. "My whereabouts are known."

The smile grew.

"So someone knows you are en route to India," she said mockingly. "Will they follow you there, do you think?"

India. Grey had not received leave from the lady to sit in her presence, but did so anyway. The weakness of his knees owed something both to the swaying of the ship and to the aftereffects of mercury poisoning—but somewhat more to the news of their destination.

Still fighting giddiness, the first thought in his head was relief that he had managed that scribbled note to Quarry. *At least I won't be shot for desertion, when—or if—I finally manage to get back.* He shook his head briefly to clear it, and sat up straight, setting his jaw.

There was no help for it, and nothing to be done now, save carry out his duty to the best of his ability. Anything further must be left to Providence.

"Be that as it may, madam," he said firmly. "It is my duty to learn the truth of the death of Timothy O'Connell—and any matters that may be associated with it. If your state permits, I would hear whatever you can tell me."

"O'Connell?" she murmured, and turned her head restlessly on the pillow, eyes half-closing. "I do not know this name, this man. Joseph?"

"No, dear one, it's nothing to do with you, with us." Trevelyan spoke soothingly, a hand on her hair, but his eyes searched her face uneasily. Glancing from him to her, Grey could see it, too; her face was growing markedly pale, as though some force pressed the blood from her skin.

All at once, there were gray shadows in the hollows of her bone; the lush curve of her mouth paled and pinched, lips nearly disappearing. The eyes, too, seemed to retreat, going dull and shrinking away into her skull. Trevelyan was talking to her; Grey sensed the worry in his tone, but paid no attention to the words, his whole attention fixed upon the woman.

Scanlon had come to look, was saying something. Quinine, something about quinine.

A sudden shudder closed her eyes and blanched her features. The flesh itself seemed to draw in upon her bones as she huddled deeper into the bedclothes, shaking. Grey had seen malarial chills before, but even so, was shocked at the suddenness and strength of the attack.

"Madam," he began, stretching out a hand to her, helpless. He had no notion what to do, but felt that he must do something, must offer comfort of some kind—she was so fragile, so defenseless in the grip of the disease.

"She cannot speak with you," Trevelyan said sharply, and gripped his arm. "Scanlon!"

The apothecary had a small brazier going; he had already seized a pair of tongs and plucked a large stone that he had heating in the coals. He dropped this into a folded linen towel and, holding it gingerly, hurried to the bedside, where he burrowed under the sheets, placing the hot stone at her feet.

"Come away," Trevelyan ordered, pulling at Grey's arm. "Mr. Scanlon must care for her. She cannot talk."

This was plainly true—and yet she lifted her head and forced her eyes to open, teeth gritted hard against the chills that racked her.

"J-J-J-Jos-seph!"

"What, darling? What can I do?" Trevelyan abandoned Grey upon the instant, falling to his knees beside her.

She seized his hand and held it hard, fighting the chill that shook her bones.

"T-T-Tell him. If we b-both are d-dead . . . I would be j-j-justified!"

Both? Grey wondered. He had no time to speculate upon the meaning of that; Scanlon had hurried back with his steaming beaker, had lifted her from the pillow. He was holding the vessel to her lips, murmuring encouragement, willing her to sip at it, even as the hot liquid slopped and spilled from her chattering teeth. Her long hands rose and wrapped themselves about the cup, clinging tightly to the fugitive warmth. The last thing he saw before Trevelyan forced him from the cabin was the emerald ring, hanging loose from a bony finger.

⚬⧢⚬

He followed Trevelyan upward through the shadows to the open deck. The bedlam of setting sail had subsided now, and half the crew had vanished below. Grey had barely noticed his surroundings earlier; now he saw the clouds of snowy canvas billowing above, and the polished wood and brightwork of the ship. The *Nampara* was under full sail and flying like a live thing; he could feel the ship—feel *her*; they called ships "she"—humming beneath his feet, and felt a sudden unexpected exhilaration.

The waves had changed from the gray of the harbor to the lapis blue of deep sea, and a brisk wind blew through his hair, carrying away the smells of illness and confinement. The last remnants of his own illness seemed also to blow away on that wind—perhaps only because his debilities seemed inconsequent, by contrast with the desperate straits of the woman below.

There was still bustle on deck, and shouting to and fro between the deck and the mysterious realm of canvas above, but it was more orderly, less obtrusive now. Trevelyan made his way toward the stern, finding a place at the rail where they would not obstruct the sailors' work, and there they leaned for a time, wind cleansing them, watching together as the final sight of England disappeared in distant mist.

"Will she die, do you think?" Grey asked eventually. It was the thought uppermost in his own mind; it must be so for Trevelyan as well.

"No," the Cornishman snapped. "She will not." He leaned on the rail, staring moodily into the racing water.

Grey didn't speak, merely closed his eyes and let the glitter of the sun off the waves make dancing patterns of red and black inside his lids. He needn't push; there was time now for everything.

"She is worse," Trevelyan said at last, unable to bear the silence. "She shouldn't be. I have seen malaria often; the first attack is normally the worst—if there is cinchona for treatment, subsequent attacks grow less frequent, less severe. Scanlon says so, too," he added, almost as an afterthought.

"Has she suffered long with the disease?" Grey asked, curious. It was not a malady that often afflicted city-dwellers, but the lady might perhaps have acquired it in the course of traveling with Mayrhofer.

"Two weeks."

Grey opened his eyes, to see Trevelyan standing upright, his short hair flicked into a crest by the wind, chin raised. Water stood in his eyes; perhaps it was caused by the rushing wind.

"I should not have let him do it," Trevelyan muttered. His hands clenched on the rail in a futile rage tinged with despair. "Christ, how could I have let him do it?"

"Who?" Grey asked.

"Scanlon, of course." Trevelyan turned away momentarily, rubbing a wrist across his eyes, then dropped back, leaning against the rail, his back to the sea. He folded his arms across his chest and stared moodily ahead, intent on whatever dire visions he harbored within.

"Let us walk," Grey suggested, after a moment. "Come; the air will do you good."

Trevelyan hesitated, but then shrugged and assented. They walked in silence for some time, circling the deck, dodging seamen about their tasks.

Mindful of his leather-heeled boots and the heaving deck, Grey strode carefully at first, but the boards were dry, and the motion of the ship a stimulus to his senses; despite his own predicament, he felt his spirits rise with the blood that surged through his cheeks and refreshed his cramped limbs. He began to feel truly himself again for the first time in days.

True, he was captive on a ship headed for India, and thus unlikely to see home again soon. But he was a soldier, used to long journeys and separations—and the thought of India, with all its mysteries of light and histories of blood, was undeniably exciting. And Quarry could be trusted to inform his family that he was likely still alive.

What would his family do about the wedding preparations? he wondered. Trevelyan's abrupt flight would be an enormous scandal, and an even greater one if word got out—which indubitably it would—of the involvement of Frau Mayrhofer and of her husband's shocking murder. He was not disposed to believe the lady's claim to have killed Mayrhofer; not after seeing the body. Even in health, for a woman to have done *that* . . . and Maria Mayrhofer was slightly built, no larger than his cousin Olivia.

Poor Olivia; her name would be spread over the London broadsheets for weeks as the jilted fiancée—but at least her personal reputation would be spared. Thank God the affair had come to a head before the wedding, and not afterward. That was something.

Would Trevelyan have bolted, had Grey not confronted him? Or would he have stayed—married Olivia, gone on running his companies, dabbling in politics, moving in society as the intimate of dukes and ministers, maintaining his facade as a rock-solid merchant—while privately carrying on his passionate affair with the widow Mayrhofer?

Grey cast a sidelong glance at his companion. The Cornishman's face was still dark, but that brief glimpse of despair had vanished, leaving his jaw set with determination.

What could the man be thinking? To flee as he had, leaving scandal in his wake, would have disastrous consequences for his business affairs. His companies, their investors, his clients, the miners and laborers, captains and seamen, clerks and warehousemen who worked for the companies—even the brother in Parliament; all would be affected by Trevelyan's flight.

Still, his jaw was set, and he walked like a man making for a distant goal, rather than one out for a casual stroll.

Grey recognized both the determination and the power of will from which it sprang, but he also was beginning to realize that the facade of the solid merchant was just that; beneath it lay a mind like quicksilver, able to sum up circumstances and change tack in an instant—and more than ruthless in its decisions.

He realized with a lurch of the heart that Trevelyan reminded him in some small way of Jamie Fraser. But no: Fraser was ruthless and quick, and might be equally passionate in his feelings—but above all, he was a man of honor.

By contrast, he could now see the deep selfishness that underlay Trevelyan's character. Jamie Fraser would not have abandoned those who depended on him, not even for the sake of a woman who—Grey was forced to admit—he clearly loved beyond life itself. As for the notion of his stealing another man's wife, it was inconceivable.

A romantic or a novelist might count the world well lost for love. So far as Grey's own opinion counted, a love that sacrificed honor was less honest than simple lust, and degraded those who professed to glory in it.

"Me lord!"

He glanced up at the cry, and saw the two Byrds hanging like apples in the rigging just above. He waved, glad that at least Tom Byrd had found his brother. Would someone think to send word to the Byrd household? he wondered. Or would they be left in uncertainty as to the fate of *two* of their sons?

That thought depressed him, and a worse one followed on the heels of it. While he had recovered the requisitions, he could tell no one that he had done so and that the information was safe. By the time he reached any port from which word could be sent, the War Office would long since have been obliged to act.

And they would be acting on the assumption that the intelligence had in fact fallen into enemy hands—a staggering assumption, in terms of the strategic readjustments required, and their expense. An expense that might be paid in lives, as well as money. He pressed an elbow against his side, feeling the crackle of the papers he had tucked away, fighting a sudden impulse to throw himself overboard and swim toward England until exhaustion pulled him down. He had succeeded—and yet the result would be the same as though he had failed utterly.

Beyond the ruin of his own career, great damage would be done to Harry Quarry and the regiment—and to Hal. To have harbored a spy in the ranks was bad enough; to have failed to catch him in time was far worse.

In the end, it seemed he would have no more than the satisfaction of finally hearing the truth. He had heard but a fraction of it so far—but it was a long way to India, and with both Trevelyan and Scanlon trapped here with him, he was sure of discovering everything, at last.

"How did you know that I was poxed?" Trevelyan asked abruptly.

"Saw your prick, over the piss-pots at the Beefsteak," he replied bluntly. It seemed absurd now that he should have suffered a moment's shame or hesitation in the matter. And yet—would it have made a difference, if he had spoken out at once?

Trevelyan gave a small grunt of surprise.

"Did you? I do not even recall seeing you there. But I suppose I was distracted."

He was clearly distracted now; his step had slowed, and a seaman carrying a small cask was obliged to swerve in order to avoid collision. Grey took Trevelyan by the sleeve and led him into the lee of the forward mast, where a huge water barrel stood, a tin cup attached to it by a narrow chain.

Grey gulped water from the cup, even in his depression taking some pleasure from the feel of it, cool in his mouth. It was the first thing he had been able to taste properly in days.

"That must have been . . ." Trevelyan squinted, calculating. "Early June—the sixth?"

"About that. Does it matter?"

Trevelyan shrugged and took the dipper.

"Not really. It's only that that was when I first noticed the sore myself."

"Rather a shock, I suppose," Grey said.

"Rather," Trevelyan replied dryly. He drank, then dropped the tin cup back into the barrel.

"Perhaps it would have been better to say nothing," the Cornishman went on, as though to himself. "But . . . no. That wouldn't have done." He waved a hand, dismissing whatever his thought had been.

"I could scarcely believe it. Went about in a daze for the rest of the day, and spent the night wondering what to do—but I knew it was Mayrhofer; it had to be."

Looking up, he caught sight of Grey's face, and a wry smile broke out upon his own.

"No, not directly. Through Maria. I had shared no woman's bed since I began with her, and that was more than a year before. But clearly she had been infected by her whore-mongering bastard of a husband; she was innocent."

Not only innocent, but clearly ignorant as well. Not wishing to confront her with his discovery at once, Trevelyan had gone in search of her doctor instead.

"I said that she had lost a child, just before I met her? I got the doctor who attended her to talk; he confirmed that the child had been malformed, owing to the mother's syphilitic condition—but naturally he had kept quiet about that."

Trevelyan's fingers drummed restlessly on the lid of the barrel.

"The child was born malformed, but alive—it died in the cradle, a day after birth. Mayrhofer smothered it, wishing neither to be burdened by it nor to have his wife learn the cause of its misfortune."

Grey felt his stomach contract.

"How do you know this?"

Trevelyan rubbed a hand over his face, as though tired.

"Reinhardt admitted it to her—to Maria. I brought the doctor to her, you see; forced him to tell her what he had told me. I thought—if she knew what Mayrhofer had done, infecting her, dooming their child, that perhaps she would leave him."

She did not. Hearing out the doctor in numb silence, she had sat for a long time, considering, and then asked both Trevelyan and the doctor to go; she would be alone.

She had stayed alone for a week. Her husband was away, and she saw no one save the servants who brought her meals—all sent away, untouched.

"She thought of self-murder, she told me," Trevelyan said, staring out toward the endless sea. "Better, she thought, to end it cleanly than to die slowly, in such fashion. Have you ever seen someone dying of the syphilis, Grey?"

"Yes," Grey said, the bad taste creeping back into his mouth. "In Bedlam."

One in particular, a man whose disease had deprived him both of nose and balance, so that he reeled drunkenly across the floor, crashing helplessly into the other inmates, foot stuck in a night bucket, tears and snot streaming over his rutted face. He could but hope that the syphilis had taken the man's reason, as well, so that he was in ignorance of his situation.

He looked then at Trevelyan, envisioning for the first time that clever, narrow face, ruined and drooling. It would happen, he realized with a small shock. The only question was how long it might be before the symptoms became clear.

"If it were me, I might think of suicide, too," he said.

Trevelyan met his eyes, then smiled ruefully.

"Would you? We are different, then," he said, with no tone of judgment in the observation. "That course never occurred to me, until Maria showed me her pistol, and told me what she had been thinking."

"You thought only of how the fact might be used to separate the lady from her husband?" Grey said, hearing the edge in his own voice.

"No," Trevelyan replied, seeming unoffended. "Though that had been my goal since I met her; I did not propose to give it up. I tried to see her, after she had sent me away, but she would not receive me."

Instead, Trevelyan had set himself to discover what remedy might be available.

"Jack Byrd knew of the difficulty; it was he who informed me that Finbar Scanlon seemed an able man in such matters. He had gone back to the apothecary's shop, to inquire after Mrs. O'Connell's welfare, and had become well acquainted with Scanlon, you see."

"And that is where you met Sergeant O'Connell, returning to his home?" Grey asked, sudden enlightenment coming upon him. Trevelyan already knew of O'Connell's peculations, and certainly had more men than Jack Byrd at his beck and call. He would have been more than capable, Grey thought, of having the Sergeant murdered, abstracting the papers for his own purposes regarding Mayrhofer. And those purposes now fulfilled, of course he could casually hand the papers back, uncaring of what damage had been done in the meantime!

He felt his blood rising at the thought—but Trevelyan was staring at him blankly.

"No," he said. "I met O'Connell only the once, myself. Vicious sort," he added, reflectively.

"And you did not have him killed?" Grey demanded, skepticism clear in his voice.

"No, why should I?" Trevelyan frowned at him a little; then his brow cleared.

"You thought I had him done in, in order to get the papers?" Trevelyan's mouth twitched; he seemed to be finding something funny in the notion. "My God, John, you do have the most squalid opinion of my character!"

"You think it unjustified, do you?" Grey inquired acidly.

"No, I suppose not," Trevelyan admitted, wiping a knuckle under his nose. He had not been recently shaved, and tiny drops of water were condensing on the sprouting whiskers, giving him a silvered look.

"But no," he repeated. "I told you I had killed no one—nor had I anything to do with O'Connell's death. That story belongs to Mr. Scanlon, and I am sure he will tell it to you, as soon as he is at liberty."

Trevelyan glanced, as though despite himself, at the door that led to the quarters below, and then away.

"Should you be with her?" Grey asked quietly. "Go, if you like. I can wait."

Trevelyan shook his head and glanced away.

"I cannot help," he said. "And I can scarcely bear to see her in such straits. Scanlon will fetch me if—if I am needed."

Seeming to detect some unspoken accusation in Grey's manner, he looked up defensively.

"I did stay with her, the last time the fever came on. She sent me away, saying that it disturbed her to see my agitation. She prefers to be alone, when . . . things go wrong."

"Indeed. As she was after learning the truth from the doctor, you said."

Trevelyan took a deep breath, and squared his shoulders, as though setting himself for some unpleasant task.

"Yes," he said bleakly. "Then."

She had been alone for a week, save for the servants, who kept away at her own request. No one knew how long she had sat alone, that final day in her white-draped boudoir. It was long past dark when her husband had finally returned, somewhat the worse for drink, but still coherent enough to understand her accusation, her demand for the truth about her child.

"She said that he laughed," Trevelyan said, his tone remote, as though reporting some business disaster; a mine cave-in, perhaps, or a sunken ship. "He told her then that he had killed the child; told her that she should be grateful to him, that he had saved her from living day after day with the shame of its deformity."

At this, the woman who had lived patiently for years with the knowledge of infidelity and promiscuity felt the bonds of her vows break asunder, and Maria Mayrhofer had stepped across that thin line of prohibition that separates justice from vengeance. Mad with rage and sorrow, she had flung back in his teeth all the insults she had suffered through the years of their marriage, threatening to expose all his tawdry affairs, to reveal his syphilitic condition to society, to denounce him openly as a murderer.

The threats had sobered Mayrhofer slightly. Staggering from his wife's presence, he had left her raging and weeping. She had the pistol that had been her constant companion through her week of brooding, ready to hand. She had hunted often in the hills near her Austrian home, was accustomed to guns; it was the work of a moment to load and prime the weapon.

"I do not know for sure what she intended," Trevelyan said, his eyes fixed on a flight of gulls that wheeled over the ocean, diving for fish. "She told me that she didn't know, herself. Perhaps she meant to kill herself—or both of them."

As it was, the door to her boudoir had opened a few minutes later, and her husband lurched back in, clad in the green velvet dress which she wore to her assignations with Trevelyan. Flushed with drink and temper, he taunted her, saying that she dared not expose him—or he would see that both she and her precious lover paid a worse price. What would become of Joseph Trevelyan, he demanded, lurching against the doorframe, once it was known that he was not only an adulterer but also a sodomite?

"And so she shot him," Trevelyan concluded, with a slight shrug. "Straight through the heart. Can you blame her?"

"How do you suppose he learned of your assignations at Lavender House?" Grey asked, ignoring the question. He wondered with a certain misgiving what Richard Caswell might have told about his own presence there, years before. Trevelyan had not mentioned it, and surely he would have, if . . .

Trevelyan shook his head, sighed, and closed his eyes against the glare of the sun off the water.

"I don't know. As I said, Reinhardt Mayrhofer was an intriguer. He had his sources of information—and he knew Magda, who came from the village near his estate. I paid her well, but perhaps he paid her better. You can never trust a whore, after all," he added, with a slight tinge of bitterness.

Thinking of Nessie, Grey thought that it depended on the whore, but did not say so.

"Surely Mrs. Mayrhofer did not smash in her husband's face," he said instead. "Was that you?"

Trevelyan opened his eyes and nodded.

"Jack Byrd and I." He lifted his head, searching the rigging, but the two Byrds had flown. "He is a good fellow, Jack. A good fellow," he repeated, more strongly.

Brought to her senses by the pistol's report, Maria Mayrhofer had at once stepped from her boudoir and called a servant, whom she sent posthaste across the City to summon Trevelyan. Arriving with his trusted servant, the two of them had carried the body, still clad in green velvet, out to the carriage house, debating what to do with it.

"I could not allow the truth to come out," Trevelyan explained. "Maria might easily hang, should she come to trial—though surely there was never a murder so well-deserved. Even were she acquitted, though, the simple fact of a trial would mean exposure. Of everything."

It was Jack Byrd who thought of the blood. He had slipped out, returning with a bucket of pig's blood from a butcher's yard. They had smashed in the corpse's face with a shovel, and then bundled both body and bucket into the carriage. Jack had driven the equipage the short distance to St. James's Park. It was past midnight by that time, and the torches that normally lit the public pathways were long since extinguished.

They had tethered the horses and carried the body swiftly a little way into the park, there dumping it under a bush and dousing it with blood, then escaping back to the carriage.

"We hoped that the body would be taken for that of a simple prostitute," Trevelyan explained. "If no one examined it carefully, they would assume it to be a woman. If they discovered the truth of the sex . . . well, it would cause more curiosity, but men of certain perverse predilections also are prone to meet with violent death."

"Quite," Grey murmured, keeping his face carefully impassive. It was not a bad plan—and he was, in spite of everything, pleased to have deduced it correctly. The death of an anonymous prostitute—of either sex—would cause neither outcry nor investigation.

"Why the blood, though? It was apparent—once one looked—that the man had been shot."

Trevelyan nodded.

"Yes. We thought that the blood might obscure the cause of death, by suggesting that he had been beaten to death—but principally, its purpose was to prevent anyone undressing the body, and thus discovering its sex."

"Of course." Usable clothes found on a corpse would routinely be stripped and sold, either by the constables who found it, by the morgue-keeper who took charge of it, or, at the last, by the gravedigger who undertook to bury the body in some anonymous potter's field. But no one—other than Grey himself—would have touched that sodden, reeking garment.

Had the fact of the green velvet dress not caught Magruder's notice, or if they had had the luck to dispose of the body in another district of the City, it was very likely that no one would have bothered examining the body at all; it would simply have been put down as one of the casualties of London's dark world and dismissed, as casually as one might dismiss the death of a stray dog crushed by a coach's wheels.

"Sir?"

He hadn't heard the sound of approaching footsteps, and was startled to find Jack Byrd standing behind them, his dark face serious. Trevelyan took one look at it, and headed for the doors to the companionway.

"Mrs. Mayrhofer is worse?" Grey asked, watching the Cornishman stumble through a knot of sailors mending canvas.

"I don't know, me lord. I think she may be better. Mr. Scanlon come out and sent me to fetch Mr. Joseph. He says as how he'll be in the crew's mess for a bit, should you want to talk to him, though," he added, as an obvious afterthought.

Grey glanced at the young man, and felt a twitch of recognition. Not the family resemblance to young Tom; something else. Jack Byrd's eyes were still focused on his master, as Trevelyan reached the hatchway, and there was something unguarded in his face that Grey's nervous system discerned long before his mind made sense of it.

It was gone in the next instant, Jack Byrd's face lapsing back into an older, leaner version of his younger brother's as he turned to Grey.

"Will you be wanting Tom, my lord?" he asked.

"Not now," Grey responded automatically. "I'll go and talk to Mr. Scanlon. Tell Tom I'll send for him when I need him."

"Very good, my lord." Jack Byrd bowed gravely, an elegant footman's gesture at odds with his seaman's slops, and walked away, leaving Grey to find his own way.

He made his way downward in search of the crew's mess, scarcely noticing his surroundings, mind belatedly searching for logical connexions that might support the conclusion his lower faculties had leaped to.

Jack Byrd knew of the difficulty, Trevelyan had said, referring to his own infection. *It was he who informed me that Finbar Scanlon seemed an able man in such matters.*

And Maria Mayrhofer had said that her husband threatened Trevelyan, asking what would happen to him *once it was known that he was not only an adulterer but also a sodomite?*

Not so fast, Grey cautioned himself. In all likelihood, Mayrhofer had only referred to Trevelyan's association with Lavender House. And it was by no means unusual for a devoted servant to be privy to a master's intimate concerns—he shuddered to think what Tom knew of his own intimacies at this point.

No, these were mere shreds of something less than evidence, he was obliged to conclude. Even less tangible—but perhaps the more trustworthy—was his own sense of Joseph Trevelyan. Grey did not think himself infallible, by any means—he would not in a hundred years have guessed the truth of Egbert Jones's identity as "Miss Irons," had he not seen it—and yet he was as certain as he could be that Joseph Trevelyan was not so inclined.

Putting modesty aside for the sake of logic, he blushed to admit that this conclusion was based as much on Trevelyan's lack of response to his own person as to anything else. Such men as himself lived in secrecy—but there were signals, nonetheless, and he was adept at reading them.

So there might in fact be nothing on Trevelyan's side, nothing beyond heartfelt appreciation of a good servant. But there was more than devoted service in Jack Byrd's soul, he'd swear that on a gallon of brandy. So he told himself grimly, clambering monkey-like into the bowels of the ship in search of Finbar Scanlon, and the final parts to his puzzle.

And now, at last, the truth.

"Well, d'ye see, we're soldiers, we Scanlons," the apothecary said, pouring beer from a jug. "A tradition in the family, it is. Every man jack of us, for the last fifty years, save those born crippled, or too infirm for it."

"You do not seem particularly infirm," Grey observed. "And certainly not a cripple." Scanlon in fact was a handsomely built man, clean-limbed and solid.

"Oh, I went for a soldier, too," the man assured him, eyes twinkling. "I served for a time in France, but had the luck to be taken on as assistant to the regimental surgeon, when the regular man was crapped in the Low Countries."

Scanlon had discovered both an ability and an affinity for the work, and had learned all that the surgeon could teach him within a few months.

"Then we ran into artillery near Laffeldt," he said, with a shrug. "Grapeshot." He leaned back on his stool and, pulling the tail of his shirt from his breeches, lifted it to show Grey a sprawling web of still-pink scars across a muscular belly.

"Tore across me, and left me with me guts spilling out," he said casually. "But by the help of the Blessed Mother, the surgeon was to hand. Seized 'em in his fist, he did, and rammed them right back into me belly, then wrapped me up tight as a tick in bandages and honey."

Scanlon had lived, by some miracle, but had of course been invalided out of the army. Seeking some alternate means of making a living, he had returned to his interest in medicine, and apprenticed himself to an apothecary.

"But me brothers and me cousins—a good number of them still are soldiers," he said, taking a gulp of the ale and closing his eyes in appreciation as it went down. "And happen as none of us much likes a man as plays traitor."

In the aftermath of the attack on Francine, Jack Byrd had told Scanlon and Francine that the Sergeant was likely a spy and in possession of valuable papers. And O'Connell had shouted to Francine in parting that he would be back, and would finish then what he had started.

"From what Jack said about the drab O'Connell stayed with, I couldn't see that he'd likely come back only to murder Francie. That bein' so"—Scanlon raised one eyebrow—"what's the odds he'd come either to take something he'd left—or to leave something he had? And God knows, there was nothing there to take."

Given these deductions, it was no great trick to search Francine's room, and the shop below.

"Happen they was in one of the hollow molds that holds those condoms you was looking at, first time you came into the shop," Scanlon said, one corner of his mouth turning up. "I could see what they were—and fond as I was by then of young Jack, I thought I maybe ought to keep hold of them, until I could find a proper authority to be handin' them over to. Such as it might be yourself, sir."

"Only you didn't."

The apothecary stretched himself, long arms nearly brushing the low ceiling, then settled back comfortably onto his stool.

"Well, no. For the one thing, I hadn't met you yet, sir. And events, as you might say, intervened. I had to put a stop to Tim O'Connell and his mischief. For he did say he'd be back—and he was a man of his word, if nothing else."

Scanlon had promptly set about collecting several friends and relations, all soldiers or ex-soldiers—"And I'm sure your honor will excuse me not mentioning of their names," Scanlon said, with a small ironic bow toward Grey—who had lain in wait in the apothecary's shop, hidden in Francine's room upstairs, or in the large closet where Scanlon kept his extra stock.

Sure enough, O'Connell had returned that very night, soon after dark.

"He'd a key. He opens the door, and comes stealing into the shop, quiet as you please, and goes over to the shelf, picks up the mold—and finds it empty."

The sergeant had swung round to find Scanlon watching him from behind the counter, a sardonic smile on his face.

"Went the color of beetroot," the apothecary said. "I could see by the lamplight coming through the curtain by the stair. And his eyes slitted like a cat's. 'That whore,' he said. 'She told you. Where are they?'"

Fists clenched, O'Connell had bounded toward Scanlon, only to be confronted by a bevy of enraged Irishmen, come pouring down the stair and rushing from the closet, hurdling the counter in their haste.

"So we gave him a bit of what he'd given poor Francie," the apothecary said, face hard. "And we took our time about it."

And the people in the houses to either side had sworn blank-faced that they'd never heard a sound that night, Grey reflected cynically. Tim O'Connell had not been a popular man.

Once dead, O'Connell plainly could not be discovered on Scanlon's premises. The body therefore had lain behind the counter for several hours, until the streets had quieted in the small dark hours of the morning. Wrapping the body in a sheet of canvas, the men had borne it silently away into the cold black of hidden alleys, and heaved it off Puddle Dock—"like the rubbish he was, sir"—having first removed the uniform, which O'Connell had no right to, and him a traitor. It was worth good money, after all.

Jack Byrd had come back the next day, bringing with him his employer, Mr. Trevelyan.

"And the Honorable Mr. Trevelyan had with him a letter from Lord Melton, the Colonel of your regiment, sir—I think he said as that would be your brother?—asking him for his help in finding out what O'Connell was up to. He explained as how Lord Melton himself was abroad, but plainly Mr. Trevelyan knew all about the matter, and so it was only sense to hand over the papers to him, so as to be passed on to the proper person."

"Fell for that, did you?" Grey inquired. "Well, no matter. He's fooled better men than you, Scanlon."

"Including yourself, would it be, sir?" Scanlon lifted both black brows, and smiled with a flash of good teeth.

"I was thinking of my brother," Grey said with a grimace, and lifted his cup in acknowledgment. "But certainly me as well."

"But he's given you back the papers, sir?" Scanlon frowned. "He did say as he meant to."

"He has, yes." Grey touched the pocket of his coat, where the papers reposed. "But since the papers are presently en route to India with me, there is no way of informing the 'proper authorities.' The effect therefore is as though the papers had never been found."

"Better not to be found, than to be in the hands of the Frenchies, surely?" Doubt was beginning to flicker in Scanlon's eyes.

"Not really." Grey explained the matter briefly, Scanlon frowning and drawing patterns on the table with a dollop of spilled beer all the while.

"Ah, I see, then," he said, and fell silent. "Perhaps," the apothecary said after a few moments, "I should speak to him."

"Is it your impression that he will attend, if you do?" Grey's question held as much incredulous derision as curiosity, but Finbar Scanlon only smiled, and stretched himself again, the muscles of his forearms curving hard against the skin.

"Oh, I do, yes, sir. Mr. Trevelyan has been kind enough to say as he considers himself within my debt—and so he is, I suppose."

"That you have come to nurse his wife? Yes, I should think he would feel grateful."

The apothecary shook his head at that.

"Well, maybe, sir, but that's more by way of being a matter of business. It was agreed between us that he would see to Francie's safe removal to Ireland, money enough to care for her and the babe until my return, and a sum to me for my services. And if my services should cease to be required, I shall be put ashore at the nearest port, with my fare paid back to Ireland."

"Yes? Well, then—"

"I meant the cure, sir."

Grey looked at him in puzzlement.

"Cure? What, for the syphilis?"

"Aye, sir. The malaria."

"Whatever do you mean, Scanlon?"

The apothecary picked up his cup and gulped beer, then set it down with an exhalation of satisfaction.

" 'Tis a thing I learned from the surgeon, sir—the man as saved me life. He told it me while I lay sick, and I saw it work several times after."

"Saw what, for God's sake?"

"The malaria. If a man suffering from pox happened to contract malaria, once he'd recovered from the fever—if he did—the pox was cured, as well."

Scanlon nodded to him, and lifted his cup, with an air of magisterial confidence.

"It does work, sir. And while the tertian fever may come back now and then, the syphilis does not. The fever of it burns the pox from the blood, d'ye see?"

"Holy God," Grey said, suddenly enlightened. "You gave it to her—you infected that woman with malaria?"

"Aye, sir. And have done the same for Mr. Trevelyan, this very morning, with blood taken from a dyin' sailor off the East India docks. Fitting, Mr. Trevelyan thought, that it should be one of his own men, so to speak, who'd provide the means of his deliverance."

"He would!" Grey said scathingly. So that was it. Seeing the scarified flesh of Trevelyan's arm, he had thought Scanlon had merely bled the man to insure his health. He had had not the faintest idea—

"It is done with blood, then? I had thought the fever was transmitted by the breathing of foul air."

"Well, and so it often is, sir," Scanlon agreed. "But the secret of the cure is in the blood, see? The inoculum was the secret that the surgeon discovered and passed on to me. Though it is true as it may take more than one try, to insure a proper infection," he added, rubbing a knuckle under his nose. "I was lucky with Mrs. Maria; took no more than a week's application, and she was burning nicely. I hope to have a similar good effect for Mr. Trevelyan. He didn't want to start the treatment himself, though, see, until we were safe away."

"Oh, I see," Grey said. And he did. Trevelyan had not chosen to abscond with Maria Mayrhofer in order to die with her—but in hopes of overcoming the curse that lay upon them.

"Just so, sir." A light of modest triumph glowed in the apothecary's eye. "So you see, too, sir, why I think Mr. Trevelyan might indeed be inclined to attend to me?"

"I do," Grey agreed. "And both the army and myself will be grateful, Scanlon, if you can contrive any means of getting that information back to London quickly." He pushed back his stool, but paused for one Parthian shot.

"I think you should speak to him soon, though. His gratitude may be significantly ameliorated, if Frau Mayrhofer dies as a result of your marvelous cure."

Chapter 18

God's Dice

Eight days passed, and Maria Mayrhofer still lived—but Grey could see the shadows in Trevelyan's eyes, and knew how he dreaded the return of the fever. She had survived two more bouts of the fever, but Jack Byrd had told Tom—who had told him, of course—that it was a near thing.

"She ain't much more than a yellow ghost now, Jack says," Tom informed him. "Mr. Scanlon's that worried, though he keeps a good face, and keeps sayin' as she'll be all right."

"Well, I'm sure we all hope she will, Tom." He hadn't seen Frau Mayrhofer again, but what he had seen of her on that one brief occasion had impressed him. He was inclined to see women differently than did most other men; he appreciated faces, breasts, and buttocks as matters of beauty, rather than lust, and thus was not blinded to the personalities behind

them. Maria Mayrhofer struck him as having a personality of sufficient force to beat back death itself—if she wanted to.

And would she? He thought that she must feel stretched between two poles: the strength of her love for Trevelyan pulling her
toward life, while the shades of her murdered husband and child
must draw her down toward death. Perhaps she had accepted
Scanlon's inoculum as a gamble, leaving the dice in God's hands. If
she lived through the malaria, she would be free—not only of the
disease, but of her life before. If she did not . . . well, she would be
free of life, once and for all.

Grey lounged in the hammock he had been given in the crew's
quarters, while Tom sat cross-legged on the floor beneath, mending
a stocking.

"Does Mr. Trevelyan spend much time with her?" he asked idly.

"Yes, me lord. Jack says he won't be put off no more, but
scarcely leaves her side."

"Ah."

"Jack's worried, too," Tom said, squinting ferociously at his
work. "But I don't know whether it's her he's worried for, or him."

"Ah," Grey said again, wondering how much Jack had said to his
brother—and how much Tom might suspect.

"You best leave off them boots, me lord, and go barefoot like the
sailors. Look at that—the size of a teacup!" He poked two fingers
through the stocking's hole in illustration, glancing reproachfully
up at Grey. "Besides, you're going to break your neck, if you slip
and fall on deck again."

"I expect you're right, Tom," Grey said, pushing against the wall
with his toes to make the hammock swing. Two near-misses with
disaster on a wet deck had drawn him to the same conclusion.
What did boots or stockings matter, after all?

A shout came from the deck above, penetrating even through

the thick planks, and Tom dropped his needle, staring upward. Most of the shouts from the rigging overhead were incomprehensible to Grey, but the words that rang out now were clear as a bell.

"Sail ho!"

He flung himself out of the hammock, and ran for the ladder, closely followed by Tom.

A mass of men stood at the rail, peering northward, and telescopes sprouted from the eyes of several ship's officers like antennae from a horde of eager insects. For himself, Grey could see no more than the smallest patch of sail on the horizon, insignificant as a scrap of paper—but incontrovertibly there.

"I will be damned," Grey said, excited despite the cautions of his mind. "Is it heading for England?"

"Can't say, sir." The telescope-wielder next to him lowered his instrument and tapped it neatly down. "For Europe, at least, though."

Grey stepped back, combing the crowd of men for Trevelyan, but he was nowhere in evidence. Scanlon, though, was there. He caught the man's eye, and the apothecary nodded.

"I'll go at once, sir," he said, and strode away toward the hatchway.

It struck Grey belatedly that he should go as well, to reinforce any arguments Scanlon might make, both to Trevelyan and to the captain. He could scarcely bear to leave the deck, lest the tiny sail disappear for good if he took his eyes off it, but the sudden hope of deliverance was too strong to be denied. He slapped a hand to his side, but was of course not wearing his coat; his letter was below.

He darted toward the hatchway, and was halfway down the ladder when one flexing bare foot stubbed itself against the wall. He recoiled, scrabbled for a foothold, found it—but his sweaty hand slipped off the polished rail, and he plunged eight feet to the deck below. Something solid struck him on the head, and blackness descended.

He woke slowly, wondering for a moment whether he had been inadvertently encoffined. A dim and wavering light, as of candlelight, surrounded him, and there was a wooden wall two inches from his nose. Then he stirred, turned over on his back, and found that he lay in a tiny berth suspended from the wall like the sort of box in which knives are kept, barely long enough to allow him to stretch out at full length.

There was a large prism set into the ceiling above him, letting in light from the upper deck; his eyes adjusting to this, he saw a set of shelves suspended above a minuscule desk, and deduced from their contents that he was in the purser's cabin. Then his eyes shifted to the left, and he discovered that he was not alone.

Jack Byrd sat on a stool beside his berth, arms comfortably folded, leaning back against the wall. When he saw that Grey was awake, he unfolded his arms and sat up.

"Are you well, my lord?"

"Yes," Grey replied automatically, belatedly checking to see whether it was true.

Fortunately, it seemed to be. There was a tender lump behind his ear, where he had struck his head on the companionway, and a few bruises elsewhere, but nothing of any moment.

"That's good. The surgeon and Mr. Scanlon both said as you were all right, but our Tom wouldn't have you left, just in case."

"So you came to keep watch? That was unnecessary, but I thank you." Grey stirred, wanting to sit up, and became conscious of a warm, soft weight beside him in the bed. The purser's cat, a small tabby, was curled tight as an apostrophe against his side, purring gently.

"Well, you had company already," Jack Byrd said with a small smile, nodding at the cat. "Tom insisted as how he must stay, too, though—I think he was afraid lest somebody come in and put a knife in your ribs in the night. He's a suspicious little bugger, Tom."

"I should say that he has cause to be," Grey replied dryly. "Where is he now?"

"Asleep. It's just risen dawn. I made him go to bed a few hours ago; said I'd watch for him."

"Thank you." Moving carefully in the confined space, Grey pulled himself up on the pillows. "We're not moving, are we?"

Belatedly, he realized that what had wakened him was the cessation of movement; the ship was rolling gently as waves rose and fell beneath the hull, but her headlong dash had ceased.

"No, my lord. We've stopped to let the other ship come alongside of us."

"Ship. The sail! What ship is it?" Grey sat upright, narrowly missing clouting himself anew on a small shelf above the berth.

"*The Scorpion*," Jack Byrd replied. "Troopship, the mate says."

"A troopship? Thank Christ! Headed where?"

The cat, disturbed by his sudden movement, uncurled itself with a *mirp!* of protest.

"Dunno. They've not come within hailing distance yet. The captain's not best pleased," Byrd observed mildly. "But it's Mr. Trevelyan's orders."

"Is it, then?" Grey gave Byrd a quizzical glance, but the smooth, lean face showed no particular response. Perhaps it was Trevelyan's orders that had caused them to seek out the other ship—but he would have wagered a year's income that the real order had come from Finbar Scanlon.

He let out a long breath, scarcely daring to hope. The other ship might not be heading for England; it could easily have overtaken them, sailing from England, en route to almost anywhere. But if it should be headed to France or Spain, somewhere within a few weeks' journey of England—somehow, he would get back to London. Pray God, in time.

He had an immediate impulse to leap out of bed and fling on his clothes—someone, presumably Tom, had undressed him and put him to bed in his shirt—but it was plain that there would be some time before the two ships had maneuvered together, and Jack Byrd was making no move to rise and go, but was still sitting there, examining him thoughtfully.

It suddenly occurred to Grey why this was, and he halted his movement, instead altering it into a reach for the cat, which he scooped up into his lap, where it promptly curled up again.

"If the ship should be headed aright, I shall board her, of course, and go back to England," he began carefully. "Your brother Tom—do you think he will wish to accompany me?"

"Oh, I'm sure he would, my lord." Byrd straightened himself on the stool. "Better if he can get back to England, so our dad and the rest know he's all right—and me," he added, as an afterthought. "I expect they'll be worried, a bit."

"I should expect so."

There was an awkward silence then, Byrd still making no move to go. Grey stared back.

"Will you wish to return to England with your brother?" Grey asked at last, quite baldly. "Or to continue on to India, in Mr. Trevelyan's service?"

"Well, that's what I've been asking myself, my lord, ever since that ship came close enough for Mr. Hudson to say what she was." Jack Byrd scratched meditatively under his chin. "I've been with Mr. Trevelyan for a long time, see—since I was twelve. I'm . . . attached to him." He darted a quick glance at Grey, then stopped, seeming to wait for something.

So he hadn't been wrong. He had seen that unguarded look on Jack Byrd's face—and Jack Byrd had seen him watching. He lifted one eyebrow, and saw the young man's shoulders drop a little in sudden relaxation.

"Well . . . so." Jack Byrd shrugged, and let his hands fall on his knees.

"So." Grey rubbed his own chin, feeling the heavy growth of whiskers there. There would be time for Tom to shave him before the *Scorpion* came alongside, he thought.

"Have you spoken to Tom? He will surely be hoping that you will come back to England with him."

Jack Byrd bit his lower lip.

"I know."

There were shouts of a different kind overhead: long calls, like someone howling in a chimney—he supposed the *Nampara* was trying to communicate with someone on the troopship. Where was his uniform? Ah, there, neatly brushed and hung on a hook by the door. Would Tom Byrd wish to go with him when the regiment was reposted? He could but hope.

In the meantime, there was Tom's brother, here before him.

"I would offer you a position—as footman—" he added, giving the young man a straight look, lest there be any confusion about what was and was not offered,"—in my mother's house. You would not lack for employment."

Jack Byrd nodded, lips slightly pursed.

"Well, my lord, that's kind. Though Mr. Trevelyan had made provisions for me; I shouldn't starve. But I don't see as how I can leave him."

There was enough of a question in this last to make Grey sit up and face round in the bed, his back against the wall, in order to address the situation properly.

Was Jack Byrd seeking justification for staying, or excuse for leaving?

"It's only . . . I've been with Mr. Joseph for some time," Byrd said again, reaching out a hand to scratch the cat's ears—more in order to avoid Grey's gaze than because of a natural affection for cats, Grey thought. "He's done very well by me, been good to me."

And how good is that? Grey wondered. He was quite sure now of Byrd's feelings, and sure enough of Trevelyan's, for that matter. Whether anything had ever passed between Trevelyan and his servant in privacy—and he was inclined to doubt it—there was no doubt that Trevelyan's emotions now focused solely on the woman who lay below, still and yellow in the interlude of her illness.

"He is not worthy of such loyalty. You know that," Grey said, leaving the last sentence somewhere in the hinterland between statement and question.

"And you are, my lord?" It was asked without sarcasm, Byrd's hazel eyes resting seriously on Grey's face.

"If you mean your brother, I value his service more than I can say," Grey replied. "I sincerely hope he knows it."

Jack Byrd smiled slightly, looking down at the hands clasped on his knees. "Oh, I should reckon he does, then."

They stayed without speaking for a bit, and the tension between them eased by degrees, the cat's purring seeming somehow to dissolve it. The bellowing above had stopped.

"She might die," Jack Byrd said. "Not that I want her to; I don't, at all. But she may." It was said thoughtfully, with no hint of hopefulness—and Grey believed him when he said there was none.

"She may," he agreed. "She is very ill. But you are thinking that if that were unfortunately to occur—"

"Only as he'd need someone to care for him," Byrd answered quickly. "Only that. I shouldn't want him to be alone."

Grey forbore to answer that Trevelyan would find it hard work to manage solitude on board a ship with two hundred seamen. The to-and-fro bumpings of the crew had not stopped, but had changed their rhythm. The ship had ceased to fly, but she scarcely lay quiet in the water; he could feel the gentle tug of wind and current on her bulk. Stroking the cat, he thought of wind and water as the hands of the ocean on her skin, and wondered momentarily whether he might have liked to be a sailor.

"He says that he will not live without her," Grey said at last. "I do not know whether he means it."

Byrd closed his eyes briefly, long lashes casting shadows on his cheeks.

"Oh, he means it," he said. "But I don't think he'd do it." He opened his eyes, smiling a little. "I'm not saying as how he's a hypocrite, mind—he's not, no more than any man is just by nature. But he—" He paused, pushing out his lower lip as he considered how to say what he meant.

"It's just as he seems so alive," he said at last, slowly. He glanced up at Grey, dark eyes bright. "Not the sort as kills themselves. You'll know what I mean, my lord?"

"I think I do, yes." The cat, tiring at last of the attention, ceased purring and stretched itself, flexing its claws comfortably in and out of the coverlet over Grey's leg. He scooped it up under the belly and set it on the floor, where it ambled away in search of milk and vermin.

Learning the truth, Maria Mayrhofer had thought of self-destruction; Trevelyan had not. Not out of principle, nor any sense of religious prohibition—merely because he could not imagine any circumstance of life that he could not overcome in some fashion.

"I do know what you mean," Grey repeated, swinging his legs out of bed to go and open the door for the cat, who was clawing at it. "He may speak of death, but he has no . . ." He, in turn, groped for words. ". . . no friendship with it?"

Jack Byrd nodded.

"Aye, that's something of what I mean. The lady, though—she's seen that un's face." He shook his head, and Grey noted with interest that while his attitude seemed one of both liking and respect, he never spoke Maria Mayrhofer's name.

Grey closed the door behind the cat and turned back, leaning against it. The ship swayed gently beneath him, but his head was clear and steady, for the first time in days.

Small as the cabin was, Jack Byrd sat no more than two feet from him, the rippled light from the prism overhead making him look like a creature from the seabed, soft hair wavy as kelp around his shoulders, with a green shadow in his hazel eyes.

"What you say is true," Grey said at last. "But I tell you this. He will not forget her, even should she die. Particularly if she should die," he added, thoughtfully.

Jack Byrd's face didn't change expression; he just sat, looking into Grey's eyes, his own slightly narrowed, like a man evaluating the approach of a distant dust cloud that might hide enemy or fortune.

Then he nodded, rose, and opened the door.

"I'll fetch my brother to you, my lord. I expect you'll be wanting to dress."

In the event, he was too late; a patter of footsteps rushed down the corridor, and Tom's eager face appeared in the doorway.

"Me lord, Jack, me lord!" he said, excited into incoherence. "What they're sayin', what the sailors are sayin'! On that boat!"

"Ship," Jack corrected, frowning at his brother. "So what are they saying, then?"

"Oh, to bleedin' hell with your ships," Tom said rudely, elbowing his brother aside. He swung back to Grey, face beaming. "They said General Clive's beat the Nawab at a place called Plassey, me lord! We've won Bengal! D'ye hear—we've won!"

Epilogue

London
August 18, 1757

The first blast shook the walls, rattling the crystal wineglasses and causing a mirror from the reign of Louis XIV to crash to the floor.

"Never mind," said the Dowager Countess Melton, patting a white-faced footman, who had been standing next to it, consolingly on the arm. "Ugly thing; it's always made me look like a squirrel. Go fetch a broom before someone steps on the pieces."

She stepped through the French doors onto the terrace, fanning herself and looking happy.

"What a night!" she said to her youngest son. "Do you think they've found the range yet?"

"I wouldn't count on it," Grey said, glancing warily down the river toward Tower Hill, where the fireworks master was presumably rechecking his calculations and bollocking his subordinates. The first trial shell had gone whistling directly overhead, no more than fifty feet above the Countess's riverside town house. Several servants stood on the terrace, scanning the skies and armed with wet brooms, just in case.

"Well, they should do it more often," the Countess said reprovingly, with a glance at the Hill. "Keep in practice."

It was a clear, still, mid-August night, and while hot, moist air sat like a smothering blanket on London, there was some semblance of a breeze, so near the river.

Just upstream, he could see Vauxhall Bridge, so crowded with spectators that the span appeared to be a live thing itself, writhing and flexing like a caterpillar over the soft dark sheen of the river. Now and then, some intoxicated person would be pushed off, falling with a cannonball splash into the water, to the enthusiastic howls of their comrades above.

Conditions were not quite so crowded within the town house, but give it time, Grey thought, following his mother back inside to greet further new arrivals. The musicians had just finished setting up at the far end of the room; they would need to open the folding doors into the next room, as well, to make room for dancing—though that wouldn't begin until after the fireworks.

The temperature was no bar to Londoners celebrating the news of Clive's victory at Plassey. For days, the taverns had been overflowing with custom, and citizens greeted one another in the street with genial cries condemning the Nawab of Bengal's ancestry, appearance, and social habits.

"Buggering black bastard!" bellowed the Duke of Cirencester, echoing the opinions of his fellow citizens in Spitalfields and Stepney as he charged through the door. "Put a rocket up his arse, see how high he flies before he explodes, eh? Benedicta, my love, come kiss me!"

The Countess, prudently putting several bodies between herself and the Duke, blew him a pretty kiss before disappearing on the arm of Mr. Pitt, and Grey tactfully redirected the Duke's ardor toward the genial widow of Viscount Bonham, who was more than capable of dealing with him. Was the Duke's Christian name Jacob? he wondered darkly. He thought it was.

A few more trial blasts from Tower Hill were scarcely noticed, as the noise of talk and music grew with each fresh bottle of wine opened, each new cup of rum punch poured. Even Jack Byrd, who had been quiet to the point of taciturnity since their return, seemed cheered; Grey saw him smile at a young maid passing through with a pile of cloaks.

Tom Byrd, newly outfitted in proper livery for the occasion, was standing by the bamboo screen that hid the chamber pots, charged with watching the guests to prevent petty thievery.

"Be careful, especially when the fireworks start in earnest," Grey murmured to him in passing. "Take it turn about with your brother, so you can go out to the terrace and watch a bit—but be sure someone's got an eye on my Lord Gloucester all the time. He got away with a gilded snuffbox last time he was here."

"Yes, me lord," Tom said, nodding. "Look, me lord—it's the Hun!"

Sure enough, Stephan von Namtzen, Landgrave von Erdberg, had arrived in all his plumed glory, beaming as though Clive's triumph had been a personal victory. Handing his helmet to Jack Byrd, who looked rather bemused by its receipt, he spotted Grey and an enormous smile spread across his face.

The intervening crowd prevented his passage, for which Grey was momentarily grateful. He was in fact more than pleased to see the Hanoverian, but the thought of being enthusiastically embraced and kissed on both cheeks, which was von Namtzen's habit when greeting friends . . .

Then the Bishop of York arrived with an entourage of six small black boys in cloth of gold; a huge *boom!* from downriver and shrieks from the crowd on Vauxhall Bridge announced the real commencement of the fireworks, and the musicians struck up Handel's *Royal Fireworks* suite.

Two-thirds of the guests surged out onto the terrace for a better view, leaving the hard drinkers and those engaged in conversation a little room to breathe.

Grey took advantage of the sudden exodus to nip behind the bamboo screen for relief; two bottles of champagne took their toll. It was perhaps not an appropriate venue for prayer, but he sent up a brief word of gratitude, nonetheless. The public hysteria over Plassey had completely eclipsed any other news; neither broadsheets nor street journalists had said a word on the subjects of the murder of Reinhardt Mayrhofer, or the disappearance of Joseph Trevelyan—let alone made rude speculations concerning Trevelyan's erstwhile fiancée.

He understood that word was being discreetly circulated in financial circles that Mr. Trevelyan was traveling to India in order to explore new opportunities for import, in the wake of the victory.

He had a momentary vision of Joseph Trevelyan as he had been in the main cabin of the *Nampara,* standing by his wife's bed, just before Grey had left.

"If? . . ." Grey had asked, with a small nod toward the bed.

"Word will come that I have been lost at sea—swept overboard by a swamping wave. Such things happen." He glanced toward the bed where Maria Mayrhofer lay, still and beautiful and yellow as a carving of ancient ivory.

"I daresay they do," Grey had said quietly, thinking once more of Jamie Fraser.

Trevelyan moved to stand by the bed, looking down. He took

the woman's hand, stroking it, and Grey saw her fingers tighten, very slightly; light quivered in the emerald teardrop of the ring she wore.

"If she dies, it will be the truth," Trevelyan said softly, his eyes on her still face. "I shall take her in my arms and step over the rail; we will rest together, on the bottom of the sea."

Grey moved to stand beside him, close enough to feel the brush of his sleeve.

"And if she does not?" he asked. "If you both survive the treatment?"

Trevelyan shrugged, so faintly that Grey might not have noticed were he not so close.

"Money will not buy health, nor happiness—but it has its uses. We will live in India, as man and wife; no one will know who she was—nothing will matter, save we are together."

"May God bless you and grant you peace," Grey murmured, reordering his dress—though he spoke to Maria Mayrhofer, rather than Trevelyan. He smoothed the edge of his waistcoat and stepped out from behind the screen, back into the maelstrom of the party.

Within a few steps, he was stopped by Lieutenant Stubbs, burnished to a high gloss and sweating profusely.

"Hallo, Malcolm. Enjoying yourself?"

"Er . . . yes. Of course. A word, old fellow?"

A boom from the river made speech momentarily impossible, but Grey nodded, beckoning Stubbs to a relatively quiet alcove near the foyer.

"I should speak to your brother, I know." Stubbs cleared his throat. "But with Melton not here, you're by way of being head of the family, aren't you?"

"For my sins," Grey replied guardedly. "Why?"

Stubbs cast a lingering glance through the French doors; Olivia was visible on the terrace, laughing at something said to her by Lord Ramsbotham.

"Not as though your cousin hasn't better prospects, I know," he said, a little awkwardly. "But I have got five thousand a year, and when the Old One—not that I don't hope he lives forever, mind, but I *am* the heir, and—"

"You want my permission to court Olivia?"

Stubbs avoided his eye, gazing vaguely off toward the musicians, who were fiddling industriously away at the far end of the room.

"Um, well, more or less done that, really. Hope you don't mind. I, er, we were hoping you might see your way to a marriage before the regiment leaves. Bit hasty, I know, but . . ."

But you want a chance to leave your seed in a willing girl's belly, Grey added silently, *in case you don't come back.*

The guests had all left off chattering, and crowded to the edge of the gallery as the next explosion from the river boomed in the distance. Blue and white stars fountained from the sky amid a chorus of "ooh!" and "ahh!"—and he knew that every soldier there felt as he did the clench in the lower belly, balls drawn up tight at the echo of war, even as their hearts lifted heavenward at the sight of flaming glory.

"Yes," he heard himself say, in the moment's silence between one explosion and the next. "I don't see why not. After all, her dress is ready."

Then Stubbs was crushing his hand, beaming fervently, and he was smiling back, head swimming with champagne.

"I say, old fellow—you wouldn't think of making it a double wedding, would you? There's my sister, you know . . ."

Melissa Stubbs was Malcolm's twin, a plump and smiling girl, who was even now giving him an all-too-knowing eye over her fan from the terrace. For a split second, Grey teetered on the edge of temptation; the urge to leave something of himself behind, the lure of immortality before one steps into the void.

It would be well enough, he thought, if he didn't come back— but what if he did? He smiled, clapped Stubbs on the back, and excused himself with courtesy to go and find another drink.

"You don't want to drink that French muck, do you?" Quarry said at his elbow. "Blow you up like a bladder—gassy stuff." Quarry himself had a magnum of red wine clutched under one arm, a large blonde woman under the other. "May I introduce you to Major Grey, Mamie? Major, Mrs. Fortescue."

"Your servant, ma'am."

"A word in your ear, Grey?" Quarry released Mrs. Fortescue momentarily, and stepped in close, his craggy face red and glossy under his wig.

"We've got word at last; the new posting. But an odd thing—"

"Yes?" The glass in Grey's hand was red, not gold, as though it contained the vintage called Schilcher, the shining stuff that was the color of blood. But then he saw the bubbles rise, and realized that the fireworks had changed in color, and the light around them went red and white and red again and the smell of smoke floated in through the French doors as though they stood in the center of a bombardment.

"I was just talking to that German chap, von Namtzen. He wants you to go and be a liaison of sorts with his regiment; already spoken to the War Office, he says. Seems to have conceived a great regard for you, Grey."

Grey blinked and took a gulp of champagne. Von Namtzen's great blond head was visible on the terrace, his handsome profile turned up to the sky, rapt with wonder as a five-year-old's.

"Well, you needn't decide on the spot, of course. Up to your brother, anyway. Just thought I'd mention it. Ready for another turn, Mamie, m'dear?"

Before Grey could gather his senses to respond, the three—Harry, the blonde, and the bottle—had galloped off in a wild gavotte, and the sky was exploding in pinwheels and showers of red and blue and green and white and yellow.

Stephan von Namtzen turned and met his eyes, lifting a glass in salute, and at the end of the room the musicians still played Handel, like the music of his life, beauty and serenity interrupted always by the thunder of distant fire.

Author's Notes and References

Most of my information on the mollies of London comes from MOTHER CLAP'S MOLLY-HOUSE: The Gay Subculture in England 1700–1830, by Rictor Norton, which includes a fairly large bibliography, for those looking for further details. (I was interested to see that—according to this reference—terms such as "rough trade" and "Miss Thing," currently in use, were in existence during the eighteenth century as well.)

While most of the locations mentioned as "molly-walks" are historically known—such as the bog-houses (public privies) of Lincoln's Inn, Blackfriars Bridge, and the arcades of the Royal Exchange—the establishment known as Lavender House is fictional.

While some characters in this book, such as William Pitt, Robert Clive, the Nawab of Bengal, and Sir John Fielding, are real historic personages, most are fictional, or used in a fictional sense (e.g., there likely were real Dukes of Gloucester at various points in history, but I have no evidence to suggest that any of them were in fact kleptomaniac.).

Other useful references include:

ENGLISH SOCIETY IN THE EIGHTEENTH CENTURY (from THE PELICAN SOCIAL HISTORY OF BRITAIN series), by Roy Porter, 1982, Pelican Books. ISBN 0-14-022099-2. This includes a good bibliography, plus a number of interesting statistical tables.

THE TRANSVESTITE MEMOIRS OF THE ABBÉ DE CHOISY, Peter Owen Publishers, London. ISBN 0-7206-0915-1. This book deals with the subject of the title, in seventeenth-century France, and is more interesting for the sumptuous details of the Abbé's clothes than anything else.

THE QUEER DUTCHMAN: True Account of a Sailor Castaway on a Desert Island for "Unnatural Acts" and Left to God's Mercy, by Peter Agnos, Green Eagle Press, New York, 1974, 1993, ISBN 0-914018-03-5. The (edited) journal of Jan Svilts, marooned on Ascension Island in 1725 by officers of the Dutch East India Company, who feared that his "unnatural acts" would bring down the wrath of God upon their venture, as upon the inhabitants of Sodom.

LOVE LETTERS BETWEEN A CERTAIN LATE NOBLEMAN AND THE FAMOUS MR. WILSON, Michael S. Kimmel, ed. Harrington Park Press, New York, 1990. (Originally published as *Journal of Homosexuality* Volume 19, Number 2, 1990.) This deals with the homosexual world in England (London specifically) during the 18th century, and contains quite an extensive annotated bibliography, as well as considerable commentary on the actual correspondence, which is included.

SAMUEL JOHNSON'S DICTIONARY. ISBN 1-929154-10-0. Various editions of this are available; a recent abridged version is done by the Levenger Press, edited by Jack Lynch. The original dictionary was published in 1755.

A CLASSICAL DICTIONARY OF THE VULGAR TONGUE, by Captain Francis Grose (edited with a biographical and critical sketch and an extensive commentary by Eric Partridge). Routledge and Kegan Paul, London. There are several different editions available of Grose's original work (which the Captain himself revised and re-published several times), but the original was probably published around 1807.

DRESS IN EIGHTEENTH CENTURY EUROPE 1715–1789, by Aileen Ribeiro, Holmes & Meier Publishers, Inc., New York, 1984. Well illustrated, with an abundance of paintings and drawings from the period, and several useful appendices on eighteenth-century currency and political events.

Greenwood's Map of London, 1827. This is the oldest complete map of London I was able to find, so I have used it as a general basis for the locations described. It's available at a number of Internet sites; I used the site maintained by the University of Bath Spa: http://users.bathspa.ac.uk/imagemap/html.

The Malaria Cure. Finbar Scanlon's notion of deliberately infecting someone with malaria in order to cure syphilis was a known medical procedure of the period—though not nearly so common or popular as the various mecury-based "cures."

Oddly enough, in very recent times, a few observations have been made of people suffering from chronic infective diseases, who then acquire a separate infection causing extremely high fever (in excess of 104 degrees) over a prolonged period. Such fevers are very dangerous in and of themselves, but what was remarkable was that those patients who survived such fevers were in many cases found to no longer have the chronic disease. So there is indeed some evidence—though still very anecdotal at this point—to suggest that Mr. Scanlon's remedy might well have worked. For the sake of Joseph Trevelyan and Maria Mayrhofer, we'll hope so!

Transvestite. The use of this word as a noun dates only from the mid-twentieth century. The practice, however, is plainly a great deal older. Given Lord John's Latin education, the use of this Latinate construction as an adjective—"transvestite commerce"—is more than reasonable.